At the sound of hoofbeats, they both looked toward the road.

"It's your folks," Susannah murmured.

Jethro nodded, recognizing his *daed*'s horse. "*Gut* thing I'm here then. Support the news I'm sure they've heard around the d-district that we're courting."

"Have they said anything to you yet?"

"*Nee.* B-but I'm sure it's coming soon. You?"

"*Nee.* Unlike you, I don't think they'll speak directly to me about it. I think it's more likely that the bishop will just send more 'eligible' men my way." She bumped him with her hip. "Thanks to your idea about the courtship that's not a courtship, when I say thanks but no thanks, most of them will be easily dissuaded."

At the sight of her teasing grin, it was Jethro's feet—not his speech for once—that stumbled. "Glad it's working out for you."

Watching the buggy crest the hill and drop from sight, Jethro cautioned himself with Susannah's words. *She doesn't want a beau. And even if she did, I wouldn't be on her list of potential candidates.* He needed to keep his heart in check.

Publishers Weekly bestselling author **Jocelyn McClay** grew up on an Iowa farm, ultimately pursuing a degree in agriculture. She met her husband while weight lifting in a small town—he "spotted" her. After thirty years in business management, they moved to an acreage in southeastern Missouri to be closer to family when their oldest of three daughters made them grandparents. When not writing, she keeps busy grandparenting, hiking, biking, gardening, quilting, knitting and substitute teaching.

Vannetta Chapman has published over one hundred articles in Christian family magazines and received over two dozen awards from Romance Writers of America chapter groups. She discovered her love for the Amish while researching her grandfather's birthplace of Albion, Pennsylvania. Her first novel, *A Simple Amish Christmas*, quickly became a bestseller. Chapman lives in Texas Hill Country with her husband.

JOCELYN McCLAY

&

USA TODAY Bestselling Author

VANNETTA CHAPMAN

Her Pretend Courtship

2 Uplifting Stories

Their Unpredictable Path and
An Unlikely Amish Match

LOVE INSPIRED
INSPIRATIONAL ROMANCE

LOVE INSPIRED®
INSPIRATIONAL ROMANCE

Recycling programs for this product may not exist in your area.

ISBN-13: 978-1-335-50832-4

Her Pretend Courtship

Copyright © 2023 by Harlequin Enterprises ULC

Their Unpredictable Path
First published in 2022. This edition published in 2023.
Copyright © 2022 by Jocelyn Ord

An Unlikely Amish Match
First published in 2020. This edition published in 2023.
Copyright © 2020 by Vannetta Chapman

This is a work of fiction. Names, characters, places and incidents are either the product of the author's imagination or are used fictitiously. Any resemblance to actual persons, living or dead, businesses, companies, events or locales is entirely coincidental.

For questions and comments about the quality of this book, please contact us at CustomerService@Harlequin.com.

Harlequin Enterprises ULC
22 Adelaide St. West, 41st Floor
Toronto, Ontario M5H 4E3, Canada
www.LoveInspired.com

Printed in U.S.A.

CONTENTS

THEIR UNPREDICTABLE PATH

Jocelyn McClay

Again, and always, I thank God for this opportunity. I want to thank Denise for letting me feed her goats, Lorelle for her wise character insight and Anthony for sharing how it feels to run toward a fire. In addition, I thank Mitch for information on clefts, Kim for responding to my questions on stuttering and SLP professionals for the difference they make in many lives. Moriah, this one's for you.

But the Lord said unto Samuel, Look not on his countenance, or on the height of his stature; because I have refused him: for the Lord seeth not as man seeth; for man looketh on the outward appearance, but the Lord looketh on the heart.
—*1 Samuel* 16:7

Chapter One

This time, he wasn't going to do it. No matter the pressure they applied. Jethro Weaver sighed and wearily shook his head. And his father, the bishop, and strong-willed mother could certainly apply considerable amounts. Turning out of his folks' lane, he gave a gentle *click* of his tongue to urge his gelding to road speed.

Ever since his wife and unborn child had unexpectedly died the previous year, his parents had been encouraging—Jethro's mouth slanted at the delicate term given the flat-out directives the bishop and his wife used—him to remarry. He loved his parents and wanted to obey them. He even understood their motive was pure. They wanted him to have a family. Large families were a gift from *Gott*. Jethro agreed.

But maybe it was a gift he wasn't meant to receive.

Maybe it didn't go with the other gifts he'd been given. The cleft lip and palate that had startled his parents when he'd been born. The stutter that frustrated him almost every time he opened his mouth, making him self-conscious around folks. Particularly around women.

Nee, going courting was the last thing he wanted to do.

His hands lax on the lines, Jethro let the gelding take his time as they started up a long hill, part of the rolling countryside in this slice of Wisconsin. It'd been different when he'd married Louisa. There'd been no courtship. He'd married the shy, frail widow of his younger brother to take care of her. *Ja,* it'd been at his parents' urging, but he'd have eventually done it on his own as she'd needed help.

Jethro slumped on the buggy seat. Although he usually succumbed to his parents' wishes, due in part to his respect for them and to his father's position as bishop of their district, he didn't relish the coming battle of wills. Because this time he wasn't going to do it. Why couldn't they let him live his life as he saw fit?

At the sudden pricked-forward ears of his gelding, Jethro glanced up the road. A battle was indeed erupting before him. Farther up the hill, a buggy was swerving perilously close to the ditch as the horse pulling it shied and reared. Jethro straightened abruptly when the animal lost its footing and tumbled over, flipping the buggy down the incline as well. At his urgent command, his startled gelding lurched ahead.

The horse swerved and reared. The lines jerked through Susannah Mast's fingers as the buggy jolted toward the ditch. She struggled to recapture the lost leather as Amos slid across the tilted seat toward her.

"Mamm!" Her eleven-year-old son's voice was high with alarm. "What's wrong with Nutmeg?"

Shoulder braced against his pressuring weight, Susannah didn't have an answer as to why their normally placid mare was suddenly shying and lunging out of control. Usually steadfast in harness, the Standardbred had been fidgety and reluctant to pull today. But it wasn't until she'd started climbing the hill toward home that Nutmeg had gone completely berserk.

"Easy, girl! Easy!" It was useless. Susannah had no control. Even as she regained the slack in the lines and struggled to settle the mare to a stop, Nutmeg fought her. Flecks of foam flew from the mare's flinging head as she hurled herself farther into the long, dried grass of the steep ditch.

A crack of fracturing wood, along with the horse's shrill whinny, split the previous quiet of the autumn afternoon. Susannah's shriek as the rearing mare toppled over the now broken buggy shaft joined it. The buggy lifted beneath her. Dropping the lines, Susannah twisted to wrap her arms around her son. Amos's straw hat went flying as she jerked him to her chest. Hunching her shoulders, she dipped her head over his, striving to protect him as the world tumbled around them.

Wincing, Susannah tightened her grasp when the edge of the buggy—door-less on the sunny October day—slammed into her back. *Please, Gott, don't let the buggy roll over on us.* Something pelted the top of her head, jerking at the pins that secured her *kapp.* A grunt escaped her, along with her breath, as her shoulder drove into the ground. Squeezing her eyes shut, she hugged her son.

One by one, Susannah's senses finally stopped whirling. Her nose was pressed against her son's head; she could smell in his hair the leather and straw of his new hat along with the haylike aroma of recently broken vegetation. A wheel squeaked as it continued to spin. At the sound of her mare thrashing in the ditch, Susannah's eyes popped open. Loosening her arms from around Amos, she capped his shoulders with her hands and carefully eased him back a few inches. His youthful face was pale, his freckles showing in sharp contrast. When he opened his eyes, they went instantly wide, the dark blue irises riveted on her.

"Are you all right?" she demanded, barely refraining from hugging him to her again.

"Ja." The word was hesitant and drawn out, almost a question in itself. "I think so?"

Praise Gott! Susannah slumped against the crumpled grass in relief as she ran a hand through his hatless dark hair. Scanning his small frame, she checked for signs of blood or possible injuries as he slowly shifted upright and away from where she sprawled. Her frantic heart rate began to ebb. Wincing at the pain in her shoulder, Susannah pushed herself into a sitting position. She was framed in the doorway of the upended buggy. Scattered around her were loose contents of the rig's interior.

The mare whinnied in distress. The horse's flailing had ceased, but the mare's labored breathing was evident. "I have to get to Nutmeg. Can you stand?"

Amos's nod was more emphatic this time. *"Ja."* They both froze when the buggy groaned, followed by a rocking sway, threatening it could tip further. They had to get out. Susannah's gaze darted across the toppled interior. Over the dash and out the open front was their best option. But should the mare begin to thrash again, they'd be within reach of flailing hooves. Though uninjured now, a kick to the head or limb would quickly change that.

At a distinct holler from the road, her heart stuttered. Twisting, Susannah looked through the buggy's open front to see Jethro Weaver scrambling down the ditch. She almost sank back to the ground in relief at the sight. Having tended to her neighbor's young son while in her preteen years, she'd known the calm and steady man all his life.

"We're all right!" She waved him away as he approached the buggy. "Check on Nutmeg!"

With an acknowledging wave, he reversed direction and more cautiously advanced to where the horse was trying to lift her head. When he settled on his haunches beside the Standardbred, Susannah heard his indistinct murmuring as he stroked the horse's neck. The old mare quieted.

Susannah struggled upright and eased into the overturned buggy. Keeping a wary eye on Nutmeg's hind feet, she hovered against the dash with Amos at her side. Jethro nodded to her as he continued to soothe and distract the mare.

"Follow me," Susannah murmured to her son. With a shaky inhale, she climbed over the dash. Using the frame of the buggy for support, she edged away from the overturned rig and clear of the metal-shod hooves before turning to watch anxiously as Amos did the same.

When they were both out of the range of danger, she gave her son another quick hug before kneeling beside Jethro at the mare's head. Nutmeg's eyes were ringed with white. In spite of the temperate October day, sweat darkened her brown neck. Susannah cooed to the mare as she ran her hand down the slick surface.

"Is she hurt?" Her gaze locked on Jethro's blue eyes, trying to decipher the concern visible there.

"D-don't know yet. Let's see." Jethro rose to his feet. Continuing to soothe the mare, Susannah watched as he worked his way down the buggy's shaft that jutted above the prone horse. His tall frame bent over the mare, the lean muscles of his forearms visible below the rolled-up sleeves of his white shirt as he efficiently unfastened the buckles and straps of the harness.

Squatting to gently rest a hand on Nutmeg's side so she knew he was there, Jethro considered the shaft and the harness leather that tracked under the mare. Tipping his flat-brimmed straw hat farther back over his sandy-blond hair, he glanced toward Susannah. Above his short beard, his lips were pressed into a pensive line, making the white scar that ran from under his nose to the top one stand out in his tanned face.

Susannah interpreted his dilemma. "I don't care about the harness or the buggy. I just want to help Nutmeg."

Nodding, Jethro set about doing what was necessary to free the mare. By the time he returned to where Susannah knelt, both she and the mare were breathing more easily.

"Let's t-try it now." With a hand at her elbow, Jethro helped Susannah to her feet. "Stand b-back," he directed her and the hovering Amos before grabbing the mare's bridle.

Susannah couldn't hear what he was saying but she knew the mare was listening as her brown ears flicked back and forth. Susannah pulled Amos in front of her, her hands tightening on his slender shoulders as she anxiously watched Jethro guide the mare into a position to rise. With Jethro's encouragement, the horse struggled to lunge to her feet. At each attempt, Susannah pushed herself onto her toes as if she could help man and horse by doing so. By the time Nutmeg staggered to a stand on the third try, Susannah was shaking as much as the horse. Scanning her side of the mare for any obvious injuries, she hurried to the trembling Standardbred.

"Careful, in case she goes d-down again," Jethro cautioned. Biting her lip, Susannah nodded as she grasped the bridle, freeing Jethro to examine the animal.

"Her legs look good," she observed in relief. There was no response from Jethro, who was making his way along the far side of the horse. Fretting for reassuring feedback, Susannah prompted, "Don't they?"

"*Ja.*"

She could almost hear a reluctant smile in his voice. Susannah took it as encouragement.

After a moment's pause, Jethro continued in a more serious tone. "She seems all right. Won't know for sure until she walks. B-but she's b-bleeding a b-bit on this side. Looks like it's coming from under the collar."

"Bleeding!" Susannah scooted around the front of the mare to see a red stain running down the mare's shoulder. As Jethro had noted, the inception point was under the leather collar that circled her lower neck. "Let's get this off."

Her fingers fumbled in their efforts to unhook the few remaining attachments. Jethro's tanned fingers gently brushed hers aside. Quickly finishing the task, he carefully lifted the collar from the mare to reveal a small gash sullenly seeping blood.

"Poor dear," Susannah murmured as she gently explored the wound. "Why there, of all places?"

Jethro was quietly examining the collar when she felt an abrupt tension charge his lean figure. When he spoke, his voice was tight. "B-because of this." Shifting the collar so she could see, he pointed to the head of a nail protruding from its interior. "Although it would've fretted her while d-driving earlier, climbing the hill t-to your p-place d-did the d-damage."

Jaw sagging, Susannah blinked in astonishment at the bloodstained nail. "How…" she said faintly before her teeth clamped together. She knew how.

"Let's see how she m-moves." Leaning the collar against the dash of the upturned buggy, Jethro gathered up the abandoned lines in one hand as he returned to Nutmeg's head. He took a firm grip of the bridle with his other to support the horse. Sharing a tense glance with Susannah, he gently coaxed the mare forward. Nutmeg reluctantly took one step, then two before slowly walking by Jethro's side along the waving autumn-golden grass in the ditch's belly.

There was no hitch in the horse's gait nor was she bobbing her head as she walked, either of which might indicate an injury. Susannah sighed in relief. Catching up to where Jethro had drawn Nutmeg to a halt, she threw her arms around the mare's neck and pressed her face against the black mane. "No limp. Praise *Gott* you're not hurt!"

Leaning back, she looked over her shoulder at the overturned buggy. Susannah's joy evaporated as her stomach clenched. Delayed reaction and overwhelming relief that Amos and the mare were safe almost made her sick. Her nose prickled with the threat of tears. Withdrawing her arms from the mare, Susannah curled her hands into fists. She blinked any renegade tears from her eyes as the sting of fingernails pressing into her palms helped her retain her equilibrium. She would not cry. Very few people had ever seen her cry. Susannah knew some wondered if she even could.

Her shock from the accident fading, the twinges and pains incurred in the tumble now made themselves known. Her shoulder throbbed. Her knee must've slammed against the dashboard. Her scalp was tender from whatever had pelted it.

Worst of all was her heart. Her heart ached. For she knew who was responsible for the dreadful incident. All evidence pointed to her hired man. What she didn't know was why. But she would find out.

She needed to fire him. And she dreaded that for many reasons, one of which was that releasing the young man would compound her issues. Lack of a hired hand would just give the bishop another reason to prompt her to remarry. He didn't think she could run the farm by herself. It wasn't like she hadn't run it alone before. But a widow with a prosperous farm was tempting for the ambitious—as well as the not so ambitious—older single men in the community, some of whom she knew had been bending the bishop's ear. Their unwanted courtships were the last thing she wanted or had time for.

"Oh, John, why did you do this? For your circumstances as well as my own." Because as much as she needed a worker, her hired man needed a job. Susannah could've dealt with his recent slothfulness. But when he harmed her animals, he had to go, no matter what that did to her own situation.

* * *

Jethro watched Susannah's brown eyes migrate from a wide-eyed dismay to a narrowed-lidded intensity. The focused ferocity of her gaze contrasted with the disarray of the rest of her appearance. A crushed prayer *kapp* hung off the side of her head, clinging precariously by a few dislodged pins. Dark brown hair, threaded with very little gray to share a clue to her age, dangled from a tangle at the back of her head. One lock had escaped completely to trail behind her shoulder to her waist.

His own eyes widened. Although he'd witnessed Susannah working hard in the fields or even hopping mad, he'd never seen her so...disheveled. Or with her hair even partially down. The only Amish woman he'd seen with her hair down had been his deceased wife, and those occasions had been rare and far between. Jethro's gaze lingered on the dangling strand where the autumn sun glowed on a few strands of red in the thick tress. The corner of his lip twitched. Somehow, the discovery didn't surprise him. Much to his delight as a shy only child for several years, he'd found Susannah a babysitter willing to be adventuresome. She'd scrambled up many trees and waded in muddy creeks in his wake, or he in hers.

But it also didn't concern him. Jethro tactfully redirected his gaze to the mare. Susannah was a neighbor and friend, nothing more. A friend who currently needed his help. Not his ogling of her partially unbound hair. That sight should be reserved for a woman's husband. And from what he'd overheard today between his parents, Susannah would soon have one of those if it were up to the bishop and his wife.

He sighed. From what he knew of Susannah, she didn't want to remarry any more than he did. They were both in a similar situation. Jethro reached out to comb his fingers through the mare's mane, freeing tangles in the coarse black strands before patting Nutmeg's dark brown neck. Too bad his and Susannah's tangles couldn't be addressed as easily. If only they could help one another with the snarls that others strove to create for them.

Jethro stilled, his eyes stared unseeing at the mane before him as a possibility struck. Heart pounding, he darted a glance at Susannah. Would she think the scheme blooming in his head *narrish*, or would the crazy thing be not to take action on the idea when it could be the solution, at least temporarily, for both their problems? He forced a swallow down a suddenly dry throat. There was one way to find out.

Jethro turned to the hovering boy. "Amos, could you d-drive m-my rig t-to your house?" The Mast farm was less than a quarter mile distant. Nodding eagerly, Amos scrambled up the ditch and into Jethro's buggy. A moment later, the *clip-clop* of hooves on the blacktop echoed behind the departing buggy, its cadence slow in comparison to Jethro's pulse.

He loved his parents, but it was time they let him run his own life. If they wanted him to go courting, so be it. But if the woman he walked out with was someone they'd think unsuitable, a widow at least ten years his senior and one toward the end of her childbearing years who couldn't give him the large family they—not he—wanted… Maybe they'd finally leave him alone. Jethro's mouth curved into a broad smile as an enthusiasm he hadn't felt in a long time unfurled inside him.

He considered again the woman beside him, the only female he'd ever felt comfortable with. If only Susannah would agree to his plan…

His shoulders sagged as he took in Susannah's pale face and disheveled appearance. He couldn't ask her now. She was still shaken from the buggy accident. Having already had one woman in his life who'd regretted her acceptance of his proposal, he didn't want Susannah to be the second, even for a fictional relationship.

Jethro rubbed the back of his neck. Besides, how was he to broach the plan convincingly, even at an appropriate time, when he occasionally struggled to get through a sentence? Although tempted to send a prayer on the matter, he didn't, knowing the scheme was his will, not *Gott's*. Pivoting to contemplate his folks' farmstead a large field's distance away, Jethro grimaced at the pressure he knew would soon come to bear from them.

The mare bobbed her head. Jethro turned back, his gaze pausing on the upturned buggy. First things first. Right now, Susannah had more pressing needs than a proposed fake relationship to an unsuitable partner.

"When we get your mare t-to the b-barn, I'll b-bring my horse b-back and pull your b-buggy out. One in the d-ditch is b-bad enough. One t-tipped would p-put folks in a t-t-tizzy." Jethro closed his eyes in frustration as he finally got the word out. At the touch of a hand on his arm, he opened them to meet Susannah's warm gaze.

"*Denki*, Jethro. I don't know how to thank you."

He smiled slightly. He hoped she'd remember that when he had the courage to propose his plan.

"You'd have d-done the same for me."

"*Ja*. But not as well." When Susannah removed her hand from his arm, the fallen lock of her hair slipped from behind her shoulder to slide into view. She glanced at it in confusion before hastily reaching up to touch the disarray of her hair and *kapp*.

A flush crept up her cheeks. Rescuing the *kapp* from its precarious perch, she tucked the pins between her lips as she corralled her escaped hair. With deft fingers, she swiftly secured the dark tresses. Quickly reshaping the dented *kapp*, she repinned the prayer covering over her now neatly coiled hair.

Giving her some privacy to put herself to rights, Jethro turned toward the road. Far down its dark surface, he could see a rig coming their way. "When I get your b-buggy t-to your p-place, I'll check over the d-damage. If it's something I can fix, I'll t-take care of it t-tomorrow." His offer had nothing to do with what he was hoping she'd agree to. It was an automatic response to a neighbor in need.

"I couldn't ask you to do that."

"You d-didn't. I offered."

"Well, the least I could do then is fix you some dinner."

"That's all right. I'll b-be fine." They were surely some of the fastest words he'd ever gotten out. Susannah was known in the district for her cooking, and not in a good way.

He glanced at her to ensure his hasty words hadn't offended. Susannah's brown eyes had lost their worry. She grinned. "Coward," she teased.

"P-probably. Or m-maybe just careful." He tugged the mare forward. By tacit agreement, Susannah fell in step beside the horse as he gingerly led Nutmeg out of the steep ditch to the blacktop.

As they started up the road toward the Mast farm, Jethro was aware that every step he took shortened the opportunity for a private conversation. To put his plan into motion and head off the queue of women his parents would soon push in his direction, he needed to secure Susannah's participation. The leather in his hands grew damp as his palms began to sweat. Jethro scowled. Maybe he was a coward. Surely facing Susannah on the question of a fabricated courtship was much better than confronting a continuous sequence of the district's single women who'd be looking for a real one. Hoping for some type of inspiration, he opened his mouth, only to close it again at the sound of an approaching horse and buggy.

Susannah winced as she looked behind them.

"What is it?" Immediately concerned, Jethro stopped the mare. Injuries didn't always make themselves initially known. Susannah may have been more harmed in the accident than she'd let on. "Are you hurt?"

"*Ach, nee.* But my ears will when he comes calling." She nodded toward the approaching rig. "Which will unfortunately be in the next day or so." Susannah slanted Jethro an unhappy look. "At least, according to the bishop."

Jethro's heart began thrumming in his ears, loud enough to drown out the *clip-clop* of the oncoming hooves on the blacktop as he watched Leroy Albrecht, a widower in the district, bear down on them. Maybe *Gott* didn't mind getting on board with Jethro's plan after all. He'd just provided a window of opportunity, one perhaps open wide enough for Jethro to clumsily wiggle through.

"Sounds like we are in a similar situation." He turned to where Leroy was drawing his horse to a halt beside them.

"Everything all right?" the portly man called through the open buggy door.

"Just fine!" chirped Susannah. "Just a little mishap that tipped us into the ditch. But we're all fine."

The man shifted to look back at the listed buggy. "Yours, Susannah? I would think you'd be a better driver at your age. Surely you know how to handle a fractious horse? I suppose I could teach you, should you have any aptitude for horsemanship."

Although Jethro heard Susannah's teeth snap together, he didn't think the sound had carried to the man in the buggy. He snuck a glance at Susannah. Her face—pale after the accident—was now as red as the late-season tomatoes in his garden.

"*Denki* for the offer, Leroy. She got away from me today when a…bee stung her, but we always get along otherwise just fine." Jethro wondered how Susannah got the words out through her gritted teeth.

"Well, should you need a lesson, you remind me when I come over. Day after tomorrow, *ja*?"

"*Ja*. So the bishop had mentioned. That's just… fine." The final word was said as if its meaning was something entirely different from the word that was spoken.

Leroy merely nodded as he lifted the lines. "See you then."

Jethro returned the man's parting wave before raising an eyebrow at his companion. "That was quite a 'fine' visit."

Susannah closed her eyes in a give-me-patience

look. "*Ach*, it would be fine if no one would bother me. The last thing I want or need right now is to have unwanted visitors come courting. I'm busy enough, especially now with having to—" She bit off what she was going to say, instead reaching to carefully stroke the mare above the bloodstain on her dark brown neck. "Any reasonable candidates would be too busy finishing fall work to go courting now."

"Leaving the unreasonable ones t-to show up?" Too nervous to stand still in case he botched this unexpected opportunity, Jethro gently urged the mare forward. "What if…something came up t-to keep them away? At least until after harvest?" he hastily added.

"That would be *wunderbar*." There was a heartfelt sigh from the other side of the mare where Susannah now walked. "Do you think you could persuade your *daed* that any courtship should wait until the winter? Or never?"

Jethro bit his upper lip, worrying the section below the surgery scar where he had no feeling. This wasn't going in the direction he'd hoped. "Ah, *nee*. It's d-difficult t-to p-persuade m-my *d-daed* about m-much of anything." He winced as he struggled over the words. "I was thinking of p-proposing—" Jethro cringed. That definitely wasn't the word he'd wanted to use. "I was thinking of an alternative. One that could help b-both of us."

"That sounds extremely tempting. Anything does to avoid having a parade of unwanted suitors make a path to my door when I've got things to do."

"How about just…one?" Jethro swallowed past the lump the size of a hay bale lodged in his throat.

There was another heavy sigh from the opposite

side of Nutmeg. "One is better than several, but even one could be too many, depending on who it is. Who are you thinking?"

Jethro worried his lip some more. It was far easier leading the mare down the road than to try to lead Susannah in this pivotal conversation. Inhaling so deeply he was afraid his suspenders would snap, Jethro breathed out his response, almost hoping she didn't hear it. "M-me."

Thankfully, Nutmeg's black-maned neck between them prevented Susannah from seeing the strain on his face. Jethro held his breath, expecting any moment to hear her laugh, followed by "Are you kidding?" His response—"*Ja, ja*, I was. Wouldn't that have been funny?"—was on the tip of his tongue.

Instead, it was silent on the other side of the mare. The only sounds were the creaking of the parts of leather harness Nutmeg still wore and the swish of long grass as the odd trio strode through it. When those, along with an occasional buzz of an insect, continued to be the only things his straining ears picked up, Jethro wondered if Susannah had heard him.

He pressed his lips together. He couldn't say it again. He'd barely been able to voice it the first time. It was a foolish idea, made incredibly so by speaking it out loud. His shoulders sagged with dejection. But since he had made a fool of himself, he was glad it was to Susannah. She was the only woman he trusted enough to do so in front of. And even with that, a sweat born of embarrassment dampened his back.

"Why?" Susannah ducked under Nutmeg's neck to appear in front of him. The startled mare wasn't near as stunned as Jethro.

He froze midstride. A quick scan of Susannah's face revealed none of the smirk he'd feared. Nor any incredulity indicating she thought he was demented. If her expression showed anything, it was a bit of concern.

Following a shaky exhale, Jethro struggled to respond. "It would b-be a reprieve for b-both of us? M-my p-parents want m-me t-to start looking for a wife again. I'm…not in a hurry t-to d-do so. B-but it's hard t-to say no t-to them. They d-don't listen t-to no when they d-don't want t-to hear it. At least when they hear it from m-me."

Susannah's mouth opened, like she was going to say something. When she didn't, encouraged, Jethro continued. "So I thought, as you d-don't want a suitor, and I d-don't want t-to b-be one, if I acted like *your* suitor—for appearances only," he hastened to add "—it would t-take care of b-both our p-problems. At least for a while."

Eyes narrowing, Susannah slowly closed her mouth. After considering him for a moment, it tipped into a slanted smile. "Your parents won't like it. You, walking out with me. I'm totally unsuitable for you."

Jethro smiled himself, relaxing for the first time since the ludicrous idea had come to him. "I know. That's p-part of the p-plan's appeal."

She eyed him a moment longer, her hooded gaze transitioning to reveal a hint of mischief in her brown eyes. "What do you propose, on this fake proposal?"

With the hand not holding the reins, Jethro stroked the short beard that proclaimed he'd been married. "I… hadn't gotten that far." He looked back down the road to his parents' small farmstead. "I suppose a start is m-making sure they see us t-together. Or hear about us from others. Which won't t-take m-much d-due t-to the healthy grapevine in the d-district." Casting a guarded glance at Susannah, he tentatively lifted a brow, aware her question didn't mean she was agreeing to his suggestion.

With a sigh, she watched Leroy's buggy top the far hill before shifting her attention to her farmyard just a stone's throw ahead. Reaching out, she ran a gentle hand down the now serene mare's nose.

"Does being a suitor include fixing the buggy?"

"Nee. It was a friend that offered t-to fix it and a friend that will." He grinned. "B-but I suppose it's something a suitor would d-do."

Susannah smiled ruefully. "Will the suitor still be a friend when the courtship has run its course? There are a number of men in the district who might come calling as suitors, but only a few who're always welcome to visit as friends. I wouldn't want to lose a long-term friendship for a short-term courtship."

"Nee." Jethro shook his head adamantly. "This one will always b-be a friend first."

She was going to say yes. Jethro didn't stop to consider why the knowledge elated him beyond outmaneuvering his parents. "Even enough to choke d-down your cooking a t-time or t-two." He almost winked at her. Jethro was momentarily stunned at the temptation. He never winked. But the urge to do so felt very good. "M-maybe that's what'll convince folks we're actually walking out. For sure and certain, no one would eat it m-more than once otherwise."

Susannah frowned as she swatted at him. "My cooking isn't that bad. And it's not like I can't cook. It's that there's always something else that needs to be

done, so the cooking either gets hurried or forgotten."
Giving Nutmeg a last pat, she ducked back under the
mare's neck.

"We'll talk about it more tomorrow when you come
to fix the buggy. It's been a while since I've had a welcomed suitor. I'm not sure I remember how."

With a soft click of his tongue, Jethro prompted the
mare into motion. Some of his exuberance receded. He
wasn't sure if he remembered how, either, as it'd been a
while since he'd been a suitor as well. And even then,
he wasn't sure he'd been a welcomed one. He'd failed
at being a suitor for the right reasons. How could he
hope to succeed when doing it for the wrong ones?

Chapter Two

She couldn't put it off any longer. Susannah drained the sink and shook the dishwater from her hands. Sucking in a fortifying breath, she looked out the window to where her teenage hired hand's push scooter leaned against the side of the big white barn.

She'd intended to talk with him yesterday, but the young man had already been gone by the time she and Jethro had walked Nutmeg back to the farm. Although her hired hand was late—again—for work today, she'd been relieved he'd arrived after Amos had departed for school and her daughter Rebecca had left for work.

John Schlabach always did what Susannah asked him to do, but there were times when he fixed his eyes on her with an unreadable expression that she felt... uneasy. Anticipating the coming confrontation, she was comforted more than she wanted to admit when Jethro had driven his rig up the lane shortly after the young man's arrival.

After drying her hands, Susannah absently pulled the dish towel back and forth between them. Although comforted by his arrival, she was also relieved that

Jethro had gone straight to the damaged buggy he'd deposited by the shed yesterday. She wasn't sure what she'd say yet if he'd come to the house to continue yesterday's odd conversation. She hadn't said yes to his nonproposal, but she hadn't said no, either. As she watched him bend over the damaged buggy shaft, a smile tugged at her.

He looked so different from the quiet, skinny child she'd been a *kinder minder* to years ago. Susannah had felt sorry for Jethro then. Never a patient woman, Ruby Weaver had been particularly short with her older son. She hadn't seemed to know what to do with him and the unexpected cleft lip and palate that'd revealed itself upon his birth. Over the years, Jethro had had a series of community-funded surgeries to correct the split in his lip and roof of his mouth. With each one, Ruby's unhappiness with the boy seemed to grow.

Noting this, Susannah had given Jethro as much positive attention as possible when she'd been with him. She'd discovered his subtle humor, his hardworking, caring character, his eagerness to please. He'd grown into a dependable, respected man in the community. One she was happy to call a friend.

Of course, he was still quiet, even reserved, around most folks. Some of that was probably due to his nature, perhaps more to his stutter. Susannah had been glad yet concerned for Jethro when she'd heard he was marrying his brother's widow. He and the fragile, emotional, Louisa had seemed an odd fit.

Susannah snorted. Now the truly odd fit would be Jethro and herself. Her lips twitched. She'd be surprised if anyone took a courtship between them seriously.

Hanging up the dish towel, her gaze lingered on the man working by the buggy. Except perhaps Jethro. Susannah felt no compunction in disrupting the bishop's plans for her life, at least temporarily, but not if it would negatively affect Jethro. Her gaze grew troubled. What if this solitary, warmhearted man got too attached in the charade? Susannah might not've been courted for a long time, but even she recalled the enjoyment of close companionship. The thrill of a certain someone paying particular attention to you. What if a potentially lonely person mistook that companionship for...something else? She didn't want him to be hurt.

Aren't you getting a bit full of yourself, Susannah? Isn't it hochmut *to think an attractive man in his prime would be interested in you when, if he overcame some shyness, he could probably have his pick of any of the young ladies in the district?*

Now there was another possibility. Maybe a fake courtship would help Jethro overcome some of his reserve. Help him become more confident to go courting in the future, as surely he would. *At least with Jethro, his interest in marriage, even if it's artificial, will be about you and not about the farm. He has his own prosperous place. Unlike some others, he doesn't need or want yours. He, at least, is straightforward in his motives.*

She was going to do it. Susannah shook her head at her foolishness but couldn't suppress the spark of excitement that flared inside her. *Ach,* the community would talk about her, gossip that she was a silly woman, but she didn't mind. It was much better than being set upon by a string of men she had no interest in. And maybe by the time their temporary courtship was over, she'd have time to identify someone who *would* be a reasonable choice—someone with maybe as much interest in her as in her farm—to come calling.

Her excitement popped like one of the soap bubbles she'd used to blow for Jethro as a child when her gaze shifted to the scooter leaning by the barn. In the meantime, she had to deal with her soon-to-be-ex hired hand. Susannah couldn't and wouldn't keep on anyone who'd intentionally hurt one of her animals. And she couldn't dawdle in the house when he might have intentions of harming another of her livestock.

Lifting the lid on a counter canister marked Sugar, she counted out enough bills to cover what she owed the youth. After a brief hesitation, she added a few more before crumpling them in a fisted hand and resolutely heading for the door.

Susannah felt Jethro's eyes on her as she marched across the barnyard. Striving for a confidence she wasn't feeling, she didn't look in his direction, but was well aware of where he knelt by the damaged buggy.

Upon reaching the barn, Susannah paused outside the door. The edge of the wood cut into her palm as she curled a hand over the open Dutch door and peered into the barn's dim interior. Inhaling a shivery breath, she called into its cavernous depths. "John?"

After a moment of stillness, there was a movement in one of the stalls. A young man stepped out of the shadows, his tall, gangly figure seeming not much wider than one of the barn's posts. When he didn't move farther, Susannah called again. "Would you please come here? I need to talk with you."

Although her heart was hammering over what she had to do, it still ached for the youth as he trudged closer. Unhooking the door, Susannah swung it open and stepped back as John approached. Following her lead, he exited into the farmyard. His eyes were unreadable under the shade of his battered flat-brimmed straw hat.

Susannah cleared her throat. "John, there was a nail in Nutmeg's harness collar yesterday. Do you know anything about that?"

The youth didn't speak. Grimacing, he shifted his feet.

"It hurt her so much, we went into the ditch. She could've been injured worse, possibly even broken a leg and had to be put down. I don't think you'd want that. And Amos was with me. He could've been hurt badly."

John was still silent. But he looked away.

"You harnessed her yesterday before we left. I think it would've been something you'd have noticed."

Pressing his lips together, John crossed his arms over his chest.

Stomach twisting with tension, Susannah continued. "Speaking of noticing, I've noticed you haven't been giving *gut* care to the animals. The chicken feed should be almost gone by now. The fact that it isn't, makes me wonder if you're feeding them the amounts you're supposed to. The bedding for the goats isn't nearly as thick as it should be, and it's long past time to be changed. You know what the chores are, John. I could attribute those things to carelessness, or laziness, both of which I'd try to work with you on. But what I can't tolerate is intentionally hurting my animals."

Her soon-to-be-ex hired hand remained studiously silent, his expression rigid.

"Why would you do such a thing, John?" The words

were no more than a whisper. Susannah was sincerely troubled and puzzled over his recent behavior.

The young man's shoulders slumped. He toed the gravel at his feet. When he finally lifted his gaze to her, Susannah almost took a step back.

"Are you going to shun me like you did my *daed*?" John's lip was curled in derision, but the effect was spoiled when his voice cracked on the bitter words. His eyes, although hot, also held a flare of fear.

"Your *daed*..." Susannah paused on a heavy sigh. She'd never mentioned Mervin Schlabach in a conversation with his son. But it was one of the reasons— primarily the reason—she'd hired him. She'd felt sorry for the boy. Susannah didn't know how much John knew about why his father had been shunned and ultimately left the community. He would've been very young when it'd happened. Surely the boy was aware...

"I would never do that." She tried a gentle smile to soften the words. "Besides, you know shunning only applies to baptized members of the church. And you haven't been baptized yet. *Nee*, John, I just need to protect my animals. Both in terms of ensuring they're given the care they need to survive and thrive, and that they're protected from harm. I... It makes me sad to tell you I can't trust you on either account. So I have to let you go."

Susannah could tell from his expression that her statement was expected.

He flinched when she swung her hand up. When she opened her fisted fingers to reveal crumpled bills, John stared at them a moment before hesitantly reaching out to pluck them from her palm. Susannah's heart clenched when he carefully flattened them before neatly refolding them to clutch in a grimy hand.

Her throat tight, Susannah nodded toward his scooter. "It might be best if you left now."

John's hard swallow was evident in his gangling neck. He turned toward the scooter, but paused briefly at Susannah's quiet words.

"I still don't understand why, John."

Jerking the scooter's handlebar toward him, he stepped onto the deck with one foot while simultaneously giving a forceful push with the other.

Susannah pressed her hands to her mouth as he careened down the lane and shot onto the blacktop.

I will not cry, she murmured into her fingertips, although she ached for the young man. Tears might threaten, but they'd never be allowed to fall. She watched until John was a speck in the distance.

Exhaling a sigh that seemed to reach down to her bare toes, Susannah lowered her hands. *Now what?* She had a busy farm and not enough labor to work it. Amos helped, but at eleven years old, he was still in school and would be until he finished eighth grade. Had she made the right decision? Would half a hired hand have been better than none? At the quiet jingle of a halter that filtered through the open barn door, Susannah firmed her lips. Not at the risk to her animals. *Ach,* she wasn't afraid of hard work. She was just troubled about determining which tasks could afford to wait.

The sunny autumn day mocked her morose mood. The tasks would just have to wait a moment more. Needing to regain her equilibrium, Susannah headed to one of her favorite places on the farm, her small orchard. The dry grass felt warm under her feet as she meandered along the avenue between the Fuji and Braeburn apple trees. Summoning a crooked smile, Susannah tried to absorb the peacefulness of the orchard instead of seeing the fruit-laden trees as more work to be done in the next few weeks. Without help.

An occasional leaf drifted by, gliding on the soft breeze. Reaching to a nearby low branch, Susannah plucked an apple as her mind churned over her options. Rebecca worked at the restaurant in town. If she had a later shift, she could help before work as it would be too dark after. Her married daughter, Rachel, might be willing to lend a hand, but with recent twins who'd made Susannah a *grossmammi*, she had enough on her plate. Perhaps Rachel could spare Miriam Schrock, the hired girl staying with them to help tend the *boppeli*, for a day.

Susannah absently brushed a hand against the faint buzzing at her ear. The serenity of the orchard ended abruptly with a sharp sting on her ankle. Automatically swatting at it, Susannah hissed at instant pain on her other foot. When she glanced down, her breath hitched at the sight of wasps swarming around her legs.

She'd unknowingly walked over a ground nest of yellow jackets.

Flinching at the stings while swatting and slapping at her legs, Susannah was rooted with distress for a moment before realizing a retreat was her best option. Snatching up the hem of her dress, she raced toward the house, frantically flapping her skirt to get the wasps out of it as she ran.

Susannah dashed up the steps to the porch, shaking her skirt to discourage any remaining insects. She didn't feel any new stings, but so many places on her legs were already throbbing, it was hard to tell. Panting, she pressed her skirt out of the way against her legs to peer down at her feet.

Welts were already rising on her ankles and lower legs. From the resonating pain, she knew some of the numerous stings were as high as her knees.

At the touch on her elbow, Susannah jumped and spun, almost stumbling down the steps in her agitation. Jethro's firm but gentle grip instantly tightened, preventing her tumble.

His gaze was sharp under furrowed brows. "Are you all right?"

"I'm not sure. I walked over a yellow jacket nest. They didn't take kindly to trespassers." Susannah tried not to wince at the pulsing pain.

Jethro instantly squatted to examine her lower legs. "Are you allergic?" His tone was as intense as his blue eyes when they shot to hers.

"I hope not. As I've made a poor choice to be a beekeeper if I am." Even as she joked about it, Susannah forced a swallow, ensuring she still had the ability to do so.

Jethro wasn't laughing. If anything, his gaze was more stern. "Have you ever b-been stung this many t-times?"

Susannah didn't think so. In fact, as places on her legs continued to throb, she knew so. She'd had a sting here and there, but never like this. Aware that allergic reactions could get worse with each sting, she touched a hand to her throat. Just because she hadn't been deathly allergic yet didn't mean she never would be.

She didn't resist when Jethro opened the door to the kitchen then gently took her hand and led her inside. "Let's get some b-baking soda and water on those stings."

Susannah had used the remedy before. She didn't look forward to the mixture drying and crumbling off all over the house, but the thought of some relief prompted her to quickly point out the cupboard where she kept her baking ingredients.

Upon ushering her to a kitchen table, Jethro pulled out a chair and helped her settle into it.

"B-bowl?" He retrieved one from the cupboard she indicated. Dumping baking soda into it, Jethro crossed to the sink where he dribbled water into it as well. Stirring the mixture with his finger, he returned to where Susannah, fighting a grimace, watched.

Setting the bowl, along with his hat, on the table, Jethro slid out another chair. Susannah frowned as he knelt beside her. When he gingerly touched her ankle, she jumped like she'd been stung again and jerked it away.

"I can do it!" The pain was momentarily forgotten at the startling sensation of his hand on her leg.

"I d-don't know if we're courting yet, b-but I suspect we're going to have our first argument." Ignoring her, Jethro lifted her foot to rest it on the seat of the facing chair. Capturing her other foot, he placed it alongside the first before he calmly reached for the bowl on the table. He regarded Susannah with a raised eyebrow. "*Ja?* Can you see t-the ones on t-the b-back of your legs, t-too?"

Their eyes collided for a moment before she relented with a frown. "*Ach, nee.* But I'll take care of the ones above the hem of my skirt." A hem that fortunately hung down well over her knees.

Nodding, Jethro dipped a finger into the bowl. It was coated with a white paste when he withdrew it.

Susannah tried not to sigh in relief at the cool comfort when he began dabbing the mixture onto her stings. Even so, he must've sensed her tension.

"I know these are hurting." He covered a few more rising welts with the white mixture. Susannah hissed in a breath as he removed a tiny barb, lost by one of the wasps, out of a welt before treating it. Jethro winced in sympathy. "It's strange t-to t-tend t-to your wounds. B-but only fair, I guess, as you'd t-tended t-to m-many of m-mine when I was young."

Susannah suspected he was just talking to distract her. She appreciated his efforts. She wanted to respond in kind. But she couldn't. Because his tending her wounds wasn't the only thing that was strange.

There was also her unexpected reaction. Susannah's breathing shallowed. Heat seeped through her, flushing her skin. Was she allergic after all?

Chapter Three

It only took a moment to determine it wasn't an allergy that was making her senses hum. This hum didn't generate from wasps or their stings. No, this was much, much worse. Her senses were humming from Jethro's soft touch.

Susannah inhaled sharply. Jethro paused in his ministrations to give her another sympathetic glance, probably assuming her distress was because she hurt. *Hopefully* assuming it was because she hurt. Because he must never know what she was feeling. For what she was feeling was ludicrous.

This was Jethro; his folks had been her neighbors since she couldn't remember when. He was at least a decade younger than she was. She'd changed his diapers when he was a *boppeli.*

Unexpectedly dry-mouthed, Susannah watched Jethro's callused but careful hands as they delicately treated her stings. He shifted, his white shirt stretching over lean but broad shoulders.

He wasn't a *boppeli* any more.

The kitchen was suddenly too quiet. Susannah filled

the uncomfortable void with nervous chatter. "I don't know. Two days in a row? I seem to have started a habit of having you tend to me."

Susannah wanted to snatch the words back. She certainly didn't want to draw attention to him taking care of her.

Jethro turned his head to glance at her, the corner of his mouth tipped in a smile. It was a neighborly look. A simple I've-known-you-all-my-life look. But when their gazes caught, they tangled. They lingered. In his eyes, the warmth shared with the tilted smile flared into something else. Awareness? Interest?

Susannah's breath caught at the sight. Oh dear! She worried about him getting too attached. What if she was the one who got the foolish notion this charade was more than what it was? That would embarrass him. And her.

Abruptly, she swept her feet off the chair. They landed with a thump on the floor, jarring the already hard, aching, itchy welts. Gritting her teeth, Susannah sat forward and extended a hand for the bowl. "*Denki*, but I can get the rest."

Jethro sat back on his heels before nodding and handing her the bowl. Pushing to his feet, he turned his back and faced her simple white-painted cupboards. "Go ahead and t-take care of them. I won't watch."

He may not be watching, but Jethro had always been a good listener. It was quiet for several seconds before the scrape of a chair sliding back and the rustle of material told him she was treating the remaining stings as he'd suggested. He stared at the metal handles on the cupboards as, one by one, he touched his thumbs to where he could feel his pulse beating at the tips of his fingers. *Now wasn't that interesting.*

Although he had hopes, he still wasn't sure what her answer to yesterday's question would be. Would the unexpected surge in his pulse at the look they'd shared cause a problem in that awkward proposal? Crossing his arms over his chest, Jethro pressed hands under his arms until all he felt against his fingertips was the cotton of his shirt. *It couldn't. It wouldn't.* He'd assured her the endeavor wouldn't affect their friendship. It would surely embarrass and dismay Susannah if he were to… what? Fall in love with her?

His face flaming at the prospect, Jethro's attuned ears picked up the quiet tread of bare feet on linoleum and the sound of the bowl being set on the counter. For numerous heartbeats, Susannah didn't move from the counter.

Clearing his throat, he offered over his shoulder, "I've heard that honey works as well."

"At least that's something I have plenty of. And it will stay on much better than this when it dries. You can turn around now."

Jethro pivoted to face her. Susannah stood by the sink, her arms crossed over her chest as well. As he regarded her, a faint blush crept up her cheeks. She hugged her arms more tightly. Jethro's lips almost twitched at the sight they must make, both of them coiled up like a roll of wire fencing. It didn't seem the time to ask about her decision, but he wanted to know, now more than ever, what might be their path forward. Maybe, as his heart finally settled back to normal, it would be better if she said no.

Although they felt as stiff as the Tinman without

oil, Jethro lowered his arms. "D-did you think about what I said yesterday?"

Her cheeks still pink, Susannah nodded her head slowly. *"Ja.* I can see some of the merits of the idea."

"And?"

"Does this count as courting?"

Jethro's pulse kicked up again. "It's an abnormal start."

Susannah smiled faintly. "I suppose that's fitting, as it's an abnormal courtship. What do we do next?"

"I'm not sure." His marrying Louisa had been more of a foregone conclusion than a courtship. Since then, other than a few awkward meals with a young woman his folks had pushed upon him—one who'd fortunately been interested in another man—Jethro had been able to avoid courtship.

Susannah shifted her weight to rub one foot against the paste-marked spots of the other. Bits of powder flaked to the linoleum floor. "Usually the intent of a courting couple is to keep their relationship unknown until it's announced in church, at least for youth in their *rumspringa.*"

Rumspringa—the years when Amish youth were allowed to explore more of the world to determine their decision regarding baptism into the church and to choose a mate—had held no interest for Jethro. Intending to do the former and having no intention of doing the latter, his runaround time had been very short. He'd attended baptism classes as soon as he'd been allowed.

"Our objective would b-be the opposite. We want p-people t-to know. We want m-my folks t-to, at least."

Susannah dropped her arms to her sides. "I suppose,

then, we need to be seen together when we wouldn't normally have a reason to be with each other, at least by your folks. That shouldn't be too hard, as they're the next farm down the road."

"B-being here to fix your b-buggy is a start. B-but I should have it d-done b-by the end of the d-day."

"*Denki*, Jethro. I appreciate your help, but I'm sorry to have kept you from your own work."

"It's not a p-problem." Crossing to the table, Jethro picked up his flat-brimmed straw hat. "Speaking of help, it looked like your hired hand went d-down the road. Is he coming b-back?"

Susannah sighed and shook her head. "*Nee*, I had to let him go after what he'd done to Nutmeg."

His gaze sharpened. He couldn't imagine purposely hurting an animal. "So it was intentional?"

It was obvious Susannah shared his sentiment. "He didn't say, but *ja,* I suspect so."

"Why?"

"That, I don't know."

"It leaves you short-handed at a b-busy time."

Susannah sagged against the counter. "*Ja.* I fear so."

"What needs t-to be d-done t-today?"

"What doesn't? I need to check on Nutmeg. I'm not sure if John cleaned the horse stalls, or the goat pen. After that, there's the garden and some remaining field work…" Her voice trailed off.

Glancing at the white residue in the bowl on the counter, Susannah shook her head wearily. "And now, the yellow jacket nest. It's too close to my beehives for comfort. If the wasps have any kind of food shortage, they'll attack my hives. If it's a big nest, they'll kill my bees and take the honey. I can reduce the entrances into the hive so the bees have a better chance of defending it. Though yellow jackets do serve some purpose in nature, to protect my bees—" her lips thinned in a humorless smile "—I'd prefer to take out the nest." She grimaced. "If I can find it."

Jethro's gaze dropped to the red welts marring the slender legs below her hemline. He'd been stung by wasps before. Some stings could feel like a baseball bat had made a solid connection. She had to be in pain. And itchy. Whether friend or suitor, he couldn't let her risk getting stung again. "I'll t-take care of the livestock when I finish with the b-buggy."

Susannah instantly straightened from her slump. "I couldn't ask you to do that."

"You d-didn't ask. I offered. What you need t-to d-do is get off your feet and continue t-to t-take care of those stings. I counted at least seven, p-plus whatever you've t-treated."

Jethro could read from her expression that she wouldn't mind doing as he'd suggested. But wouldn't. At least not yet. She'd always been a stubborn female. "Susannah, m-most of m-my crops are already in for the year. I have a b-bit of t-time t-to spare t-to help." He gave her a half smile. "It's what friends, if not suitors, d-do. P-plus, it gives m-my folks m-more of a chance t-to see m-me here," he reminded her.

Susannah regarded him with lowered brow before finally conceding with a sigh, "I could use any help you can provide."

He nodded. Having been pushed frequently in his life, he knew when not to. "How d-do you p-plan t-to find the nest?"

Wincing, she bent to scratch at the red welts on her

legs. More powder drifted to the linoleum floor. "I need to catch a wasp, mark it and follow it back to the nest and mark the nest when I find it. Later this evening, when all the wasps are inside, I'll pour soapy water…or—" Opening the cupboard from where he'd gotten the baking soda behind her, she shifted a few jars around. "Molasses. I should have enough of that to seal the nest. The wasps get trapped in the thickness."

Jethro eyed her dubiously. "How d-do you p-plan to catch a wasp and m-mark it?"

Susannah glanced over her shoulder with a wry smile. "Carefully. With gloves, a lidded cup and this." She withdrew a bag of powdered sugar from the cupboard.

Jethro raised his eyebrow. He wasn't going to ask. "Find a b-big p-pair of gloves. I'll catch the wasp."

She opened her mouth like she was going to argue. Closing it again, she bit her lip and rubbed one leg against the other again. There was now more powder on the floor than her legs. "I won't argue with that today."

"Why d-don't you sit for a m-moment with ice or something while I t-take care of the livestock? Then we'll catch a wasp."

An Amish woman rarely had time to sit during the day. Even under the circumstances, he didn't think Susannah would make an exception. Surprisingly, she nodded. She must be in considerable pain, indeed. Pulling out a drawer, she retrieved a plastic bag before hobbling to the gas-powered refrigerator and withdrawing a handful of ice from the freezer section to drop it into the bag.

"You m-might also t-try a sweet p-pickle juice compress. The alum in it is supposed t-to help." With that suggestion, Jethro headed out the door.

* * *

Two hours later, he and Susannah were standing in the shade of one of her apple trees. Jethro's shirt sleeves were rolled down. On his hands was a worn leather pair of gloves. Susannah attention flicked around their surrounding area, searching for potential captives for the cup she held, its bottom covered with a powdery white substance.

Her distraction gave him a chance to study her profile. Her features were relaxed, but the strain of the day's pain was evident in her tanned face. The only hint to her years was the creases at the corners of her eyes. Ones that crinkled when she smiled. He remembered her as always smiling when he was young. But with running a farm while nursing an ill husband before losing him around a year ago, and taking care of her family alone since, she hadn't had a lot to smile about. Neither of them had.

Susannah had had a nice smile. It surprised Jethro how much he wanted to put another one on her face.

"I can understand how you got your reputation, or lack of it, for b-baking skills. You d-don't use your groceries for cooking b-but for farm work. M-molasses and sugar for wasps. B-baking soda for your legs. I think I'll stay and see what you feed the goats t-tonight."

As Jethro intended, her lips curved at his teasing. The tenseness in her shoulders eased fractionally. He found himself relaxing as well.

He'd only been six when a teenage Susannah had married Vernon Mast. The rumored reason had been to save her family's farm after her father had died. Jethro hadn't been and still wasn't one for rumors, but his *mamm* was. Six was a young age to listen and re-member conversation, but Susannah had minded him frequently when his *mamm* wasn't able, and he'd liked her. She'd been…fun, a rarity in his life back then. She had never stared at his scar, which'd been much more prominent. Perhaps what'd struck him the most was that she'd always been patient while he'd struggled to communicate. That was probably why he spoke more easily with her than any other woman.

Whatever the reason, Jethro had wondered when she hadn't come around anymore. His *mamm* had shushed him when he'd asked about her absence and told him Susannah had her own family to attend to now. As had Jethro's *mamm*, since his little *bruder* had soon ap-peared. His perfect little *bruder*. Jethro stared unsee-ing at the ripe apple in front of him as his shoulders rose over a deep sigh.

"It's not as bad as rumors claim. As the youngest *dochder*, by the time I arrived, my folks had given up on having a *sohn*. So while my older *schweschdere* mostly stayed inside and helped my *mamm*, I was out-side working with my *daed*." Susannah's gaze shifted to the collection of white buildings down the little rise. "It's not that I can't cook or bake. It's just that I'd still rather be outside, and frequently am. So sometimes food is a little too done or…"

"Not d-done enough? Or b-both at once?"

She scowled as she idly shook the powdered sugar inside the container. "You heard about that?" She peered at him. "Of course you did. I'm sure everyone has. Still, it had a benefit."

Jethro raised an eyebrow.

"Now I'm only asked to provide bread and church

spread on Sundays and other gatherings." Her eyes crinkled as they joined her grin. "It cuts down on what I have to prepare. Especially when Rebecca makes the bread."

They both froze at a nearby buzzing sound. Susannah flinched when a striped yellow jacket flew idly over her shoulder to land on a small branch nearby. As it worked its way to a dangling apple, Jethro carefully took the cup from her. Removing the lid, he cautiously raised it above the distracted wasp with the cup below. When the wasp lifted off the branch, Jethro slammed down the lid, knocking the yellow jacket into the cup. Quickly securing the lid, he rocked the now vibrating container to and fro, coating the startled wasp with the white powder.

"Now what?"

"Now we let him out to betray his community."

His lips quirked. "You're vindictive for an Amish p-person. What happened t-to t-turn the other ankle?"

"Both ankles have turned hot. And aching. And itchy." Susannah looked up at him with an impish expression. "The wasps are hungry. I'm planning on sharing the contents of my cupboard with them. It's a neighborly thing to do. What more could they want?"

Gazing down into her face, Jethro's fingers tightened on the container. He knew he needed to be careful about what he wanted in this courtship he'd suggested. It was to be an act. Something to fool his parents. It wouldn't do if the only thing that ended up foolish about their ploy was him actually falling for Susannah.

Hours later, Susannah headed for the orchard, a heavy jar of molasses in her hand. The time had fled since they'd released the wasp and watched it zigzag a path before settling in the grass to disappear from view. Creeping closer, Jethro had identified the hole in the ground and carefully stuck a stick trailing a bit of white fabric at the entrance.

Her heartrate accelerated as she climbed the hill in the tranquil moonlit night. Not because of the uncertain task ahead, but because of the man at her side.

Jethro had gone into town to obtain a part for the wrecked buggy, teasing Susannah that he'd get lunch while he was there. She'd countered that she didn't mind, it saved her from stopping to fix something on the farm. She'd kept busy—as always—while he was gone. But what was new was the breathless lift to her heart when his rig had driven up her lane later in the afternoon.

Upon finishing the buggy repair, Jethro had joined her in the garden, harvesting the last of the squash and pumpkins, and pulling the vines to prepare the patch for tilling in fertilizer. Amos had returned from school by the time they'd finished. Her son had assisted Jethro in doing chores while she'd gone inside to prepare supper. And took her time doing so to ensure it was one of her better meals. When Jethro hesitantly took a bite after she'd invited him to stay once they'd finished chores, he'd met her watchful gaze and raised his eyebrows in appreciation. And lifted Susannah's heart further.

Saying he couldn't let her face the nest alone in case the wasps rallied for an attack—and besides, his rig needed to be parked in her yard just in case someone should drive by—Jethro had stayed until darkness had settled and the full moon had risen. He'd listened quietly while Amos told of the softball game at recess and Rebecca had shared news of the potential sale of the restaurant in town.

The evening had been…nice. Too nice. It touched on an ache that was far different from the residual stings throbbing around Susannah's ankles.

Don't get used to it. This is only temporary. Jethro is a man in his prime. He has a successful farm of his own. He doesn't need to marry an old widow to get one. Tucking the jar against her side, Susannah crossed her arms over her chest.

"Cold?" Jethro murmured. The autumn's evening temperature had dropped as quickly as the earlier setting sun.

"Nee." She nodded toward the stake with its pale streaming material. "Just hope this works."

A barred owl in the surrounding dark fringe of woods called its iconic cry. *Whocooksforyou?* Before they'd gone a few more steps, another owl answered from farther in the distance. *Whocooksforyouall?*

Jethro bumped his shoulder against hers. "I know who d-doesn't."

Susannah's heart squeezed at the action. *Don't get any ideas. It doesn't mean anything. The man is just practicing before we take this courting act public.* But from the way her pulse skittered, she didn't think Jethro needed any practice. "Provoke me all you want, I'm still not giving up the jar."

They'd had a quiet yet intense debate over who would crouch by the nest and pour the molasses. Jethro didn't want Susannah to risk getting stung again. Susannah silently figured the stings might do her some good at the present. Get her mind off the moonlit night and the unexpected attractiveness of the man beside her, and remind her that Jethro was there for a purpose. And it was because he *wasn't* looking for a wife, not because he was.

Unscrewing the jar's lid, she crept up to the stake. Absent of artificial light, as any light would attract the wasps, it took a moment of searching to find the hole in the tall grass. When she knelt and poured the molasses down it, she flinched at the initial buzzing. But as more thick brown substance flowed into the hole, the sound was increasingly muffled. She tipped the jar upside down for a moment to prompt the sluggish material to drain out. Recapping the lid, she stood and stepped back.

Jethro relieved her of the now empty jar. "There. Your b-bees are safe."

Susannah nodded, hoping that was the case. She'd check tomorrow.

"I've never heard of a female Amish b-beekeeper," Jethro observed as they started back down the hill to where her white barn and house gleamed in the reflected moonlight.

Susannah smiled softly at memories. "My *daed* kept them. As he had no sons, I'd take care of the hives with him. When he was gone, I just didn't want to look up on the hill and not see them there anymore. So I kept a few of them."

Jethro nodded as he walked silently beside her. His steps slowed as he looked up until he drifted to a halt.

Susannah presumed he was gazing at the stars. She stopped, tipping her head back, as well, to take in the magnificent display. With the clear night, along with the absence of ground lights in the Amish neighborhood, the overhead glow seemed to press so close you could almost reach up to touch it.

"And something I've never d-done is walk in the m-moonlight with a woman. It's nice." His gaze remained on the stars, but Susannah heard his quiet murmur in the stillness of the evening.

She had to lower her head so she could swallow past the sudden dryness in her mouth. "You don't have to say that. There's no one to hear or see us."

When he looked at her, she could easily make out his crooked smile. "P-perhaps. But m-my *m-mamm* has sharp eyes, sharp ears and a nosy nature. And her kitchen window faces this way."

Susannah turned to squint at the farmhouse across the field. All she could make out was a very faint glow from inside the house, most likely from a gas light or lantern. "If she is, she's not seeing much."

"We can fix that." He extended his hand to her.

For an instant, Susannah stared blankly at his work-roughened palm. She'd never walked in the moonlight with a man, other than with her late husband while looking for escaped livestock. And she'd never held hands with one, just for connection's sake. Not even her husband. Her breathing shallowed. Remembering Jethro's jolting touch earlier today, she tangled her fingers into her apron. "If we jump into it too fast, they might suspect it's not a real courtship."

Crossing her arms over her chest, Susannah began walking again. "It has gotten considerably chillier, hasn't it?" She hoped he wouldn't be upset, but her senses were already foolishly affected by the surprising pleasantness of the earlier evening with Jethro and her family and the current alluring surroundings. It wouldn't do to agitate them further.

She blew out a quiet breath in relief when Jethro fell into step beside her, seemingly unoffended. Side by side, they ambled down to the farmyard to where he'd already harnessed his Standardbred as they'd waited for full darkness. Jethro climbed into the buggy. "T-tomorrow," was all he said before directing his horse down the lane.

Watching the rig depart, Susannah absently rubbed her hands together before reaching down to scratch at her ankles. She frowned with concern. Not for her itchy and achy skin, but her heart, which was acting in a similar manner.

Be careful, Susannah. He's not for you. He's young. He needs someone who can give him a family. And that's not you. Remedies involving baking soda and pickle juice won't do anything to heal a broken heart.

Chapter Four

Susannah wiped down the countertop, her movements brisk with agitation. She had so much she needed to be doing today instead of playing hostess to an unwanted suitor. But Bishop Weaver had been adamant when he'd cornered her after church last Sunday.

It'd been a year since Vernon had died. It was time for her to remarry. The farm was too big for her to run alone. His admonishing recitations were like the order of hymns in their church service; he'd been voicing the same ones to her every church Sunday in the same sequence.

Striding to the table, Susannah scrubbed furiously at a spot of honey dripped by Amos at breakfast. She was accustomed to running the farm by herself, even with a husband. Both while Vernon had been sick and before, when he'd found things he'd rather do than work the farm that Susannah had inherited as the youngest girl in a family of daughters. *Ja*, it was difficult, particularly without a hired hand. But now with Jethro's help...

She paused while swiping the dishrag over the rest

of the oak table. *With Jethro's help.* His help made a big difference. Both on the farm and as a pretend beau, which would hopefully make this the last visit of an unwanted suitor, at least for a while.

As far as a wanted one…her gaze drifted to where Jethro had parked his buggy by the barn when he'd arrived a short while ago. She'd had a lot of time *not* sleeping last night after their moonlit walk to think about that. *Ja,* she'd had flickers of awareness that Jethro was no longer a *boppeli* or little boy. And she was no longer an immature girl. Nor was she married anymore. And neither was he.

They were both single adults.

The flickers had been…preposterous. And that's how she needed to treat them. Even if no one saw through their sham, the community knew they were totally unsuitable for each other. As did she. So any wayward flickers would just have to be extinguished. She could do that. She was well acquainted with stifling longings over the years and being satisfied with what she had.

Crossing to the sink, Susannah dropped the dishrag into soapy water with a splash. She supposed she should provide some refreshments for the pending visit, although she didn't want to encourage the unwanted guest. The goats had taken longer than expected this morning. She usually enjoyed her time with them but they'd put her behind today and left her little time to get ready.

Shooting a glance at the clock, she realized her potential suitor was to arrive in fifteen minutes. Susannah froze at the *clip-clop* of hooves coming up the lane that drifted through the open window. The only thing she liked less than a courting widower was an overeager one.

With a waist-deep sigh, she brushed a quick hand down her apron and headed to the kitchen door in time to see Leroy Albrecht descend from his buggy. Although she'd known his deceased wife, they hadn't been close friends. Still, Susannah had a great deal of admiration for the departed Mrs. Albrecht. Anyone who could live with Leroy had more patience than Susannah could ever summon. She'd rather spend the day with the goats. While she watched, her assigned suitor rubbed his hands together as he glanced around her well-kept farm with an assessing expression. *Ja*, she'd definitely rather spend it with the goats. She held the door open for him with a gritted-teeth smile and a false welcome.

Without pausing to respond to her greeting, Leroy made his way to the oak table, slid out a chair and settled into it. The last place Susannah wanted to be was sitting across from his florid face. Flicking on the gas oven, she pulled a mixing bowl from the cupboard.

"I thought I'd mix up some cookies."

Leroy nodded in agreement. "I'd sure appreciate that. My wife, Arleta, was *wunderbar* in the kitchen. It's essential my next one is as well. I'd heard about your cooking, so when the bishop mentioned I should pay you a call, I was apprehensive. But I thought, for sure and certain, she can't be as bad as they say."

In the process of beating the butter and sugar in the bowl, Susannah paused an instant before her wooden spoon whipped a little faster. *Oh I can't, can I?*

"I don't think there's much more important work for a woman to do than to take care of her man. 'Course it's well known that you've always been a hard worker on the farm and that's important, too."

Ja, Susannah decided. *I can.* Jerking the baking soda down from the cupboard, she jiggled the box to determine the quantity inside. Leroy's wife had needed to be a hard worker. Because he certainly wasn't. Retrieving her measuring cups, Susannah poured a heaping amount of baking soda into the quarter cup measurer and dumped it into the batter.

"That's why I've been seeking out the more—" Susannah could feel the man's eyes on her as he hesitated "—mature widows."

Susannah wasn't feeling very mature as she added three times the amount of salt the recipe stated before eyeballing an amount of flour and spices and beating the batter more vigorously than any electric mixer could. The man couldn't see what she was doing anyway with her more...mature figure in the way.

Snagging a cookie sheet from a lower cupboard, Susannah banged it on the counter to drown out whatever he was droning on about how his late wife cooked and baked so wonderfully. After spooning the dough onto the sheet, she popped it into the oven and turned to face her unwanted guest.

"My wife was a *gut* housekeeper." Leroy shifted to gaze around the rest of what he could see of her home from the kitchen. Susannah watched his eyes linger on the two baskets of laundry she'd pulled from the clothesline last evening and hadn't yet had time to put away. Leroy grimaced at the evidence that she might not be up to his standards, but his expression when he turned back to Susannah indicated he'd overlook the fact if necessary.

A flush unrelated to her vigor in stirring the batter climbed up Susannah's neck.

"It sure was a dry drive over. If you wouldn't mind getting me a drink?"

"*Nee. Nee,* I wouldn't mind at all." Reaching for a pitcher, Susannah fixed a drink that would be a fitting companion for the upcoming cookies.

It wasn't a surprise when a short time later Leroy decided she wouldn't be much of a match for him. Susannah was still smiling at the expression on his face when, after dubiously considering the flat blob of cookie on his plate, he bit into it. When he took a drink, her unwelcomed suitor's eyes bulged and his face reddened to a degree that she wondered for a moment if she'd have to hurry down to the phone shack to call in Gabe Bartel, the community's local EMS.

Fortunately, Leroy recovered quickly, shoving away from the table so forcefully the glass of lemonade tipped over. With a wary glance in her direction, he headed for the door.

"*Mach's gut.*" Susannah called a cheery farewell as it slammed behind him. With a satisfied smile, she grabbed a dishcloth to clean up the mess.

The first thing Jethro noticed when Susannah responded to his knock on her door with a greeting to enter was a pitcher of what looked like lemonade on the table, along with some curious-looking cookies. In a hurry to get his chores done to help at her place, he'd left his farm without eating breakfast and only gulping down a hasty cup of coffee.

Hoping she wouldn't mind, he grabbed a glass from

the drainer, strode to the table and poured it full of lemonade.

"Don't drink that," Susannah directed without turning around from where she worked at the sink.

Jethro paused with the glass halfway to his lips.

Turning to face him, she reached for it. "It isn't for you. You won't like it."

Jethro eyed the pale yellow liquid in the glass. It looked like perfectly good lemonade to him. After cleaning out the barn, he could almost taste its tartness cutting through the dust that seemed to coat his mouth. Pushing back the brim of his hat with his opposing wrist, he rubbed it across his sweaty forehead.

"You d-don't share lemonade at your house?"

"Not when I make it to chase away potential suitors." Susannah's lips twitched as her hand dropped and she propped it on her hip. "Go ahead. Try it. Let me know if I was successful."

Now eyeing the glass suspiciously, Jethro cautiously took a sip. At the first taste, he scrunched his eyes closed and puckered his mouth. Upon recovering, he set the glass on the table and nudged it farther away with a forefinger. When he glanced at Susannah, she was watching, the smile in her brown eyes matched by the one on her lips.

"D-did it work?"

She wrinkled her nose. "I hope so. He left fast enough. A bit of vinegar in the lemonade helped. But time will tell. Don't eat the cookies, either."

It seemed a shame. They were cooling on the rack on the table. Although haphazard in size and shape, hungry as he was, they still looked tempting.

"Probably enough baking soda in there to use them

as a salt lick." Susannah pursed her lips. "I don't like to waste things, but I hesitate to even feed them to the goats. Contrary to myth, goats don't really eat everything. They're pretty good about avoiding things that aren't good for them. Which would include these cookies."

"The visit needed such d-drastic m-measures?"

Susannah poured his glass into the sink, rinsed it and refilled it from a pitcher of tea in the refrigerator. "Some people can't take a subtle hint. Or they're determined. But not as determined as I am in not wanting to marry that particular person."

From the barn, Jethro had watched Leroy Albrecht drive his rig up the lane. He'd smiled when the man had hitched up his trousers and strode confidently to the house. Jethro hadn't been able to see Susannah's expression when she'd met her visitor at the door, but recalling her reaction to the man yesterday, he'd been tempted to watch the show and finish the barn work later. But he liked his own privacy and extended it to others accordingly. Still, it would've been amusing. He knew Leroy well enough to be aware of the man's appetite. The cookies must be bad, indeed, if they were able to drive him off.

As he eyed the cookies, his stomach growled. Loud enough for Susannah to hear as she frowned. "Are you hungry?"

Jethro scratched his beard. "P-probably not enough t-to t-try those."

Susannah nodded with wry acknowledgment as she opened a cupboard door. "I think I have other options. Hmm, there's some cookies from the Bent N' Dent, or there's bread and church spread."

As a busy widower, Jethro was well familiar with food from the local store that sold damaged package and expired goods. Opportunities for homemade bread and the popular peanut butter, marshmallow crème Amish mixture came less frequently. And as far as he knew from Sunday meals, both the offerings were safe. "Church spread sounds *gut*."

Taking his glass of tea to the table, Jethro sat as Susannah efficiently cut a few thick slices of bread and set them, a butter knife and a jar of spread in front of him.

He sighed as he slathered some of the creamy mixture onto a slice. "I think the b-buggy is fixed. B-but I t-took a look at the harness t-today. I need t-to get some things t-to repair the p-places I had t-to cut t-to free the m-mare when she was d-down. Should've remembered them yesterday." He been too distracted thinking of their recent arrangement, but he wasn't going to admit that. "I need t-to go b-back t-to Miller's Creek t-today so you have a harness when you need it." Taking a bite, he eyed her thoughtfully. "Want t-to go with m-me?"

He'd anticipated the words before she hastened to say them. "I don't have time."

Finishing the rest of that piece, he nodded understandably as he chewed. "T-true. B-but d-do you have t-time to m-make another b-batch of goat-rejected cookies for an unwanted visitor?"

Susannah scowled at him. "The goats didn't reject my cookies. I refuse to feed the cookies to them. And what does that have to do with a trip to town?"

Jethro picked up the second slice of bread. "It'd b-be a chance for folks t-to see us t-together. Get word out of our…relationship. M-might stop some future visits," he said, tipping his head toward the cookies. "B-besides, I figured you m-might need some groceries, the way you use up yours on first-aid, wasp slaying and wasted cookies."

Sinking into a chair across the table from him, Susannah narrowed her eyes in a mock glare. Jethro concentrated on smearing the second slice with church spread to keep his lips from twitching.

She huffed out a breath. "I suppose there's merit in that."

Jethro lifted the bread to his mouth to hide his smile. "Out of curiosity, who are m-my…competitors? Who else would m-my *d-daed* b-be sending your way?" Although he was familiar and, to his knowledge, on good terms with everyone in the district, Jethro minded his own business and didn't pay attention to the social undercurrents of the community. He knew the men who weren't married, but not those who might want to be.

Susannah fiddled with a cookie on the cooling rack. "There's a few I've caught casting occasional unexpected glances my way recently." When Jethro didn't say anything, just raised an eyebrow, she continued, although with obvious reluctance. "It seems like Henry Troyer is ready to marry again. I think after the…challenges that Lydia gave him, he wants some help with the rest of the *kinder* at home."

Jethro nodded. Henry was a *gut* man who'd lost his wife a few years ago. Jethro might not pay much attention, but even he'd noticed that one of Henry's older daughters, Lydia, had been more than a little fast. He hadn't been too surprised when he'd heard she'd gone to live with relatives in Pennsylvania.

"Thomas Riehl's children have moved to Indiana to work in the factories where they build recreational vehicles. I would imagine he's lonely." She furrowed her forehead. "And I suppose David Neuenschwander."

Jethro raised his eyebrows at the name. "D-David? He's an old b-boy."

"Just because he never married, doesn't mean he doesn't want to."

Heat crept up Jethro's neck at her gentle chiding. If he hadn't married Louisa at his parents' urging, and her reluctant acceptance, he'd probably be an old boy—the Amish term for an older bachelor—too. "Well, I know he's *gut* with horses. I heard that when Samuel Schrock gets a really skittish one from the t-track, he leaves them with D-David for a b-bit t-to work with them b-before he b-brings them home." And if Samuel, the local horse trader, who was an excellent horseman himself, trusted David, the man must really have a gentle touch with the animals.

Susannah wrinkled her nose. "I don't mean to imply that they're not *gut* men. They are. I just don't have time or interest right now in trying to determine which might be a *gut* man for me and my family. And for the farm."

Brushing the crumbs from his fingers, Jethro stood from the table. "I guess that m-means we go into t-town t-today t-together and let them think you've p-picked m-me."

Susannah's gaze trailed after Jethro as he headed out the door to ready his buggy for the trip. Her fingers tapped on the table as she considered the men she'd mentioned, all the men in the district for that matter.

Jethro was indeed a good pick. Her lips slanted in a rueful smile as she rose from the chair.

But while he might be a *gut* man for her, Susannah knew she wasn't the right wife for him.

Chapter Five

Susannah's pulse surged as Jethro settled onto the buggy seat next to her. It felt odd to be sitting on the left side—the wife's side—of a seat again. She twisted her hands in her lap. Did she really want to be doing this? Agreeing to Jethro's plan when they were isolated on the farm was one thing. But actually taking it public in their community? She smoothed out her apron before resting her damp palms on it.

Certainly, it might give her some peace from the unwanted visits of men the bishop directed her way. But at what cost? She normally wasn't one who worried about what people thought of her, but—sneaking a glance at Jethro's strong, solid profile—would they laugh at a foolish older woman for encouraging a courtship from a man more than ten years her junior? One who could, and should, be seeking a spouse closer to his age?

Jethro certainly didn't seem to mind what people might think. He turned his head and, finding her attention on him, gave her a smile. "If we d-don't see m-my folks t-today, how fast d-do you think it will t-take the news t-to reach them?"

Knowing the speed of the Amish grapevine, Susannah rolled her eyes. "Probably before we can even get back to the farm."

Jethro nodded in satisfaction.

"You're that eager for them to find out?"

"Ja." His smile migrated from teasing to melancholy. After several minutes with only the sound of the buggy wheels and the cadence of his gelding's hooves on the blacktop, Susannah didn't think Jethro was going to say any more. His gaze was fixed on the road ahead of them, his mind obviously somewhere else.

When he caught her still watching him, Jethro grimaced. "I d-doubt they'll ever stop, b-but I want them t-to consider what they're d-doing a b-bit longer b-before they p-push m-me on the d-district's women again."

Susannah's eyes widened when she watched the strong column of his tanned throat bob in a hard swallow. She heard him clear his throat as he turned his face away. Whatever Jethro was going to say next, it was difficult for him. When he spoke, it was directed toward the far ditch. Sitting breathlessly still, Susannah listened intently, her gaze fixed on the back of the sandy-blond hair that stretched to his shirt collar from under his straw hat.

"I'm... I fear the way you feel about Leroy coming courting is the way..." With his face still turned away, he dipped his chin. His voice dropped in volume so she could barely hear his words. "It's the way women would feel if I came calling."

Her heart clenched. Without thinking, Susannah reached out to grasp the work-roughened hands holding the lines. "Oh *nee*, Jethro. I'm sure that's not true."

Facing forward, his profile revealing a wistful smile, he shrugged one shoulder. "Isn't it?"

"*Nee.* Not that I've been listening to that kind of talk, but I'm sure your courtship would be welcomed."

He snorted softly. "B-because I'm the b-bishop's only son. B-because of the size of m-my farm. B-because I can p-provide for them."

His words struck too close to home for Susannah to immediately respond. Her husband had married her for her farm. And she had done more of the providing. It'd taken a long time to accept that as her primary worth.

Withdrawing her hand, she curled it into a loose fist at the memories. But she couldn't let this *gut*, sensitive man believe that was all he had to offer. She'd been thinking of their subterfuge only as how it might keep her from unwanted courtships. Not how much it might help Jethro avoid the same, potentially painful, activity. Having heard his reluctant admission, Susannah resolved to help protect her self-conscious friend. Even if she'd endure a bit of ridicule herself in doing so. If he wanted a fake sweetheart, she would be one for as long as it lasted.

"You have many more qualities than that. But you'd grow *hochmut* if I sat here listing them all."

"Well, p-proud is one thing I'm not."

"Humility is a quality we should all strive for. And speaking of that, I'm not proud of the way I treated Leroy." Dropping her gaze, Susannah picked absently at a stain in her apron. "I shouldn't have done what I did. I hope *Gott* forgives me for my rudeness." She sighed. "Leroy has some *gut* qualities. They're just… not what I'd look for in a husband."

The squeak of the seat signaled Jethro had shifted

his position. She looked up to find him facing her, one sandy-brown brow lifted. "What would you look for in a husband?"

Caught in a trap of her own making, Susannah crossed her arms over her chest. "You think I have a list, like I do with groceries?" When he just smiled, she scowled. "*Ach*, that is difficult, as I'm not looking." She couldn't brush Jethro off when he'd just shared something very personal. Directing her attention to the twitching ears of the bay in front of them, she gave the question serious consideration.

Although affection wasn't the reason they'd married, over the years she and Vernon had grown to love each other in their own ways. But if she were to look for a spouse for reasons other than an imminent need to protect the farm, there were characteristics Vernon hadn't had that Susannah would appreciate. And ones he'd had that she could do without. She supposed that was the way of all married couples. But as for what she'd specifically look for...

"Hardworking." She made a face at her choice of words. "I know that's not the most romantic thing, but... I would appreciate that in a partner."

"Romance? Is that important?"

She shook her head. "*Nee*. Not for me. Romance doesn't get the chores done. Or the fields planted in a timely manner. Besides, I'm too old for romance now."

Jethro thoughtfully ran his fingers through his short beard. "You think romance is limited t-to the *youngies*? Hmm. I walked in the moonlight last night with a woman who looked just like you. She was skittish about it, b-but I d-don't think she was t-too old for romance."

"She's an old fool if she lets a little moonlit walk

turn her head and forget other, more necessary, things regarding a man who's courting her."

"M-must not've b-been you then, 'cause I d-don't see you as old nor a fool, nor ever forgetful of necessary things."

"I should hope not," was all Susannah said, but she fought a blush at his words.

Traffic, both car and buggy, picked up as they approached Miller's Creek. They'd already passed a few buggies going in the opposite direction, the occupants casting them curious looks along with waved greetings. Although resolved to start the charade, Susannah curled her fingers around the edge of the buggy's seat as she pasted a smile on her face. She could feel the weight of all the glances as they drove down the main street.

"If I was courting a woman, I'd p-probably t-take her t-to lunch." Jethro nodded toward the Dew Drop as they approached.

Despite her recent determination, Susannah hesitated. Driving through town in the buggy was one thing, but sitting with him in a restaurant so soon? And taking the time to do so when there was work to be done at home?

Jethro read her reluctance. "P-perhaps another t-time."

Susannah gave him a grateful smile. "I just thought of two more qualities that are *gut* to have in a husband. Thoughtful. And kind. I'm sure many other women would think the same. And you are both of those, Jethro Weaver. In fact, another comes to mind, as well—patient."

"Hardworking and p-patient. I have d-draft horses

with those t-traits. M-maybe I'll send them t-to d-do future courting for m-me. B-but they like to eat. And so d-do I. The b-bread and church spread was *gut* earlier, b-but if I d-don't have something m-more soon, m-my stomach will d-do m-most of the t-talking on the way home. If we eat in t-town, you won't have t-to t-take t-time out t-to fix something when we get back. That is, if you were going t-to feed m-me."

She scowled, because he was right. "I'll pick up some deli sandwiches and chips when I'm getting my groceries. Will that do?"

Nodding, he winked at her. Susannah blinked in surprise at the unexpected sight and the absurd breathlessness it caused. When they pulled up in front of the hardware store, she climbed out her side of the buggy as Jethro did, meeting him at the rail provided for Amish customers as he secured the gelding.

"D-do you want to come in with m-me t-to get what's needed for the harness?"

"*Nee*, but I want to make sure I reimburse you for all these parts when you're finished." Skeptical of his innocent look, she furrowed her brow. "I mean it, Jethro. You said a friend was fixing the buggy. I wouldn't take advantage of a friend like that."

"I suppose you're right. If I was getting p-paid in m-meals, that one's thing. B-but it sounds like m-my p-payment is either starvation or a b-bellyache."

Susannah jabbed her elbow into his lean waist. "If it was, it's no more than you deserve. I'm walking down to the Piggly Wiggly to do my shopping."

"Sounds *gut*. This shouldn't t-take long. I'll m-meet you there."

Nodding, she turned away before pivoting to walk

backward a few steps. "Do you prefer any particular kind of sandwich and chips?"

"I t-trust you," Jethro replied as he headed into the hardware store.

Susannah pondered his comment as she walked the short distance to the grocery store. She didn't think Jethro trusted easily. Not on things more than sandwiches anyway. He'd placed his trust in her participation of this charade. Whatever came of it, she would ensure he wasn't hurt.

Fifteen minutes later, her gaze was shifting between the two cellophane-wrapped sandwiches in her hands. Turkey and Swiss? Or roast beef and cheddar? Which would Jethro prefer? *Ach,* she might as well get both. Whichever one he didn't want, she'd put it in the refrigerator and Amos would be happy to eat it when he got home from school.

"I heard about your buggy accident! I'm so glad you're all right." Susannah looked up to see a petite, older woman had stopped beside her.

She greeted Naomi, a widowed Amish woman she'd known for decades, with a smile. "*Ja.* It was a bit of an adventure." Susannah didn't elaborate. She intended that no one beyond her and Jethro would know about the nail that'd caused Nutmeg to put them in the ditch. Although most in the community probably already knew she'd let John Schlabach go as her hired man, they could only speculate as to why. She didn't want to cause his *mamm,* Lavinia, any distress. The woman had had enough trouble in her life.

Behind her glasses, Naomi's eyes widened with curiosity when Jethro stepped up beside Susannah. Aware of the avid attention, Susannah sighed inwardly. *Here we go*. If they wanted to get word out about their "relationship," there wasn't a better place to start. "Which one do you want?" She handed Jethro the sandwiches in her hands. "I couldn't decide."

Jethro debated between the two. "B-both? These and chips will d-do. At least until we get home t-to the cookies that await there." He gave Susannah such a big smile, she bit her cheek to stifle a laugh.

Naomi glanced from him to Susannah's cart. At the collection of ingredients inside, her mouth sagged. "You're baking?" The words were said in the same tone she might have used if Susannah had said she was going to drive trotters in the afternoon's harness races in Milwaukee.

Susannah muzzled her instinctive objection. She could bake, to an extent. But the widow was one of the more acclaimed cooks in the district. And was knowledgeable, even *hochmut*, of the fact, if truth be told. Still contrite over her actions with the widower Leroy, an idea sprang to Susannah.

"You're too right, Naomi. Now that Jethro is joining my family for several meals—" she curled her toes in her tennis shoes at the exaggeration "—he'd probably appreciate it if I improved my skills. If you would have the time, I'd surely appreciate some quick lessons in the kitchen." It was a struggle to get the words out, but Susannah reminded herself it was for a greater purpose.

"Why, of course." Naomi puffed up like the sole rooster in a chicken pen.

"*Denki*. Sometime next week then?"

"*Ja, ja*. Just let me know."

"Oh, I sure will," Susannah assured her. "Are you ready to head home then?" she asked Jethro. With a nod, he put the sandwiches inside the cart and positioned himself to push it. Susannah smiled again at the older woman. "You'll be helping me out considerably, Naomi. I can't thank you enough." Following Jethro to the checkout, she could feel the widow's inquisitive gaze burning through the back of her *kapp*.

"Now we've gone and done it," she muttered to Jethro as they loaded the grocery bags into his buggy.

"I guess it was a successful t-trip into t-town then."

"Did you get what you needed for the harness?"

"That, t-too."

Susannah blew out a breath, not wanting to think about repercussions of what they'd now initiated. "Then I guess we're set."

Lost in their own thoughts as they ate their sandwiches, it was a quiet ride home.

Jethro helped her carry the groceries inside. "Was it as b-bad as you thought?"

"I suppose today was the easy part. Folks who saw us were probably too shocked to say anything. To us, at least," she added wryly.

"Still all right t-to d-do this?"

Although he was trying to hide it, Susannah noted his hopeful expression. "*Ja.* I suppose I don't mind the others talking now. And again when the charade has run its course." A realization had struck today when they'd passed the Dew Drop where Rebecca waitressed. "But what shall I tell my children? I don't want them hurt by this fake relationship." She pressed steepled hands to her chin as she studied Jethro. "I don't want anyone hurt."

"D-do you think they would b-be?"

"I think they enjoyed your company the other night."

As did she, but she wasn't going to admit that. "I don't want them to get too hopeful that it's real. Or will become permanent." It was a reminder for herself as well.

Jethro scratched his ear. "I supposed while we coo in p-public, we could argue all the time we're t-together in front of Amos and Rebecca."

"Coo?" She arched her eyebrows. "I'm not quite the cooing sort."

"That's for sure and certain. You're m-more apt to snarl."

"I do not snarl," she retorted.

With a wink and a smile, he climbed into the buggy to drive the gelding to the barn. He paused lifting the lines when she called out to him. "Jethro, most women also appreciate a sense of humor in a man when looking for a husband. I suppose what you have could be called that."

He didn't say anything as he backed the gelding, but Susannah could see the broad grin on his face. A smile on her own, she returned to the house to put up the groceries.

He was still in the barn, presumably repairing the harness when Susannah put on some gear and checked the beehives to ensure they hadn't been bothered by the wasps. From the hill, she saw him emerge from the barn. When Susannah noticed that he was working his way toward the hill, she started down. They met halfway.

"I've got some extra chores at home that have t-to b-be d-done, so I need t-to go."

"I understand. I'm just glad for the help you've provided."

"I m-may not b-be able t-to get b-back for a few d-days as I finish up my field work. I'd b-be glad t-to help you find another hired hand, b-but harvest is a hard t-time of year t-to d-do so. Will you b-be all right?"

"*Ja.* If need be, I'll keep Amos home from school. He's a *gut* student and will quickly catch up." She was oddly reluctant to have him go. "Speaking of field work, do you think we planted enough seed in our little project to get it started?"

"I'd b-be surprised if we d-didn't. Gossip grows like weeds and d-doesn't require m-much cultivation."

They walked in quiet companionship back to the farmyard where she waved him off.

As she put away the limited gear she'd donned for the bees, Susannah wore a pensive smile, considering the man she'd spent a good part of the day with and the discussions they'd had. Her eyes narrowed as she contemplated the qualities she might want in a husband before widening when she realized how many of those characteristics Jethro possessed. Or did Jethro have those qualities and therefore they were the ones she was thinking she'd like in a husband?

Susannah frowned as she strode outside to attack the most strenuous task on her list. Something where she'd need to focus and have very little opportunity to think. Because it was very foolish to be thinking what she was thinking. They had an agreement. It was to be a fake courtship. It certainly wouldn't do to actually consider Jethro as a husband.

Chapter Six

Narrowing his eyes, Jethro leaned forward as he caught sight of a rig approaching on the opposite side of the road. With a huff of disgust, he settled back on his buggy seat. He was acting like a schoolboy, eager at even the possibility of seeing the girl he was sweet on. At his age, he should know better. Their situation wasn't even real. There's no audience that he needed to smile for today. No one to witness his pretend calf eyes. Just because the rig was approaching the crossroad Susannah lived on didn't mean that it would be hers.

Jethro's lips twisted in a self-mocking smile as he focused on the advancing horse, looking for any sign that it might be Nutmeg. At the faint sideways fling of the trotting bay's left front leg, a trait he'd noticed was indicative of Susannah's mare, his smile widened. It didn't mean that it wasn't, either.

Straightening in the seat, Jethro finally made out a smiling Susannah inside the buggy. His casual return wave as she swung onto the crossroad belied his accelerating pulse. Watching her rig move down the road, he unconsciously turned his gelding down it as well. Cocoa's ears rotated back, as if asking what was going on with the abrupt change of plans. Jethro could understand. He was asking himself the same thing.

Nothing said the only reason he was on this road would be to see Susannah. He hadn't checked on his folks since the day of Susannah's buggy accident. He could probably stop in there. But while Jethro didn't mind his *daed* and *mamm* talking about his rumored romance—as they surely were since the grapevine'd had almost two days to ferment since his and Susannah's trip into town—he didn't want them talking to him about it. At least not yet.

And why couldn't he stop in to see Susannah? They *were* supposedly courting. Although practical Susannah might wonder at his visit. He could always say his reason was that he wanted to see how she was coming along on her harvest with so little help.

As he approached the corner of her property, a reason for stopping suddenly presented itself. Goats. Goats were all over Susannah's farmyard. And based on the burst in speed of her buggy ahead of him, not where they were supposed to be. Jethro clicked Cocoa to a faster pace. When Susannah swept into her lane, he was right behind her.

Drawing the horse to a halt, he quickly set the brake and jumped down from the buggy. Dashing to Susannah's rig, he gave her a hand as she scrambled down as well.

"What happened?"

"I don't know." Her wide-eyed gaze swept over the goats scattered around the farmyard before settling on the pen where creaking hinges bore evidence of the open gate. "They were secured before I left today."

"What d-do you need m-me t-to d-do?"

Sighing, Susannah took stock of all the escaped goats. "If you'd make sure they stay off the road, that would be helpful. I'll get feed and see if I can coax them in. Usually they come running at the sight of the pails."

Nodding, Jethro turned to do as she asked, only to halt in his tracks at her dismayed exclamation. Pivoting, he found Susannah with her lips as compressed as the fists at the ends of her stiff arms.

"What is it?" he urged.

"The bucks are out, too," she muttered, pointing first to a larger spotted goat before moving her finger to indicate another animal, this one roan. "This wasn't an accident. Someone released them." Her voice dropped. Susannah looked more sad than mad at the discovery. Suppressing a surprising urge to reach out in comfort, Jethro kept his arms firmly at his sides.

"*Ach*, I guess I'll be kidding a bit early this year." She looked up at him with a wry smile. "And we'll have to figure out later who is papa to whom."

He frowned in sympathy, knowing she kept careful genetic records. "Will it impact any future sales?"

"It might. Particularly as Eclipse is a LaMancha breed and Artemis is a Nigerian Dwarf goat."

As no goats were currently inclined to head for the road, Jethro relaxed his stance. Although Susannah seemed more discouraged than upset, Jethro determined his primary task was to cheer her up. "I d-don't understand—" he gestured toward the smooth profile of the larger male goat's head "—why anyone would want a goat without ears."

"They have ears," Susannah mildly chided. "They're

just very small and without cartilage, called 'gopher' ears. I think it makes them distinct. They have a hardy character and *wunderbar* temperament, along with being a solid producing dairy goat with high butterfat content." She smiled. "You should never judge anything by the outward appearance."

Jethro could've lost himself in her brown eyes. He found his hand reaching for her before he jerked it back. She was talking about goats. Not him. He pulled his gaze away. When *Gott* admonished about the dangers of envy, He probably didn't have goats in mind.

With relief, Jethro saw a few of the does working their way across the yard toward the ditch. "I'll keep them off the road. See if the feed works. When we get them in, we'll check if any further d-damage had b-been d-done."

Susannah's smile fell at the reminder that the goats hadn't gotten out by themselves. With a brisk nod, she headed toward the barn. No fools, a couple of the goats already began trailing behind her.

By the time she exited the barn, a red plastic pail in each hand, most of the goats had fortunately congregated in the goat pen. More of them, including the bucks, came trotting through the gate at the sound of feed being poured into the pans strewed about the pen.

Leaving the road, Jethro began working his way toward some of the stragglers. Lifting their heads at his approach, the goats quickly decided the food and the sanctuary in the pen was more appealing than forbidden grazing and the advancing stranger. They scrambled to join the others.

He reached the gate as Susannah was swinging it shut. "Are they all here?"

She ran a silent count as she looked over the multi-colored collection of goats in the pen. "*Ja*. Fortunately." Wrapping a chain around the gate, she secured it to the adjacent post.

"You want to sort out the b-bucks now?"

"*Nee.* I'll let them finish eating and settle a bit. Besides, I need to check out their pen and see how they got out."

Jethro tugged on the chain she'd just fastened. It held firmly. He glanced at Susannah. "How d-do you think they got out?"

Susannah pressed her hands over her cheeks. "I can't prove it, but I think John Schlabach, my ex-hired man, let them out." Her shoulders slumped. "It doesn't appear that any of them are hurt, and I'm truly grateful for that. I wish I knew why he was doing this. Even though I had to let him go, I tried to be fair about it." She shook her head dejectedly. "But I recently discovered my timing was truly awful."

They started walking in unison toward the small shed and pasture where Susannah kept the bucks. "His *daed* hit another car while driving drunk and died last weekend. John would've just found out. I'm sure he's upset. I don't know why he put the nail in Nutmeg's collar, but that's probably why he accused me of wanting to shun him like his father was. Apparently he blames that on why Mervin left the community for the *Englisch* when John was a boy. Considering how he was treating his wife, Mervin probably didn't treat John well, either. I recall the older children left home in different ways as soon as possible."

"That d-doesn't change the fact that Mervin was his father. Sometimes feelings for p-parents are…complicated. A child wants to b-be loved no m-matter what a p-p-parent…" It was particularly hard to get the word out. "D-does."

He assumed his *mamm* loved him. At least, he hoped so. Was that the reason he'd always sought her approval? Jethro's lips twisted, making him aware of the numb section where the surgeons had joined his cleft together. He knew she was capable of the emotion, as he'd seen her shower it on his younger brother, Atlee, who'd been killed in a fall during a barn-raising over five years ago. Atlee, who'd left a young wife. Whom Jethro had married, knowing his mother would approve as she'd been the one encouraging it. The only time Jethro had outright contradicted Ruby Weaver was when she'd wanted him to take a secret child Atlee had fathered with a woman other than his wife from the child's mother. He'd refused. The girl and her mother now had a *wunderbar* father and husband in Samuel Schrock.

Jethro scowled as he looked across the field to his folks' farm. His father had been different. Bishop Weaver had been a hard taskmaster, but if you did a job well, he'd give you a nod. It'd been enough. At least it'd been some acknowledgment. The bishop had seemed easier on Atlee when the younger boy had gotten old enough to help. But that could've just been Jethro's perception.

He wasn't going to dwell on it. That was in the past. His gaze slid to the woman walking beside him. He wasn't seeking his parents' approval now. That was for sure and certain.

Susannah's brow was furrowed. "I felt sorry for John. I wanted to help him and Lavinia. Although the community has provided support for her since Mervin left, she's still struggled. I thought the money John brought in would help them both. But it seemed that whatever I told him to do, he wanted to do it a different way. Or at a different time. I tried to work with that, because, at first, when he would do tasks, he worked hard. But later, even that stopped. It was almost as if he wanted me to notice him defying me. And when he hurt Nutmeg… *Ach*, I couldn't allow that." She shook her head wearily. "He didn't seem surprised when I had to let him go. It was almost as if he thought, since his father had been shunned, then he needed to break the rules as well. If his *daed* was an outcast, then he needed to be, too."

Jethro had no advice to offer. Having no *kinder*, he couldn't say how best to raise them. And he doubted that his childhood was a good example to follow.

Other than a fence panel pulled down, they found no further damage at the bucks' pen. Jethro helped Susannah wire the panel back into place.

After brushing the dirt from her hands, Susannah propped them on her hips and smiled up at him. "I can't thank you enough, Jethro. I'm so glad you stopped by." She tilted her head. "Why did you stop by?"

Jethro deflected the question. "D-do you think he m-might have d-done anything else? The b-bees perhaps?"

Frowning, Susannah took a few quick steps that gave her a better view of the hives on the hill. Shading her eyes with her hand, she scrutinized the area for a long moment before turning back to Jethro. "They look all right from here. I don't think he'd bother them up close. Having been stung a time or two, he was very wary around the bees."

"You want m-me t-to check in the house for you? Will you b-be all right here b-by yourself?"

Susannah shook her head as they turned in that direction. "I'm sure it'll be fine. John wasn't much of one for going into the house, either. And Amos will be home from school soon."

When they returned to the farmyard, Jethro was reluctant to go. At the sound of hoofbeats on the blacktop, they both looked over toward the road.

"It's your folks," Susannah murmured.

Jethro nodded, recognizing his *daed's* horse. "*Gut* thing I'm here then. Support the news I'm sure they've heard around the d-district that we're courting."

"Have they said anything to you yet?"

"*Nee.* B-but I'm sure it's coming soon. You?"

"*Nee.* Unlike you, I don't think they'll speak directly to me about it. I think it's more likely that the bishop will just send more eligible men my way." She bumped him with her hip. "Thanks to your idea about the courtship that's not a courtship, when I say thanks but no thanks, most of them will be easily dissuaded."

At the sight of her teasing grin, it was Jethro's feet—not his speech for once—that stumbled. "Glad it's working out for you."

They both held their breaths as the rig visibly slowed as it approached Susannah's lane. When the buggy crept by the end of the drive, Jethro belatedly lifted his hand to wave. He couldn't see into the shadows of the buggy whether his greeting had been returned. He and Susannah smiled at each other when they simultaneously hissed out an exhale as the rig continued past before increasing speed again.

Watching the buggy crest the hill and drop from

sight, Jethro cautioned himself with Susannah's words. *She doesn't want a beau. And even if she did, I wouldn't be on her list of potential candidates.* He needed to keep his heart in check. It reminded him of why he was going into town.

Jethro glanced at the rig he was driving today, the one that had a flat open buckboard extending behind the enclosed driver's seat, the style labeled by the *Englisch* as the Amish pickup truck. He needed some materials to fix a fence. He would do well to keep one around his heart.

"Are you going to the cider frolic tomorrow?"

"D-don't know." He hadn't really thought about it. Although he didn't need any cider, he enjoyed picking apples, and it was a good opportunity to visit with others in the district.

"If you decide not to go, would you mind helping me?"

"Of course. Will you and Amos b-be harvesting? D-do I need to b-bring m-my team?"

"*Nee.* Just your arms and your patience." Susannah's eyes were sparkling.

Jethro's mouth grew dry at the sight. He knew what he'd like to do with his arms. Put them around her. He bit down hard on his tongue. *Fences, remember?* Apparently he couldn't erect them fast enough. He cleared his throat. "I d-don't understand?"

"My *dochder* Rachel hasn't been out much since she had the babies a few weeks ago. I'm going to watch them so she, Ben and their hired girl can go to the frolic, along with Amos and Rebecca. I need your help with the twins."

His help with the twins? His heart lurched with trepidation tangled with longing at the prospect. Any hope of a child in his life had been lost when his pregnant wife had died. At the thought of a baby in his arms, Jethro knew it wasn't just fences he needed to erect around his heart. It was walls.

Chapter Seven

Any trepidation Jethro felt about the afternoon was eased when he stepped through the door the next day. Glancing around Susannah's kitchen, he wondered if the goats had gotten out again and invaded the house this time. "D-do you need some help?"

"Now why would you ask that?" Susannah's tone was as crisp as the black-edged cookies on the nearby cooling rack.

"I suppose it's b-because it looks like you d-do? Or m-maybe b-because I know you d-don't have enough t-time t-to keep running into t-town for ingredients that d-don't end up very—" He touched one of the cookies on the rack. It disintegrated under his finger. "Useful."

"*Ach*, Amos wore out the knees on his pants. They were getting too short anyway. I was working on some new ones for him while these were in the oven. I fear I was sewing seams when I should've been watching the time." Her shoulders slumped, along with her expression. "I told Rachel I'd have something for her to take when she dropped off the *boppeli* and now I'm behind."

"And she agreed t-to t-take them?" Jethro couldn't

help himself. It felt *gut* to be able to tease. The concept of joking with his *mamm* or deceased wife would've been like trying to milk a goose. Ridiculous and uncomfortable for all parties.

Susannah turned away from the counter to give him a mock glare. The effect was spoiled by the faint traces of flour along one side of her hairline.

"What can I d-do to help?" Crossing to the sink, Jethro washed his hands in preparation.

"Run to the store for me and buy some?"

He laughed then stepped up beside her. "You can d-do it. I'll m-measure and you d-dump and stir. Where's your recipe?"

Susannah tapped an index card lying on the counter, its surface stained with spatters of long gone baking episodes. Jethro ran his finger down the list of ingredients. Since the butter and eggs were already out, he searched the cupboard from where she'd pulled the wasp supplies days ago for the rest of what he was looking for and set them on the counter.

Susannah plunked a few measuring cups down on his side of a large bowl before selecting a wooden spoon from a collection of similar cooking utensils in an upright canister on the counter. Measuring out the butter, he handed it to Susannah. While she whipped it vigorously, he dumped the appropriate amount of sugar into the bowl.

"Ach!" She shot him a frown as, still stirring, she slid the bowl farther down the counter.

Preparing the next sequence of recipe items, Jethro raised an eyebrow. *"You* of all p-people are going t-to b-be p-picky about how the ingredients are added? D-don't you t-trust m-me?"

With an exaggerated sigh, she scooted the bowl closer again, and he added those ingredients as well, albeit more slowly. "B-besides, it's not as if folks have high expectations for any b-baked goods of yours."

Susannah huffed softly. "Well then, it's time I surprise them."

"Oh, with what's running along the grapevine about us, I'm sure we're already d-doing that." Rescanning the card, he measured the rest of the ingredients, checking with Susannah for approval to add them before he did so. When everything was in the batter, he put the supplies away while she continued to stir. Using the side of a hand, Jethro slid a small heap of flour, left over from her earlier efforts, off the counter into the palm of his other cupped hand. "You're a m-messy cook."

Leaving the spoon in the bowl, Susannah dusted her hands off on her apron. Jethro gently snagged one to turn it palm up. With a smile, his eyes met her soft brown ones as he deposited the residue from his cupped hand into it. His smile faded as their fingers tangled. Susannah's lips parted, drawing his attention.

Jethro ached to kiss them. His chin dipped. He froze. He'd never kissed a woman other than Louisa. And that was only once. Conscious of the numbness of the scarred section of his lips, he'd been self-conscious about kissing. Louisa's reaction to his one attempt reinforced that he'd had reason to be. It might've been his kiss. It might've just been him. He hadn't been her choice, after all. Either way, he couldn't bear to see the same reaction on Susannah's face. Clearing his throat, Jethro withdrew his hand and stepped back.

He winced as some of the debris between their hands scattered to the linoleum. "I'll sweep that up."

Striving to clear the sudden tension that pervaded the room, Jethro retrieved a broom and a dustpan from a tall, narrow cupboard as he tried to remember what he'd said just before…before he'd almost made a huge fool of himself. "Knowing you're so m-meticulous about everything on the farm, the state of the kitchen surprises m-me."

Having emptied what was in her hand into the trash, along with the burned cookies from the last batch, Susannah was now spooning dough onto cookie sheets. She tilted her head as her brow furrowed. Jethro hoped she was thinking about his question rather than his near blunder.

"I think it's because the farm was my *daed's* and my domain. I didn't spend much time in the kitchen with my *mamm* and older *schweschdere.* I learned we might live in the house, but our livelihood came from the farm. After my *daed* died, the farm was passed down to me as the youngest. I appreciated that Vernon tolerated my lack of enthusiasm for housework, understanding I'd rather be outside working, though I suppose he should've, as he married me for it. But then, there were other things he'd rather be doing than farming as well. Fortunately, Rachel and Rebecca enjoyed working in the house, so some semblance of order was maintained and we didn't starve."

She put the cookie sheets into the oven.

Glancing outside when something caught his attention in the window, Jethro saw a horse and buggy arrive. "D-does Rachel know? About us? About what we want folks to think of us, I mean?" Jethro hastily corrected himself.

Susannah watched her *dochder* descend from the

buggy. "*Nee.* She's not a gossiper, neither is Ben. But she might unintentionally mention you are here today."

"That's what we want, right?"

Although she hesitated a moment, Susannah nodded. "*Ja.* That's what we want."

Jethro's stomach twisted. He read in her expression that any wanting regarding their relationship would be more he, than we.

By the time Rachel came inside like a whirlwind, her arms full with twins, the cookies were out of the oven and cooling on racks. Rachel's husband, Ben, was a step behind, carrying a handmade bag of baby supplies, while Miriam Schrock, their hired girl—as was Amish custom to help a new mother for a while—smiled from the doorway.

"Are you sure you don't want to come with us today?" her *dochder* asked with the breathlessness of a new mother coordinating an outing with two infants.

Ja, Susannah was sure. She wasn't ready to face all the eyes of the district on her and Jethro, now that word was surely out about their relationship. After the recent, unexpected moment in the kitchen when their hands had touched, she was afraid she'd blush like a *maedel* if anyone glanced at the two of them. Which was ridiculous, as she wasn't a young girl anymore, they hadn't done anything, and this whole thing was just a ruse.

"Most definitely," she assured Rachel, relieving her daughter of her grandson, Eli. "I've been to many cider frolics, but I've never before had a chance to watch my *kinskinder* for the afternoon."

"Are you sure you can handle them by yourself?"

Susannah arched an eyebrow at Rachel. "I've handled a *boppeli* or two before. And I won't be by myself. I have help." Susannah pivoted to thrust Eli into Jethro's arms. At the sight of his wide eyes and dropped jaw, she couldn't prevent the smile that curved her lips as she turned back to take Amelia from her daughter's hands.

"If you're sure?" Rachel's curious gaze shifted between Susannah and a stunned Jethro, who now held her infant son.

"I'm sure. Now go enjoy." Although she gazed down into her granddaughter's sleeping face, in her peripheral vision Susannah could see Ben's callused hand clasp around Rachel's slender one. Her smile widened at the action. An expectant couple with a surprise marriage, Ben and Rachel had struggled during the early months of their union. Although confident they'd work it out—they had to, as Amish didn't believe in divorce—Susannah was thrilled to see them getting along so well now. Always elated to see her twin grandchildren, Susannah was also glad to give their parents a chance to socialize as a couple.

"They ate just before we came. I should be back in a few hours. But I packed bottles for them just in case they get hungry." Pulling them out of the bag, Rachel put them into the refrigerator.

"I'm sure we'll be fine. Won't we, Jethro?" Susannah swiveled to look at her pretend suitor, in part to ensure he was doing all right with the unexpected babe. When she saw the pair, her breath caught in her throat at the tender expression worn by the bearded man as he gazed at the infant. Jethro didn't look up at her question. Throat suddenly clogged with an emotion she couldn't define, Susannah had to clear it as she turned back to her daughter. "We'll be fine," she repeated hoarsely.

She tipped her head toward the cookies on the counter. "Don't forget to take those. They just need packing up."

At her mother's request, Rachel automatically extended the hand not entwined with her husband's toward the cookies. Casting a dubious glance at them, she hesitated. "Are you sure?"

Susannah grasped at the chance to regain equilibrium shaken by the sight of Jethro with the *boppeli*. She rolled her eyes. "After all those years of living with me, you should've realized by now that I know my own mind. *Ja.* I'm sure. But to protect your reputation in the community, you can announce to everyone that you didn't make them, I did. And they're delicious." Susannah bit her cheek at the exaggeration. "Jethro helped me with them. We're a *gut* team."

Rachel fixed Susannah with such a warm look that Susannah wondered if it'd been intended for the babe in her arms instead of her. "*Ja.* I can see that you are, *Mamm.*" Her quiet murmur caused the flush Susannah had been hoping to avoid earlier to blossom across her cheeks. She needn't have worried. Rachel had already shifted her attention to efficiently packing up the cookies. "Where are Amos and Rebecca?"

"They didn't know if you'd have room in the buggy. Besides, I think they both wanted to get there early in order to spend as much time with their friends as possible."

Rachel nodded. Handing the cookies to Ben, she tenderly stroked a finger down the cheek of each of her sleeping *boppeli*.

"We'll be fine," Susannah reassured her yet again.

With a final wave, Rachel and Ben followed Miriam out of the kitchen. It seemed unnaturally quiet as the door swung shut behind them.

Braced this time for the disconcerting impact the man holding the infant gave her, Susannah looked at Jethro. "She didn't leave us any cookies."

Jethro lifted his gaze from the baby and smiled. "Is that *gut* or b-bad?"

"It would've been nice to taste them. Just in case."

"You have t-to t-trust us, Susannah. As you said, we m-make a *gut* t-team."

"Well, I appreciate your help today, as these two definitely take a team." She smiled as she recalled that Jethro, neighbor of Rachel and Ben, had been the one to come get her the night the twins had arrived. He hadn't stayed to see them then. In fact, this might be the first time he'd been around a small babe.

"Shall we sit down?" She nodded toward the chairs in the living area. "One thing I always want to enjoy and never take for granted is holding a *boppeli.*"

As she eased into her rocker with the baby in her arms, what felt like a rock settled in her stomach. She'd forgotten that Jethro had never had a chance to hold his infant child. It'd been lost, along with his wife, before it was born. Her stark gaze fastened on the man settling into a nearby chair. "Oh, Jethro. I'm so sorry. I didn't think…"

He lifted his eyes from the sleeping boy. "It was *Gott's* will. Although I…" He dropped his attention back to the infant. "It wouldn't have mattered, but I sometimes wonder if the child had…" Careful not to disturb the baby he cuddled, he touched the scar on his upper lip with his free hand. "I worried about giving that to any children. It...wasn't always easy."

Susannah's eyes closed as she thought of the babies, the two she'd lost due to what she and her husband passed on to them. The Amish had begun with a limited number of families. Due to the requirement of being baptized into the church to be married, over the generations, the gene pool had narrowed. Recessive hereditary diseases were showing up in their children. Ones like the Crigler-Najjar syndrome, a genetic disorder causing severe jaundice that her affected babies hadn't survived.

When the infant shifted in her arms, Susannah opened her eyes to take in Amelia's thankfully beautiful skin. As if to reassure her *grossmammi*, the infant momentarily blinked open her clear blue eyes before they disappeared again under fluttering fragile lashes.

"Is it genetic?" she asked quietly.

"I don't know."

They lapsed into silence. Susannah didn't know if Jethro had noticed, but his stuttering was diminished as he held her grandson. Were his thoughts on that? Or were his thoughts, like hers, on the genetic issues both of them had witnessed in their community? Her gaze focused on Amelia's tiny perfect fingers, curled into a little fist that rested against her cheek as she slept. Perhaps Jethro was thinking about the wonder of *Gott's* creation that a *boppeli* was?

A wonder that she would experience now as a *grossmammi*, not a *mamm*. It was enough. It was more than enough.

She glanced at Jethro through lowered lashes. He was a compelling sight with the child in his arms. It

was a *gut* thing their courtship wasn't real. If they were
to get married, there might be a possibility of little ones
as, with children being a gift from *Gott*, their church
didn't believe in birth control. It would be *Gott's* will,
but would there be more heartbreaking issues like the
ones they'd already experienced?

Susannah knew Amish women who'd had babes in
their later years. She also knew risk factors increased
with age, for the mother and the child. Her arms tightened around her granddaughter. She couldn't bear to
lose another baby. Her arms and her heart had felt dev-
astatingly empty after the two she'd lost. To remarry,
and risk losing more? It didn't bear thinking about. To
take her mind off the disturbing direction, she asked
the first thing that popped into her head.

"Is the cleft related to your…" She hesitated to bring
up his speech. It'd never been an issue to her, but she
knew it was to him.

"Stammer? I don't think so. When I was in school, it
was b-before they'd built the Amish one, so, like you, I
went to the p-public school. B-because of my stammer,
I saw a speech pathologist." His brow creased slightly
in reflection. "She helped me a lot."

"Did it ever go away?" After Susannah was married, she'd been so busy with the farm and her own
young family, she hadn't had time to interact with the
neighbor boy she'd once babysat.

"*Nee*. B-but it got m-much better. Until I left school
after eighth grade and didn't work with her anymore."

"Who was it?"

"Mrs. D-Danvers," he said with a faint smile.

Susannah's instantly pictured an older *Englisch*
woman. "I remember her. She's retired now. I see

her sometimes in town. Maybe she'd work with you again?"

Jethro's smile faded. He gave a barely discernible shake of his head, his focus returning to the baby in his arms. Susannah's breath caught at the tenderness in his expression. If she could make a secret list of character traits she'd like in a husband, tenderness would definitely be one of them.

"*Nee*. It is what it is. I'd rather just keep my words few since it t-takes me t-twice as long to say them. Save them mainly for m-my livestock and close friends." His gaze briefly lifted to meet Susannah's.

Warmed more than she should be by the obvious inclusion in that category, Susannah dropped her own gaze to watch as sleeping Amelia scrunched up her face before the tiny rosebud lips curved into a smile. Concerned that the sensations that flowed through her were way too cozy and tempting, Susannah sought a topic to stop the wayward emotions in their tracks.

"Your *daed* has been bishop here a long time, *ja*?"

Jethro frowned. "Since just b-before I was b-born, I understand."

"He must've been very young when he was chosen."

"*Ja*. I heard he became a m-minister shortly after he was b-baptized and m-married, and when the b-bishop d-died the following year, m-my *d-daed* was selected to replace him." Jethro inhaled deeply.

Susannah winced inwardly as his speech tightened up again.

"Knowing that I was also agreeing to serve as leader if selected was the only thing that m-made m-me hesitate about b-baptism into the church. I hold m-my b-breath every election, hoping *Gott* d-doesn't choose m-me. Although I d-don't know why He would, when folks would surely rather watch a field of alfalfa grow than listen t-to m-me t-try t-to p-preach."

Susannah smiled. While church members chose the nominees, *Gott* chose the minister from the nominees by determining who would pick up the *Ausbund* hymnal containing a scripture verse. The lifelong job was rarely sought and although it was considered an honor to be chosen, she'd seen grown men sob with dismay when a hymnal was opened and revealed as the one containing scripture. She couldn't imagine what the task of preaching for twenty minutes to an hour without notes on a regular basis would do to Jethro.

What she *could* imagine, as she watched him totally absorbed by the infant he cradled, was Jethro as a father. He would be a *wunderbar* one. With a surprising pang, she shifted so she could rest the arm holding Amelia against the extension of the chair. The babe, although weighing but a few pounds, grew surprisingly heavy in an unsupported arm. A bit like her heart as she considered the man across from her. *Ja*, it was a good thing their courtship wasn't real. Jethro needed a family she couldn't give him. Closing her eyes to what had suddenly become a painful sight, Susannah hoped for him that he would find someone who could. Pressing her free hand against her stomach, she attempted to stifle the regret that immediately pooled there at the thought.

Chapter Eight

The bishop had obviously pressed Leroy Albrecht to call on her again. Susannah wasn't surprised. Bishop Weaver surely knew now of her and Jethro's courtship and wanted to ensure his neighbor didn't get any ideas about a permanent relationship with his only son. Instead of confronting it head-on, Bishop Weaver seemed intent on sending more suitable candidates in her direction.

A couple of them had stopped by a few days ago on Visiting Sunday. Susannah felt no compunction on gently dissuading them by indicating she was seeing someone else. She was. Just not seeing him all the way to matrimony. And these were nice men. But not ones she saw herself marrying, even if she were looking. If she ever changed her mind, it wouldn't do to burn any bridges in case later they were the only ones to cross the void. Although Susannah didn't feel a void now, when Amos was grown and in charge of the farm, it might be nice to have some companionship.

But regarding Leroy, she wanted him to come over. At the appropriate time. Unsurprisingly, he'd been very reluctant when she'd issued the invitation. That was why she appreciated the bishop's pressure in his case. Without it, Leroy might not've grudgingly accepted.

Although Susannah didn't bring many desserts to community gatherings, she had definitely helped serve her share. Just as she noted any nuances of her goats' behavior while feeding them in case one was sick or needed attention, she was very observant when feeding others as well. In fact, she'd noticed more than once that Naomi had discreetly placed extra servings of desserts next to Leroy at the meals on church Sundays since shortly after the man had been widowed. Leroy had noticed the food, but not who'd nudged the plates near him. Susannah figured it was long past time Naomi got credit for her efforts. She also figured Naomi wouldn't mind someone who truly appreciated her skills in the kitchen sitting at her table on a regular basis.

At the sound of a muted clatter, Susannah looked out the window to see Leroy's rig coming up the lane. "Looks like we have some company," she chirped as she whipped a wooden spoon more quickly around the bowl of cake batter, the pace in sync with her accelerated heart rate.

"Oh, were you expecting anyone?" Naomi asked, as she was dusting a cake pan farther down the counter.

"*Nee*, good thing you brought over an example of what a *gut* dessert should look like." Fixing an encouraging smile at the widow, Susannah hoped her plan would work. She didn't know how many more visits she—or Leroy—could take. Or how much more time she could waste in her kitchen when the farm needed her elsewhere.

Naomi rose on her tiptoes to look out the window. "Leroy Albrecht is here?" Her question, accompanied by a faint blush, ended with a squeak. She glanced at Susannah. Her narrowed gaze seemed to ask, *How many men do you need to come courting?*

Sliding damp palms down the sides of her apron, Susannah crossed to the front door. Pinning on a bright smile, she opened it to see Leroy sitting in his buggy, wearing a morose expression as he stared at the house. Upon seeing her, his shoulders lifted in what she assumed as a sigh—either that or a fortifying breath. Slowly climbing down from the buggy, he secured his horse to the rail and plodded to the door at a pace that suggested he'd rather be any place else.

"Leroy." She ushered him through the door. "How pleasant to see you today." For the first time since she'd noticed the man's gaze on her, Susannah meant it. "I've been baking. It'll take a few minutes, but I can treat you to a warm spice cake."

Leroy froze in his tracks, preventing Susannah from shutting the door. His face paled. "I… I don't know that I'll be able to stay that long."

"You'll at least have time for a cup of *kaffi* since you came all this way." Her plan wouldn't work if she couldn't get him through the door. Placing a firm but gentle hand on his shoulder, Susannah urged him toward the table. "And, if you don't have time to wait, Naomi, would you mind cutting into that streusel cake you brought over? It would go wonderfully with *kaffi*. I'll just get some plates out."

Susannah scooted over to the cupboard to retrieve two plates. Setting them on the table, along with a couple of forks, she returned to where she'd left the bowl on the counter. "Naomi," she said over her shoulder, "why don't you sit for a minute and keep Leroy company while I finish this up?"

Her hands slowly stirring the cake batter, Susannah kept her ears tuned to any sounds behind her. When she heard the first, then the second, chair move on the linoleum floor, she exhaled inaudibly in relief. At the continued silence, other than the quiet *tink* of a fork against china, she turned to the two seated at the table. "So how is it?" she inquired cheerfully.

Leroy's plate of cake was already half empty. His eyes were closed in blissful appreciation as he slowly chewed. "Mmm." He opened them to stare at the intently watching woman on the other side of the table. "This is *wunderbar.*" Under his gaze, Naomi flushed rosily as she reached up to tuck her gray-threaded hair under her *kapp.*

"Naomi is one of the best bakers in the district. Has been for some time. I imagine you've sampled some of her desserts before at church dinners. But then, maybe not. If you don't eat early or have someone hold a piece back for you, there generally isn't any left." Susannah bit the inside of her cheek. She felt like an auctioneer at a mud sale, keeping up a patter to encourage bidders.

"If I haven't before, I'll be sure not to miss them now." Leroy took another bite, his eyes closing again in obvious approval. "This is how a wife should be able to bake."

Susannah turned back to scowl at the batter in the bowl before her. Keeping her actions quiet so as not to disturb the couple behind her, she slid the prepared cake pan closer and poured the batter into it.

"My Absalom was very happy with my baking. His

favorite was my shoofly pie. He liked it even better than this streusel cake."

That a way, Naomi, Susannah silently cheered at the older woman. Stealing a glance at the table, she hid a smile as Leroy served himself another piece.

"I'd be happy to try it sometime," the widower mumbled around another forkful.

"I'd bake more, but when I don't have a purpose to bake for, it takes some of the enjoyment from it. It's no fun baking for one. And, lately, it's challenging to get things done outside. Even with my small place, by the time I feed the horse and care for his needs, along with other tasks, it doesn't leave me much time in the kitchen, which is where I'd rather be. And speaking of my horse, I've been having a problem with him lately."

Tuned in to the conversation behind her rather than the cake she was sliding into the oven, Susannah raised her eyebrows. Perhaps Naomi didn't need her help, after all. The widow seemed to be doing fine on her own. But just in case, Susannah inserted, "Leroy is a *wunderbar* horseman. Just ask him."

And so Naomi did. While the two at the table discussed the merits of Standardbreds purchased from the track versus those raised for Amish buggy work, and the decision to shoe horses one way as opposed to another, Susannah cleared up the counter.

"Sure would be nice to have someone so knowledgeable take a look at my gelding," Naomi sighed at the end of one of Leroy's monologues.

Susannah figured that was as good a nudge as any. Opening the oven door, she peered at the underdone cake. "This should be out soon and we can sample it as well. Of course, it'll be nowhere near to Naomi's, but I've been working on it and I'm sure…"

Leroy's chair scraped back from the table. Brushing cake crumbs from his graying beard, he hastily stood. "Well, I need to be going. Got things to do, you know. Just thought I'd drop by." He smiled at Naomi and even Susannah had to admit it made him look almost appealing. Almost.

To Naomi, the expression must've been considerably appealing indeed. She shot a beseeching glance at Susannah. Hastily interpreting it, Susannah shut the oven door with her hip and crossed her arms over her chest, mostly to hold in her laughter. "*Ach*, that's too bad. If I remember correctly, didn't you mention, Naomi, that you wouldn't be able to stay long today, either?"

The widow beamed as she pushed back from the table as well. "*Ja, ja.* I've got to be going as well. Chores, you know."

Leroy paused at the door. "Well, I suppose I could follow you home and see what issues you might be having with your horse."

Susannah quickly returned the rest of Naomi's cake to its traveling container. She thrust it and its contents into the widower's unresisting hands. "Why don't you take this along and enjoy it while you discuss those issues. In a few minutes my own cake will be out, which is more sweets than I need. Unless you'd like to take some of that along as well?"

She smiled as the older pair made hasty goodbyes and fled from the kitchen.

Snagging a spatula, she scraped the bowl before putting it in the sink. With a finger, Susannah swiped some batter from the spatula, tasting it thoughtfully as she watched Leroy help Naomi into her buggy. Considering her skill set in the kitchen, it was not bad work for an afternoon. Not bad at all.

Susannah carried two baskets loaded with jars of honey into the Dew Drop the next day. Her eyes swept the interior of the restaurant, which contained only a scattering of customers in the midafternoon. Recalling Rebecca's comments about the restaurant's potential sale, Susannah's hands tightened on the basket's handles. The Dew Drop was a much needed outlet for her honey and other items. Hopefully, the new owners would continue to allow her to sell them here.

Rebecca waved to her from where she was clearing a table. Nodding in return, Susannah set the baskets on the floor and began to restock the shelf space allotted to her in the wooden cupboard by the checkout counter. Thrilled that sales for herself, as well as some of the other local Amish craftsmen she shared the cupboard with, had been good this fall, she quickly emptied one basket and started on the other. Having placed all from the second basket that would fit on the shelf, Susannah gave the display a final satisfied survey before grabbing the handles and glancing around the restaurant for a quick farewell to her daughter. Not seeing Rebecca, she shrugged and strode toward the door.

Before she reached it, it swung open to admit a quartet of older *Englisch* women. Although she hadn't had any of them in the limited years that she'd gone to the local public school, Susannah recognized them as teachers, apparently retired by now. Among them was Mrs. Danvers, the speech teacher whom Jethro had mentioned as being such a help to him in his early years. Appreciative of what the woman had done then for the shy young boy he would've been, Susannah gave the woman a smile and brief nod. To her dismay, while the other three drifted on to a table, Mrs. Danvers paused in front of Susannah.

"Mrs. Mast?"

Susannah hesitantly nodded acknowledgment.

"You probably don't know me. I used to teach in the public school system, dating back to when the Amish children in the area attended before they set up their own school." The older woman smiled, her face creasing in graceful lines. "I've tried to keep track of some of those previous students. One of those that I had was Jethro Weaver. I understand you two have been seeing each other recently."

Susannah's eyes widened at the woman's comments. One of Jethro's and her objectives was for their artificial courtship to be discussed along the Amish grapevine. She never imagined it would make the jump to an *Englisch* one.

Mrs. Danvers reached out to gently pat one of Susannah's hands curled around the basket handle. "He was one of my favorite students. Such an earnest, hard-working boy."

Smiling faintly at the image of Jethro around her son Amos's age, Susannah had to agree. "*Ja*. He was just speaking last week of what a huge help you were to him back then." Encouraged by the woman's warm expression, she continued, figuring that as Jethro held his former teacher in high opinion, he wouldn't mind if she shared their conversation. "He said he spoke better when you were working with him."

Mrs. Danvers' smile ebbed. "I was afraid that

might've been the case. Although he did well in our sessions and his teachers at the time said there was much improvement, I don't think he had much encouragement at home."

The woman's observation didn't surprise Susannah at all. She hadn't witnessed that Jethro'd had much encouragement at home, regardless of the topic.

"I worked with him for a number of years. Due to issues from the cleft lip and palate as well as the stutter. Children born with clefts frequently need SLT." At Susannah's blank look, the older woman's smile reappeared. "I'm sorry. After years in the field, the lingo just slips out. Speech and language therapy."

"Is stuttering common with clefts?"

"No, not really. One of the reasons I would've liked to have spoken with his parents at some point. Stuttering tends to run in families. It would've been interesting to know if anyone in their family stuttered."

Susannah blinked in surprise. "Stuttering does? I assumed maybe clefts were but not the other."

"There are some genetic relationships in both." Mrs. Danvers acknowledged her companions, who were now waving at her from their table. "I enjoy getting out with friends, but I have plenty of free time. I'd be happy to work with Jethro again if he'd like."

"Oh, that isn't for me to say. You'd have to ask Jethro." Susannah's response was instantaneous. Jethro had said as much. He was sensitive about his stutter and valued his privacy. But…what if working with the speech teacher again for a while would help him? She'd witnessed how, when he was more relaxed, as he'd been holding the babe, the stutter was diminished. Maybe this would help him when their charade was over. Susannah felt a pang at the thought. She really was enjoying Jethro's company. Their agreement was for the short term as Jethro didn't want to face courting anyone right now. But with a newfound confidence, he might not find it so onerous. She wanted that for him.

"Wait. *Ja.* That might be *gut*. He is a fine man just the way he is. But being able to speak better, or be more relaxed when he speaks, might help him in… other ways." She couldn't say "in self-confidence." That would seem to be intruding on Jethro's privacy. Hopefully, Mrs. Danvers, with her years of knowledge on the topic, would understand what she meant.

The older woman's compassionate smile indicated she did.

"Denki so much for what you've done for him."

"It's no problem. As I said, he was one of my favorite students." With a small nod, Mrs. Danvers went to join the three other women.

Susannah watched her thoughtfully as the woman reached their table. With a shrug, she slid the basket handles up her arm, exited the restaurant and stepped directly into the path of Ruby Weaver, the bishop's wife—and Jethro's *mamm*.

Chapter Nine

Susannah halted so abruptly the basket handles slid down her arms. Only a frantic grab prevented them from tumbling onto the sidewalk along with the few jars of honey that remained in one.

Ruby Weaver stopped as well, her blue eyes raking Susannah from her *kapp* down to her tennis shoes. Susannah had never noticed that Jethro's were the same color. His were so warm and kind while his mother's seemed cold and flat. The realization helped Susannah rein in her galloping heart rate at the unexpected meeting. If his folks were unhappy with their supposed relationship, it was no more than what she and Jethro had expected. Remembering this was for him, Susannah straightened. And smiled.

"*Guder daag*, Ruby." Accustomed to working with livestock and having recently been stung by wasps, Susannah knew enough to be wary of unpredictable creatures. A category that included the bishop's wife. Hoping to escape with the simple "good day," Susannah continued toward her nearby buggy.

"Is that what you're catching him with?"

Inhaling slowly as she kept her smile on her face, Susannah turned around. "Pardon?"

"Honey." The woman nodded her head at the remaining jars in one of the baskets. But her gaze on Susannah indicated the word had nothing to do with what a bee provided and everything to do with what she thought Susannah was granting to her son to entice his attentions.

Susannah would've laughed at the insinuation if it hadn't been so insulting. Her smile turned rueful as she regarded the older woman. "You obviously don't know your son." Cocking her head, Susannah held Ruby's frowning stare as she recalled the young Jethro she'd cared for and the current one she was beginning to care for in a much different way. Even though their courtship wasn't real, she wasn't going to let this woman denigrate Jethro. "Perhaps you never did. Which is your loss. He is a *gut* man and a dutiful son. One you don't deserve. The man he's become is more credit to him than you."

Ruby's eyes narrowed and her mouth puckered like she'd taken a gulp of Susannah's vinegar-infused lemonade. Shaking her head sadly, Susannah continued to her buggy, opened the door and stored her baskets on the floor.

"You don't deserve him, either."

She wasn't surprised to hear the words behind her. Slowly pivoting, she found Ruby had followed her to the edge of the sidewalk. "You're probably right about that. But he's a grown man and it's for him to decide, ain't so?"

Maybe this time he wants to choose his own wife instead of having his parents force a bride upon him once again. Susannah bit her tongue to keep the words from escaping her mouth.

Suddenly having no more energy for the conversation—she'd already said more than she should—she yanked the lead loose from the hitching post, causing Nutmeg to fling up her head in surprise. Instantly contrite, Susannah crooned an apology to the mare. Making a point to control her movements—she refused to give the impression she was intimidated or running away—she climbed into the buggy. With a stiff nod to the still watching woman, Susannah backed Nutmeg onto the street and headed home.

She was disgusted to find herself still shaking a full block away. *You've gone and done it now.* She'd never crossed the bishop's wife before. She'd never really crossed anyone before. *If Ruby wasn't upset initially, ach, you put her well on her way there.*

Susannah's lips twisted. *I wonder if Jethro can court me if his parents find some reason to put me in the Bann?*

It was a possibility. It hadn't happened in their district, although Bishop Weaver—frequently prompted by his wife—could be strict. But Susannah had heard stories from others that in dysfunctional churches, leaders had shunned members for personal reasons. Women for not having their *kapps* made correctly. Or having hair that frizzed and wouldn't lay down flat enough under their head covering. So it could happen. Susannah was more worried about what being in the *Bann* would do to Amos and Rebecca than to her relationship with Jethro. If she was shunned, she couldn't eat at the same table as them. Or take anything from their hand. They would be greatly distressed, as would she.

Her trembling finally ceased a mile out of town when she determined that Bishop Weaver and Ruby surely knew Jethro enough to realize that—dutiful son not withstanding—shunning the unsuitable woman he was courting would only push him further in that direction. Finally relaxed as she turned down the road toward her farm, Susannah shook her head. All this emotion for a relationship that wasn't real to begin with. Although, her fingers twitched on the leather lines, as often as she was seeing Jethro, it was feeling more real all the time.

And if it really was real, then she'd have Ruby Weaver as a mother-in-law. Susannah almost giggled at the thought. Wouldn't that be something? They would surely clash on occasion. On *many* occasions. They wouldn't find her frail like Jethro's first wife. Would the bishop and his wife go so far as to try to put their own daughter-in-law in the *Bann* if she crossed them, unintentionally or not? What would the district think of that? *Gut* thing their courtship wasn't real. And why did that acknowledgment make her feel a little wistful?

Jethro unhitched Cocoa from his buggy and led the gelding to where his father's rig was parked by the barn. He'd kept a wary eye on the house as he'd driven up the lane, bracing himself for the kitchen door to swing wide and his *mamm* or *daed*, or most likely both, would stomp out of their house to give him the lecture he was sure they felt was needed.

When the door didn't open and a scan of the farmyard revealed his *mamm's* buggy was missing, he breathed a little easier. A peek through the large open barn doors confirmed it held no occupants other than a slouch-hipped bay in the stall and a yellow-and-white cat curled up on a hay bale. As both their attentions were turned toward the back of the barn, Jethro paused to peer into the shadows as well.

Seeing nothing, he smiled faintly. He couldn't have picked a better time to check on the issue his *daed* had mentioned he was having with his buggy when he'd seen him briefly in town. His father, wearing a frown, had stopped him yesterday outside the hardware store. Jethro had been afraid the discussion he'd been expecting but trying to avoid—his unacceptable courtship of Susannah—was about to begin. He'd looked around with dread, afraid of someone overhearing the lecture. His knees had almost sagged when his father had asked if he'd take a look at his buggy, which had been pulling oddly.

Distracted by relief and an immediate interruption by a church member, Jethro hadn't been able to interpret the problem based on the bishop's short description. He'd determined to take the rig for a drive today to get a better idea of the issue. At least then he'd know what to fix. A last glance around the barn confirmed the bay horse and cat as his only company while fixing the buggy. He much preferred their company to his folks', who would be leaning over his shoulder, haranguing him on how he should fix his life to suit them while he tried to do the repairs.

Jethro eyeballed the buggy as he hitched up his gelding. Other than expected wear in some areas, he couldn't see anything obvious prior to climbing into the buggy.

As he drove down the lane, ears tuned to any sounds the conveyance might be making, Jethro reflected that his ability with repairs was something he'd at least felt was appreciated while he was growing up. His father wasn't good with mechanics, proclaiming his talents lay elsewhere. Jethro didn't know if his *daed* meant that his skills were more people-related.

Recalling some memories of his youth, Jethro snorted. He didn't see that, either. He supposed there were others in the community who'd disagree, thinking the bishop was doing a good job. The role, one his father had been in for longer than he could remember, certainly rested easily on his father's shoulders.

Jethro was glad someone was good in that position. Even though, when he was baptized into the church, he'd had to accept that, if so chosen, he would serve in the lifetime role of minister, it was a job he never wanted. As he'd shared with Susannah, his only security had been that the congregation knew how he spoke, and they didn't want to suffer through a note-less sermon from him any more than he did.

At the end of the lane, Jethro automatically turned Cocoa in the direction of Susannah's farm and let the horse pick its own pace up the hill. He hadn't seen her since they'd watched the *boppeli* together when Rachel and Ben had gone to the cider frolic last Saturday. He smiled at the memory. He'd longed to stop by on Visiting Sunday the next day. But since word was out about their relationship and she might not think it necessary to be in frequent contact, that had kept him away.

Jethro's lips twitched. He'd always been prompt about attending to his folks' needs, but the possibility of seeing Susannah had him rushing over now at his earliest opportunity. He rubbed a hand over his face, feeling the scar above his lip as his smile faded. When had it changed from liking to see Susannah to wanting to see her, to *needing* to see her? Not even to speak to, just to know she was near.

His heart rate, and his mood, picked up when he caught sight of Susannah. She was out in the orchard, picking up windfall apples. The rig had passed a few fence posts before Jethro reminded himself that his focus was to be sensitive to the sounds and motions of the buggy, not wondering whether the lovely apple picker would welcome an unexpected visit from him. Returning to his task, he directed the confused gelding to weave its way back and forth in their lane. Finally, he felt what his *daed* had noted. The buggy was pulling more to one side. But that wasn't all.

Tuning out the *clip-clop* of the gelding's hooves on the blacktop, Jethro narrowed his eyes in concentration. There it was. A peculiar rattling sounded from beneath his feet. Jethro estimated it to be somewhere near the front axle. When he eased the gelding into a trot, he felt a slight give in the buggy at the change of pace. He couldn't be certain of the exact issue until he got back to his folks' farm and climbed underneath, but at least it gave him some idea of what to address.

Guiding the gelding into Susannah's lane to turn the rig around, Jethro suppressed the urge to continue up the lane, park the rig and walk up to the orchard to help her. Picking up fallen apples with her would be much more interesting than staring at the undercarriage of his *daed's* buggy. But one was something he said he would do. The other…well, it was just what he wanted to. Jethro learned long ago not to expect to get what he wanted. With a final wistful glance toward the orchard, he checked for traffic before backing onto the road.

Now reluctant to waste any time fixing the buggy, he urged the gelding to a prompt pace. This time as the buggy surged forward, neither the rattling sound nor the give of the buggy beneath him was subtle. As they started down the hill, a sharp squeal followed by a pop startled the horse. Cocoa bolted, taking the shaft, all the way to the shaft eyes, away with him.

The fleeing reins whipped through Jethro's startled hands. He snatched at them, securing the tail end of the leather, only to be jerked almost to the dash for his efforts. The buggy—with no horse attached—was racing down the hill. Realizing the gelding would be better off away from the runaway rig, Jethro released the reins. Frightened by the bouncing shaft behind him, the horse raced away. An occasional spark flew up as hardware on the apparatus skidded along the blacktop.

Jethro shot a glance down the road. His breath whistled out in relief. No one was approaching. The last thing he wanted was to crash into someone or to force them to drive into the ditch to evade him. He hoped Cocoa would be all right. At least the horse was outracing the buggy and wouldn't be part of the impending wreck.

The buggy hurtled down the hill at breakneck speed. Jethro rapidly debated his own escape. *I'm sorry,* Daed. *There're going to be a few more things to repair on your old rig.*

The buggy didn't have a storm front. The open area increased his avenues of escapes. But that way could be deadly. He'd do better jumping to the side. With a white-knuckled hand wrapped around the right front corner of the rig, Jethro considered the amber grass of the ditch that blurred by at increasing speed.

He glanced through the open front of the buggy in time to see the gelding swing safely into his folks' lane. Now for him. If the rig kept going straight, the road flattened out beyond the farmstead. The buggy would slow to a less frantic speed. But any bump or rock in the road could throw it off. And with traffic of steel-wheeled buggies and metal horse shoes, the surface was far from even.

It was the ditch then.

Jethro slid to the edge of the seat. Bracing both hands on the sides of the door, he scanned the ditch ahead. No boulders loomed to hamper his fall. Snagging a ragged breath, Jethro launched himself through the door.

Chapter Ten

Ducking his head, Jethro attempted to roll on impact. Weed stems stabbed his face as he landed with a thud, his breath exiting in a whoosh. Bright stars whirled in his head as he lay momentarily motionless, waiting for the world to stop spinning. His mouth filled with the telltale metallic taste. Groaning, he rolled over and pressed a hand against the insistent throbbing in his head. *What happened to the buggy?* Pushing onto his knees, Jethro spat a bloody mouthful into the ditch before lurching to his feet. With help of the long stems of grass, he pulled himself out of the ditch.

The buggy had veered toward the left side of the road. Heading for the ditch, it'd hit the embankment of his folks' lane. The abrupt stop had flipped the buggy over and into the ditch on the far side. It lay on its top, one wheel obviously broken, the other three still spinning.

Swaying slightly as he surveyed the wreck, the blood drained from Jethro's face at the horrific thought of his parents taking that frantic ride. Neither of them was spry enough to have made the jump from the buggy.

Then a flash of movement in the farmyard drew his attention. Expecting to see his horse, Jethro was bewildered to observe a young man rushing his scooter down the lane. When he looked in Jethro's direction, the youth's pale face was visible beneath his battered straw hat.

"Hey! Wait!" Jethro started a stumbling run in the boy's direction, the stiffness in his limbs slowing his pace. Without pausing, the youth darted out the far side of the lane. Jethro slowed to a rough jog and then a walk as the boy sped away down the road.

"Are you all right?" The frantic call came from behind him.

He looked back up the hill to see Susannah scrambling over the fence from the orchard before plunging down into the ditch. He waited while she clambered up the steep edge and hurried to his side. With a light hand on his shoulder, she scrutinized him from his missing hat to the mud ground into his pants and the toes of his boots.

"Your face is bleeding."

Jethro dabbed at his lip and other stinging spots on his cheek. He wasn't surprised when the tips of his fingers came away bright red. He furrowed his brow in pretend dismay. "Oh *nee*. D-do you think it will scar?"

What spared him a swat on his arm for the poor joke was most likely the concern that anywhere it landed would already hurt. An accurate assumption.

"Come to compare b-buggy wrecks?" He nodded with a rueful smile in the direction of the upturned vehicle.

Although she eyed him cautiously, Jethro was relieved when Susannah picked up that he wanted to make light of the situation. "Seems like an odd way to court a girl."

He found it even hurt to smile. "Maybe she's an odd girl."

"She is that, for sure and certain." Frowning, Susannah turned to consider the wreck. "I think we might need a warning sign on this road."

"Hmm." Wincing, Jethro rolled his shoulders experimentally before crossing his arms at his chest. "I think we need one on the b-boy instead. I'm p-pretty certain that was your former hired hand racing away on his scooter. I think he m-might have b-been in the b-barn when I came to work on the b-buggy."

Staring down the road in the direction of the vanishing youth, Susannah sighed as she twisted her hands together. "Do you think the accident was intentional?"

"*Ja.* I know enough about b-buggies t-to know what just happened d-doesn't easily d-do so. Not without help." The admission was hard. And concerning.

Susannah folded her arms as well. "I thought the reason he was sabotaging my place was because he was unhappy with something I told him to do. Or the lectures I gave him when he seemed to be willfully trying me. But that wouldn't be the case with what happened today." She contemplated the wrecked buggy. "Were you the intended target? Or the bishop?" she murmured.

Jethro shook his head, stilling abruptly when it throbbed in protest. "I hardly know the b-boy. I d-don't know why he'd t-target m-me."

"If not you, then the bishop. But why?"

His troubled gaze shifted from the wreck to the farmyard. "I d-don't have an answer t-to that right now.

But what I d-do know is that I need to find m-my horse." He started for the lane, gritting his teeth against aches that loudly objected to his determined stride.

Susannah walked by his side. The gelding hadn't gone far. Shaking and lathered, it stood next to Jethro's buggy. Jethro talked soothingly as he freed the horse from the broken shaft before running a careful hand down its legs. "Ready t-to go back to our house b-boy? T-too m-much excitement for you here?"

"Is he all right?"

"Looks that way." Jethro sighed heavily as he stroked the horse's sweaty neck. "I'm so glad."

"You want to leave him here and drive one of my horses?"

What he wanted to do was wrap his arms around her and just hold her a moment. Just to absorb her warmth, practicality and support. Just to take a moment to appreciate the fact, although he was sore and knew he'd be stiff later, that it wasn't worse. Just to dwell a bit in the possibility of a future with this woman. Instead, he ran a final hand down the gelding's slick neck.

"We'll see how he is after taking a look at the b-buggy. If he's sore or skittish at all, I m-might t-take you up on that."

A quick search in the barn revealed a bag of horse treats. He gave Cocoa a few before leaving him inside with the other horse for company. Then he headed to the wreck at the end of the lane.

Jethro longed to take hold of Susannah's hand as they studied what had been an old but still usable buggy. Along with the broken wheel, the buggy's front end was crumpled. The axle was bent. He could see the impact from the flip over the lane had caused one wall to separate from the roof of the buggy. There would be no repairing it. Jethro trembled again at the thought of his parents as passengers during the wild ride instead of himself. He exhaled shakily. "I guess I owe my *daed* a new rig."

"I'd say he owes you his life," Susannah countered quietly. "No guarantee it wouldn't have happened to him on the hill with the same results to the buggy and…" Her voice faded away.

She didn't have to say it. Jethro already knew. And much worse results for his folks.

Later that afternoon, as he and Bishop Weaver stood at the end of the lane, absorbing the scattered debris, Jethro was almost tempted to wrap his arms around his *daed* in a tight embrace. The moment the impulse arose, he suppressed it. His *daed* would be shocked and annoyed by the display of affection. Jethro had learned that years ago at the age of six when his father had been gone for a week, having traveled to Ohio for a gathering of church leadership.

Thrilled to see his *daed* after spending a week being alternatively ignored or chastised by his mother, Jethro had run to him as soon as the bishop had climbed off the bus with a gathering of other Amish men. Throwing his arms around his *daed's* lean waist, Jethro had hugged him, his more approachable parent, with all his strength. A gruff, "Stop that, boy," had been followed by a grip prying his stick-thin arms from his father's torso. Hanging his head, Jethro had shuffled to the side as the bishop said his farewells to the men he'd traveled with and greeted his wife and younger son. Jethro had never attempted to hug either of his parents again.

"I'll confirm what caused it after I get it p-pulled out. From the way the whole shaft came away, it had t-to b-be intentional. I saw the Schlabach b-boy racing from the farm on his scooter. Susannah has had some issues with him earlier." Jethro stroked his beard as he turned to his father. "Any reason he m-might t-turn his attention t-to you as well and wreck your b-buggy?"

The bishop's mouth compressed into a lipless line as he studied the carcass of the buggy. But Jethro had an impression the wreck wasn't what the man was seeing. With a shrug, he pivoted to retrieve the team of Belgians he'd brought over to pull the damaged rig out. At his father's abrupt, "Wait!" he paused. Expecting to hear a comment about the Schlabach boy or even the damaged buggy, Jethro stiffened at the bishop's choice of topic.

"You need to stop seeing Susannah Mast."

"What?" Jethro cocked his head, unsure that he'd heard right. For sure and certain, he'd been expecting the subject to come up at some point. He'd even made himself scarce just to evade the conversation. But he hardly expected it to be now, when there seemed other much more pressing issues for the bishop than directing his adult son's private life.

"She will wreck your life, surely as this buggy is wrecked."

Jethro turned around to face his father. "Susannah is a *gut* woman."

"*Ja*. But not for you. You need someone who can give you children. A family. Susannah can't do that. She is better matched with an older man who wouldn't be looking for that in a wife. You'd do better to look to her daughter. She's not that much younger than you. You could build a life, a large family, with her."

"I know what I need." Jethro hardly recognized his voice as he ground out the words. He liked Rebecca. She was a sweet girl. But the thought of courting her instead of Susannah coated the back of his throat with bile.

"You need to obey your parents. Honor your father and mother, as is commanded."

Jethro easily identified the biblical verses. Ones that'd been drummed into him since before he could remember. At this moment, they stabbed at him. He'd strived to obey his folks all his life, even at the price of his own happiness. It'd been worth the cost, for he did honor his parents. But what he was feeling for Susannah was not wrong. It gave him a spark of contentment—happiness—he hadn't felt in a long, long time, if ever. It was something worth fighting for. Still, his stomach clenched and sweat beaded on his forehead as he countered his father.

"I've d-done that all m-my life." The headache that'd never fully dissipated since his dive into the ditch throbbed anew. "As b-bishop, you'll be glad to hear that I know scripture as well. What about 'fathers, p-provoke not your children to wrath'? I've already m-married a wife you've chosen for me. My b-brother's. I would've stayed married to Louisa. B-built a life with her. B-but it wasn't *Gott's* will. This t-time I will m-marry whom *I* choose."

"It isn't *Gott's* will that you marry Susannah."

Jethro walked over to the waiting team of Belgians. The large heads of the normally placid geldings were lifted, eyes rounded and chestnut ears pricked forward at the raised voices. Drawing in a ragged breath, Jethro concentrated on monitoring his tone as he walked the team past the bishop on his way down into the ditch. "Isn't His? Or isn't *yours*?"

Conscious of his father's gaze on him, Jethro focused on safely hitching the Belgians to a section of the broken buggy. His hands were shaking so badly, it took him three tries to attach the now wheel-less shell of the buggy to the team. With a quiet command, the geldings lunged into their collars to pull their load out of the ditch and into the bishop's yard. Briskly unhooking that piece, Jethro returned for another, relieved to see that his *daed* had gone into the house.

He wished he could sort out the wreckage of his emotions as quickly as the debris scattered in the ditch. He didn't like conflict. That didn't mean he couldn't face it when necessary, but doing so troubled him. Greatly. Jethro snorted as he urged the Belgians up the lane with the second load. One more reason why he hoped never to be a minister who might have to address a misbehaving flock.

But on this, he wasn't misbehaving. As he'd told his *daed*, Susannah was a *gut* woman. A woman any man would be happy to have as a wife. Wasn't his father urging other men to court her? Why not him? Surely it wasn't wrong to want to marry the woman of your choice. And Susannah was everything he wanted.

Securing the geldings, Jethro returned to the ditch to collect smaller pieces, ones he didn't need the team for, from the wreck. He wanted this courtship to be real. He wanted Susannah as his wife. But that wasn't the arrangement they'd agreed to. Susannah had given him no hint that she wanted anything else than a brief reprieve from other suitors. Unwanted suitors.

Gathering the last few pieces he could find in the tall grass, Jethro gazed across the field to Susannah's farm. Oh, how he longed to be considered as a serious suitor by this woman. Because what he was feeling for her was anything but temporary.

Chapter Eleven

There were already a dozen rigs in the farmyard the following day when Susannah secured Nutmeg to the rail. Upon gathering the cleaning supplies she'd brought from the buggy, she waved a greeting to the woman she spied on the porch industriously applying her broom. Her good friend, Willa Lapp, paused in her sweeping as Susannah came up the stairs.

"Do you think I can convince them to plan a frolic to help me clean my house?" Susannah jested.

"Maybe if you're preparing for a church service or a wedding. I'll make the suggestion that they do yours… right after they do mine." Willa smiled as she eyed Susannah's assortment of rags and bottles. "They're going to give you a hard time about not bringing food."

Susannah grinned in response, knowing what was coming. "They'd give me a harder time if I had."

With a sympathetic nod, Willa put the broom in motion again. "*Ach,* that's for sure and certain."

Opening the door, Susannah found several other women bustling around the roomy kitchen. Bumping the door with her hip to close it, she stayed just inside,

out of the flow of traffic, as she responded to the cho-
rused greetings. "Where do you want me?"

"Not in here, that's for sure," quipped a gray-haired
woman near the stove. Laughter circled the room.

Susannah heaved a wounded sigh. "I'll remember
that, Waneta Gingerich. And next time you host church,
I'll bring several desserts and make sure to transfer
them to your dishes and serve them up saying 'Waneta made this.'"

"Anyone who knows us wouldn't make that mistake," came the prompt retort, followed by more chuck-
les.

"Actually, I had a cookie or two of yours at the
cider frolic that weren't bad at all. I thought they were
safe when I saw Rachel bring them in. When I com-
plimented her on them and she said they were yours,
you could've knocked me over with a feather. And not
because I was sick from them, either." Mary Raber, Rachel's mother-in-law, winked from the doorway.

"I've been working on my skills," Susannah said,
tamping down her unexpected delight at the comment.
"I'll just have to keep sneaking them in somehow so I
can prove it to all you doubters in the district."

"I don't know. According to Naomi, you have a
whole new set of skills." Ruth Schrock, the wife of
the owner of the furniture business in town and Ben's
boss, raised her eyebrows from where she'd just handed
her young daughter to one of the preteen girls who'd
watch the smaller children while their mothers cleaned.

Susannah, along with the rest, turned to look at the
older woman who was currently doing dishes. Naomi's
cheeks grew rosy as she turned away from the sink.

"*Ja.* The reason Leroy Albrecht is courting me now is because of Susannah's skills as a matchmaker."

Susannah's eyes weren't the only ones that widened at the news. A quick review of the kitchen revealed many speculative glances now aimed her way. Susannah stifled a snort at the attention. Single women, both widows and those who'd never married, as well as mothers with many daughters who were perennially in search of something that might help their children find a spouse, were eyeing her with consideration. Content to remain a widow, Susannah was in the minority in the community.

Her desire to smirk quickly faded as she acknowledged many were not smiling. Marriage was a matter of economics, companionship and a foundation for children. Just because her marriage had primarily been of the former and latter didn't mean that others didn't long for those as well, in addition to the allure of companionship. Her attitude wasn't entirely fair to her husband, Vernon. They'd developed a comfortable companionship over the years. Just not—her heart gave a couple distinct thuds at the abrupt realization—companionship like she'd been relishing lately with Jethro.

Uncomfortable with the direction of her thoughts and the attention aimed her way, Susannah lifted the supplies in her hands. "Since I won't be in the kitchen, where do you want me to start?"

Although they were preparing the farmhouse for Hannah Bartel—she and her husband Gabe were moving from the small apartment they'd been living in over the quilt shop in town—Waneta was in charge of the day's cleaning frolic. Wiping her hands on her apron, the gray-haired woman stepped forward. "I don't think anyone has been upstairs yet. Would you mind starting up there? We'll send others up as soon as possible."

"*Ja.* Sounds *gut,*" Susannah hastened to assure her. Sounded very good in fact, as it might forestall any curious questions arising from Naomi's announcement. With a smiling nod for those in the kitchen and others she passed working in the main-floor rooms, Susannah opened the door to the narrow stairway, trotted up the steps and stepped into the first bedroom.

The old farmhouse had been empty for a year or so following the passing of its *Englisch* owners. Although smaller than many houses built by the Amish, it still had two bedrooms upstairs and a small bath. Sturdy, it would be a nice place for Hannah and Gabe, the local EMS provider. According to their district's rules, new Amish owners had a year to convert an *Englisch* home to Plain standards. Susannah wondered how many of those who'd purchased homes waited until the eleventh month before leaving the power grid.

She wasn't sure what Hannah and Gabe's plans were. Gabe was Mennonite. In order to marry him, Hannah hadn't been baptized into the church and so wasn't subject to the rules of the *Ordnung.* Even so, the couple, widely accepted in the Plain community, tried to abide by the lifestyle Hannah had grown up in.

Susannah studied the empty room. At least there was no carpet here to pull up. As Amish didn't use electricity, which meant no vacuums, carpets were difficult to keep clean. Most of the floors in the district were wood like this or covered with linoleum with some woven rugs here and there to provide warmth and color. Susannah had dragged her share of rugs outside to beat the dust out over the years.

Setting her cleaning supplies on the floor, Susannah rolled up her sleeves. The house was much more spacious than the couple's current apartment where they'd resided for the past year. It would be exciting for them to move into a new home, something Susannah had never done. As the youngest daughter in a family with no sons, she'd inherited the farm when her folks had died, her father passing when she was in her teens. Susannah knew her husband had considered the farm more appealing than any personal attributes she might have had. Her and Vernon's youthful marriage had been based on expediency; she'd needed help on the farm and he'd needed an occupation, although farming wouldn't have been his first choice. And it'd showed.

To shed the melancholy thoughts, Susannah grabbed some supplies and headed into the bathroom. The little room filled with the sharp smell of vinegar as she poured it, along with a sufficient amount of water, into the bucket.

Returning to the bedroom, Susannah frowned at the shadows in the room. Although every square inch of the room would be scrubbed, the dim lighting made it difficult to see. If it were up to her, she'd immediately repaint the room in a brighter color. In the meantime, she narrowed her eyes at the small white rectangle by the doorframe and drummed her fingers against her leg. Had they been working in natural light downstairs, or was the electricity still on in the house? And were those working today using it? There was one way to find out.

Striding to the door, she put her thumb under the switch and pushed upward. With a soft click, the room brightened, making the problem areas much easier to see. *Gut!* Now if only she was left alone to work, the fact that she was using it up here wouldn't be known.

Even as the thought crossed her mind, the door to the stairway creaked open, followed by the hesitant tread announcing someone was coming up the steps. Scowling, Susannah clicked off the light. Selecting a large rag, she dipped it into the vinegar solution and began wiping down the walls. She was halfway across the first one when, at a sound at the door, she turned to see Emma Beiler poking her head into the room.

"How's it going up here?" the petite woman asked.

"Pretty well. Not a large room, so it shouldn't take too long."

"Do you want some help?" Emma stepped through the door.

"*Denki.* That would be appreciated. Would you mind starting on the opposite side?"

"Sure." Snagging a rag, Emma dipped it into the bucket and began scrubbing the far wall. The two worked in silence for a while before Susannah heard the other woman clear her throat.

"You know…what Naomi said in the kitchen got me thinking…"

Susannah blinked at the smudge on the wall before her. *"Ja?"* she responded as she re-wet the rag and went back to work. Absently scrubbing at the dark spot, her attention was focused on the woman across the room. Emma and her twin sister Elizabeth had never been married. Perhaps five years or so older than Susannah, Emma produced the straw hats many in the community had worn for as long as Susannah could remember, running the business out of the sisters' little house. Always thinking of Emma and her twin as a unit, Susannah had never thought of one of them as wanting a marriage of her own. She frowned at the stubborn smudge. Which had been foolishness on her part.

Their culture placed such importance on marriage; there was unfortunately a stigma on being older and single. If it was uncomfortable enough for a woman, it was even tougher for a bachelor. Unmarried men were less common than unmarried females because if either sex were to leave the Amish life, it was more likely the men. Beyond the advantage of numbers, because the men did the proposing in their society, it was assumed if an older man was single, he either couldn't get anyone or he was too particular. Dubbed an "old boy," it wasn't a flattering term.

"I was wondering… If you wouldn't mind… If you could think of someone who might be interested…"

Feeling for the woman, Susannah turned to face Emma's tentative expression. "Getting Naomi and Leroy together was more of an accident than anything else. But if I can, I'd be happy to send someone in your direction." Her heart clenched at the hope in the other woman's face. "Did you have anyone in mind?" she added lamely.

"*Nee.*" It was said with a sigh. "But I haven't thought about it for a long while."

Susannah bit her lip at the obvious wistfulness. "Are there any particular traits you might be looking for?"

"Breathing?" Emma smiled before cocking her head and considering the ceiling for a moment. "And kind."

"I'll keep those in mind." That and more for the obviously lonely woman. But there was one thing Susannah wanted the woman to be certain of before she assumed a role she wasn't looking for and wasn't sure she was capable of. "Although I might not find anyone."

"I know that. But then again…you might."

They worked further in silence. When she'd completed wiping down the walls on her side of the room, Emma set her rag with the rest of the supplies. "I need to get back downstairs and finish the task I was working on before…our talk. *Denki* again."

"Thank you for your help. Oh, would you send someone up with a dry mop or broom I can throw a rag over to wipe down the ceiling?"

"I'll let someone know as soon as I get downstairs."

A short time later, the door creaked open again followed by footsteps on the stairs. Susannah turned as someone entered, carrying not one mop, but two. She relaxed at the sight of Linda Esh. There'd be no request for a matchmaker here. Linda was already a wife and mother of a large family.

"Emma said you needed this?"

Taking one mop, Susannah leaned the other against the wall. *"Ja. Denki."* When Linda didn't retreat back down the stairs, Susannah shrugged. Draping a large rag over the mop, she started systematically wiping it over the ceiling, clearing it of an occasional cobweb.

The odor of vinegar was strengthened when Linda returned to the room with a fresh bucket of solution. Fishing out another old cloth diaper Susannah had brought as rags, the woman dampened it and began cleaning the windows. Susannah was halfway across the ceiling when the woman cleared her throat.

"About what Naomi said downstairs… My oldest *dochder* seems to be overlooked by the young men in the district and I was wondering…"

Susannah's brisk motions across the ceiling slowed as her brows rose.

"I've heard that the bishop thinks it's time his son marries again. Jethro's quiet, but he's a *gut* man. He'd be quite a catch."

Susannah froze at the woman's words. She stared at the ceiling where her mop was pressed, the edges of the rag dangling down. Her emotions were suddenly as frayed as the edges of the old cloth. Apparently she and Jethro hadn't been doing such a good job in presenting themselves as a courting couple. Either that or the woman was intentionally ignoring the news, knowing as Susannah did that the notion of the two of them together was foolish.

It wasn't surprising someone thought of Jethro as a prospective husband. The bishop's frequent pushing of his son toward courtship was Jethro's reason for entering into their agreement in the first place. But still, to hear it voiced aloud? Susannah felt like she'd unwittingly swallowed the vinegar solution and her stomach was now rebelling. In the silence behind her, she knew she needed to say something. But the thought that someone was particularly interested in Jethro, *her* Jethro… Lowering the mop handle, Susannah rubbed her uneasy midsection.

Fortunately, the other woman filled the quiet when she moved to the next window. "There's also the older Raber boy, who just came back from the *Englisch*. But you'd always worry that he might leave again. Besides, Aaron always seemed a bit wild. Or maybe the youngest Schrock *bruder*, Gideon? His older *brieder* seem to be doing all right. Anyone can see the Schrocks are fine-looking and responsible men."

Susannah silently blew out a breath as the discussion moved away from Jethro. She couldn't blame the woman. As a mother, you always hoped for your children to make a good match. She wanted the same for Rebecca, who was Linda's oldest daughter's age.

"I will keep your comments in mind. But you need to know that what happened with Naomi and Leroy was just..."

The second and final window complete, Linda set her rag next to the bucket. Her smile was lopsided, her cheeks slightly pink with what could be exertion from cleaning or embarrassment. Susannah knew which it would be for her. "I understand. But I wanted to ask before others did."

Susannah nodded numbly as the woman exited the room. Spotting the extra mop, she almost called the woman to take it back downstairs. The last thing she wanted after the two previous helpers was more company. Quickly finishing the ceiling, she prepared to mop the floor. And cringed when she heard the door creak at the bottom of the stairs.

That was the way it went for the rest of the morning. When one woman went down, another was soon mounting the stairs. Even though Susannah began to direct them to a room she wasn't working in for a task, new helpers at some point poked their head into where she was and brought up her unexpected and unwanted role as a matchmaker.

Susannah tried to guide the conversations to the upcoming election for minister. All acknowledged that it was an honorable role to serve *Gott* in such a way, although many admitted few wanted to be chosen for the lifelong, unpaid position. And then they worked the discussion around to what they'd be interested in as a match for themselves. Or their children. Or their sisters. Even their grandchildren.

Susannah didn't know whether to clean faster to avoid any more private moments with those seeking her questionable matrimonial skills or to take her time in case it would be worse downstairs among the others. Although appreciative of the revolving help, she was thrilled for a few moments' respite when there were no new footsteps on the stairs.

Shaking her head, she scoured the sink in the small bathroom. *I'll probably hear the door's creak in my dreams. What have I gotten myself into?* The idea had been amusing at first—connecting Leroy, her unwanted suitor who wanted someone talented in the kitchen, with Naomi, who was proud of the fact that she was. But it wasn't so amusing any more.

With an ear tuned for any noise from the door, Susannah replayed some of the conversations as she rinsed the sink. *Well, now I know what the single women in the district want in a husband.* Furrowing her brow, she polished the faucet handles. *If I were talking to a matchmaker*—she rolled her eyes at the notion of herself in the role—*what would I look for in one?* Jethro had asked her that once. Originally mocking the question, she'd later struggled to answer it. The discussion had been gnawing at her at odd moments ever since.

If and when she had to marry, Susannah was going to make sure it was someone she wanted. She'd make a list of qualities, much like what she looked for in a buck when matching with her does. If you wanted specific characteristics, you needed to identify and look for them, especially when you were working with a small herd. Her lips twitched. Or community. Otherwise you got what you got.

If she remarried, she didn't expect a love match. She

hoped for a good working relationship and help with the farm. A hardworking man. Patient around livestock. She smiled as she recalled Jethro's comment about his draft team going courting for him. Mechanically inclined would be helpful as well.

Susannah paused while shifting her attention to the tub. It would also be pleasant to have someone she enjoyed being around. Today, Emma had requested a kind man. That was certainly an attractive quality. The other traits women had mentioned—a good sense of humor, fun, able to laugh but serious when necessary, someone who listened—Susannah could agree with.

She bent over the tub. *Jethro is hardworking. He's good with livestock. He can fix anything. He's...* Sitting back on her heels, Susannah stared unseeing at the beige tile above the white tub. Jethro had all the qualities she looked for in a husband. It was almost as if she'd been describing him. *Oh dear. And when had he become my Jethro? That wasn't our agreement at all.* Theirs was only to be a fake relationship. He wouldn't appreciate her getting other ideas.

This time when the squeak of the door interrupted her thoughts, she was relieved. Hannah Bartel stopped in the doorway. A contented wife of less than a year, Hannah wouldn't be looking for a match for herself, she had no single sisters that needed a union, and no marriage-age children. This should be a safe conversation.

Hannah inhaled with appreciative slowness as she surveyed the bathroom. "It smells clean in here. Looks like you're finishing up. My timing is *gut* as I've been instructed to tell you that lunch is ready."

"Sounds *wunderbar*." Gathering her supplies, Susannah looked up to find Hannah studying her.

"So…you and Jethro, huh?"

Susannah's hand tightened on the handle of her bucket. She didn't respond. Couldn't respond. Despite her and Jethro's agreement, following the unexpected emotional turmoil of the morning, she hesitated to mislead this woman.

Hannah wore a sweet smile. "I'm glad. He's a *gut* man. He deserves happiness. Take care of him. I know you'll be *gut* to him."

Would she? Susannah wasn't so sure, now that she was aware of other women—more suitable than her—who were interested in Jethro. Maybe the best thing she could do for him was to free him from their fake relationship so he could pursue a real one. She swallowed against the lump in her throat as she followed Hannah downstairs. Why did the thought make her feel as empty as the vacant rooms she'd just cleaned?

Chapter Twelve

Susannah drew Nutmeg to a halt, wondering if she was making a mistake in stopping here on her way home from the cleaning frolic. At least she knew Lavinia Schlabach was home. John's *mamm* was hanging clothes on the line. She stepped out from between the sheets that billowed in the breeze to see who had driven up her lane. Susannah remained on the buggy seat, unsure of how to proceed. She'd known Lavinia for years, liked and respected the woman, but they weren't close friends. How did one accuse a woman's son of potentially dangerous activities without offending her? And that, on top of having fired the youth the previous week, probably removing a needed income source for the family.

Still, while what John had done to her had been nuisances—although she didn't put hurting Nutmeg in that category—they hadn't been potentially deadly like the situation with the bishop's buggy. What had caused the sullen boy's normally harmless actions to take a more dangerous turn?

When Lavinia shaded her eyes in an effort to identify who had arrived, Susannah knew she couldn't delay longer. Fastening her jacket against an inner chill as much as the drop in October temperature, she climbed down from the buggy and started across the shaggy yard. The laundry on the line attested to the financial challenges Lavinia had endured. The sheets flapping in the light wind were worn and bore patches, as did the socks that spun on the small, circular rack hanging from the main clothesline. Still, the dress of the woman standing among these, although worn as well, was neat and clean, as was her lean figure.

Susannah sighed after a quick scan of the laundry. No pants or shirts hung with the other items flapping in the breeze. John was Lavinia's youngest child and the only one living at home. John wasn't here. If he was, his clothes surely would've been on the line. Still, even if he wasn't living at home, his mother might know where he was.

"Hello, Lavinia." Susannah stopped a few feet from the clothesline.

"Susannah." There were a few beats of silence while Lavinia studied her before continuing. "I know why you're here. I don't know where he is. I haven't seen him since the day he came home early from your place."

"I'm so sorry I had to let him go. I don't know what he mentioned, but he'd intentionally hurt my mare. I couldn't allow that."

Sighing, Lavinia dropped her head. "It's all right. I understand. He'd been sorely troubled since he heard of his father's passing."

"I'm sorry about that as well."

"You needn't be. It was *Gott's* will. Mervin left the

Amish…and me, over ten years ago. I shouldn't say it, as he was my husband, but they've been a better ten years than the ones that came before. I appreciate all the district has done for me, both before he left and after. I don't know what I would've done without their intervention and support." Her prematurely lined face lifted in a rueful smile. "Including the money that's been provided over the past decade."

"We take care of each other. That's as it should be." Figuring it might make it easier for the woman to talk if they weren't facing each other like unintentional adversaries, Susannah grabbed an item from the nearby basket and a handful of clothespins and hung it on the line. A moment later, Lavinia did the same.

"John saw some things he shouldn't have. He experienced some things he shouldn't have, either. The older ones were bigger and quicker to get out of the way. I tried to protect him as much as I could, but I was dealing with the same thing. Still, John took it very hard when Mervin was…" The woman's voice drifted off as she bent to the basket and hung up a few more items.

Susannah stayed silent as well, letting Lavinia determine what she wanted to share. Many things had been attempted to impact Mervin Schlabach's behavior—visits by the ministers, the *Englisch* jail, shunning—until the man had left the community for an unsettled life among the *Englisch*.

"Before he went, Mervin was always talking poorly about the ministers. Bishop Weaver, David Petersheim and your husband. I think John blames them for what happened."

Susannah's fingers tightened on the clothespin as she hung a ragged towel. The information was enlightening and disturbing. She and the Weavers had been targeted. David Petersheim had passed away a few years ago and his family had moved out of the area. And therefore, apparently, out of the troubled boy's reach? "Doesn't John know when someone is excommunicated from the church, the district must be unanimous in the decision?"

"That's not what he'd heard from his father before he left. It was never Mervin's fault. Not surprising when he never showed remorse. I'm afraid he poisoned the boy's thinking. Mervin would fly off the handle at everything. I suppose I wasn't surprised, but it was still painful when John started stealing. When I'd confront him on it, it was like he was anticipating it." Lavinia shook her head sadly as she asked quietly, "Did he steal from you?"

"Not that I know of."

"I'm glad of that at least. John never had a *gut* role model. At least when the older children were little, my folks lived in the connected *daadi haus* and had some influence. They passed when John was an infant, so after that it was just… Mervin."

Susannah nodded solemnly, knowing remarriage hadn't been possible for Lavinia. Even though the man had left her, she could never divorce him, as they would always be married in the eyes of the church.

"But we always managed, with the help of the community." Having hung the last item in the basket, Lavinia crossed her arms over her narrow chest and stared toward the road. "I worry for John. I don't know where he's staying. Folks tell me when they catch sight of him. I've heard some folks have been missing eggs and such. I just want him home and safe." Sighing, she picked up the empty basket. "Wish I could tell him that he's striking out at the wrong folks. The only one to blame was his *daed*. But he doesn't want to hear it." When she turned her gaze to her visitor, its bleakness cut straight through Susannah's heart. She couldn't imagine not knowing Amos's whereabouts, and that he needed help wherever he was. There were no limits to a mother's love.

"Would you like some *kaffi*?" The suggestion was tentative.

"Denki." Susannah recognized it as more a plea to talk than anything else. Even with the many things waiting for her at home, it was an offer Susannah couldn't and wouldn't turn down. "That would be *gut*." She followed Lavinia into the house.

The muffled chatter made Susannah smile. Leaning on the smooth branch of the apple tree, she watched Jethro, Rebecca and Amos picking apples from a tree several yards away. The air was crisp with the scent of the ripe fruit, the faint hum of insects and a nippy reminder of cooler weather to come. The descending sun cast a relative glow over the orchard. Susannah's smile slipped as she inhaled sharply. The day seemed brighter when Jethro was around. At least Rebecca and Amos seemed to think so. They'd been thrilled when Jethro had happened by while they were using some time before chores to harvest the fruit. Susannah had been as well. But she wasn't going to show it. Particularly after the cleaning frolic yesterday.

She should really stop this farce. Jethro didn't need her help anymore. Based on what she'd heard yesterday from some women in the district, he wouldn't even need to go courting. Several interested parties would find a way to make a trail to his door.

As for her reason for the fake courtship, Jethro had brought his team over yesterday while she'd been gone and completed a large share of the field work. Now, with just a few big days in the field, she and Amos should be able to complete the rest of the work. Since finishing it before colder weather arrived had been her stated purpose for evading unwanted suitors, the motivation no longer existed.

But had that really been her reason? Susannah acknowledged her real motivation had been that she didn't care for any of her potential suitors like she now cared for Jethro. She rubbed a hand over her forehead. How could she tell him that she wanted to make their pretend courtship real? He'd be embarrassed to hear his former babysitter confess she wanted to be his… what? His wife? Envisioning the awkward admission, and equally embarrassing rejection, Susannah turned as red as the surrounding apples.

She'd been the one to insist that whatever happened, they stay friends. But it was too small of a community for that. It would be painful enough to continue to see him with whomever he'd eventually choose as his wife and their growing family over the years.

Sniffling, Susannah brushed the back of her hand against the faint prickling in her nose. Her head lifted at the sound of Rebecca's laughter. At the other tree, she watched her daughter grin as she caught an apple dropped by Jethro, who'd climbed up the tree's trunk to reach some of the higher branches. Susannah's breath caught as he smiled in return from his precarious perch.

Her stomach twisted at the sight. Jethro had been more quiet than usual lately. What if he was already losing interest in her and turning his interest elsewhere? To someone whom he'd also been around lately who was pretty and charming—and much more appropriate for him? What if she had to watch Jethro court, marry and raise a family with her own daughter? It made sense. Closer in age, Rebecca could give him a family. What if in the future Susannah would babysit her grandchildren—his children—the ones she couldn't give him?

Susannah's face contorted briefly at the image of having the man she cared for as a son-in-law. When Jethro looked up and caught her gaze, she ducked her head. Pivoting, she grabbed at the first apple she saw. Jethro would be a *wunderbar* husband for Rebecca. As a mother, Susannah couldn't ask for a better partner for her daughter. But she didn't know if she could bear it. And for that reason, she needed to break off their fake engagement and point him in the direction of other women in the community. At the thought of losing their cherished connection, her hand clenched around the apple, denting the fruit.

"Are you all right?"

Jethro raised his eyebrows when Susannah flinched at his words. Surely his father hadn't had the same distasteful lecture with her that he'd had with him? That was more his mother's tactic than his father's. But that was entirely possible, too. He longed to touch Susannah on her shoulder, to gently prompt her to face him, but he didn't really have the right to do so. Yet. Although she'd smiled when he'd arrived, Susannah hadn't said much, which in itself was odd. Instead of staying by her as he'd wanted to when he'd found them in the orchard, he'd allowed himself to be drawn away by Rebecca and Amos. But when their eyes met and she'd seemed distraught, it would've taken a six-horse draft hitch to keep him away.

Finally, her shoulders straightened and she turned to face him. "*Ja.* Certainly." Her voice was as peculiar as the smile it accompanied. It definitely didn't emanate from her eyes as it normally did. Her eyes weren't smiling at all. They were troubled.

Jethro took a step closer.

Breaking his gaze, Susannah bent to put an apple in the basket at her feet. "I wanted to thank you for your help yesterday."

He'd come over, hoping to see her. After the conversation with his father, he'd wanted to be with her. To replace the uneasiness he'd felt with the joy that always filled him when he was near Susannah. They'd covered many more acres than he'd expected, but his draft team had been tired by the time he'd finally given up and left when she'd never come home.

Because she seemed uncomfortable facing him, he plucked a few nearby apples and set them in the basket. "Glad t-to d-do it. It was p-part of our arrangement."

He frowned when her face paled to a color more closely matched to the *kapp* she wore than her normally tanned cheeks. She moved to another branch. One farther from him. There were still plenty of reachable apples on the one she'd left. "Speaking of that. Your name came up at the cleaning frolic at Hannah Bartel's yesterday. More than once." Susannah tossed a smile over her shoulder that was more dismal than the one she'd offered him before.

Other than their fake relationship, which he'd gladly have folks talk about, Jethro wasn't fond of being a topic of discussion. Had his mother gotten to Susannah? From where he'd been working, he could see her rig had been home all day yesterday. Had she gotten a ride to the gathering?

"About our courtship?"

"*Nee.* Apparently we need to do a better job of that. Or perhaps—" she cleared her throat "—we should end it. Because these were women who would like you to be courting them or their daughters." The small branch bowed before springing up again with the force of which she'd tugged the fruit from the tree.

Jethro's stomach dropped. He scowled as he reached for a pair of apples. With a grunt, he briskly snapped them off at the stem. The last thing he wanted to do was end their courtship. As for there being women in the district who wanted him to come calling? That was certainly a surprise. But useless information. He didn't want to even think about courting someone else. He was much more interested in figuring out a way to have the woman whom he was pretend courting want to make it real.

And from what Susannah was saying, he was doing a pretty poor job of even faking a relationship. More evidence of why he should avoid courting in general. Sweat beaded on his forehead as he jerked a few more apples from the branches.

"Don't you want to know who they were? Aren't you even slightly curious?"

"*Nee.*" He pulled down another couple handfuls of apples. "If we're supposed t-to b-be courting, why are they asking you about wanting to walk out with m-me?" Jethro glared at the fruit in his hand before he put it in the basket. He could see his *daed's* hand in this somehow. His folks knew a direct approach didn't always work with him. He wasn't surprised they'd try another method to break up what they presumed to be an inappropriate relationship of his.

When Susannah didn't respond from where she worked on the other side of the tree, Jethro darted a frowning glance in her direction. Was she trying to push him off on other women? A blemish on the apple in his hand caught his eye. Well, that was something he could certainly relate to. Cocking his arm, Jethro pitched it far into the connecting field and watched it bounce hard before rolling into the grass. Susannah couldn't possibly be caring for him, as he was her, if she was that eager to get rid of him.

"Apparently I've gained a reputation as something of a matchmaker. That's why they were asking me. Naomi and Leroy are now seeing each other after my 'baking lesson.' She announced that I was the one that brought them together. I was working upstairs. It was a regular parade of women who came up to see me after that. Some wanting someone to court them. Some wanting a match for their daughters. A few of the single men in the area were specifically mentioned. One of them was you."

Putting a trio of apples in her basket, she turned to him and mused ruefully, "Maybe my skills at cooking up something weren't meant to be in the kitchen. Maybe I'm better at blending people together instead of ingredients."

The tension in Jethro's shoulders relaxed. Perhaps she wasn't trying to get rid of him, after all. "B-be careful. There m-might still be m-mishaps waiting to happen. My favorite is the fork you baked into the corn bread."

Plucking an apple from the tree, Susannah threw it at him. Catching it one-handed, Jethro contentedly sighed at this more Susannah-like action as he looked it over. Rubbing it on his sleeve, he took a bite.

"The goats had made a commotion outside. I ran over to the window to make sure they were all right, which they fortunately were, and when I got back, I'd forgotten that I'd propped the fork on the edge of the bowl. It slid into the batter when I wasn't looking."

Jethro took another bite from the apple. Now that Susannah seemed closer to normal, he was comfortable enough to ask, "So, was there anything that m-made you think of cooking up something else for m-me?"

Grimacing, Susannah twisted her hands together as she looked away. "Actually, it was a little bit disturbing to have someone ask about seeing the man that I'm supposedly seeing."

It was like the sun coming out, the way her words warmed his heart. Jethro wanted to embrace the apple tree beside him. Embrace Susannah. He pitched the apple core into the field, much more gently this time. "As you say, we need to do a better job with our own courtship. How would you like to go to the auction with me tomorrow?"

She went still at his words. Above the simple neckline of her dress, her slender throat bobbed in a hard swallow. When she finally looked over at him, her eyes were troubled, wistful. But she nodded.

Chapter Thirteen

Swishing water over the blade, Jethro tapped it on the corner of the sink basin to dislodge any shaving cream before raising it. He was always very careful shaving around the scar. The last thing he wanted was to nick it and make it even more pronounced. He'd prefer not to shave the area at all, and to grow a mustache. But although Amish men grew beards when they married, mustaches were forbidden, because along with the fact that they were associated with the military that'd persecuted early Amish centuries ago, they were considered *hochmut*.

He supposed that might be true as it was surely pride that tempted him to grow one to cover the scar. Opening his mouth to stretch the skin above his lip taut, he began to shave the area. He'd been told his first surgery, the one to join the lip, was when he was six weeks old. There'd been…what? Six or seven others since then?

Lowering the razor, Jethro scowled into the mirror. His nose was still asymmetrical. People didn't seem as aware of it as he was. Or were mature enough not to mention it. Still, he was glad that, save the one in the bathroom, there weren't any mirrors in the house.

Most of the surgeries had been when he was younger. He didn't remember them. Except once when he'd been in the hospital and old enough to notice there were those with more obvious scars than his. Since then he'd learned there are some scars that were more on their soul than their physical being. Something perhaps less easily healed than split skin.

Well, his scars or his stammer couldn't define him if he didn't let them. Was he going to continue to? Susannah didn't seem to mind and that's what mattered. He loved her. The shoulders in the mirror rose and fell in a deep breath at the acknowledgment. Being with her these past few weeks had taken a respect and affection and cemented it into so much more. She made him happy. It was a novel feeling. He was determined to make her feel the same way.

So he'd better not blow this date. He set the razor down with a shaking hand. Other than taking a female out to dinner, one who'd been forewarned by his parents to accept, his dating experience was limited.

Already knowing he was going to be baptized and join the church, Jethro's *rumspringa* had been short. Since Jethro hadn't thought he'd marry, there'd been no point in a long running-around period. He'd had no desire to go to singings and frolics, and even less to face rejection should he have asked to take a girl home afterward.

The girls had the pick of many other men in the community before they'd consider him. Jethro ran a thumb over the scar above his lip. His parents had never mentioned anyone in their family history with it, but he'd always wondered if his cleft was genetic and if there were risks in passing it on. Still, he'd been stunned and overjoyed when Louisa had reluctantly mentioned she was pregnant. When he'd lost them, he'd been lost for a bit, too. The babe had been his chance to be a father, even though the notion had petrified him.

Jerking the plug from the sink, Jethro drained his shaving water and ran a bit more to splash over his face. If only painful memories could be washed away like clumps of shaving cream. Casting a final look in the mirror, he grimaced as he touched the ends of his hair. His bowl cut was curling up at the ends. It needed to be cut again. Not that it mattered, but he wanted to look nice. At least as nice as possible.

Good thing he hadn't thought ahead about asking her for a date. If he had, he'd have been too nervous to get the words out. Although he could tell Susannah had been reluctant to do so, to his elation, she'd said yes. Well, nodded it, anyway. Jethro wanted to keep her in the habit of saying yes. There was a bigger question down the road, if he could work up the nerve to ask it, that he was hoping she'd say yes to as well. One that would make this courtship no longer fake.

The fact that some folks hadn't seemed to notice that they were courting, puzzled him. If Jethro had anything to do with it, this was the day they would definitely put that ignorance to rest.

Jethro's nervousness surged anew when Susannah settled next to him on the buggy seat. She looked so neat and vibrant in her white cap and apron over the dark green dress visible under her light jacket.

"Are you looking for anything in particular today?"

As if noting the way his eyes feasted on her, a hint of pink flushed Susannah's complexion.

"B-besides m-making sure I'm seen with you? *Ja.* Looking for a new b-buggy for m-my *d-daed.*"

"Surely he's not expecting you to replace it." Susannah eyed him with concern. "The wreck wasn't your fault."

"*Nee.* He's b-buying it. I'm just looking them over t-to advise the b-best choices for him t-to b-bid on."

Susannah nodded. "He trusts your judgment."

Jethro's smile froze for a moment before disappearing completely as he replayed the words the bishop had spoken to him regarding the woman currently seated on his left side. *It isn't* Gott*'s will that you marry Susannah.* His grip tightened on the leather in his hands.

"On this matter, anyway." Jethro rolled his shoulders. The bishop would be there today. He would see them. That was *partly* the intent of this outing. To show his father that he would make his own decisions. Jethro inhaled sharply. He wasn't going to let his father bother him. An elemental joy hummed within him at spending the day with Susannah.

"I'm going to look at the ponies." Amos poked his head over the seat back into the space between Jethro and Susannah. The empty space Jethro longed to bridge by linking his hand with hers.

"Don't go thinking we're going to replace Ginger." Susannah turned to remind her son.

"Ah, Ginger is okay. Just because you want to look at something new doesn't mean you're not happy with what you have." The boy rested his arms across the leather. "I just like to look at ponies."

Jethro enjoyed the chatter between mother and son.

"Why does someone who doesn't like to b-bake name her horses after spices?"

"Says the man who drives a horse named Cocoa," Susannah teased. "For me, it was the one place I knew what to do with them."

"That's right. You use m-more ingredients on the farm than in the kitchen."

With a smile, Susannah glanced over her shoulder at the other passenger in the back seat. "Anything in particular you'll be looking at, Rebecca?"

Amos snorted with the disgust of a younger brother. "She's just coming so she can look at the *youngies*."

"I am not!" The retort, followed by an affronted sniff, was instant. "I want to check out the crafts, particularly the quilts."

Jethro suppressed a smile at Rebecca's protest. From casual observations of her at social gatherings and the restaurant where she worked, he knew she wasn't averse to looking at men her age. He swiveled his head to see, like her mother previously, the young woman's pretty cheeks were flushed. The sight brought back another admonishment from his father—that he should look toward the daughter instead of the mother for a spouse. Jethro had no doubt that Rebecca would make someone a fine wife someday, but it wasn't going to be him.

"And maybe stop at the bake sale to see what they have."

Jethro turned back in time to see Susannah's lips twitch at her daughter's subtle nudge.

"*Ja, Mamm.* Can we get a cake or cookies so we can have something *gut* at home for once?"

The twitch morphed into a wry grimace at the reminder of her nonexistent baking skills. Susannah sighed. "You may choose one item each."

Jethro felt like sighing as well. In contentment. He was part of a family. A happy, teasing family. At least for the day. And if he could somehow convince the woman sitting next to him he was worthy, he would be a permanent member. Jethro's eyes widened. If things went as he hoped and Susannah married him, he'd become father to the two seated behind him. A father. Jethro shifted the lines to one hand to press a palm to his mouth. When Louisa and his *boppeli* had died, the unexpected hope of being a father that'd grown with his wife's pregnancy had died with them. Even though they weren't of his body, he would be proud to be a father to these fine young people.

"Are you all right, Jethro?"

He looked over at Susannah's quiet question. Because it was worth taking the risk, he surreptitiously reached out to grasp her slender hand that rested between them on the seat. She smiled at him quizzically. But Jethro's heart thrilled when she held it for several heartbeats before pulling free.

Faint heat rose up Susannah's neck when Jethro helped her down from the buggy. And she let him. It wasn't as if she hadn't climbed down from a buggy by herself a hundred—*nee,* a thousand times before. The flush rose higher when she saw all the interested gazes that turned their way.

This is why we came together today, after all. Although she shouldn't have agreed. She should've followed her better nature and let him go. Let him pursue a more suitable relationship. But when she was with Jethro, when he smiled in that shy, hopeful way…surely a little more time with him wouldn't hurt? She'd told him other women would welcome his attention, certainly that was enough? As he now knew he had other options, if he wanted to pursue them, he'd break it off with her, wouldn't he? But instead, he'd asked her to join him today, further cementing their charade. Susannah tried, and failed, to suppress the joy that thrummed through her at the knowledge.

Once out of the buggy, Amos and Rebecca hastily went their separate ways. Glancing at her, Jethro gestured to the stream of people walking toward the tents and assortments of good in the short distance. "B-business first?"

Nodding, Susannah fell into step beside him. When they located the used buggies for sale, Jethro went over each one, carefully examining them while Susannah visited with nearby friends whose husbands did the same. When Jethro returned to her side and indicated he was ready to go whenever she was, a few eyes widened. But it was the smiles that widened when the glances shifted between the two of them that thrilled Susannah.

A smile took up permanent residence on her face as they sauntered, arms or elbows occasionally brushing—each "accidental" bump sending happy jolts through Susannah. By tacit agreement, when Jethro spotted his father, she hung back, drifting over to the booth of baked goods while he went with the bishop to point out the buggies he'd recommend. Before she turned to stare at the breads, cookies and doughnuts, she saw the bishop narrow his eyes when he spied her nearby. But he didn't say anything. At least, not directly. But what might he say to Jethro? The thrill abated as she tucked a wayward strand of hair behind her ear.

"I set aside what Amos picked out. He stopped by earlier, saying you were letting him choose one."

Susannah looked up to see Ruth Schrock's grinning face. She arched an eyebrow. "I noticed no one asked me to contribute to the sale."

Ruth mirrored her expression. "I noticed you found other things to keep you busy." She glanced in the direction of where Jethro was walking with his father.

Susannah's gaze followed the pair as well. When they disappeared in the crowd, she turned back to Ruth. "Am I being foolish?"

The auburn-haired woman put her hands on her hips. "Susannah Mast, you are the least foolish person I know, and that includes myself."

"Denki." Susannah exhaled through pursed lips. "It's just that he's…"

"That he's a *gut* man and you, not being foolish, recognize that?"

"Ach, he could do so much better than me."

Ruth handed her a bag of cookies that bore a tag with the name Amos Mast. "Maybe as a baker. But not as a wife and partner." When Susannah reached for some money, Ruth shook her head. "It's on me. Although I know we're not supposed to have one, you need something to feed your ego. I know you'll make him very happy, and I can see that he's already doing that for you."

It was true. Relieved more than she could admit by Ruth's words, Susannah smiled gratefully. Before she could leave the table, another woman stepped up beside her. It was Linda Esh, who'd inquired about Susannah's matchmaking services for her daughter at the cleaning frolic. And specifically mentioned the bishop's son.

"I see that Jethro Weaver is here today. He's looking particularly fine. Have you had a chance to talk with him yet?"

Susannah opened her mouth but nothing came forth. Glancing over, she caught Ruth's droll gaze. Closing her mouth, Susannah cleared her throat. "*Ja.* I've been talking with him ever since he picked me up to go to the auction with him today."

The woman narrowed her eyes. With a pointed look at the bakery items on the table and the bag in Susannah's hand, she muttered, "At least my daughter could feed him," then stomped away. Susannah turned away as well, but not before an outrageous wink from Ruth prompted her to smile.

The smile expanded when she saw Jethro coming toward her. Susannah had to agree with Linda. Jethro was looking particularly fine. His blue eyes were so kind, so steady. Lit with frequently unspoken humor if you shared a glance at the right time. Like the one they were sharing now. Susannah curled her fingers more tightly around the bag of cookies to ensure she didn't reach for his hand.

"Finished?"

"With that. B-but not with the t-time I want t-to spend with you." With a brief touch of his hand on her arm, they melted back into the crowd.

It took more than a few miles on the trip home for Amos to finish talking about his adventures that day. And probably only then because his mouth was full of the cookies. Susannah let him eat his fill as Rebecca shared her day. When she'd ended her stories and leaned back, Susannah snuck a glance at Jethro. And found him looking back at her.

It'd been a wonderful day. The best day. They'd giggled like children together. They'd talked with good friends as if they were a couple. They'd avoided his parents and anyone else who'd looked at them askance. There'd been very few who had. When Jethro laid his hand palm up on the seat between them, Susannah didn't hesitate to entwine hers with it. And treasure his grasp the rest of the way home.

She'd started the day worried that encouraging this mock courtship was the wrong thing to do. Now she was wondering how to make it real. Because to her, it was. Her breath hitched as Jethro gently ran his thumb over the back of her hand. The amazing thing was that he seemed to want that, too. Susannah slowly exhaled. This wasn't part of their plan. But plans could be changed, couldn't they?

Chapter Fourteen

Jethro did another quick count of the bags on the wagon, ensuring the number matched what he'd calculated as he'd loaded them. Upon confirmation, he reentered the back door of the feed store to pay. His steps paused when he saw the older man and woman at the counter. He smiled faintly. Mrs. Danvers, who'd worked with him when he'd gone to the *Englisch* grammar school, hadn't changed much over the years. Although pleased to see her—he'd always greatly respected his speech teacher—Jethro didn't want to visit. But even though he stayed in the back of the store stacked high with bags of different kinds of animal feed, the alert woman caught sight of him. With a brief word to her companion, she headed his way.

Sliding his hands down the sides of his pants, Jethro tried to dry his suddenly sweaty palms. Would she expect him to be able to talk like he had as a student when they were meeting regularly? She had been so helpful. It shamed him that his speech had regressed since then. Particularly when he wanted to make a good impression. Which made him nervous, because he wanted to do so. Which affected his speech. It was a frustrating cycle. Shifting his feet, Jethro glanced longingly at his wagon. The store's proprietor could put this load on his bill. The man knew what he'd intended to pick up and that he was good for it. But it was too late...

"Jethro! How nice to see you."

Dry-mouthed, Jethro considered a greeting. *D* was one of the letters he'd always had issues with, along with *m*, *p*, *b* and *t*. Why couldn't her name have been Mrs. Stuart?

Perspiration trickled down the center of his back. "Hello," he finally inserted into the awkward silence.

If Mrs. Danvers noted his evasion, she didn't let on. She shared the kind smile he'd always remembered. "I was just talking about you the other day."

Immediately tensing, Jethro eyed her warily.

"I ran into Susannah Mast. I understand she's a good friend of yours."

The stiffness in his shoulders eased and Jethro gave an acknowledging nod. If anyone was to discuss him, he would rather it be Susannah. He knew he could trust her with his self-consciousness regarding his speech. After all, he feared he was already well on his way to trusting her with his heart. "*Ja*. She is."

"She indicated it would be good if you and I worked together on your speech again."

Jethro went rigid. His heart pounded in denial. He'd never known Mrs. Danvers to lie. Or to exaggerate the truth. Why would Susannah tell his old teacher the exact opposite of his expressed wishes the only time they'd discussed it? Was she ashamed of him now that folks truly thought they were a couple? Had she grown tired of listening to his stammer as they spent more time together? Crossing his arms tightly over his chest, Jethro stepped back.

"*Nee*. No," he repeated, just in case the *Englisch* woman didn't understand his original dialect. "I d-don't want any m-more lessons." His face heated as he stumbled over the words. Retreating farther, his escape ended when he bumped against a hip-high stack of cattle feed.

Mrs. Danvers' smile faded. Her brow creased with concern, but she nodded mildly as if she knew when to withdraw as well. "It was just a thought. If you're ever interested, I'd be happy to work with you. Since retirement, my husband and I are looking for anything to keep us active and out of each other's hair. Something you're probably not familiar with as I'm sure you're always busy." Jethro wanted to wince under her compassionate gaze. "And probably are now, so I'll let you go. It was very nice to see you again, Jethro." With a graceful smile, she returned to where the older man waited for her at the store's front door.

Jethro quickly paid his bill and left the store. On the way home, his stomach felt as if the load of feed in the wagon behind him sat upon it. And upon his heart. He'd trusted Susannah. She'd been the only woman he'd ever trusted and loved. Well, that would teach him. His shoulders sagged despondently until it seemed they should be resting on his thighs instead of his elbows.

As he couldn't trust his own choices, he might as well do what his folks wanted him to do. At least then he wouldn't have to bear their disapproving glares, comments or reproachful silences. His mouth twisted. They'd give him some time to dwell on his own poor choice before the I-told-you-so lecture, one followed shortly by instructions on when and whom to court.

Jethro stared between the ears of his draft horses to the road ahead, seeing his future as gray and unchanging as the pavement under their plodding hooves. Under his parents' pressure, he knew he'd eventually marry again. The thought made his stomach churn further. The woman would be a wise choice, according to his parents. But for sure and certain, not someone he loved.

The lines drooped in his hands. Good thing he didn't have to worry about the Belgians going anywhere. Jethro shook his head morosely. He could live without love. He'd done it before. It was just...he'd been happy. With Susannah in his life, the sun seemed brighter, his burdens lighter. He'd never felt that way before.

Maybe there'd been some mistake? Some misunderstanding? He straightened in the seat at the possibility. Surely it would be reasonable to see her and determine the truth? Better than letting hurt and fear fester on some simple misinterpretation. Reaching the corner for her road, Jethro turned the Belgians. By the time he swung them up her lane, the weight of both the big draft animals seemed to be resting on his chest as well as the feed. When he saw Susannah working in the garden with her own team, he set the wagon's brake and stiffly climbed down.

She waved when she saw him. A greeting he didn't return. When she reached the end of the row, Jethro closed the distance.

"*Guder daag.* I didn't expect to see you today. Although I'm glad I am. What brings you by?" Her smile accompanied the words as she bent to clear dried vines from the machinery.

"I saw M-Mrs. D-Danvers in t-town t-today." Jethro gritted out the words.

"*Ja*? I ran into her the other day at the Dew Drop."

"So she said."

Apparently alerted by his tone, Susannah stopped what she was doing. Dusting off her hands, she straightened to give Jethro her full attention.

"D-did you t-tell her that she should work with m-me on m-my speech?"

Her eyes shifted. The brown eyes he'd loved and trusted shifted as they acknowledged what he'd said. Jethro's hope faded as his heart sank.

"*Ja*. I told her that it would be *gut*. That it might… help you."

At least she didn't lie. But each word was a blow to Jethro. Each word reinforced the knowledge that she didn't find him worthy as he was.

"Everyone seems t-to have an opinion on what is *gut* for m-me. Like I'm incapable of d-deciding for m-myself." His voice was hoarse. Jethro swallowed against the ache in his throat. "I thought you were *gut* for m-me. B-but apparently I'm not *gut* for you. Or m-maybe just not *gut* enough."

Every remembered mockery of his speech stabbed at him. He'd thought she'd been different. That she hadn't minded his speech. His mistake, in letting himself care for someone.

"Jethro, it's not that at all." To her credit, Susannah looked stricken. Considering him silently, she sighed heavily.

And what did the sigh mean? That he was trying her patience, as if he were a child or imbecile? The notion struck Jethro almost as painfully as knowing his speech bothered her.

"You're trying to pick a quarrel." A corner of Susannah's lip tipped up in a smile, although it was a trembling one. "Two cannot quarrel when one will not."

Jethro didn't want to hear the old Amish platitude. "I'm not quarrelling. I'm t-trying t-to understand why the only woman I t-t-t…" Closing his eyes, he paused to take a deep breath; to continue as he was would only reinforce her obvious low opinion of him. "T-trusted… would b-be ashamed of me." Heat rose up his neck and flushed his cheeks. "Would d-do exactly what I p-p-particularly d-determined not t-t-to." She was ashamed of him. The knowledge was agony.

"So if I can't even t-trust you, I m-might as well court some of those other women I've b-been t-told that I should b-be seeing. B-but spare m-me your newfound role, b-because I d-don't need you t-to b-be m-my m-matchmaker. I wanted you as m-my wi—" He struggled to swallow. "The last thing I want is t-to have you b-be m-my m-matchmaker."

Blinking rapidly as if there was something in her eyes, Susannah's compressed her lips into a thin, quavering line. "That would probably be for the best," she murmured huskily.

Nodding curtly, Jethro spun on his heel and strode to where he'd left the Belgians. Where he hoped he'd left them, because his vision was initially so blurred that he couldn't see clearly. Thankfully, his direction was good. Swiftly taking his seat, Jethro guided the draft team out of the farmyard.

Although he longed to look back, he didn't. He couldn't. The sooner he moved on from his mistake, the better. Or so his mind said. His heart said something different entirely. Fortunately, his mind was well accustomed to taking charge.

Which is why, as soon as he reached home and unloaded the feed, Jethro reloaded the wagon with the plow Ben Raber had asked to borrow and drove it over to the neighboring farmstead that Ben was renting. Jethro didn't want to be alone with his fractured emotions. For once, he wanted company.

You'd always wanted Susannah's company. Jethro hushed his wounded heart.

As he entered the lane, Jethro saw that Ben's brother, Aaron, was there. It was an effective distraction. For the first time since the feed store, a faint smile touched his lips. He was glad the two brothers had reconciled.

Aaron had left their Amish community early last year. When Ben had abruptly married Rachel—long understood as Aaron's girlfriend—the community had been surprised. Probably none more so than Aaron when he'd returned to find his brother not only married to Rachel, but parenting twins with her. Fortunately, the brothers seemed to be getting along fine now. Although Ben was much more settled than the restless Aaron. *Maybe marriage did that. Settled you.* Although, Jethro hadn't really felt settled and content when married to Louisa. His throat clogged immediately. *I would be if I married Susannah.*

But that wasn't happening. He needed to look elsewhere. So when Jethro saw a woman he knew was single hanging up the wash in the Rabers' yard, he asked her out.

The moment they'd sat down at the Dew Drop, Jethro was already wishing he hadn't come. Already wishing that he was either at home or at Susannah's. But that wasn't an option any more.

"Is something wrong?"

He looked up to find his date's curious gaze on him. "*Nee.*" Jethro rubbed a hand over his face. There was nothing wrong other than his heart was broken. Surely it would recover. Although he couldn't imagine when.

Inviting Miriam Schrock to dinner had been a mistake. He hadn't had an appetite ever since his and Susannah's discussion. *Discussion* seemed too pleasant a word for something so painful. Or so foolish. Because what if she hadn't really meant it the way he'd taken it? What if it hadn't really been that at all, like she'd said? *Ja,* this whole thing had been a mistake. The only thing he wanted to eat right now were the words he'd spoken to her in hurt and anger. He'd even happily eat some of Susannah's awful cookies, as long as she was there beside him.

Glasses of water appeared on the table between him and Miriam. When Jethro glanced up, he almost sank through the booth at the sight of Rebecca's impassive face. The usually vivacious girl was totally devoid of expression. He'd forgotten Susannah's daughter waitressed here. At the curious look of the woman across from him, he opened his mouth. It was a few moments before any sound came out. *"D-d-denki."* Jethro dropped his head as embarrassing heat rushed up his neck and into his cheeks. He clenched his fingers around the menu.

"Are you ready to order? Or do you want a few minutes?" Rebecca's tone was as stiff as her face.

Jethro's stomach knotted. What he wanted was to leave. He was betraying Susannah by being there. He was betraying himself. He'd been *hochmut.* It was pride that'd gotten him into this. Pride that'd wrecked the best thing that had ever happened to him.

"Maybe a few minutes would be *gut*." Rebecca nodded and left at Miriam's quiet words. Jethro shot an appreciative glance across the table. Miriam didn't deserve this. He shouldn't have involved her in this... this—whatever this was.

Earlier this afternoon, so tightly twisted up inside he was surprised he could stay upright on the wagon's seat, Jethro had walked straight over to where Miriam Schrock was hanging up the laundry. He didn't know who was more surprised when he stopped in front of her. Her, him or the watching Raber brothers.

He hadn't wanted to ask out any of the women who might've been asking after him. He didn't want it thought by Susannah or anyone that she was acting as his matchmaker. But before he lost his nerve, he'd wanted to ask someone, as he'd proclaimed to Susannah that he would. And Jethro knew Miriam wouldn't have been on the list.

Miriam had recently arrived in the area to be a hired girl for Rachel and her twins. Hopefully, she was similar in personality to her brothers. Jethro was friends with Malachi, Samuel and their younger brother, Gideon. When he'd haltingly asked her to dinner, her eyes had widened. After stating that she'd need to ask Rachel first, Miriam went to do so while he and the Raber brothers unloaded the plow. When she'd returned, after a hooded gaze at Aaron, she confirmed that Jethro had a dinner date.

Now guilt swamped him at involving Miriam in his troubles. Would his spontaneous action affect his relationship with the Schrocks? Wouldn't that just be great? In one fell swoop, he would wreck his friendship with Susannah and sabotage the one with the Schrocks.

"Why did you ask me out?"

Jethro cringed. For sure and certain, Miriam was more straightforward than her brothers.

"Did you and Susannah have a fight? I won't be used to make someone jealous."

That was far from his intent. Jethro had wanted to assure himself that other women thought enough of him to date him. Was that trying to make Susannah jealous? The concept was alien to him. The only association he'd ever had with jealousy had been his feeling toward his little brother, Atlee. Atlee, who'd been perfect and cherished by their parents. No matter what Jethro had done, he hadn't garnered similar reactions. After a while, he'd quit trying to please them, determining to simply do things that he'd thought were right.

But wasn't he doing just as his folks had wished? Ending his relationship with Susannah and courting someone they'd consider more appropriate?

Jethro grew cold at the realization. He wanted to beat his head on the table. Instead, he shook it miserably.

"*Nee*," he muttered belatedly.

Miriam gave him a sympathetic smile. "Do you really feel like having dinner?"

Jethro smiled glumly. When the woman he'd asked out to a meal recognized he didn't want to be there, it proved that he was a disaster at courting. His shoulders dropped in defeat. "Not really. I apologize, M-Miriam. This hasn't b-been m-much of a d-date."

She slid out of the booth. "That's all right. You can make it up to me by stopping at the Dairy Mart to pick up some food on the way out of town."

"I'll b-be glad t-to d-do that." Tossing enough bills on the table to cover his embarrassment in entering the restaurant in the first place, he followed Miriam out the door.

Her matter-of-fact conversation interspersed with periods of companionable silence helped steady Jethro on the way home. Miriam was a wonderful girl, which Jethro was certain the local single men would soon discover. But she wasn't for him. There was only one woman for him.

And he'd just destroyed any chance for a relationship with her.

Chapter Fifteen

Susannah shifted on the hard bench. Ordination Sunday was always particularly long. Normally, she loved church. But today she'd rather be home, still quietly grieving over her and Jethro's parting the other day. How had it all gone so wrong?

She straightened when a hush descended in the barn. Bishop Weaver and Minister John Stoltzfus were returning after being cloistered following the church members' voting to fill the ministerial vacancy. Watching them, Susannah furrowed her brow. Although their expressions matched the solemnity of the occasion, the bishop looked unsettled. Almost as unsettled as herself. Preventing her gaze from finding Jethro on the men's benches where they sat opposite the women in the barn had been more difficult that she could've imagined.

It was even worse when it invariably settled on him like a bee returning to its hive. More devastating was to find him looking back, his dear face so grave, his blue eyes shadowed. She'd spent more time with downcast eyes this service than she had the whole year to date.

As the day continued, lead had settled in her stomach. *Gut* thing she'd have another two weeks before church was held again. Maybe by then it wouldn't hurt so bad to see him. Susannah bit her cheek. Or to hear in the meantime that he was now actively courting others. She didn't know who'd needed more comfort the other day when Rebecca had come home from the Dew Drop after having seen Jethro there with another woman— her or her daughter. If she had wondered whether her children supported their relationship, she now knew they had. Fully. She wished she'd told them the truth about the fake courtship. But then, toward the end, she'd denied the truth herself.

She forced her attention to where Bishop Weaver was laying five *Ausbunds*—denoting five candidates— side by side on the table set up between the men's and women's benches. Even though she didn't have a husband who might have to select one of the hymnals today, Susannah's heart started pounding. Amish believed a minister was chosen by *Gott*. That He would lead the appropriate candidate to select the hymnal containing a bible verse, a selection confirming that man into the life of minister, perhaps later, even bishop, whether the man sought the role or not.

Bishop Weaver visibly swallowed. "The candidates for minister receiving three or more votes are…" The barn was preternaturally quiet. It was as if those present had ceased breathing for a moment. Even the pigeons in the loft, cooing earlier to the amusement of some during the church service, were silent. Susannah understood. The job was a blessing. It was also a burden. The job was unpaid, untrained and for a lifetime. And ministers were expected to speak without notes for twenty minutes to an hour on Sundays, not knowing which sermon he'd be preaching until just prior to the service.

Everyone waited to hear the names, afraid that theirs, or their spouse's, would be mentioned. A glance down her row revealed more than one of her married bench mates had reached out to grasp the hand of a nearby friend.

Bishop Weaver cleared his throat. When a *boppeli* in one of the young mother's arms emitted a small cry, there was a ripple through the congregation as everyone tensed.

"Isaiah Zook." Even in the challenging acoustics of the barn, the bishop's hoarse voice was easily heard in the hush. Susannah followed the turn of heads on the other side to find the dairyman. He was staring straight ahead, his expression set.

"Malachi Schrock." A sharp inhalation from the row behind her identified the location of where the furniture business owner's wife sat with their young daughter.

"Elmer Raber." Susannah winced fractionally when she heard Ben's *daed's* name. Elmer was a quiet, reserved man. If chosen, the role would weigh heavily on him.

"Henry Troyer." A widower of a few years, Henry was a pleasant man and successful farmer. Although his sons were doing fine in the community, his older daughters had given him some trials of late. One lived separately from her husband, although on the same property. Another had moved out of state after her heavy pursuit of a potential spouse had driven all the men away.

Without Jethro and her fake courtship, Henry might've been one who'd eventually come calling. Susannah swallowed. When word was broadcast that their relationship was over, he might come calling still. If he did, she'd find some way to dissuade him. After what she'd almost had with Jethro, *nee*, she didn't want to court anyone.

"And Jethro Weaver."

Susannah's breath froze in her lungs. Her ears began ringing. Aware of exactly where he was sitting, her gaze shot to Jethro. His face was so white, the faint scar showed in contrast. His eyes locked with hers. She wanted to weep at the despair in them. To race between the benches separating the men and women and throw her arms around him.

While the rest of the congregation was motionless, there was subtle movement in the third row behind Jethro. Her tense gaze shifted in time to see smirks on the faces of three young men, ones recently baptized. Susannah's suspended breath exhaled in a rush. *Oh, you young fools. You don't know what you've done.* She knew what this role would do to Jethro. Although a godly man, it was the last position he wanted. Splinters of the worn plank pricked into the palms of her white-knuckled grip of the bench. Susannah's gaze darted back to Jethro as he slowly rose to take his place with the other candidates at the center of the barn.

One by one, the men selected their hymnals in the order they'd been called, leaving Jethro with no choice at all. Even so, he hesitated, his shoulders rigid under his *mutza* suit as he picked up the last hymnal from the table. Trudging back to his seat, he sat cautiously, as if he was afraid the bench, as well as his world, had shifted from beneath him.

Susannah understood, particularly having been a minister's wife. And that had been to a man who'd become more than comfortable with the role. Vernon had grown to relish preaching on Sunday. She'd wondered at the time if he'd taken some inappropriate pride in appearing more spiritual than others.

Jethro would never enjoy preaching, even without the stutter. He'd also be totally ill at ease in counseling those out of line with the *Ordnung's* rules.

Heart pounding so frantically she could feel it pulse at the tips of her fingers, Susannah watched as the bishop nodded for the candidates to open their hymnals. One by one, in the order they'd selected them, they did so. The rustle of pages could be heard as Isaiah Zook opened his book. When no slip of scripture was found, his shoulders sagged in relief. A soft exhalation came from along Susannah's bench, where Isaiah's wife sat.

While the dairy farmer was obviously relieved, the tension grew for the remaining four men on the bench. All attention now focused on Malachi Schrock. The young man's face was expressionless, but a bead of perspiration tracked down the side of his brow. Opening his hymnal's cover, he slowly flipped through the pages. When no piece of paper was found, the furniture maker's eyes closed at his reprieve. This time, there was no mistaking the muffled squeak from the row behind Susannah as Ruth Schrock shared her husband's relief.

Elmer Raber's hands shook as he spread wide the book in his lap. As he paged through it to find no note, he started breathing so rapidly, Susannah would've been concerned for the older man if she wasn't so afraid for the man she loved.

Why it would take a moment like this to make her realize it, Susannah didn't wonder. All she knew was that she ached to wrap her arms around him. Ached to comfort and support his tense figure. Breathing so shallowly she was lightheaded herself, she did what she could. She held his gaze. She wanted to shout the words to give him strength but knew that was the last thing she could do. She wanted to take his burdens away, share this one for the lifetime it would be, if that's what he needed.

It was down to just two. Henry Troyer's book wobbled on his knees as he opened it. When he slowly fanned the pages, there was a communal gasp as a slip of paper fluttered to the barn floor. Henry grimaced, his previously pale face turning red. His eyes filled with tears.

Susannah's breath finally normalized as she watched Jethro reach over and grip the man's shoulder in a consoling clasp. As Henry struggled to compose himself, Jethro withdrew his hand and, with a deep breath, opened his own hymnal. When no notes revealed themselves, he closed it with a soft thud. His head tipped back and his throat bobbed in a heavy swallow.

A hand settled on Jethro's shoulder. Bishop Weaver stood behind his son, his head bowed. The material of Jethro's suit crinkled under the bishop's tightened fingers. Jethro reached up to pat his father's hand with his own. A huge sigh lifted Ezekiel Weaver's gaunt shoulders as he nodded before removing his hand. Susannah didn't know if a word had been spoken between the two men, but apparently the bishop was also relieved that Jethro hadn't been selected. Because he knew his son and didn't think he could do the job? Or because he knew the job and knew what taking on the role would do to his son? For Jethro's sake, she hoped the latter.

When Jethro lifted his head a moment later, he looked straight into Susannah's eyes. As their gazes locked, the obvious relief in his eyes shifted to a question. A question that brought Susannah's breathlessness back. But for a different reason. Because it wasn't for the role he'd just missed. It was for the role he wanted. Did she want it, too? Could she? Should she? Breaking eye contact, she stood from the bench when the service was over. Needing something to do with her hands, she brushed off the back of her skirt while she looked anywhere but at Jethro. Using the hasty excuse of needing to milk her goats after the lengthy service, she left for home, giving Amos a distracted permission to linger with a school friend.

Jethro drew the gelding to a halt in front of Susannah's front gate. His palms were sweating. Was he making a mistake? He was almost as nervous as he'd been earlier during the ordination. What if he'd misread her expression? What if the poignant gaze they'd shared when he'd been frightened beyond himself had been a delusion of his pounding heart and heightened senses? He'd searched for her but, like many others with livestock to care for, she'd left soon after the ordination service. Or was that why she'd left so soon? Had it been intentional, so she wouldn't have to see him? Jethro exhaled through pursed lips. Surely the bees in Susannah's hives weren't buzzing as much as the thoughts in his head.

He climbed down from the buggy and secured the gelding to the rail. Rubbing the back of his neck, he turned his attention to the front door. Should he look for her in the house, or would she still be in the barn doing chores? What should he say when he found her?

Guder owed, Susannah. I'm thinking you've forgotten or forgiven me for our recent discussion, because today you looked at me like you might...care for me so I hurried through chores so I could drop by to see if it was so. That didn't seem an appropriate start. Besides, with his stutter amplified by his tension, he would probably struggle through the lengthy sentence.

The front door swung open.

He'd have to think of something soon because wiping her hands on her apron as she stepped onto the porch was Susannah. Without hesitation, she headed down the walk toward him. Jethro stood transfixed as she came through the gate. He was still frozen when she walked up to him. He only began to melt when she wrapped her arms around him. Instinctively, reverently, Jethro returned her embrace. Eyes drifting closed, he rested his cheek against her prayer *kapp. I would struggle through giving a hundred hour-long sermons just to have this moment.*

"Oh, Jethro, I was so anxious for you. And the other day, when I spoke to Mrs. Danvers, I certainly didn't mean..."

"I know," he murmured into her hair. "I'm sorry I d-didn't t-trust you."

Jethro opened his eyes to see her upturned face. They met her soft gaze before dropping to her lips.

Lips that he longed to kiss. Automatically dipping his head, he hesitated before drawing back. Who was he fooling? She wouldn't want his kisses. Louisa hadn't. And she'd been his wife. Keeping Susannah enfolded in his arms, he focused his attention on the porch behind her as he worried his top lip. He felt the bite of his teeth along its length, except for the section that had no feeling.

Jethro winced. "I'm not *gut* at this."

Susannah's eyes reflected her puzzlement. "At what?" She tightened her embrace. "You've proven yourself to be *gut* at anything. You'd even have been a *gut* minister, had you been chosen."

"I can't kiss."

She blinked in confusion before a slow grin spread over her face. "Is that a rule for bishops' sons?"

Although he thrilled at her teasing, his fear of her rejection was too great to respond to the joke. "*Nee*, my kisses aren't *gut*."

Susannah's smile abruptly faded as her brow creased over brown eyes turned fierce. "Who told you that?"

The admission was painful. "Louisa d-didn't like to kiss m-me."

Susannah cocked her head as she solemnly studied him. "That sounds like her problem."

"*Nee*. It is m-mine. Where m-my lip is joined, I d-don't have any feeling. I d-don't kiss well."

"*Ach*, let me be the judge of that." At his doubtful expression, her grin returned. "Maybe we should try and see. Perhaps, instead of your lips, it was the pairing of the two of you."

Jethro couldn't help but smile at her logic. Was it possible? He and Louisa had definitely not been a love match. But dare he try? Louisa rejecting him was one thing. He had married her out of duty, not out of affection. Whereas his feelings for Susannah... Jethro didn't think he could bear it if she rejected him as well. But could he bear to never kiss this woman?

His gaze knotted with Susannah's until, as both their eyes drifted shut, Jethro lowered his head and gently touched his lips to hers. Lifting his head a few moments later, years of fear that'd strangled the edges of his soul melted away when he opened his eyes to the look in Susannah's.

She tipped her head as her smile widened. "I think if you're unsure about it, you should keep practicing."

Again, he liked her logic. And so he did. When he raised his head a second time, Susannah sighed. Jethro knew it to be a contented one. One that he shared.

"You are definitely *gut* at this, Jethro Weaver."

Jethro felt good. Everything about this woman made him feel good. So good that he blurted out the words he'd never expected to say again. "Marry me."

Susannah's mouth rounded such that, had one of her honeybees been flying by, she'd have been in danger of inviting the creature in. Was her shock because she wanted to? Or because she didn't want to?

"You didn't stutter."

"My heart is m-making up for that. Marry me."

"Oh, Jethro. I don't know... This isn't what we planned."

"It m-may not b-be what we p-planned b-but it's what we want. Or, at least, what I want. T-today I was faced with t-taking on a role I'd have for the rest of m-my life. I've realized the role that I want for the rest of m-my life is t-to b-be your husband. Marry me, Susannah."

"It would be foolish. We'd be making a mistake."

"Okay then. M-make it with m-me. I've m-made others. This is one I'll happily live with."

Now it was Susannah who chewed on her lip. Then her fingertips. Followed by pressing both hands to her face until all that was revealed were her eyes. Eyes that wanted to say yes, Jethro could tell. But would she?

When finally, hesitantly, the word escaped through her fingers, Jethro thought his heart would burst with joy.

Chapter Sixteen

Jethro ran the comb over the Belgian's sweaty hide. He felt good about what he and the team had accomplished today. This would finish the field work for him for the year, freeing him up even more to help others where needed. Primarily Susannah, although he knew from what he'd done earlier that her work should be almost completed as well. Too bad. It was a handy excuse to see her.

At the clatter of buggy wheels coming up the lane, he paused. His head lifted at the sound, closely followed by his pulse rate. Was it Susannah? He hadn't wanted to leave her yesterday. The memory of their shared embrace lingered on his lips. In his arms. In his heart. His face creased with a smile. Maybe she missed him as much as he missed her. With an eager step, Jethro strode for the barn door. Swinging it open, he stepped out and—

What was his mother doing here? Once again, Jethro's pulse surged, but for an entirely different reason. It was accompanied by a tightening in his stomach. If she was going to try to talk him out of seeing Susannah, she'd wasted the trip over. He ducked back into the shadows of the barn but guilt swept over him at his cowardice. Leaning out the door, he waved so she'd know where he was before he went back to work. By the time the Belgian he was grooming swung his head toward the door, indicating the unwanted company had arrived, Jethro had made sure he was on the far side of the gigantic cream-colored horse.

He didn't speak, just continued running the brush and rubber comb over the horse's broad shoulder, smoothing out hair that'd become matted with sweat under the harness collar. In the silence unbroken except for the rhythmic sweeps of the tools on the horse's hide, he waited, shoulders hitched, for his *mamm* to say what she wanted, as surely she would. She always had. He waited. And waited. And waited.

Having brushed this side of the horse so thoroughly the animal would probably glow in the dark, Jethro sighed. Reluctantly, he worked his way around the gelding until he was on the same side as his mother. Shooting a wary glance over his shoulder, he saw her quietly sitting on a bale of straw, hands folded in her lap as she watched him. It was unsettling. Jethro's usually fluid motions were stiff in the continued quiet. The Belgian nudged him with his gigantic head at the odd behavior, almost knocking him over.

"Your *grossdaddi*, my father, died before you were born."

Jethro paused in midstroke at her flat statement. Whatever he'd been expecting her to say, it wasn't this.

"You never knew him. Or my younger *bruder*."

He turned fully to face her. He'd never heard that his *mamm* had a younger *bruder*. He'd heard said that his *grossmammi* had died in childbirth and that his *grossdaddi* had never remarried after her death. But when no word had ever been mentioned of siblings on his *mamm's* side, he assumed she'd died when his *mamm* was born.

"I was eight when my *bruder* was born. It wasn't spoken of then. Still isn't." Her thin face reddened a bit. "But I think my *mamm* lost several *boppeli* between me and him. And when Atlee was born, we lost her."

Jethro frowned. Furrowing his brow, he crossed his arms over his chest. "Atlee?" It'd been his younger *bruder's* name. His perfect, pampered, younger *bruder.* His deceased younger *bruder* who'd left a widow whom Jethro had married to take care of. At his *mamm's* insistence.

His mother's face was stiff. "Your younger *bruder* was named for mine."

Jethro slumped against the Belgian. Fortunately, the horse stood firm as a living wall.

"I understand Susannah Mast was stung by some ground-nesting yellow jackets."

Tensing at Susannah's name, Jethro was ready to defend her should his *mamm* say anything derogatory. Where was his mother going with this? Why, after all this time…? His eyes widened at the sight of her white knuckles, visible in her clenched hands. In the silence, her shoulders lifted in a deep inhale.

"My father was a hard worker. He expected everyone else to be as well. He was a…tough taskmaster. I learned to do everything successfully. Even take care of my little *bruder.*

"One day when my *vader* was gone, my *bruder* went out to mow the hay. At seven, and small for his age, he was too little to do it by himself. He wouldn't have been able to, if I hadn't helped him harness the team. I shouldn't have. But he wanted to do it. He wanted to pull his own weight, he said. He wanted to do something helpful for *Vader*. Atlee knew, as I knew, that *Vader* was disappointed in him."

She looked down at her tightly entwined hands. "Whereas I did everything *Vader* asked, and even more so as I got older and wise enough to anticipate him, Atlee didn't. He dawdled. He daydreamed. He was sickly. It was surprising he survived infancy, as I was the one taking care of him, and I didn't know what I was doing, never having been around a new *boppeli* before. Fortunately, a neighbor came over frequently to check on him. And me. And we got by. The two of us got by better than Atlee and my father did. Not only did Atlee have to be told twice to do something, he had to be told through me. *Vader* didn't even want to talk with Atlee. You see… Atlee stuttered."

Jethro froze. He was barely able to breathe as he stood there listening. The Belgian behind him stomped his bucket-sized foot on the floor. Jethro felt the reverberation through his work boots, but the sound didn't register because all his hearing was focused on what his mother was saying from where she sat on the bale.

"So I helped him harness the team that day. We had Belgians as well." Her eyes remained downcast. "Big, strong horses. I watched him drive the team out to the field with the mower. Figured it would be *gut,* like Atlee thought, to have *Vader* come home and see the work finished. Maybe be able to tell *Vader* what he'd done himself. I went back to the house to work. I looked out the window from time to time to check on him."

His *mamm* seemed fascinated with a blade of straw that'd escaped from the bale. She ran the toe of her black shoe over it, rolling the blade back and forth until she pressed so hard one end of the blade lifted off the barn floor. When she spoke again, her voice was hoarse. "I never imagined they'd drive over a yellow jacket nest. The horses panicked with the stings. Atlee couldn't handle them. It all went wrong." Her face paled. The only evidence of where her lips were was a telltale quiver.

Jethro tilted his head forward to hear her last whispered words.

"I didn't protect him when I should've."

He needed to sit. Stumbling away from the horse's side, Jethro sagged against the stall wall. He continued to slide down the rough wood until he rested on the barn floor, his back braced against the boards.

"Shortly after your father and I married, he was chosen as minister. Thanks to my upbringing, even though I was a young bride, I knew I could handle the role. I was going to be an exceptional minister's wife." She hunched a shoulder. "I succeeded. When the previous bishop died in the following year, Ezekiel was chosen to replace him. It's an esteemed role, a weighty responsibility in the district. I was going to do everything to help make him a successful bishop and do all that was right as a bishop's wife."

She looked over to where Jethro, knees drawn up with his arms around them, had propped himself against the stall wall. "You were born shortly after he took the position. I was excited to be a mother. I was going to care for you like I hadn't been able to care for my *bruder*."

Her gaze shifted away. "It was…obvious from the moment you were born that you were going to need some help. We knew we'd have to take you to a hospital. Especially when we couldn't get you to eat. With the cleft…"

Jethro hissed in a breath when his *mamm's* face crumpled. He'd never seen her as anything other than stern and daunting. She quickly regained control. If he hadn't been watching, he wouldn't have seen it. "I couldn't nurse you. I wasn't able to feed you. Not even with a bottle. I'd successfully undertaken every other role, but I couldn't take care of my own child. We took you to a local hospital. They sent you to the large one in Madison. I couldn't stay with you. I sat at home, all ready for a baby. But had no baby for a week. They finally sent you home with special bottles that had special nipples that you could handle. Several weeks later, you had your first surgery to close the split in your lip.

"Things improved, as you could at least eat. But when you had cereal for the first time…" She shook her head. "You had no roof of your mouth. As you explored the strange texture with your tongue and tried to figure out what to do with it, it all came back out your nose. I'd always been able to do everything. But I couldn't effectively take care of my own child. Like I didn't with my little brother."

Plucking straw out of the bale on which she sat, she picked at the golden blades. "Like most Amish, we don't carry health insurance. As a community, we take care of each other. But it was everyone taking care of us. All the time. There were so many surgeries. None of them nearby. You had to stay at those places overnight. Every one cost thousands of dollars. As the district's church leader, we should've been helping others. But it wasn't that way. For years, it was always us the community was constantly holding fundraisers for. I was ashamed to have cost the district so much work and money."

Jethro's mouth was dry. He tightened his grip of his knees as if to hold himself together. It was such a different conversation than the one he'd expected when he'd seen her rig drive up the lane. His *mamm* had never spoken of this to him. He wasn't sure what to do with the unexpected history. It explained many things, but it didn't erase the loneliness of his childhood.

For a moment, his *mamm* held his gaze before dropping hers back into her lap. "When Atlee..." She swallowed. "When your *bruder,* Atlee, was born, I didn't feel like I didn't know what to do, like when my little *bruder* was a *boppeli,* or that I wasn't enough, like when you were. I could take care of him. I was going to protect him, like I hadn't my *bruder,* or you, when you were always taken from me to have the surgeries that brought you back swollen and bruised." She wore a sad smile. "And I did. Maybe too well. As you turned out better without my help, than he did with it."

Her mouth twisted ruefully. "Susannah Mast told me that. She said the man you'd become is more a credit to you than me. She also said I didn't deserve you."

The heels of Jethro's boots skidded along the barn floor as he abruptly straightened his legs. Susannah had said that? Far from being ashamed of him as he'd mistakenly thought, she'd been defending him to his mother? His lips curved in a slow smile. It was understandable he'd always been comfortable around Susannah, had from the time he was little. He was right to trust her then and now. To love her. For he did. Deeply.

Heart swelling with emotion, he almost didn't hear his mother's words.

"You are besotted with her. Always have been, from the first time she came over to watch you when you were a *boppeli* and she a young girl. But you don't need a *kinder minder* now, Jethro, you need a wife who can give you a family."

Jethro found himself standing before he was aware of moving. He'd moved so quickly, the nearby Belgian jerked his head as high as the lead attached to his halter would allow, causing the post to which it was attached to creak in protest. Running a hand down the muscular neck, Jethro frowned as he saw his fingers were trembling. Sweeping his palm again against the horse's warm flesh, Jethro wasn't sure if the action was more calming to him or to the animal.

He wanted to keep his back to his mother. To reject what she was saying and maintain his attention on the gelding instead. But that wasn't the man he'd become. Pivoting, he saw she had also risen to her feet. "As you've said, I've t-turned out b-better without your help. I d-don't need it now in choosing who is right for m-me as a wife."

There was no hint of the earlier vulnerability in the woman who faced him. His *mamm* pursed her thin lips as she studied his face, as if weighing his resolve. Squaring his shoulders, Jethro met her gaze. His heart thudded as if he'd recently been the one in the harness pulling equipment instead of the Belgians. In fact, he'd rather put on the heavy horse collar and pull a plow across the field instead of engage in this confrontation. But he would if he had to. He'd endure anything he had to, if the reward was a life with Susannah.

His *mamm* didn't say another word. Dipping her chin slightly in acknowledgment, she turned and headed for the wide barn door. If her heavy stride was less than the confident one he'd previously known, it wasn't surprising. The conversation had probably been as wearying to her as it'd been to him. Possibly more so, as it seemed like a bottled-up lifetime had been uncorked in an abrupt moment. Jethro bent to pick up the brush and rubber comb he'd dropped when he'd slid down the wall. What she'd shared wouldn't make any difference. It was his *mamm's* past. Whatever it was supposed to mean to him, one thing was clear: Susannah was his future. A future, for the first time, that he was looking forward to.

Tilting her head, Susannah put a hand on the wheel to stop the treadle sewing machine. *Ja.* There had been a knock at the door. With a distracted glance at the shirt she was making for Amos, she rose and walked across the large common room to the door. Her son was outgrowing his shirts as well as his pants every time she turned around. She might as well start cutting down some of Vernon's old clothes to see if they'd work to help keep up.

She'd packed them away for that possibility after he'd passed on. Which closet had she put them in? Running through the possibilities in her head, Susannah pulled open the door, a smile of greeting on her lips. But when she saw her visitor, Susannah wished she hadn't finished fall plowing earlier today. She'd rather be out in the field. Or in town running some errands. Anything would be better than facing the stern-jawed woman standing on the porch.

There was no need to guess what this visit would be about.

"Ruby," she greeted the bishop's wife flatly. "Won't you come in?"

Without a word, Jethro's *mamm* stepped into the house. Inhaling a girding breath, Susannah slowly closed the door behind her. *I'm a grown woman. Who loves a grown man who I think loves me. A man who doesn't need his parents' approval to marry. She can't quell the joy we shared together yesterday and that we can have in the future if we don't let her.*

"Would you like some *kaffi*?" Susannah gestured to the chairs by the table.

After only one step into the kitchen, Ruby confronted Susannah. "I want you to stop seeing my son. Stop putting ideas into his head about a relationship with you, when you are far from what he needs." The older woman cocked her head as her blue eyes tried to pin Susannah against the door.

"You're a *gut* woman, Susannah Mast. No doubt, you're hardworking, among many other qualities. I admire you. And I think you're a *gut* enough woman to know my son needs something different than the life you can give him. Sure and certain, you've always been *gut* with him. Right now, it might seem that marriage between the two of you would also be *gut*. That it would work. But what about a few years down the line? When your childbearing years are completely gone and his aren't? When he looks around at the families other men his age have. A family you would be keeping him from. Let him go." Her words, although quietly spoken, rang through the silent kitchen.

Ruby shook her head sadly. "You think I don't know

my son? I do. He's lonely. He's lonely for more than just the companionship you can give him. He needs a family more than anyone I've ever known. A family you can't give him. It's true, I might not've done right by him. But I want to do right by him now. I'm asking you, as a mother, to help me do right by him now." Ruby lifted one of her hands, seemingly in supplication. It fell back to her side. The woman turned away, but not before Susannah thought she saw tears glistening in the woman's eyes. Surely that'd been a trick of the light through the window. Ruby Weaver...crying?

Susannah's rebuttal shriveled in her dry mouth. Anticipating this confrontation, she'd prepared herself for many arguments. But not how to respond to a mother's love in doing what she thought was best for her only son.

She loved Jethro. She wanted to marry him. The relationship they had was unlike the companionable partnership she'd developed over the years with Vernon. *Ja*, this love had that, but it also had joy. Enthusiasm. Peace. Hope. Anticipation for the future. But was the anticipation all on her side? Like the early part of their mock courtship, was she thinking too much about how the relationship would benefit her and not what it would ultimately do to Jethro? Had he become too caught up, or perhaps even trapped, in the pretend that he felt he had to make it real? All of the reasons, good reasons, of why she'd earlier determined the relationship was foolish seeped back in through the cracks in her resolve that Jethro's mother had just created.

What would she want for Amos, should he be in the same position? Would she want him to marry a woman who possibly couldn't give him a family? Who couldn't give him a biological son or a daughter to inherit his own farm at some point? He'd already lost one child. She'd lost two. Unbidden, the image of an enthralled Jethro tenderly holding her infant grandson, Eli, filled her mind. Immediately joining it were memories of how patient he was with Amos. How good with Rebecca. Just because he would be a *wunderbar* husband for her didn't mean she'd be an equally *wunderbar* wife for him. She couldn't do that to Jethro. Not when she loved him.

Susannah suddenly felt so weary, like the residue after a dam had burst under the weight of an unusually heavy storm. *Maybe I am old.* Shuffling around Ruby, she crossed to the kitchen table and sank onto one of the chairs. With a bleak smile, she considered her unexpected guest as she repeated her earlier question. "Would you like some *kaffi*, Ruby?"

While she could defy the bishop's wife if the woman tried to badger her adult son, could stand in the way of anyone attempting to browbeat him, Susannah wouldn't argue with a mother who loved her child and wanted what was best for him. Not when she would do the same.

Chapter Seventeen

Jethro's eager stride slowed when Susannah stepped out of the barn. After the distressing interaction with his *mamm* today, he'd needed to see her. Even before the sound of his mother's horse's hoofbeats had faded away, Jethro had been counting the minutes until he could see Susannah as he'd hurried to finish up chores and other necessary tasks at his farm.

"Your *mamm* came to see me today."

Dread pooled in Jethro's stomach at Susannah's somber words. At her somber expression revealed even in the gathering dusk. His legs were filled with lead. He stopped—his breath, his heart, his gaze fixed on her face. Her closed-off expression. Jethro tried to swallow but his throat wouldn't cooperate. He should've come sooner. He should've gotten to Susannah before his mother had.

"D-don't listen t-to her." He was surprised he could get the words out through his stiff lips.

Wincing, Susannah shook her head. "But she made sense, Jethro."

"*Nee. We* m-make sense. The t-two of us t-together."

How could he be so motionless when he was shaking to pieces inside?

She lowered her chin until, instead of her sorrowful brown eyes, he was facing the *kapp* pinned neatly to her brown hair. "*Nee.* We don't. I've lived a phase of my life that I can't get back for you, Jethro. You need someone who can go through that phase with you."

He lurched forward a step. "*Nee.* Let them say what they will, but I *know* what I need. I *know* the feelings I have for you." *Why does everyone think I can't feel? That I don't know my own mind? That they all know better? I'm a grown man. I've done what they wanted before. Am I not allowed to live my own life?* When Susannah lifted her head, his heart fell, as he could see in her pale, resolute face that, *nee*, in this, he wasn't allowed. At least not a life that would have Susannah in it as he'd dreamed.

This was so much harder even than she'd feared. Confronted by Jethro's desolate expression, Susannah was afraid she would shatter and blow away on the chilly October breeze. Or maybe the cold was all internal. If so, then she feared she'd be cold for a long, long time. Regardless of how much she wanted to respond to his entreaty, for him, she had to remain strong.

She shook her head. "You're mistaking the feelings you have for me for something else. You think it's…" She couldn't say *love*. If she used that word with him, it would be to tell him that she'd grown to love him more than she could ever have imagined. Which is why she had to do this. "It's comfort. What we have is a…comfortable companionship." Her throat was raw as she framed the words. What they had, what she felt they had, was so much more. But she could tell by his face that he wouldn't accept her decision unless she made him.

"You're imprinted on me, Jethro. Like a duckling. I gave you attention when you needed it, then and now, and we're—" she swallowed "—friends, and you've mistaken that for something else. That's all."

When he winced, she wanted to grab the words back.

"I thought you were so m-much m-more. I'd hoped you were so m-much m-more." His voice was hollow.

"You'll thank me later. We can still be friends."

His jaw clenched. "I d-don't need this kind of friendship. I can't d-do this kind of friendship."

"It's all we can have, Jethro." She couldn't stand it if they lost that connection as well as everything else. That'd been her fear from the beginning. If only they hadn't started down this charade! But if they hadn't, she wouldn't have the moments together she knew she'd treasure for the rest of her years. Closing the distance between them, she touched her hand to his dear, cherished face. "It's probable I can't give you a family." Her eyes squeezed shut for a moment at the memory of the two babies she'd lost. "You need a family."

She could feel his shuddering sigh through her fingers before he gently kissed their tips. "You'd b-be m-my family."

"Oh, Jethro." She smiled sadly as she lowered her hand, surreptitiously curling her fingers in to hold his kiss. "You think that now, but in ten years when I'm old and gray and you don't have anyone to inherit your farm, you'll think otherwise. You'll find a woman your age that would've worked out better for you and you'll regret that you were stuck with me."

"I'd never regret it. And Amos can farm it for m-me when he's grown."

"*Nee*, Jethro. This time, my answer is *nee* and it must remain so."

Gutted at her own words, Susannah wheeled and returned to the barn door on quavering legs. Slipping inside, she closed the door and hooked the latch before sagging against it. Face contorted, she remained propped there as she listened for sounds indicating the actions of the man on the other side. At last, she heard the retreating crunch of boots on gravel.

"Are you all right, *Mamm*?" Amos, his arms full of straw bedding for the stalls, was staring at her in concern.

Nee. She was anything but all right. But she would be. She had to be. It would just take time. Susannah feared it would be a long time.

"*Ja*," she assured him as she pushed upright. "It's just…been a long day."

With a doubtful nod, he continued on his way.

Moving away from the door, Susannah entered the first empty stall and crossed to the open window in time to watch Jethro's buggy travel down the lane. When even the glow of the orange caution triangle indicating a slow-moving vehicle faded from view, she turned from the window. And burst into tears. Not wanting to draw Amos's concerned attention again, she jerked open the barn door and stumbled through.

Once outside, she headed for the orchard. Her crying became unchecked. By the time she'd climbed up the hill in the light of the rising slivered moon and reached the trees, her head ached and her breath was coming in little hiccups.

"This is why I don't cry," she muttered through the thickness in her nose and throat. Lifting her apron, she dabbed at her eyes. *I did the right thing.* Jethro's face, his eyes so wounded, sprang into her mind. Tears began to leak anew. *Then why doesn't it feel like the right thing? Not for him, not for me. You're just thinking about now. You can't just think about now, you have to think about later, years later.* Slumping against the smooth trunk of one of the apple trees, the purported "years later" seemed empty and lonely as she wadded the serviceable cotton into a fist. But she could eventually find someone for companionship. She'd had companionship before.

Her mouth, numb from the crying, began to quiver. *Now I want love. Is that wrong? I did the right thing.* Maybe if she repeated it enough, she could finally accept it in her heart. *I did the right thing. I did the right thing.* It became a sob. One hand wrapped around her heaving stomach, Susannah used the other to wipe away the tears that made the thin moon just a blur.

Her breathing slowly quieted from hiccupping gasps to slow, steady breaths. Susannah tipped her head back against the tree. Another reason she didn't cry. For when she did, she was exhausted afterward, wrung out, like a dishrag that'd been twisted and squeezed. Emptied of everything. Like her heart…

Jethro didn't remember climbing back into the buggy. He didn't recall directing the gelding down the lane. Blinking distractedly, he realized they were headed toward the crossroad that would lead him to his own farm. Cocoa must've made the determination, as Jethro wasn't conscious of doing so. His gaze flicked momentarily to the side mirrors as the shapes of Susannah's and his parents' barns receded with every hoofbeat. At least the horse had turned away from his folks' farm. They were the last people he wanted to see right now.

What a fool he'd been. He'd allowed himself to hope. As he'd never really let himself want before, he'd had little cause for hope. Life had been a steady diet of disappointments. Disappointments that Jethro had thought were his due. But with Susannah, he'd hoped. Hoped that she'd love him for himself. Loved him in spite of himself. Loved the inner man even through his outer issues.

Why are you surprised when she didn't want you? She doesn't need another farm. She has a prosperous one. She doesn't need a tighter relationship with the district's bishop; she's already their closest neighbor, and regardless of their opinion on this, a respected one.

He fingered the lines. The gelding's ears flicked back in his direction, as if to ask him what he was thinking. Jethro's brow furrowed. His eyes narrowed as he stared ahead. *Susannah didn't need to agree with his parents to cultivate their good opinion. She frequently didn't agree. So why now?*

He saw not the starlit night with its fingernail moon but Susannah's pale face. Her rigid figure. Her glistening eyes. *Glistening? Susannah never cried. Her hand against his mouth had been quivering. Because she was mad? Nee. Because she'd been trying not to cry. Why would she want to cry? Because she didn't want to say what she was saying when she sent him away?* He scowled in disgust. *Why do I strive to hang on to some kind of hope?*

You're wallowing in your misery like a pig in the mud, Jethro. Quit fooling yourself. Why continue to pursue a woman who doesn't want you? Like Louisa didn't, even when she had you.

But Susannah was different. If there was any possibility he could convince her to take a chance on them, wouldn't it be worth it? Just a chance, as small as a single stalk of straw in a full hayloft, that he could convince her to say yes, would he be a fool for not taking it? Jethro's jaw shifted as his teeth clenched.

Yes.

Oh, Lord, please don't let me make a mistake in this.

He'd spent a lifetime knowing his needs were always second to others. Second to Atlee's when he had come along. Second to his father's responsibilities as bishop. Second to Louisa's needs. Second to his mother's determination to be the bishop's wife she'd envisioned.

He needed Susannah. He needed her positive outlook. He needed her strength. He needed her acceptance. He needed her love. And he'd thought he had it. *Dear* Gott, *don't let me be wrong in that.*

He'd dated women his folks had directed him to. Even married one. If she'd lived, he'd have stayed married to Louisa for the rest of his days. But she hadn't. Was he going to let them chose a second one? *Gott* had given him a chance and he'd found love when *Gott* had dropped a buggy wreck on this very road. How many more chances would *Gott* give him if he turned his back on this one?

As for him needing a family, he'd have one with Susannah. He'd be proud to help raise Amos. Although a bit strange as Ben was near his age, he'd happily be *grossdaadi* to the twins, and any additional children

Ben and Rachel, or for that matter, Rebecca and Amos whenever they married, would have. As everyone was so worried about him having a family, he'd found one he'd love to call his own.

Jethro drew the already confused gelding to a stop in the middle of the road. He loved his parents, he truly did. But as the *Biewel* said many times, a man shall leave his father and mother. It was time they let him. Let him make his own mistakes, if that's what this was.

But he knew it wasn't.

Resolute, he didn't even look for a field lane in which to turn the rig around. Looking both ways— there'd been too many buggy wrecks on this road as it was—Jethro ensured there were no lights from an on-coming car. Backing the gelding until the rear wheels of the buggy teetered into the far ditch, Jethro turned in the direction from which they'd come. The direction Jethro hoped would hold his future. A future he would choose. One with Susannah in it as his wife.

Eager to have the discussion with his parents that would free him for a better one with Susannah, he urged Cocoa to a greater pace. As the silhouettes of the farms came into view, Jethro leaned forward abruptly in the seat and asked the gelding for all the speed the horse possessed.

At the rapid staccato of hoofbeats, Susannah peeked through the branches to see a buggy racing down the road. Jethro's rig. Heading for his folks. To argue with them? Or agree?

As well as being a good man, Jethro was a good son. Although he might not agree with his parents in this, he would always honor them. *She had done the right thing.* Sniffing, Susannah wiped the remnants of tears from her face with her hand. She needed to get back to the barn and help Amos finish up chores. At least her nose had cleared enough that she could finally breathe again. With a deep sigh, she straightened from the trunk. A few strides later, she paused for another deep, exaggerated inhalation.

Was that smoke?

Stooping, she ripped up a handful of grass and tossed it into the air. As the fragments drifted across the orchard, she spun toward the opposing direction. The smell was stronger. Definitely smoke. The dark night quickly revealed the source. An orange glow haloed the bishop's house. Now that her eyes were on it, even across the large field that separated them, Susannah could see flames lick up one side of the building. Her legs were moving before she fully processed the sight.

"Amos! Amos!" she screamed as she sprinted for the barn. To her great relief, her son popped out of the barn door.

"Get the pony and race to the phone shack! Call the fire department and tell them Bishop Weaver's house is on fire!" Susannah dashed past where Amos stayed rooted, mouth agape. "Hurry!"

For a brief second, Susannah thought about grabbing Nutmeg and racing the mare the short stretch to the bishop's farm. Determining she could be at the Weaver's place before she could bridle the mare and later deal with the frightened animal around what was sure to be a dangerous situation, she pivoted for the lane.

In the distance, she heard the frightened whinny of a horse. The silhouette of Jethro's rig was visible as he rushed up the lane in front of the burning building. Susannah pumped her legs harder. Although he was a member of the local volunteer fire department and knew what actions to take, Jethro was alone. Alone at a fire in his parents' home. Were his parents inside?

Her heart was pounding. Energy fueled by adrenaline poured into her limbs as the fence posts between the farms flashed by in swift succession. Susannah couldn't feel her feet hitting the ground, but they must've been as she could hear the rapid slap of them on the blacktop. Her knees tangled in the confines of her skirt. Staggering, she almost went down before regaining her balance. Grabbing a handful of fabric, she jerked it up out of the way of her legs.

Halfway to the house she heard the clatter of the pony's hooves on the blacktop behind her, the sound barely discernible over her panting breath. Amos was on his way to call for help. Thank *Gott* he frequently raced the pony, even when she'd discouraged it. They'd make a fast trip to the phone shack.

The light surrounding the Weaver house had intensified. Now instead of just on one side, flames were creeping over the roof. Susannah frantically scanned the yard for any sign of figures in the fire's glow. *Jethro, where are you? Oh, don't go in alone! Where were the Weavers? Were they home?*

As Susannah swung into the lane, she saw that the buggy, pulled by the unfettered, spooked horse, had circled the farmyard and was heading back down the driveway toward her. Knowing the danger of a loose runaway with the impending traffic, Susannah staggered to halt in the middle of the lane. One hand on a trembling thigh, she stretched out the other to stop the frightened animal. To her relief, the horse skidded to a standstill a few feet from her. Susannah snagged the rein just under the bit and stroked a hand along the gelding's sweaty neck.

"That's a boy," she soothed between pants. Scanning the area, Susannah searched for a place the horse would be safe. With a gentle tug on the rein, she trotted the skittish animal across the blacktop to a field entrance. Ensuring the rig was well clear of the road, she secured him to a post that supported a field gate. Breathing nearly recovered, she raced back across the road. Her steps slowed to an appalled walk up the lane.

The fire's crackle and pop made it almost seem alive. Orange flames assaulted the house from multiple locations. Shades of smoke rose up into the sky. Susannah felt like she was caught between two dimensions. Searing heat flushed her skin that faced the fire. The dropping temperature chilled the side away from it.

Mesmerized by the horrifying sight before her, Susannah at first didn't separate the sound from the fire's ominous rumbling. When she recognized that whatever it was, it wasn't of the fire, she frantically searched the yard. Several heart-pounding seconds later, she located a dark shape on the ground, yards from the front door. Cringing against the hostile heat, she rushed to the figure.

The bishop lay on his back, his lanky legs bent at the knees. His chest rose and fell with wheezes interspersed with harsh coughing. The man's gray hair was in tangled disarray around his hatless head. His face was slick with sweat.

"We have to get farther away. Can you move?" Susannah bent to grab his arm.

"*Ja*," he wheezed. "I think so." He struggled up on his elbows to stare with a shattered expression at his home.

"Come on," Susannah urged. With a hand on his forearm, Susannah propelled him to his feet. As a clumsy team, they staggered step-by-step until the gravel of the driveway was under her feet. She kept him upright until they'd crossed the grass on the driveway's far side. Hoping they'd come far enough, for now at least, she helped the bishop sink down next to the water trough that served as part of the livestock enclosure.

"Where's Jethro? Where's Ruby?" she gasped.

The bishop's face was white in the flickering light of the fire. "He went back in to get her."

Chapter Eighteen

Susannah jerked upright to stare at the front door of the house. The fire had taken possession from when they were outside it only moments before. Flames flared through the nearby window. In the glow, the house's white paint pocked with blisters. She choked on a sharp inhalation, smoke and despair clogging her throat.

Jethro was in the burning house.

A dark blur darted across the yard. Jethro? Or were her eyes, beleaguered with tears and smoke, playing tricks on her? Was it Ruby? The figure in the erratic shadows turned, exposing a pale face. Susannah launched herself toward it. She shrieked and stumbled when a small explosion rocked the night. Flying glass and debris burst from a side window, knocking the figure down.

Staggering to regain her footing, Susannah focused her attention on the downed body. The fire roared a victory after the blast. *Oh, please, please let Jethro be all right!* At the faint whine of a siren, she whimpered in relief. A quick glance revealed a pulsing blue light that penetrated the night sky beyond her farm. Her strides diminished to a jarring halt as she neared the motion-less figure. It was too small to be Jethro. Too short to be Ruby. Who then? She dropped to her knees beside it.

The slender chest was wracked with coughing. When the body jerked with laboring breath, Susan-nah helped it turn to the side. She gasped at the sight of John Schlabach's grimy, gaunt face.

"Are you hurt? Can you get up? We have to get out of here!" she yelled over the rumbling behind her.

The house groaned as if complaining when its in-terior began giving way under the onslaught of the flames. Susannah's stomach churned at the sound. At her ex-hired hand's feeble nod, she jerked him up, pull-ing him away from the now fully engaged house even before he completely regained his feet. As they crossed the driveway in a staggering run, Susannah prayed she wasn't doing further damage to any injuries the boy might've sustained in the blast. When they reached the pasture fence, she braced him against the boards.

"Did they get out?" Susannah barely heard the words interspersed in John's coughing and wheezing. "Are they all right?" He bent over at the waist as he panted. Susannah placed a light hand on his back in support. Under her fingers, she could feel the ridges of his spine. Her eyes, burning from the smoke, closed in despair. Where was Jethro? Was he out? Was he safe? Torn with the need to search for the man she loved, to scan for any sign of him, she remained instead with the boy who needed her.

The sound of sirens battled with the roar of the fire and the crash of shattering glass. Occasionally a shrill whinny from a frightened horse—the one she'd secured across the road and ones in the barn—were discernible. Susannah wanted to weep with relief when Gabe Bartel's pickup swept into the lane. As John was now standing upright beside her, she waved the local EMS provider on to where she'd left the bishop. And Jethro? Were he and his mother out of the house? *Oh, please, Gott, let them be out.*

Distant sirens indicated more help was on the way. Would they be too late? Or was it too late for her and Jethro to have any chance at a future? If he were only safe, Susannah would happily spend the rest of her life as his wife, if that's what he wanted. Regardless of what others thought best. When her son loved like she loved, she wouldn't stand in his way.

John was crying. Tears tracked from his bloodshot eyes over his grimy cheeks to drip off his chin. "I only wanted to hurt them a little. Hurt them like they hurt my *daed*. The bishop and the ministers drove him away. If they hadn't done that, things would've been better. He wouldn't have left. He wouldn't have died like he did."

Susannah cringed at the mumbled words. She didn't know what to say. The boy was seeing a version of reality that existed only in his mind. But a child longs to love his parents. She wrapped her arms around John's shoulders and drew his thin, unresisting frame to her.

"What if I've killed them? I didn't mean to kill them. I just wanted someone to hurt like I hurt." The boy gasped in air between sobs. "I kept thinking he'd come back and he'd be different and it would be all right. We'd be a family again."

Hot tears dripped against her neck. Were they John's, or hers? Susannah didn't know. She didn't care. The only thing she cared about was seeing Jethro emerge from the growing inferno a short distance away. John shuddered in her arms. *Ach, nee.* She cared about this troubled boy. And what might become of him. How incredibly disheartening if Mervin Schlabach destroyed another life beyond his own.

Susannah stroked gentle fingers through the youth's grimy hair. "For all have sinned and fallen short of the glory of God, John. It's normal to want to love your parents. *Gott* wants you to love your parents. But sometimes parents don't always make the best choices. For themselves, or for their children," she murmured. "You're not your father, John. Confession is well on the path to repentance. You can determine your life going forward. *Gott* can change it. We are here to help you."

Vehicles bearing the emblem of the Miller's Creek volunteer fire department roared up the lane. Doors slammed as men launched from vehicles. Susannah shifted with the trembling boy she supported until she could look back toward the livestock trough where she'd left the bishop.

Her arms sagged from around John's frame when she saw not one but three figures beyond the EMT garbed in his bulky reflective gear. One of them was on the ground, leaning against the bishop, the face partially covered by an oxygen mask. The other was standing, facing her direction. Slight steam vapors wafted from him. Stunned, Susannah watched as Gabe draped one wet towel around the man's neck and another over the top of his head. Then she burst into tears.

John glanced up at her in surprise before he, too, looked in that direction. His body began quaking again with sobs. "I didn't kill them. I'm so thankful I didn't kill them."

Flashing lights and sirens intensified as more trucks parked along the lane when fire departments from other towns arrived to join the fight.

Susannah's gaze remained locked on the man draped in towels. He took a step in her direction before Gabe stopped him with raised hand. The EMT rose from where he'd been attending the Weavers and turned his full attention to the one who'd saved them.

Jethro was alive.

Susannah's legs gave out. If it hadn't been for John, she would've crumpled to the ground. At the touch on her shoulder, she twisted to see David Neuenschwander, one of the Amish volunteer firefighters, beside them.

"I've got John." Under his helmet, a smile was evident on the older man's kindly face. "Why don't you go see if Gabe needs any help?"

Susannah nodded mutely. Through the ashes that drifted down between them, she saw the bishop struggle to his feet. He stumbled over to wrap his arms around his son. Jethro wobbled under the embrace, but his father held him steady. His attention on her approach, Jethro tipped his head to something the bishop must've spoken. He said something back before patting the older man's shoulder. With a nod, Ezekiel lowered his arms and settled back down beside his wife.

Susannah's heart lurched as, without breaking eye contact, Jethro started in her direction. A few coughs punctuated his progress, but his arms were as strong as Susannah could ever hope for when they wrapped around her. She even relished the heavy smell of smoke that permeated the shirt under her nose, as she could feel the powerful beat of his heart beneath it.

"I was so afraid." She breathed the words. "I didn't see you. When I heard the explosion…" Burrowing deeper into his embrace, she tightened her arms around the waist that was damp with sweat and the towels that still draped him.

"We couldn't get to the front d-door. *Gut* thing, as the small p-propane tank that feeds the lamp blew right when we would've passed it. We went out through the mudroom into the side yard."

"Your *mamm*?"

"She's all right."

Susannah's face contorted in relief as tears leaked anew. She flinched at the crash of timbers behind her, but now the roar of the fire was accompanied with the hiss of the water beginning to suppress it. Safe in Jethro's arms, she took in the surreal scene in the normally tranquil farmyard. Red and blue lights flashed, highlighting the safety stripes on the gear worn by the men who were spread over the property manning fire hoses. Although the house couldn't be saved, they were ensuring none of the other buildings were caught up in the inferno.

"Are you truly all right?"

"*Ja*. Gabe checked me over p-pretty *gut*. For smoke inhalation, b-burns, heat exhaustion. Wouldn't let m-me come t-to you until he d-did so." She felt a kiss against her hair. "B-but he couldn't stop me from coming t-to you, Susannah. Nothing could stop me. You b-better get used t-to it. I'll always come t-to you."

Smiling, Susannah looked into his dear, dear face. "Do you remember when you asked me about the qualities I'd look for in a husband? I just realized that persistence is a very important one. In fact, I've been doing a lot of consideration lately regarding the qualities I'd look for in a mate. I'm still not sure what all they are, but it doesn't matter, as the mate I'd been looking for was you."

Jethro's arms flexed around her. "*Gut* thing. As I've known m-mine was you for a long t-time." His heavy sigh, although interspersed with a few coughs, was heartfelt. "I'm sure one of the qualities wasn't a stutter."

"Jethro, I never hear the stutter. I just hear you." Her gaze rested on the bedraggled couple huddled together by the trough under Gabe's watchful eye.

"What about your folks, Jethro? Are you all right without their approval?"

"I have it. We have it." His smile flashed white in his soot-covered face. "I was willing t-to give m-my life for them. I can surely be t-trusted to m-make a *gut* decision who b-best to spend that life with."

"They're right in that I can't give you children or a family. My only value to contribute is the farm."

"What's your farm got t-to d-do with us? I d-don't want you for your farm. I want you. In fact, you can d-deed the farm over to Amos right now if you wish. Or anyone else, for that m-matter. As for a family, you're my family. Your children will be my family. I can't imagine one I'd want m-more."

Susannah closed her eyes against the surrounding chaos and opened them to see only the man who held her. A man she couldn't imagine wanting more, either.

Epilogue

Jethro's hand tightened on Susannah's as they sauntered up the hill to the orchard. The moonlight reflecting on the snow in the clear night was all the light they needed. Even though the cold November temperature nipped at her nose, she was happy to forego her gloves to feel the hand enfolding hers.

The apple trees, their branches draped in a light snow, were dormant for the winter. Susannah looked from their frail skeletons to the one far across the field of Bishop Weaver's house. Although the fire had rapidly been controlled, between it and the resulting water damage, little in the house had been salvageable. The district had promptly rallied to provide the bishop and his wife with everything they might need.

Initially, the couple had moved into the apartment in town above The Stitch quilt shop, recently vacated by Hannah and Gabe Bartle. For the rest of this winter, at least, they were moving into Jethro's house. His place was now with Susannah, his wife.

"Do you think they'll move back here again in the

spring? The community would certainly build a house for them."

"I d-don't know. It depends how my *mamm* would feel about it at the t-time. It makes her…uncomfortable t-to have the district continually p-providing for her."

"We could build a *daadi haus* and have them move in here."

Jethro stared at her as if he'd never heard of the term for the onsite residence that housed the older Amish generation.

"You would let m-my p-parents, m-my *m-mamm*, m-move in right next d-door?"

"Why not? They've been my neighbors all my life. And they're your parents. They are always welcome. Although we won't have grandchildren for them." She worried her lip before drawing in a deep breath. "Are you sure you won't regret that?"

"We've gone over that. M-my only regret would be in not sharing every m-moment of m-my life that I p-possibly can with you."

Susannah sighed, comforted more than she could say by his words. And so glad that his life hadn't ended on that night.

The bishop hadn't pressed charges against John. As was their way, he forgave the remorseful youth, working instead with the authorities to release the boy on probation into his mother's care. With some additional guiding influences.

Stroking his thumb in slow circles over the back of Susannah's hand, Jethro seemed to read her thoughts. "I'd heard the old b-boy, D-David Neuenschwander, will no longer be an old b-boy when he m-marries

Lavinia Schlabach. Seems the new matchmaker had something to d-do with that."

Smiling, Susannah tipped her head back to take in the brilliance of the stars overhead in the crisp clear night. "I'm glad for him. I'm glad for them all. He's a gentle, patient man. I figured, if those qualities would do well for a troubled horse, they might help a troubled boy as well. And a woman who'd waited a long time for a *gut* man. It was just a matter of getting them together to see it themselves."

"I think their courtship surprised everyone."

"More so than ours?"

Jethro grinned. "If anyone had p-paid any attention to the way I looked at you, they wouldn't have b-been surprised."

"Well, I was surprised." She lifted their joined hands to her cheek, where she rested his chilled fingers against it before turning her head to place a soft kiss on them. "In the best way." She thought about the misunderstanding that'd temporarily broken them up. "You spoke with Mrs. Danvers regarding your speech?"

"*Ja*. B-but I won't b-be working with her. I wouldn't have chosen this, b-but it's who I am. She d-did suggest some t-tools to help me relax when speaking that will improve the stuttering. I'm relaxed with you. See, it's better all ready. B-because if you're content, I'm content." Releasing her hand, he tucked her against him as he wrapped his arms around her.

Leaning back against his chest, Susannah rested her hands on the ones clasped at her waist. "I'm content. I'm so much more than content."

"I walked with a woman here once who t-told me she was t-too old for romance. Is she still t-too old?"

"*Nee.* Never. Maybe I just never knew what it was."

"I'm glad I, of all p-people, got to be the one t-to show you."

"Romance," she mused. "Well, that might be a quality in a spouse I wouldn't have looked for—" she entwined her fingers with his "—but I'm glad my husband has it."

"I l-l-love you."

Pulling out of his arms, Susannah turned to meet his gaze, her eyes widened with awe before they narrowed with concern. Jethro had never struggled with that letter before. When she saw the breadth of his smile, she relaxed.

"For the first t-time in m-my life I'm glad for the stutter. I've never t-told anyone I loved them b-before. I wanted to linger over the words."

He kissed her. And he lingered over that as well.

* * * * *

AN UNLIKELY AMISH MATCH

Vannetta Chapman

This book is dedicated to Ms. Peggy Looper, who inspired in me a real love for the art of storytelling.

Being confident of this very thing,
that he which has begun a good work in you
will perform it until the day of Jesus Christ.
—*Philippians* 1:6

But when he was yet a great way off,
his father saw him, and had compassion,
and ran, and fell on his neck, and kissed him.
—*Luke* 15:20

Chapter One

Susannah Beiler was carrying a to-go bag holding half of a cinnamon roll in one hand and her coffee in the other when she stepped out of Cabin Coffee and started across the street. At that exact moment, a large Ford pickup truck careened to the curb. Her friend Deborah pulled her back with a laugh and a smile. "Wouldn't do to have you flattened on the streets of Goshen on this beautiful spring day."

After all she'd been through the last two years, it would be ironic. Susannah shook off that thought and would have walked across the street that was now clear, but Deborah stepped back under the canopy of the coffee shop and nodded toward the truck. "Do you ever wonder why people act like that?"

The music was blaring at such a high level that the vehicle was practically rocking. The truck sported a bright blue paint job with streaks of lightning painted down the side, a large chrome bumper and spinning tire rims.

"Why would you jack it up so high?" Susannah crossed her arms, tapping her right index finger against her left arm. Sometimes she felt like she didn't understand other people at all.

"And who would want to purchase such big tires? They look as if they'd fit a tractor."

"*Ya*, I'm not sure what the point is."

They glanced at one another when a young man jumped out of the truck, empty fast-food bags and soda cans trailing after him. He noticed the girls, smiled in a cocky *Englisch* way and then realized they were staring at the litter that had escaped from the truck.

"Oops." He snatched up the trash and tossed it into an adjacent trash can before once again flashing them both a smile.

He was a bit taller than Susannah, but then, most men were. He was also built like the mule her *dat* kept to watch over the goats—stocky and muscular. Blue jeans, a T-shirt that sported the logo of some rock and roll band, and sandy-colored hair flopping into his eyes and curling at his neck completed the picture.

Deborah laughed, but Susannah shook her head.

She couldn't abide rude people, and this guy seemed oblivious that the truck was obnoxious and the music was too loud.

The driver of the truck had put the vehicle into Park and jumped out. He had bright red hair sticking out from his ball cap, but other than that he could have been a twin to the first guy. As Susannah and Deborah watched, he walked up to his buddy, and they performed some complicated handshake.

"Take care, man."

"You know it." The first guy reached into the truck and snatched out a ball cap and a faded backpack.

"Later."

"Much."

The driver hopped back into the truck and sped away. The sandy-haired guy winked at Susannah and Deborah, pulled a cell phone out of his pocket and proceeded to stare at it as he walked in the opposite direction.

"Clueless," Susannah said, rubbing at the brow over her right eye. "He'll be lucky if he doesn't fall off the sidewalk the way he's staring down at that phone."

"Maybe."

"Are you kidding me?"

"I'm only saying that just because he's different doesn't mean that he's bad."

"I didn't say he was bad."

"Uh-huh, but the look you gave the both of them would have frightened a small child."

"Really?"

"Definitely. You've always been able to do that—stop someone in their tracks." Deborah linked their arms together and turned them toward her buggy. "Are you sure you don't want to be a teacher?"

"I'm not sure of much, but I am sure of that."

"Which is just as well, because you're a fabulous quilter."

"Danki."

"Off we go to the fabric store, then."

Which cheered up Susannah immensely. Even if she didn't purchase anything, being around bolts of fabric had a way of encouraging her on the darkest of days. During the worst of her chemotherapy treatments, she'd often stopped into the local fabric store simply to enjoy the smell and touch of new fabric. When she was too sick to piece or quilt, she'd sometimes sit with a basketful of different-colored cotton swatches, dreaming of what she would sew as soon as she was better.

There was something about brushing her fingertips over the cotton, envisioning the pattern she would use and the quilts she would make and picturing the smiles on tourists who purchased them. Quilting was her way of spreading joy, and wasn't that what a person of faith was supposed to do?

Deborah was describing her *dat* having to battle his way through a thicket of thorny brush to free a goat that had managed to become ensnared. The goat had taken one look at Deborah's *dat* and scampered off in the opposite direction, leaving him wondering why he'd thought he needed to save the animal in the first place. "'Goats are resourceful animals, Deborah. Never forget it,'" Deborah finished with a spot-on imitation of her *dat*. She always could tell a good story, and they were both laughing by the time they reached the fabric store.

Susannah enjoyed the rest of the afternoon.

She forgot all about the *Englischer*.

And she arrived home humming a tune and feeling immeasurably better than she had when she had awakened that morning. Some days she still woke terrified that the cancer had returned, certain that she was about to be plunged back into the cycle of doctor's visits and tests and treatments. Some days were still harder than others.

But her day had improved, and her mood had lightened with it.

"Mind fetching the mail for me?" Her *mamm* had been up since before sunrise—they both had. While Susannah did her best to help with household chores, her *mamm* often shooed her away, telling her to go rest or step outside for a while or spend an hour in her quilting room. At the moment, her *mamm*'s apron was a mess, her hair was escaping from her *kapp* and her hands were covered in bread dough. Two loaves were already baking in the oven and two she'd finished kneading sat on the counter.

Sometimes Susannah wondered why they still made the bread from scratch, since loaves were certainly cheaper to purchase at the grocery store. She did love the smell of fresh-baked bread, though.

"And please take your *schweschdern*. They're full of energy today."

Sharon and Shiloh dropped the dolls they were playing with and ran toward the front door.

"Sweaters first," Susannah said. Though it was the last week of April, the afternoons cooled quickly. The twins reversed directions and ran for their cubbies. When the girls were born, her *dat* had placed cubbies in the mudroom with their names marked at a level they could now easily read.

"They sound more like puppies on the loose than children," Susannah said.

She adored her little *schweschdern*. Her *mamm* had been twenty when Susannah was born and forty when the twins came along. They were the siblings she never thought she'd have, and she prayed every day that they hadn't inherited the gene that had caused her ovarian cancer. She didn't want anyone else to have to endure such a thing, especially not her *schweschdern*.

"Like I said—full of energy. I wouldn't mind if you stayed out with them a half hour or so, give them time to run some of it off."

Susannah thought her mother was one of the most

hardworking women she knew, but twin five-year-olds could wear anyone down.

"Finish that bread and then sit down with a cup of tea. I have a feeling you've earned it today."

The twins catapulted back into the kitchen.

"I'm ready." Shiloh reached for her hand.

"Me, too. I wonder if we have a letter from *Mammi*." Sharon dashed to the front door.

"Don't run too far ahead," Susannah called out.

The girls looked identical—white-blond hair, blue eyes and a thin build. The only physical difference that was easy to spot was that Sharon had freckles and Shiloh didn't. Their personalities were quite opposite. Sharon was always running ahead—energetic, enthusiastic and fearless. Shiloh preferred to hang back and carefully watch. She also liked holding hands, while Sharon proclaimed that was for babies.

By the time Susannah and Shiloh descended the front porch steps, Sharon was already waiting at the lane—hands on her hips, a scowl on her face and a whine in her voice. "Why are you so slow? Come on already."

The day was one of those glorious spring days that Susannah often daydreamed about in the winter. The leaves were a green so bright they caused you to blink, and the flowers planted earlier that month had burst into a rainbow of color. The sky was blue, the sun shone brightly and the weather was cool enough to require a sweater but without a cold north breeze.

Perfect.

They picked wildflowers as they rambled down the lane.

Both girls stooped to watch ants carrying tiny pieces of grass.

And they fed carrots to Percy, their buggy horse, who was grazing in the field that ran alongside the lane.

Susannah's mind called up all the things she had to be thankful for—her family, her health, a community that had supported her through a difficult time and now a perfect spring afternoon.

Ten minutes later, they reached the mailbox. Susannah had her hand inside, trying to reach to the back, where it seemed at least one piece of mail always managed to land, when Shiloh stepped closer and Sharon began to bounce from foot to foot.

"Someone's coming," Sharon said.

Susannah shielded her eyes against the afternoon sun, at first curious and then disbelieving and finally completely confused. What was *he* doing here?

Micah Fisher had taken his time finding his way out to the farm. He'd figured that as long as he was in town, he might as well check things out. Then he'd realized he was hungry again, so he'd stopped by the coffee shop where the two Amish ladies had been standing. He ate a leisurely lunch and used the time to charge his phone since he wouldn't be able to do so at his grandparents' farm.

The sun was low in the western sky by the time he hitched a ride to the edge of town. The driver let him out at a dirt road that led to several Amish farms. He'd never been to visit his grandparents before. They always came to Maine. But he had no trouble finding their place. His *mamm*'s instructions had been very clear.

As he drew close to the lane that led to the farm-house, he noticed a young woman standing by the mailbox. A little girl was holding her hand and another was hopping from foot to foot. They were all three staring at him.

"Howdy," he said.

The woman only nodded, but the two girls responded with "Hello"—one whispered and the other shouted.

"Can we help you?" the woman asked. "Are you... lost?"

"*Nein.* At least I don't think I am."

"You must be if you're here. This is the end of the road."

Micah pointed to the farm next door. "Abigail and John Fisher live there?"

"They do."

"Then I'm not lost." He snatched off his baseball cap, rubbed his hand over the top of his head and then yanked the cap back on and down to shield his eyes. "Say, don't I know you?"

"Absolutely not."

"But I've seen you before...in town, when I first arrived. You were standing outside the bakery with a plain-looking girl."

"If you mean Amish, we all are."

"No, I meant plain." He smiled to suggest he was teasing, though honestly the other girl had been so pale as to be translucent and had worn the traditional white *kapp* and a gray dress. She could have been a cloud or a puff of fog or a figment of his imagination.

But the girl in front of him?

She wasn't someone you'd quickly forget—daring brown eyes, a *kapp* pulled so tightly that not a hair escaped, which only served to accentuate the exquisite shape of her eyes, bright color in her cheeks and a sweet curve to her lips. Her dress was a pretty dark green with a matching apron.

And she was his neighbor?

Perhaps *Gotte* had provided him an ally through this trying time of his life.

Micah stepped forward and held out his hand. "I'm Micah—Micah Fisher. Pleased to meet you."

"You're not *Englisch*?" Instead of shaking his hand, she reached for her other sister. They had to be siblings from the way they looked up at her and waited to see what she'd do next.

"Of course I'm not."

"So you're Amish?" She stared pointedly at his clothing—tennis shoes, blue jeans, T-shirt and ball cap. Pretty much what he wore every day.

"I'm as Plain and simple as they come."

"I somehow doubt that."

"Since we're going to be neighbors, I suppose I should know your name."

"Neighbors?"

"*Ya*. I've come to live with my *daddi* and *mammi*—at least for a few months. My parents think it will straighten me out." He tugged his ball cap lower and peered down the lane. "I thought the bishop lived next door."

"He does."

"Oh. You're the bishop's *dochder*?"

"We all are," the little girl with freckles cried. "I'm Sharon and that's Shiloh and that is Susannah."

"Nice to meet you, Sharon and Shiloh and Susannah."

Sharon lost interest and squatted to pick up some of the rocks lining the caliche lane. Shiloh hid behind her *schweschder*'s skirt, and Susannah scowled at him.

So, not an ally.

"I knew the bishop lived next door, but no one told me he had such pretty *doschdern*."

Susannah's eyes widened even more, but it was Shiloh who peeked out from behind her skirt and said, "He just called you pretty."

"Actually, I called you all pretty."

Shiloh ducked back behind Susannah.

Susannah narrowed her eyes as if she was squinting into the sun, only she wasn't. "Do you talk to every girl you meet that way?"

"Not all of them—no."

"And do you always dress like that?"

"What's wrong with how I'm dressed?"

"And why did you arrive in a pickup truck?"

"Because a friend offered to bring me."

"An *Englisch* friend?"

"Say, what is this—the third degree? It feels like it, and as far as I know, I've done nothing to land me in trouble."

"Yet." Susannah snatched up Sharon's hand and turned back toward the bishop's house.

"It was *gut* to meet you," he called out, knowing it would fluster her. Just his luck that the girl next door would be a killjoy. He'd met enough Amish girls like her to fill the back of a pickup truck twice over.

They were so disapproving.

It rankled him.

It also made him want to do something reckless, like throw a party or take off for points unknown or walk back to town and see a movie. But he didn't do any of those things. He didn't know anyone to invite to a party—yet. All of Goshen was unknown, and he wasn't even sure they had a movie house. Plus, he had no money to pay for a movie.

He sighed heavily, considering what lay before him. He'd promised his parents that he would come to Goshen and stay for at least six months. He realized he might as well walk up to the farmhouse. There was no point in avoiding it, but first he pulled out his phone, tapped the Snapchat button and held the phone up in front of him.

"I've arrived at the far reaches of northern Indiana. Let's hope I can survive life on the farm." He made what he hoped was a hilarious face, added a filter and frame, and then clicked the post button. Sticking the phone into his back pocket, he trudged down the lane toward his grandparents' house and what was probably going to be the longest six months of his life.

Susannah wasn't going to bring up the subject of their new neighbor to her parents. She actually was trying to forget him. She liked her life exactly as it was. The last thing she needed was trouble living next door, and Micah Fisher definitely looked like trouble.

They'd paused to bless the food and had just begun passing around the dishes of ham casserole, fresh bread, carrots and salad when Sharon starting chatting away about their encounter with Micah.

"He's tall and he talks funny."

"He wears a crazy hat," Shiloh added.

"And he wanted to shake Susannah's hand, but she didn't want to."

"And he said we were pretty—he said we were *all* pretty." Shiloh pulled in her bottom lip as she concentrated on cutting up her ham into small bites.

Her *dat* helped Sharon to scoop a spoonful of carrots onto her plate. "John mentioned to me that the boy was coming to stay with them for a while."

"He hardly seems like a boy." Susannah felt a slow blush creep up her neck when both her parents turned to stare at her. "What I mean is that he seemed to act like a *youngie*, though plainly he was older—I'd guess around twenty."

She could tell that her explanation hadn't cleared up anything, so she backed up and told them of seeing him in town, of the truck and the trash and the *Englisch* clothes. She didn't bring up the cell phone. That felt like tattling. No doubt his grandparents, and her *dat*, would know about it soon enough.

"Not everyone is as settled as you are, dear. I believe *Gotte* used your illness to mature you." Her *mamm* buttered a piece of bread—hot, fresh and savory. Perhaps homemade was better.

"And hopefully to make you even more compassionate toward others." Her *dat*'s smile softened his words. "No doubt Micah is trying to find his way as many of our youth are—though, as you say, he's hardly a *youngie* anymore. Just turned twenty-five, if I remember correctly from what John said."

"The same as you." Her mother looked pleased, as if sharing the same age would make them best pals.

Susannah didn't think that was likely.

Her life had finally settled down. She had no desire to complicate it with the likes of Micah.

The rest of the meal passed in a flurry of conversation. Sharon chattered on about the kittens in the barn and how she was planning to name each one. Shiloh had read another of the picture books from the library, and she insisted on describing it in great detail. Her *mamm* reminded Susannah that church would be at the Kings' on Sunday, and that they had agreed to go over and help Mose prepare on Saturday. And her *dat* described a young mare that had been brought in for shoeing. "Four white socks and a patch on her fore-head—pretty thing."

Susannah heard the conversations going on around her, but her mind kept volleying between the log-cabin quilt she'd started the day before and the new neighbor next door.

She didn't want a new neighbor.

Why couldn't things stay as they were?

She couldn't have explained what made her think so, but somehow she was certain that the comfortable rhythm of their days was about to change.

And then, as if to confirm her thoughts, her *dat* said, "Oh, I forgot to mention that Micah is going to be working in my shop a couple hours each afternoon. Perhaps we can have him over for dinner sometime."

The smile on her *mamm*'s face told Susannah there was no use arguing with that.

Well, she'd just have to endure Micah's presence though she did not and would not approve of his *Englisch* ways.

Her *dat* had said he was staying awhile.

Micah had mentioned a few months.

Surely it couldn't be for a terribly long time. He wasn't moving in, and he hadn't been carrying any luggage, just the denim backpack. With any luck, he'd be gone by the first day of summer.

As was his habit, her *dat* took the twins out with him to do a final check of the animals. Susannah and her mother were cleaning the dishes when the conversation returned to Micah.

"Do you think you might like him?"

"Oh, I'm pretty sure we're polar opposites."

"Not always a bad thing."

"It's not going to happen, *Mamm*." The words came out more harshly than she'd intended. "We've spoken of this. I don't believe… That is, I'm sure what you're thinking of isn't *Gotte*'s plan for me."

"You mean marrying."

"*Ya*. I mean marrying."

"Because of your cancer—which is gone."

"Gone, yes, but it could come back, and more than that, the whole experience has left me changed."

"In more ways than one." Her *mamm* turned to study her though her hands remained in the sudsy water. "You've turned into a fine young woman, Susannah—a godly woman."

"You're changing the subject. Any man—any Amish man—would want a houseful of children." Susannah refused to meet her mother's gaze. Instead, she focused on the plate she was drying.

"Just because Samuel felt that way doesn't mean every man feels the same."

"We both know that Samuel and I were…mismatched. His breaking up with me, it was hard, but I felt immediately better once it was done."

"But…"

"But I learned, *Mamm*. I learned that men have certain expectations from marriage."

Why was it that speaking of this always brought tears to her eyes? She'd grown accustomed to the facts—to the limitations—of her life, but it seemed as if a certain part of her heart remained bruised. "How does the proverb go? 'No woman can be happy with less than seven to cook for'? I suspect no Amish man can be happy with less than seven to provide for."

"Children come to us in different ways."

"You're speaking of adoption—which is rare in an Amish community."

"Rare but not unheard-of." Her *mamm* wiped her hands on a dish towel, reached out and put a hand on each of Susannah's shoulders, turning her toward her.

Susannah couldn't resist the need to look up, to look into her *mamm*'s eyes and face her dreams and fears head-on.

"I'm only saying that you shouldn't assume you know *Gotte*'s plan for your life. Our ways are not *Gotte*'s ways, and that's something to be grateful for."

Once Susannah nodded that she understood, her *mamm* picked up another dish and slipped it into the dishwater. Susannah swiped at the tears that had slipped down her cheeks, feeling foolish and wishing she could keep a better rein on her emotions.

Her melancholy wasn't about Micah. It was about her parents' expectations for her life. Micah, she felt nothing except pity for—and perhaps a tad of irritation.

"Just wait until you meet Micah, then you'll understand."

"Will I, now?"

"I'm more likely to marry Widower King."

"Who is a fine man and a *gut* addition to our community."

"And he's thirty-five years old."

"Is he, now?"

They shared a smile. Her *mamm* knew very well

how old Mose King was and that Susannah didn't have an ounce of romantic feelings for the man.

"You wouldn't have to worry about not being able to have children," her *mamm* joked.

"Indeed—six would be plenty, especially when those six are three pairs of twins."

"And all boys."

"All of them *full of energy*." Susannah purposely used her mother's words from earlier that afternoon.

They finished cleaning up the kitchen and walked onto the front porch to watch for her *dat* and the twins.

"I understand your not being interested in Micah, though you'd do well to remember that our first impression of someone isn't always the best."

"Fair enough."

"There's something else you should know, though."

Susannah sank into the rocker beside her *mamm*. She thought that twilight might be her favorite time of day. Something in her soul felt soothed by watching the sun set across their fields and her *dat* walking hand in hand with the twins toward the house.

"Micah's parents have been corresponding with Abigail and John. When it was decided he would move here, they shared the letter with both me and your *dat*. He's had a bit of a hard time, which is why he's here."

"Okay." She said the word slowly, tempted to add an *I thought so*.

"What I'm saying is that Micah will be here for at least six months—"

"Six months?" Susannah realized her mouth was hanging open and snapped it shut.

"And he'll be here helping your *dat* every day, so it

could be that *Gotte* has put him in our path for a special reason."

Susannah stifled a groan.

"There's a real possibility that what Micah needs most is not a girlfriend but simply a friend, and that's something that we can each be."

Chapter Two

Micah's first night with his grandparents went fairly well. It was the next morning that things took an unpleasant turn, when they laid down the law, so to speak.

His *dat*'s parents were in their midsixties—not too old to farm, but old enough that they should be slowing down. That wasn't happening. His *daddi*, John Fisher, was built like an ox. Micah's mother had always said that Micah inherited his size from the man, but Micah didn't see it. He was as muscular as the next guy, but his grandfather's forearm look like corded rope. *Forearm*—singular. He'd lost his right arm in a harvesting accident when he was just twenty years old. It had made him tough and intolerant of weakness of any type.

He was also a very serious man. Micah couldn't imagine that they'd come from the same gene pool.

Abigail Fisher was stern as well, but with a soft spot for her grandchildren. Growing up in Maine, Micah had seen his *mammi*'s letters arrive weekly. They always contained a paragraph addressed to each of the eight children. Her Christmas presents were always mailed well before Christmas Day—practical items, lovingly made. And his *mammi* and *daddi* visited occasionally, though certainly not every year.

In truth, Micah felt as if he hardly knew his grandparents, and though he loved them as he thought grandchildren should, he didn't think they had much in common. In fact, from the expression on his *daddi*'s face he wasn't sure the man really wanted him there. So why had he agreed to this ridiculous plan? How was Micah supposed to become a different person—*a more mature person* in the words of his *dat*—by living in a different state for six months?

Daddi didn't look up until they'd finished eating. Then he cradled his coffee mug in his left hand and waited until he was sure he had Micah's attention. "We expect you to work every day."

"Okay. That's fair." Micah brushed his hair away from his eyes and sat up straighter. "I can start looking for something today."

"No need to do that. I have it all arranged."

"All arranged?"

"To begin with, you'll be expected to carry your share of the work around here—the same as any grown man. I realize that will be different from what you're used to back home. I'm aware that your parents have coddled you."

Micah frowned at the last biscuit on his plate and focused on not saying the response that immediately came to mind. His thoughts scrambled in a dozen different directions, trying to think of a way to forgo the lecture that was surely headed his way.

"It's true, Micah." His *mammi* peered over her reading glasses at him. "There's no need to look hurt when your *daddi* is only stating the obvious. I spoke to your *dat* and *mamm* about this on several occasions."

"This?"

"She's referring to the way your *schweschdern* spoiled you—all of them did, really. It's not a surprise, you being the last child and only son."

Micah had seven older *schweschdern*, and it was true that they doted on him. He'd never washed a dish or helped prepare a meal. If he suddenly had to cook for himself, he'd probably perish from starvation. When he was young, he'd thought that was the life of every Amish boy, but as he grew older he'd learned his situation was a bit unique. The entire family had treated him as if he was a special gift left on the doorstep on Christmas morning.

Spoiled? *Ya.* He had been, but who in their right mind would turn that down? What was he supposed to do? Ask his siblings to be mean to him?

"You'll work with me in the fields every morning," his *daddi* continued. "There will be no more sleeping in."

Micah nearly choked on the sip of coffee he'd been in the process of swallowing. His *mammi* had called up the stairs at 5 a.m. sharp to wake him. That was sleeping in?

"After lunch you'll go to the bishop's and help in his farrier shop."

"The Beilers are *wunderbaar* people." His *mammi* might have winked at him, or she might have a twitch in her right eye. Micah couldn't tell. "This way you'll be learning two trades. Your *daddi* can teach you everything about farming—"

"Something your *dat* should have done already."

"And the bishop can teach you about horses."

As if he didn't know about horses. He was Amish, in spite of the way they were speaking to him. Micah felt the hairs on his neck stand on end, like a cat that had been brushed the wrong way. Why had he ever agreed to come to Indiana? What they were describing sounded worse than boot camp, which he only knew about from his friend Jackson, who had given him a ride from Maine.

Up before the birds.

Early-morning drills.

Work all day.

Collapse into bed at night.

Rinse and repeat.

His *daddi* gulped down the rest of his coffee, pushed his chair back and stood. The sleeve of his right arm had been sewn into a pocket, so that his stump rested inside it. He held his left hand in front of him—palm down—and made an invisible circle that included the three of them as well as the empty chairs, which he supposed his cousins had occupied before moving to Maine. In fact, it seemed the entire family was there, so what were his grandparents still doing in Goshen?

"We are your family—your *mammi* and me and all of your kinfolk here in Goshen. Your family in Maine loves you, as do we, but it's time for you to grow up, Micah. It's time to become a man."

And with that pronouncement, he turned and strode from the room.

Micah pulled in a deep breath, pushed himself away from the table and started across the room after him, but *Mammi* called him back.

"Best go upstairs and change first. I put proper clothing in your dresser and on the hooks. Your *daddi*—well, he won't abide the blue jeans and T-shirts."

The day seemed intent on continuing its slide from bad to worse.

"Anything else I should know? Any other changes I need to make?" He tried to sound lighthearted, but the words came out sarcastic and gruff. Too late to bite them back, and his *mammi* didn't seem to even notice.

"When you're done with the day's work, I'll cut your hair."

"What's wrong with my hair?"

"And he knows about the phone. As long as it isn't in the house—as long as he doesn't see it—he'll tolerate it. Just don't push him."

"I shouldn't push him?"

"He's old-fashioned, I know."

"You think?"

"But he's also a fair man." She stood and walked over to where he waited. His *mammi* barely reached his shoulders, but she was a formidable woman, and for some reason he couldn't identify, Micah wanted to make her proud. Reaching out, *Mammi* put a hand on his shoulder and waited until he met her gaze. "He's a *gut* man, and he cares about you. I suspect the changes will be difficult at first, but in the end, you'll thank him."

Micah seriously doubted that.

A quick glance at the clock told him it wasn't 6:30 a.m. yet.

The day was shaping up to be a long one.

He cheered himself with the thought that he only had 179 to go.

* * *

By the time they stopped for lunch, Micah was yawning and eyeing the hammock strung up in the backyard.

"Thomas expects you at one o'clock sharp, so you best hurry." His *daddi* nodded toward the sandwich on Micah's plate. "You can eat that on your walk over."

Micah started to protest but then realized he'd probably prefer eating alone. At least he wouldn't have to listen to his *daddi*'s plans for their work the next day. He was too tired to even consider more fieldwork, and the day wasn't half-over.

Why had he never listened to the stories of how severe his *daddi* was?

If he had, he wouldn't have agreed to this exile.

He tried to hold on to his bad mood, but the weather was fabulous, and he had over a dozen comments on his social media pages. He'd fetched the phone from the barn as soon as he'd left the kitchen. He paused at the fence line long enough to answer the comments and snap another picture to post.

It would probably be a bad idea to take the phone over to the bishop's. Thomas Beiler was no doubt even more strict than Micah's *daddi*.

He glanced around for a place to hide it, but all he could see was fence line and fields, so he shoved it into his back pocket. Fortunately, on his way to the bishop's shop, he spied Susannah coming out of a small building set next to the house.

He called out to her and then jogged to where she was waiting.

"Do me a favor?"

"Like what?"

She was holding a basketful of fabric scraps. He pulled the phone from his pocket, picked up the stack of fabric and dropped the phone, then covered it back up. "Keep that for me until I'm done working."

"Why would I do that?"

"So I won't get in trouble on my first day in your *dat*'s shop."

"If you knew you would get in trouble, why did you—"

"Thanks, Susannah. You're a peach."

Instead of smiling, she glared at him, which caused him to laugh.

"I don't see what's so funny."

"You are. You just don't know it." He turned and walked backward so that he could point at her. "You're going to be my new best friend."

"Oh, I doubt that."

"You'll see."

"Uh-huh."

"Just don't use up all my battery playing *Candy Crush*."

"What is…"

But he never heard the rest because he realized it was five minutes past one and he was late. No doubt the bishop would relay that to his *daddi* and he'd be given extra chores, or perhaps they'd deliver yet another lecture. He absolutely hated lectures. It was difficult to sit there and act respectful and pretend to listen. He just did not understand old people. Best to avoid such a confrontation, so he broke into a run.

He was surprised when Thomas greeted him with a smile and no rebuke. "I was happy to hear you'd be here for a few months. I can use the help."

"Don't know as I'll be that much help."

"Does your mind work?"

"Excuse me?"

Thomas tapped the side of his head. He was tall for an Amish man, probably close to six feet. His beard was peppered with gray, and crow's-feet stretched out from his eyes. He struck Micah as a man who smiled easily.

"Does your mind work? How did you do in school?"

"Oh, I did fine."

"Then the work won't be too hard for you to learn. It's difficult physically... I'll give you that. But anyone who is willing to learn the trade will always have a job."

"*Ya*, always plenty of horses when Amish are around," Micah joked.

"Exactly. Now, let's get to work on Widower King's buggy horse."

Micah had never considered that he'd be straddling the leg of a thousand-pound beast. He'd lived around horses all of his life, but feeding a horse or harnessing it to a buggy was one thing. Getting that horse to raise its foot so you could trim away its hoof was another.

"A horse's hooves are like our fingernails. They must be trimmed and exfoliated." Thomas proceeded to show him how to cut off the excess growth, then clean and check the hoof for overall health. "It's important that the horse trusts you. If you appear confident and act like you know what you're doing, the horse will relax."

"But I don't know what I'm doing."

"You will. Soon enough you will. See this triangle-shaped thing at the bottom of the hoof?"

"Sure."

"That's the frog. It acts as a shock absorber of sorts. We need to clean it up. Don't want any ragged ends."

"Why?"

"*Gut* question. We clean it so the dirt and muck is able to get out of the foot easier. Next we trim the hoof wall. Hand me the curved blade there on the shelf."

Micah quickly did as asked. When Thomas was finished, he used a hoof nipper to trim the outside of the hoof wall, and then a rasp to even out everything.

"I never realized there was so much detail to shoeing a horse."

"Few people do—they count on their farrier. Think of it as job security." Thomas looked up and smiled. "Now let's see what sized shoes we need."

Susannah was tempted to find an excuse to visit her *dat*'s shop. How was Micah doing? And did he know anything about trimming hooves or shoeing horses? She knew firsthand that what her *dat* did was hard work. She'd sat in his workshop often enough and even helped him occasionally. She loved being around the animals whether they were buggy horses or workhorses.

It took her an hour to separate her fabric scraps by size and color. It was amazing what could be salvaged from one project to use in another. The process soothed her until she picked up the last piece of fabric and spied Micah's phone in the basket. Why did he have such a thing? How much did he pay for it? And who did he stay in touch with?

Other Amish rebels?

Someone in his family who had left the faith?

Or maybe an *Englisch* girlfriend?

She dropped the phone into her apron pocket. It didn't matter to her what Micah did with his phone, and she would set him straight that it wasn't her place to keep him out of trouble. She didn't think he was going to fit into their community very well. She didn't think he even wanted to.

There's a real possibility that what Micah needs most is not a girlfriend but simply a friend...

Remembering her *mamm*'s words caused her to feel a twinge of guilt. Perhaps he had a good reason for having the phone, though she couldn't imagine what that might be.

She didn't have to wait long to find out.

She was pulling laundry off the line while Shiloh and Sharon played on the trampoline when Micah came walking around the corner of the house.

He headed straight to the water hose and preceded to roll up his sleeves and wash his hands and arms. He even swiped some of the water on his neck, wetting the hair that curled there, and then he doused his face.

"We have indoor bathrooms."

"I like washing up with a water hose."

Susannah handed him a clean hand towel.

"Danki."

"Gem gschehne."

He rubbed his face dry, then his arms, and finally remembered that water was dripping down his neck. When he was finished, he held up the towel and asked, "Where should I—"

"I'll take it."

"Do you need help with the laundry?"

She inclined her head toward the empty clothesline.

"I could help fold."

"Do you know how to fold clothes?"

"How hard can it be?" He peeked into her basket. "Oh. Looks like you've already folded everything."

"It's easier to do while you pull the items off the line."

"I knew that."

"Sure you did." She moved closer to the trampoline so she could keep an eye on the girls.

Micah followed and plopped down on the grass. For reasons she couldn't quite fathom, she did the same. It wasn't that she was interested in Micah, but she was curious as to what made him tick. How did he become so unorthodox? And why? What was the point of rebelling against their conventions?

"Actually, I know nothing about housework." He picked up their conversation as if there hadn't been a long, awkward silence. "I'm the baby of the family."

"Is that so?"

"Seven older *schweschdern*."

"What was that like?"

"I loved it, but apparently…according to my *daddi*, I was spoiled and it's time for me to grow up and become a man."

"Ouch."

"Yeah. Hence my exile here in Goshen for six months."

"When you say it that way, it sounds like a long time."

"It is a long time—a lifetime practically." Micah leaned forward and lowered his voice. "Not sure I'm going to make it if every day is like today."

"Why's that?"

"It's all so…grim."

The sun was setting in a beautiful splash of color, the horses were pastured in the field, Sharon and Shiloh played happily a few feet from her, and dinner was nearly done. "I don't understand."

"What?"

"Grim. How can you call this…" She took an exaggerated gaze around them. "How can you call it grim?"

"The work is endless."

"You didn't enjoy helping *Dat*?"

"Actually, that part was rather interesting."

"But…"

"But I'd already spent five hours in the field. I've done nothing but work all day. And tomorrow will be the same. It's just so…boring."

She fought the urge to defend their lifestyle, even their farm. So what if he didn't like it? Why should she care what Micah Fisher did and didn't like?

"If excitement is what you want, then *ya*, I agree that Goshen isn't the place for you."

"I knew you'd understand."

"And the work is endless because it's a farm. That's pretty much the definition of farmwork."

"I do not see the point."

Susannah didn't know what to say to that, so she asked, "How did it go working with *the horses*?"

"Better than I thought it would be. I only got kicked once."

"Once usually does the trick."

"You've helped your *dat* shoe horses?"

"Of course."

"Not exactly girl's work."

"So now you're a traditionalist?" She reached into

her apron pocket, retrieved his phone and dropped it into his hand. "Except for that…"

"Have you ever owned a phone?"

"Nein."

"Did you play around on mine?"

"Of course not."

"It's not going to burn your fingers, you know."

"And yet it's forbidden."

"It's discouraged. There's a difference." He winked at her.

She refused to let his charm muddle her thoughts. "Does that usually work?"

"What?"

"Winking at girls."

"Not sure I wanted it to work. I was just being… friendly."

"Ah."

He stuffed the phone in his pocket and said, *"Ah,* what?"

"That's what people who flirt say…that they were just being friendly."

"So you think I was flirting with you?"

Susannah almost laughed, but she didn't want to encourage his silliness. The twins continued to jump on the trampoline, giggling and calling out to one another.

"Watch me, Susannah. I can flip." Sharon jumped and then fell onto her back. "Did I do it?"

"You didn't do it," Shiloh said.

"I did, too. Tell her, Susannah. Tell her I did."

"Almost. Keep practicing."

Micah flopped onto his back, staring up at the sky. "Your *dat* isn't what I expected."

"How so?"

"Well, he's a bishop."

"Ya."

"I thought he'd be more conservative."

"Don't tell me he was watching TV again while shoeing the horses."

Micah propped himself up on his elbows, then smiled at the twins, who were trying to get his attention. "I mean he seems rather open-minded. He asked all about our community in Maine, which many of the old folks don't even want to know about. They think it's much too progressive."

"Is it?"

"I don't think so. Plus, look at this place." He waved at the backyard. "Trampoline for the kids."

"They need somewhere to play."

"A new little modular house."

"That's my sewing shop, where I quilt."

"I wondered what all those pieces of material were for."

"They're scraps and they're for sewing."

"Do you have an electric sewing machine in there?"

"I do not." Her cheeks warmed, not because he was teasing her but because of the way he was looking at her. She stood and picked up her laundry basket. "Dinner will be ready in a few minutes. I assume you're staying."

"I wouldn't miss it."

Sharon jumped closer to the edge of the trampoline and held onto the netting, which prevented her from falling out. "Come and jump with us, Susannah."

"Yeah, come and jump." Shiloh was actually sitting on the trampoline, not jumping. She was careful even there, as if the thing might throw her onto the ground.

"It's time to help with dinner. Come on inside."

"Just five more minutes...please."

It always made her smile how their voices could become one when they wanted something. Usually Sharon and Shiloh seemed like complete opposites, but when they joined together, they reminded her of two halves of the same whole.

"I have to go in, and you know *Mamm* doesn't like you out here alone."

"I'll stay with them," Micah said. "Unless you need me to help cook."

"Have you ever cooked before?"

"Nein."

"Then no—we don't need your help."

"I'll just stay here, then. I promise to keep an eye on them."

Actually, he did better than that. By the time she'd climbed the porch steps and looked back, Micah had removed his shoes and was pulling himself up onto the trampoline.

Not that he could ingratiate himself to her by playing with the girls. His comments had bordered on rude—first calling them progressive and then boring. Or, had it been the other way around? Regardless, he obviously didn't like it here and she didn't think he'd last even a week.

Which was absolutely fine with her.

The longer he stayed, the higher the risk he would be a bad influence on someone in their community. The last thing her friends needed was an Amish bad boy complete with long hair, *Englisch* phone, ball cap and blue jeans. Though he had been wearing more traditional clothes today. Where had those come from? Were they stuffed in his backpack?

Not her business.

She guessed he'd probably grow up eventually, but she didn't think it would be today or tomorrow or anytime in the near future.

That boy was trouble with a crooked smile.

The sooner Micah Fisher was out of their lives, the better. If he needed a friend, he could find one back home in Maine.

Chapter Three

By the time Sunday rolled around, Susannah's feelings regarding Micah had grown even more complicated. He'd shown up the second day with a fresh haircut but the same born-to-be-wild attitude. Her *dat* was happy with his work, but Susannah was growing increasingly uneasy around him. Micah reminded her of a wild horse temporarily corralled. It was only a matter of time before he broke out and then his grandparents would be heartbroken and her *dat* would be in need of another helper.

She spent much of the service praying that God would forgive her uncharitable feelings and clear the confusion in her mind. Since her *dat* was the bishop, she was aware that she was scrutinized more closely than others.

So even as her mind wandered toward Micah, she kept her attention on the person preaching.

When it was time to pray, she closed her eyes and petitioned her heavenly Father for clarity.

When it was time to sing, she stood and raised her voice with the others around her.

And as soon as the service ended, she hurried toward the serving area, not pausing to give their new neighbor a second glance. She worked at filling cups with water and lemonade. When she saw Micah walking toward her, she quickly changed tables to help with salads. It wasn't that she was avoiding him, but he would simply want to tell her more about Maine, a subject she'd heard quite enough about. When she finally had a few free moments, she snagged Deborah.

"Care to walk out into the pasture?"

"I can think of nothing I'd rather do." Deborah jumped up from her seat and grabbed her sweater from the big bag she carried around. Deborah was the only Amish person Susannah knew who carried what amounted to a baby bag though she had no baby. It was sometimes quite amazing what Deborah could pull out of that bag.

"Tell me about Micah," Deborah said as soon as they were out of earshot of the others.

"What's to tell?"

"Does he seem to be behaving himself?"

"*Dat* hasn't complained."

"I'm not surprised. Your father is the bishop. Of course Micah would be on his best behavior around him."

"*Ya*, I suppose."

"Betty heard that Micah had an alcohol problem when he was living in Maine. That's why his parents sent him here."

"Alcohol?"

"Or maybe it was drugs… She wasn't really sure."

Susannah sighed and pressed her lips together.

"You might as well say it," Deborah teased.

"Then I would be as bad as Betty."

"Oh. So you don't want to be a gossip, which you would be if you pointed out that Betty is a gossip."

That was such a convoluted statement that it made Susannah laugh, which helped her relax a little. "I guess I was thinking that Betty has been somewhat bitter since Joshua left the faith."

"And left her for an *Englisch* girl. I saw them in South Bend the other day."

"At the college?"

"*Ya.* They looked…um…close. Arms wrapped around each other. Kissing in public." Deborah made a wide-eyed, somewhat disgusted expression.

"Your *dat* is still consulting at the college?"

"He is. Their agriculture students want to know all about our Plain and simple ways."

Which caused them both to laugh.

"Perhaps they should come help in the fields—then they'd really understand."

"They're actually going to do that sometime in the next few weeks."

"Seriously?"

"Uh-huh."

"You're going to have *Englischers* traipsing around in your fields?"

"We are."

"Maybe we should send Micah over. He seems to speak their language."

They'd made it to the corner of the property where Mose King had made a bench out of a felled tree. After checking that there were no critters hiding beneath it, they both sat down and studied the scene in front of them.

Most of the women and a good number of the men were spread out in chairs under the trees.

Boys of all ages were playing baseball, with a few of the men standing on the edge of the ball field, providing sideline advice.

The younger children were in a play area that Mose had made for his own children. It looked like a school playground. There was a seesaw, a swing set and even a sandbox that he kept covered with a tarp when it wasn't being used.

Susannah thought that playground was a sign of something—thoughtfulness, adoration, maybe devotion. "*Mamm* thinks Mose would make a *gut* husband."

"I'm sure he would…for someone his own age."

"*Ya*, my sentiments exactly."

"That's another thing I heard about Micah. He was apparently dating an older woman—who he dumped, and according to the grapevine, that wasn't the first relationship that he broke off for no reason."

"There's always a reason."

"I suppose."

"It's kind of sad that we're so interested in everything he did wrong there."

"Are you defending him?"

"Not at all. It's only that… Well, *Mamm* reminded me that everyone deserves a fresh start. Don't they?"

Deborah pulled her skirt up an inch or so and proceeded to pull stickers from her socks. "I guess. The only thing is that I'd rather these people who need a fresh start get it somewhere else."

Which pretty accurately mirrored Susannah's thoughts, though somehow, spoken out loud, they sounded rather judgmental and unfair.

"What do you mean?"

"I guess I was thinking that what Micah Fisher does in Maine is his own business, but what he does here… Well, here he stands to hurt other people with his actions."

"Meaning what?"

Deborah shrugged and pretended to look for something in her purse. Susannah put her hand on top of the bag and left it there until her friend looked up.

"What aren't you telling me?"

"Apparently Micah sneaked out of his house on Friday night and met up with Caroline Byers."

"I have trouble believing that's true. He's been here less than a week. How could he—"

"I heard it from Caroline herself. She said it was harmless. Said they just happened to be downtown at the same time to hear a local band, but Betty heard them talk about meeting up again on Thursday."

Susannah had at least a dozen questions, but none of them really mattered. Most of them were none of her business. She settled for asking, "Her parents let her do that?"

"*Nein*. She sneaked out. Are you even paying attention?"

"I am now." Susannah jumped up, crossed her arms and paced back and forth in front of Deborah. "Caroline is young and impressionable. I can see how she'd fall for someone like Micah in a second, but I'm not sure that's a *gut* idea."

"Finally."

"Finally what?"

"Finally you're paying attention and concerned. I

mean, the guy practically lives at your house. Maybe you could say something to him."

"I'm not sure that I could, or even that I *should.*"

Deborah began to fiddle with her *kapp* strings, something she only did when she was holding back.

"What else?"

"Well…one of the boys claimed they saw him smoking."

"He doesn't smell like smoke, and I should know… He's eaten with us three times now."

"There was also talk of his carrying a flask in the back pocket of those blue jeans and…you know…taking a sip now and again."

Susannah flopped back down beside Deborah. "I don't know if I'm more aggravated about the gossip—"

"Unless it's true."

"—or Micah's behavior."

That sat between them a few minutes until Susannah realized they needed to start back to help put out a snack for the children. It was nearly three in the afternoon and some of them would be going down for a nap soon.

They were halfway toward the main group when Deborah asked, "Are you going to talk to your *dat*?"

"*Nein.* He wouldn't want to hear about it unless it was something I saw myself. He has no patience for gossip." She turned abruptly so that Deborah nearly bumped into her. "If anyone else talks to you about Micah, about his behavior, you tell them to come to my *dat* directly. *Dat* will speak to him, but only if the report is a firsthand account."

"Okay. I should have done that to begin with. I guess I was a bit stunned by it all."

"Understandable, but now that we know about his reputation we need to take steps to protect our *freinden*."

"What kind of steps?"

"Well, I can keep a closer eye on him when he's at our farm. I can certainly watch for the smoking and drinking."

"I doubt that he's likely to do either of those things around your *dat*."

"But there would be signs, and I just don't..." She looked toward the picnic tables, where she should be helping. Instead, she tugged on Deborah's arm and pulled her in the opposite direction. "It's just that I don't want him to be unfairly judged. He seems like a *gut* guy, just a bit lost."

"Reminds me of my *bruder* when he was on his *rumspringa*."

"Exactly."

"Only Elias was seventeen at the time."

"And Micah is twenty-five."

A shout rose up from the baseball field, where none other than Micah had apparently hit a home run and was jogging around the bases to the cheers of all watching.

Susannah pinched the bridge of her nose and squeezed her eyes shut. After taking a deep breath and letting it slowly out, she tried to shake off the feeling of trepidation. It was a beautiful Sunday afternoon, and so far at least, Micah had done nothing against their *Ordnung*—at least nothing she'd witnessed.

"We'll give him a fair chance but keep our eyes on him."

"Sounds reasonable." Deborah nodded so hard that her *kapp* strings bounced.

"And above all else, we'll make sure that he doesn't set his ball cap at any of the girls in our group."

"Like Betty."

"Or Caroline or any of the other girls we've grown up with. The ones who aren't married… Well, some of them are too quick to fall in with a guy."

"Their biological clocks are going ticktock."

"Exactly."

Deborah tucked her arm through Susannah's. "The good part is that he's not planning on staying, from what I've heard."

"He said as much to me, as well. Hopefully he can serve his time at his *daddi*'s and then go home to break hearts."

"*Gut* idea. We don't need any of that sort of drama around here."

Which echoed what Susannah had been thinking. Personally, she'd experienced enough tragedy in the last few years with her cancer diagnosis, treatment and the breakup with Samuel. She knew firsthand what it was like to have your dreams ripped away, to have your heart shredded to the point that it felt raw. If she had anything to do with it, that would not be happening to her friends. Even if it meant she had to take matters into her own hands.

The following Thursday, Micah had finished shoeing a dappled gray mare under the watchful gaze of Thomas. Then the bishop had been called off to visit with one of the old-timers who had taken a turn for the worse, and before Micah knew it, he was being babysat by Susannah.

"I can take the man's money and put it in the box."

"What man?"

"The man who owns the mare."

"Yes, but you don't even know the man's name. Mr. Hochstettler has been bringing his horses here since I was a *kind. Dat* likes for our customers to have personal service."

"They're Amish. Where else are they going to go to have their horses cared for?"

"Not the point, according to *Dat*. The point is that we treat every customer as if we value their business—which we do."

"Fine. I didn't remember the man's name, but you could tell me that and leave."

"Do you know the mare's name?"

"*Nein* and what difference does that make? Are you going to tell me that the mare needs to feel valued, too?"

"Of course she needs to be valued. Have you ever owned a mare?"

"Never needed to. I had my parents' buggy horses to use in Maine, and I have my grandparents' here."

"But one day you'll be a man with your own family and your own horses." Susannah had been grooming the mare, which definitely did not fall under the services of shoeing a horse in Micah's opinion. She stopped what she was doing and pointed the brush at him. "When you have your own horses, you'll understand why it's important to appreciate them and treat them with respect."

Micah rolled his eyes and then started laughing. He couldn't help it.

"What?"

"Nothing."

"Just say it."

"You couldn't even see over that horse if you weren't standing on a crate, and yet you're lecturing me."

"What does being short have to do with anything?"

Micah raised his hands in surrender, but he continued to laugh. Most days Susannah aggravated him, especially when she reminded him of his nagging sisters. But then, other times, he caught a glint of mischievousness in her eyes, and he wondered what else was going on underneath her perfectly starched *kapp*.

"Say, I'm thinking about asking Caroline Byers to this weekend's spring festival in town. What do you think?"

"Terrible idea." Susannah resumed brushing the mare, but much more vigorously.

"Why's it terrible?"

Now her lips were forming a tight, straight line, as if they'd been glued together. He knew that expression well enough.

"Just say it. What's the problem?"

"She's too young for you, that's what!" Susannah brushed the mare so vigorously that it turned its large muzzle toward her. "Sorry, Smokey."

"Smokey?"

"That's her name. If you'd bothered to find out, you would know that."

"You seem awfully cranky all of a sudden."

"I'm not cranky!" She jumped off the crate, cleaned the horse brush with a metal tool and slammed it onto the tool shelf. Next she picked up the currying comb, which looked somewhat dangerous the way she was brandishing it in his direction. "Pick a girl your age, Micah."

"Wow. Okay. Well, I hadn't thought of it that way, but I guess I see your point. How about Betty Gleich?"

Susannah closed her eyes as if praying for patience and shook her head so hard he feared her *kapp* would pop off.

"What's wrong with Betty? I know for a fact she's over twenty-one."

"She's twenty-two, and she just went through a rather rough breakup."

"What does that have to do with me?"

"Did you not say only twenty minutes ago that you only had—and I quote—one hundred and seventy days left in this awful place?"

"Sounds like something I might have said."

"Obviously you hate it here."

"You don't understand. If you'd been to Maine, then you'd appreciate how much more beautiful it is than your much-loved Indiana. If you could experience the hunting, the fishing, the wildness of the place. It's just—"

"You'd be in your precious Maine right this minute if you hadn't been banished."

"Ouch."

"Again—your word, not mine."

"Fine." He named off four other perfectly eligible girls, all of whom Susannah disapproved of him dating for the most ridiculous reasons and sometimes for no reason she'd share at all.

His mounting frustration was threatening to get the better of him. He tried to mentally order himself to calm down, but the way Susannah was frowning at him was not helping matters. "What is your problem?"

"My problem?"

"You know, I don't need your permission to date someone, but now I'm curious. What's your beef?"

"Beef?"

"Apparently I'm not *gut* enough for any of the gals in your district."

"It's not a question of whether you're *gut* enough for them."

"Then what?"

"You're leaving, that's what. You're leaving, and they'll get attached to you, and then it will hurt them when you go."

"I'm not proposing to them, Susannah. I'm asking them out on a buggy ride."

"One thing leads to the other."

Micah threw up his hands and walked out of the far-rier shop. The sky was dark and brooding, a perfect reflection of his mood. Well, Susannah Beiler was not the boss of him. He could ask out whomever he liked.

He stomped back in to tell her that and caught her with her cheek pressed against the mare, a look of utter desolation in her eyes. Now he felt like a heel, and he didn't even know what he'd done.

"Hey…it's not that bad."

She stood up straighter, gave the mare one last pat and returned the crate to its place along the wall.

"You can't expect a guy to hang around for six months and not go on a single date. Surely you can see that."

"Why?"

"Why? Because it's not natural."

"There's nothing wrong with being alone, Micah."

"Maybe not for you, but I haven't decided I want to be single the rest of my life—apparently you have."

"This discussion isn't about me."

Now her chin rose as if she needed to defend herself—oh, the many faces of Susannah Beiler. If she ever came down from her high horse, she might be an interesting person to get to know.

"Look, I'm sorry." He yanked off his hat and stared at it—a straw Amish hat. Why couldn't he wear his ball cap? Glancing up, he realized Susannah was waiting. He forced himself to refocus on the problem at hand. "I didn't mean to offend you, but you're so…"

"What?"

"Serious. You're so serious, and life is just waiting for us to enjoy it." In three long strides, he was at her side. Grasping her by the shoulders, he marched her toward the open barn door. "See that? The clouds and the rain and the turbulence?"

"I see it."

"But behind all of that are more things that we can't begin to imagine—sunshine and new experiences and memories waiting to be made. Life is out there, Susannah. We're supposed to be living it."

"And you can't do that without dragging some poor girl along with you?"

"Why should I?"

Susannah rubbed at her forehead as if she'd quite suddenly been slapped with the worst headache imaginable. Finally, she pulled in a deep breath and turned to stare up into his face.

"Then take me."

"Huh?"

"If you must take someone on these jaunts around our little town, take me."

"But…you don't even like me."

"That's beside the point."

"No, I think that is the point."

"You're not looking for love, Micah. We both know that. You're looking for a buddy to pal around with, and there are plenty of men your age in our district."

"All paired up. I've already tried that route."

"Then take me, like I said."

"You're going to pal around with me? Miss Susannah Beiler, who does everything by the book? That should be a load of fun."

"I do not do everything by the book."

"You cleaned the horse brush before putting it on the shelf. Who does that?"

"You're changing the subject. Is it a deal or not?"

"A deal?"

"I go with you to enjoy life, and you leave the girls in my district alone."

"Wow. There's a proposal that is hard to turn down."

"So it's a deal."

She held out her hand, which reminded him of meeting her out on the lane, offering his hand and her refusing it. He couldn't help laughing as he clasped her small hand in his large one.

"Fine. It's a deal, but you're going to regret it."

"I have no doubt that is true." And then she turned and strode toward the house.

"I thought you needed to be here when Mr. Hochstettler came by," he called out to her.

Rather than bothering to answer, she simply gave him a backward wave.

So, he was going to date the bishop's daughter.

Or rather, *not* date her.

It would be like having a chaperone along every

time he went to town. He kicked the door of the barn, startling the mare.

"Easy, Smokey. It's just me, doing a stupid thing to top off another stupid thing."

One hundred and seventy days.

Somehow, that seemed like an even longer stretch of time than it had an hour ago.

Chapter Four

Susannah went with Micah to hear a music duo on Friday. She had to resist the urge to remind him that they were Amish and their *Ordnung* strongly discouraged listening to worldly music. But she didn't have to point that out. Micah taunted her with it as soon as they were in the buggy and driving away from her parents' farm.

"Guess your *mamm* and *dat* didn't want you to go tonight."

"Why would you say that?"

"First of all, because it's with me."

"For reasons I can't fathom, my parents have taken a real liking to you."

"Huh." He looked pleased for a brief moment, but then he slouched his shoulders and rammed his hat down on his head. "Wish I could say the same for my *daddi*."

"I'm sure your *daddi* likes you."

"*Nein*. He might love me. He's supposed to love me, but like me? I'm pretty sure that isn't the case."

"Why would you say that?"

"A guy can tell."

"Give me an example."

"Okay." He pulled the buggy out onto the main road, then glanced at her and smiled, as if he was sure he could prove his point—even though his point was that his own *daddi* didn't like him. "I asked him to go fishing, and he said no."

"Maybe he was tired."

"I asked him to play checkers, and he said no."

"Maybe he's not good at checkers and hates losing."

"I even asked him if he'd like to walk outside with me and see an owl's nest that I found."

"Maybe he doesn't like owls."

Micah laughed, stretched like a cat and looked immensely proud of himself. "Enough about my problems, but admit that your parents did not like the idea of your going to an *Englisch* concert."

Susannah shrugged and refused to make eye contact.

"Oh, my gosh. You never had a *rumspringa*!"

She shook her head and closed her eyes. He really was incorrigible. She wasn't about to explain that she'd been going through her cancer diagnosis and treatment when her friends were enjoying their running-around time.

"I hit the nail on the head. I knew they didn't approve of your going to hear Jason Wright and the Red River Posse band."

"What does that even mean? Red River Posse?"

"Well, a posse is a group of individuals who are sort of deputized. You know, they help out the sheriff."

"And Red River?"

"In Texas."

"And Jason Wright?"

"I think it's a play on the word *right*, like being right, not wrong."

"Ridiculous."

"Uh-huh." Now he did looked pleased. "Just as I thought. You're going to hate it."

"I might not hate it. I happen to like music."

"You do?"

"Sure. I've been known to hum a melody as I sew."

"What kind of melody?"

"Uh...the only kind I know. Songs from church." She rushed on when he gave her an I-told-you-so look. "That's not the point. Did you specifically pick this to do tonight because you thought I'd hate it? Are you trying to—" she waved a hand at the passing roadside "—ditch me?"

"Oh, no. You're not getting out of this that easily by saying that I'm trying to ditch you. Uh-uh. I'm not ditching anyone. I'm glad that the bishop's daughter is having a night out on the town. Besides, you're my only option if I'm not allowed to date anyone else."

"I'm not the boss of you, Micah."

"Exactly. But you know how to put the pressure on, just like a woman."

"Oh, good grief."

"So if I'm being pressured not to date other girls in your community, then you have to stick to our deal."

"Fine by me."

They rode in silence for a minute, but then Micah returned to his original question. "So, were your parents upset...about where we were going?"

"*Nein*. I'm a grown woman. I can go wherever I want."

"But you've already joined the church."

"Which doesn't mean I can't enjoy an evening in the park."

"Uh-huh."

"If a band happens to be playing, there's no rule that says I have to cover my ears."

"I see."

"It's not like I have a radio hidden away in my sewing room."

"Already I'm corrupting you."

She slapped his arm, but in truth it was a relief to get away from the farm for an evening. It had been a long time since she'd done something that didn't involve her family or her girlfriends or her sewing. She loved all those things, but it felt good to do something different. Maybe Micah was a bad influence or maybe he could be for some people, but she would be more careful than that. She had decided not to worry about anything this evening.

She actually had fun at the park. There were booths set up where people were selling homemade items like jewelry and T-shirts and even ball caps. Micah put one over her *kapp* that was pink and had the word *Princess* spelled out in glitter. Susannah told the woman it was beautiful and carefully placed it back on the table.

The local pizzeria had a booth where they were selling giant slices, but Micah insisted on buying a large pizza. Susannah couldn't remember the last time she'd eaten two slices of pizza, but when Micah dared her to eat another piece she actually found she was still hungry. Maybe it was from all the walking around they'd done.

And the music wasn't so bad. They saw a few other Amish families enjoying the fine May evening, though none were actually sitting up front listening to the band like they were. She waved each time she saw someone from their district.

"What's wrong?" Micah nudged his shoulder against hers. "I rather liked that song. It was all about bull riding, which I saw once in Maine. Maybe you'd prefer love songs."

"Oh, it's not that. I waved at the Kings."

"Mose King? Isn't he the one you told me was a widower? The guy your *mamm* wants you to marry? Point him out to me. I want to see if he has hair sprouting out of his ears and uses a cane."

She slapped his arm. "Not Mose, his brother and sister-in-law—Frank and Ida. I waved when they looked toward us, but they turned away as if they didn't see me."

"They probably didn't see you." Micah nodded his head to the left and right. "Lots of people here."

"I guess you're right."

He pulled back and widened his eyes in mock surprise. "Excuse me? Could you say that again?"

Which made her laugh, and then she stopped worrying about the Kings.

Susannah helped her mother clean their house the next day. Since it wasn't a church weekend, they were having dinner for their closest neighbors—which would include Micah and his grandparents.

"I'm interested to see how they react around him," she confessed to her mother as she dumped the pail of dirty water on the flower beds.

"What do you mean?"

"Well, according to Micah, his *mammi* is strict but kind."

"Abigail is a *gut* woman."

"But his *daddi* is beyond strict. Micah says he doesn't think his *daddi* cares for him very much."

"Why would he say such a thing?"

Susannah shrugged, then plopped down beside her mother in the porch swing. The twins were playing with a set of jacks on the far side of the porch. The sight of their heads nearly touching as they leaned over the jacks and ball made Susannah extremely happy. Was it just two years ago that she was worried she wouldn't see them grow up to be young girls? Yet, here they were. She was thankful for that, for every day she had with her family.

"Where'd you go?" her *mamm* asked softly.

"Just thinking about how grateful I am to still be alive."

"I thank the Lord for that very thing every day when I rise and every evening when I go to sleep. It's a frightening experience to almost lose a child."

Susannah cornered herself in the swing so she could study her mother. "I guess it's easy for me to forget how hard that time was on you."

"That's the thing… When tragedy is in our past we do forget about it, but it changes us, Susannah. Just like you are a more serious young woman—a more grateful and mature one—because of your illness. I'm changed, too, as is your *dat*. We realize more than we ever did before how precious each day is."

They pushed the swing for a while as the girls' laughter spilled toward them. Susannah's mind drifted back toward Micah and his grandfather. As if sensing the turn in her thoughts, her *mamm* stood up and brushed dirt off her apron. "John Fisher loves Micah.

I have no doubt about that. I didn't know him before the accident…"

"The one where he lost his arm?"

"*Ya*. I didn't know him then, but I imagine it changed him just as your experience with cancer changed you. We can never know how a person's path through this life twists and turns. We only know where they are right now. But John? Well, it's been hard for him."

"Because of his disability."

"That and probably how strangers look at him—no one wants to be pitied."

"I hated when people looked at me that way—when I was going through the worst of the chemo."

"John has endured those looks all of his life. People mean well, but sometimes they allow your disability to define you, and none of us want that." She reached for Susannah's hand and pulled her off the swing. As they walked inside to prepare lunch, she added a final comment on the subject. "John does love Micah. Abigail has shared with me that they are both worried about the boy, and John intends to do his best by him. Sometimes that's not an easy thing."

That evening Micah took her moonlight fishing. As they walked across the back fields to the pond, Susannah felt as light as one of the swallows darting through the last of the sunset. She realized in that moment that she felt happy, really happy for the first time in a long time. Glancing at Micah, she wondered if that had anything to do with him.

But that thought was ridiculous.

It wasn't Micah that was changing the way she looked at things.

But it could be that doing things she wasn't used

to—going to the park and listening to bands and fishing in the moonlight—was pulling her out of a lingering depression that had started when she'd first been diagnosed.

"Tell me you're not thinking of changing your mind." Micah shifted the backpack across his shoulders. "I even brought *Mammi*'s cookies and coffee."

"I'm not going to change my mind, but I don't believe we'll catch anything. You can't fish by moonlight."

"Can, too."

"How do you know if you've caught anything?"

Micah reached into his pocket and pulled something out. As he shook his closed fist, she heard a jingle sound.

"Bells?"

"Yup. Small ones." He was carrying two fishing poles, and he waved them in front of him. "Plus, I rigged these up with fluorescent line."

"Now, that was a waste of money."

"You won't think so when we catch a lot of fish."

They didn't catch a lot of fish, but somehow that didn't matter too much to Susannah. Sitting on the dock in the moonlight, she thought that she hadn't ever seen a more beautiful evening. The moonlight resembled the soft glow from a lantern. If she focused, she could just make out the fishing line stretched out from Micah's poles. He'd attached the bells on the end, and each time they rang she laughed.

"You're scaring off the fish."

"I'm sorry, but I've never fished with a bell before."

"Have you ever fished before?"

"Some." She almost said "before my cancer," but

then she realized she hadn't told him about that part of her life. Did he know? Had someone else told him? Maybe not. Maybe that was why she liked being around him. Micah didn't treat her as if she might break.

A few minutes earlier she'd thought he was going to make good on his threat to push her into the water. He'd only stopped when she'd grabbed one of the poles and said she'd take it with her. She enjoyed people treating her like a normal person. Maybe that was what she'd been missing.

"Oatmeal cookie for your thoughts?" He held up a cookie, and when she reached for it, he moved it out of her reach. "Uh-uh, you have to tell me what you were thinking about first."

"Right. Okay. Well, I was thinking about something my *mamm* said, that hard times change a person."

"Ya?" He handed her the cookie and then scooted the thermos of decaf coffee closer to her. "What kind of hard times?"

"I guess it could be anything, but the point is that you're not the same afterward. Maybe you start out carefree and end up serious. Or maybe you start out sure of everything, every turn your life is going to take. Like you have it all planned out. You know?"

"I've never planned much," Micah admitted.

"Say you did, and then something happened to change everything."

"Everything?"

"Ya."

"Huh. I guess that would make me more cautious." He reeled in a little of the fishing line, then asked, "Is that what happened to you? Is that why you're such a rule follower?"

"I'm not a very good rule follower. I went to a concert with you last night."

"And it didn't corrupt you a bit."

"True, but I need to be careful, or I might start singing about pickup trucks and mud on my boots."

She picked up one of her flip-flop sandals, waved it at him and then sat it back down. "Imagine that—an Amish woman in cowgirl boots."

Micah picked up the other shoe and studied it. "This looks nothing like a boot. Maybe if I threw it into the water, it would change and become a boot."

"Give me that shoe back."

But Micah had already jumped up and was holding the flip-flop over his head. "This? You want this?"

"Micah, don't you dare…"

"Sounds like you're issuing an ultimatum."

"I need that shoe to walk back to the house. You don't want me walking barefoot through the fields."

"It's good for a person to walk barefoot. Helps you to feel connected to *Gotte*'s green earth."

Susannah was standing on her tiptoes, trying to wrestle the shoe from his hands, and Micah was moving backward to avoid her, a big dopey grin on his face. Then he took one too many steps backward at the exact moment that she rested a hand on his chest so she could keep her balance and reach up higher with the other hand. His eyes found hers just before they splashed into the water.

She came up sputtering, shocked that she was now thoroughly wet. Then she heard something that was becoming quite familiar to her—Micah's laughter.

He pointed at her head. "You have moss on top of your *kapp*."

"Oh, so you think that's funny. Is that why you're laughing?" She reached down into the water, grabbed a fistful of the slimy green stuff, then lurched toward him and tossed it on top of his head. After that, it was rather a free-for-all of water splashing and moss throwing.

Micah was the one who noticed that her flip-flop had drifted toward the middle of the pond. He swam out to it with sure, easy strokes. She waited near the dock in the moonlight, standing in water up to her waist and wondered where he'd learned to swim like that. His shadow in the moonlight reminded her of a large fish cutting through the water.

It occurred to her that Micah was a nice guy and a good-hearted man. He was certainly not difficult to look at. That thought caused her cheeks to burn with embarrassment, and she was grateful for the darkness. He wasn't interested in her, and she certainly wasn't interested in him—not that way. They were just hanging out together, helping him through a tough time until he was able to return home. She'd do well to keep that thought front and center.

When he returned and presented her with the shoe, she grabbed it from him with what she hoped was a curt "I'm going to get even for this."

Walking out of the water, she paused at the edge to put her shoes on her feet and squeeze water from her dress. She didn't realize he was behind her until he spoke—his mouth close to her ear and his words a mere whisper that sent goose bumps down her arms. "You look awfully pretty in the moonlight, Susannah Beiler."

Which set off every emotional alarm she possessed.

Was he flirting with her?

Did he think she had been flirting with him?

What was she doing standing in the moonlight with Micah Fisher? She was supposed to be keeping an eye on him—keeping him out of trouble.

Before she could work any of that out, Micah said, "Let me gather up our stuff. Then we can walk back by the road. It'll give our clothes time to dry off a bit."

The route would be longer, but Susannah found she didn't mind.

A small part of her wished the night could go on and on.

Micah whistled through his Sunday morning chores, maybe because he knew they were going over to the Beilers for lunch. There was something about Susannah that intrigued him. It wasn't that he was falling for her—she was much too serious to be his type—but she was easy to be around.

And she was a challenge.

He was honest enough to admit that he loved a good challenge.

The morning devotion time with his grandparents was a bit trying. His *daddi* had an obvious focus in mind. They began in the book of Psalms, reading how *Gotte* would establish the work of their hands—whatever that meant. Then moved to Proverbs, where they spent a good twenty minutes on a verse about sluggards and how such persons were doomed to an unsuccessful life. Finally, they ended up in Colossians, where Paul wrote that whatever they did they should do with all their heart.

Micah tried to stay focused.

He didn't fidget or peek at the clock in the kitchen even once.

But he did feel resentment building in his soul. Did he not work hard every single day? What did his grandfather want from him? And why had his parents banished him to Indiana when it was obvious that he belonged in Maine?

By the time they'd finished the final prayer, Micah was feeling agitated and needing to burn off some steam. He felt like he could hit a baseball a hundred times and still have energy to spare.

"We'll be driving the buggy over to the Beilers' place." His *mammi* had followed him into the mudroom, where he'd grabbed his hat and jammed it on his head.

"*Danki, Mammi*, but I'll walk."

He didn't wait for an answer.

He didn't bother to explain.

He needed out of there and away from their disapproving stares.

Being outside in the sunshine helped. He wasn't normally a morose person. Sometimes, though, he felt backed into a corner. For the life of him, he could not understand what people wanted from him, what they expected. He chewed on those thoughts for the first half of his walk, but as soon as Susannah's little sewing shop came into view, his mood improved.

Last night had been fun.

He'd almost kissed her just to see what it would be like.

But the way her eyes had widened... Well, it had caused him to pat her awkwardly on the arm and walk away.

Had Susannah never been kissed?

Why wasn't she dating?

She was a smart girl with a pleasant personality. She apparently was a very good quilter, as there were often people stopping at her little shop to purchase quilts. She was patient with her sisters, and she was pretty to boot.

Why wasn't she married?

He forgot that question and his aggravation with his grandparents as soon as he started helping Susannah carry out food to the picnic tables. Her little sisters—Sharon and Shiloh, who looked so much alike that he still couldn't tell them apart—had taken a liking to him. They followed him like baby ducks waddling after their mama.

In truth, they reminded him of his own *schweschdern* back in Maine—they were older, but he rather missed having them around. He could always make them laugh, and they thought he was ever so clever.

Shiloh and Sharon helped him and Susannah set up a volleyball net.

They insisted on showing him the new kittens in the barn and the baby goats in the pasture.

They sat beside him as everyone ate lunch.

"You need to finish eating, Sharon." Susannah nodded toward her sister's plate with a stern look.

Which, of course, made Micah laugh because Susannah looked so serious and Sharon looked so frustrated. And then he remembered that Sharon was the one always running ahead. She also had freckles sprinkled across her cheeks and the bridge of her nose.

"Why are you laughing at me, Micah? I don't want to eat. I want to play."

"*Ya*, but the playing is not going anywhere, and you need to eat to have lots of energy."

"*Mamm* always says I have plenty of energy."

"That's because you knock things over a lot," Shiloh commented as she was carefully attempting to cut a piece of ham with a knife and fork.

"Want some help with that?" he asked.

She nodded enthusiastically, but Susannah shook her head in disapproval. "How will she ever learn?"

"How will she learn what?"

"*If* you do it for her, how will she learn?"

"I'm watching him do it, Susannah."

"*Ya*, you're watching, but your hands are smaller. When your hands are bigger you'll be able to do it yourself."

Shiloh studied her palms, then held them up for all to see. "Still small."

He couldn't have said why he felt so comfortable around Susannah and her sisters, but the afternoon flew by. Micah's grandparents left early, *Mammi* claiming she had a terrible headache.

"Is she okay?" Susannah asked.

"She gets migraines sometimes. Says the only thing to do for them is lie down in a dark room."

"Should you have gone home with them?"

"They'd probably rather I didn't." He laughed at the look of dismay on Susannah's face. "What I mean is that it's quieter when I'm not there."

"How much noise do you make?"

"Not that much, but they're used to living alone."

"How did they end up here without any family?"

"Their oldest daughter—my *aenti* Grace—married and moved to Maine when the Unity community was first established in 2008."

"How did she happen to meet a fellow from Maine?"

"Her husband, Otis, had been looking for cheaper land, moving every few years, trying to find a less crowded area. Lots of eligible men in Maine and not a lot of women, since the communities are smaller. My other *aentis* had soon married and moved there, as well. Then my *dat* would visit, and the way he tells it, he loved being out in the wild. In fact, that's our family motto. It's sort of a joke. *Less people and more wild animals*."

Susannah rolled her eyes and shook her head at the same time. Ha! He was getting to her.

"My *dat* says he wouldn't want to live anywhere else, that he's glad I grew up there."

"But you weren't born there?"

"*Nein*. I was actually born in Wisconsin."

"Wisconsin?"

"Before he settled on Maine, my parents moved every few years. According to my *mamm*, they'd move to a place, get settled and then the community would double in size and my *dat* would start looking in the *Budget* for another place to move."

"So why haven't your *daddi* and *mammi* moved to be with the rest of the family?"

"That's a really good question, one that I've been asking myself, but I haven't figured out the answer. Maybe they were waiting to see if we'd all actually stay there."

"Sounds like your *dat* plans on staying."

"*Ya*, he does. The problem is that the other communities in Maine are quite strict. Fort Fairfield, which is the northernmost district, was originally a Swartzentruber district."

"I've heard of them. More conservative?"

"Much. They're not allowed to hire drivers unless it's for an emergency, no close relationships with non-Amish people and their clothes are even more Plain." He bumped his shoulder against hers as they walked toward the adjacent field. "That pretty peach color you're wearing wouldn't be allowed."

"I can't imagine you living in a community that strict."

"Well, where we live in Unity isn't that strict, but there's still the influence of the other groups."

"Maybe that's why you're such a renegade."

"I'm a renegade?" He stopped in his tracks, hands on his hips. "You have offended me deeply, Susannah Beiler."

"Sure I did."

They walked to an old swing suspended from a tall maple tree. "Have a seat."

"What?"

"Sit down. I'll push you."

"You want me to get in the swing?"

"Sure and certain. It'll make you feel free. Make you feel as if you could touch the sky." He stepped closer. Already he was learning that she spooked easily. Susannah was accustomed to her personal space. Anytime he stepped within that space, she looked like a colt about to bolt. Rather than let him in her space, she plopped down into the swing and raised her feet.

"So push me already."

Soon they were both laughing, and Micah was wondering if he could talk her into fishing again. But they were interrupted by Sharon, who ran up and said, "*Dat* wants to see you both. In the house."

"Are we in trouble?" He was kidding, but the look

on Sharon's face said that he might have nailed it with his question.

"Both of us?" Susannah asked.

"*Ya*, that's what he said. I have to go. We found a bird nest over by the barn, and I'm watching the babies try to fly." She fairly screamed the last part as she ran in the opposite direction.

"Does she ever slow down?"

"Only when she's sleeping."

Apparently their afternoon free time was over. Micah pulled Susannah to her feet, and they trudged toward the house, in step with one another.

"Any idea what this is about?" He tried not to sound worried. Why should he be worried? It wasn't as if he'd never been called in to see the bishop before. He should have expected this, though somehow he'd begun to hope that things could be different in Goshen.

"*Nein.*"

"Your *dat* didn't say anything at breakfast?"

She shook her head, glancing at the adults gathered around the picnic table.

When they walked into the house and saw that Thomas was there with one of the other preachers— some guy by the name of Atlee—Micah sensed they were in trouble. He could understand why he might be. Not that he could think of anything in particular, but there was always something. It was actually rather a surprise that he'd made it nearly two weeks without being reprimanded by someone.

But Susannah? He couldn't imagine why she'd been called in.

"Have a seat." Thomas indicated the couch, so they sat side by side. Thomas sat in a rocker, and Atlee was in a rather large upholstered chair. He was a small older man, and the chair pretty much dwarfed him.

"I'll get right to the point," Thomas said. "I've had two different families come to me this morning with concerns about your behavior."

"Mine?" Susannah's voice screeched like a hoot owl.

It made Micah smile, which caused Atlee to frown.

Micah quickly schooled his expression in an attempt to appear more serious.

"Can't think of any reason there would have been concerns," Micah said. "I pretty much just worked all week."

"And I was working on that new quilt order I had."

"I'm sure you both did work very hard." Thomas's expression softened. "This was about the weekend, beginning with Friday night at the park."

Susannah crossed her arms and frowned. "I can't think of anything we did wrong at the park."

"Perhaps we shouldn't think of this as right or wrong, but rather something that someone saw and was concerned about. You two are old enough to realize that it matters how we're perceived by the community at large. We're to be examples of Christ, and we're to set ourselves apart from the world."

"Of course." Micah stared at the floor, because if he looked up, Thomas would see that he was about to lose his temper. He just had no patience for this sort of thing.

"You went to the park in town?" Thomas asked.

"*Ya*. I told you that, *Dat*. You said it would be fine."

"And you stayed to hear the concert?"

"In fact you moved and sat up front, if accounts are correct." Atlee studied them through large round glasses.

Micah blew out a noisy breath, then he sat up straighter. "We did, and I asked Susannah if it was all right before we did so."

"And I told him it was. *Dat*, there's nothing wrong with listening to music. We didn't get up and dance. We didn't waste money on a CD that we could bring home and play on a hidden music player we keep in the barn."

Thomas sighed heavily, then scooted to the edge of the rocker, his elbows braced on his knees.

"Why do we sing?"

Micah glanced up, wondering if this was a trick question. He was surprised to see a twinkle in Thomas's eyes when he'd expected to see condemnation.

"To express our moods," Micah said.

"Because it lifts our spirits," Susannah added.

"All right. Those are both *gut* reasons. But you've forgotten the Biblical reason—to give glory to *Gotte*. Singing, it's an act of worship, just like when we pray or observe communion or when we wash one another's feet."

Micah shifted uncomfortably in his seat. He wasn't sure where Thomas was going with this. This wasn't the standard lecture he'd received back home from his bishop or his *dat* or even from his *daddi*.

"We're even admonished to keep singing in the Bible. Paul told us to encourage one another with psalms and hymns and spiritual songs." Thomas paused, then added, "I suspect that isn't what you were listening to at the park."

"Nein," Susannah said softly.

"More like songs about pickup trucks and mud and boots."

"Ah." Thomas slapped his leg, as if they were finally getting to the crux of the matter. "We could relate to that if it was a buggy instead of a pickup truck."

When Micah dared to look at him again, he was grinning. "We want to be separate from the world, though I've been known to listen to a country tune myself once in a while. You both know Jethro. He gives rides to Amish folk, always has his radio turned to country music. I heard a lady named Alison Krauss sing 'Amazing Grace' once. It was beautiful indeed."

"So why are we in trouble?" Micah asked.

"I didn't say you were. I only said people were concerned."

"Then there's the matter of last night." Atlee cleared his throat and pushed up his glasses. "Perhaps we should move on to that."

"All we did last night was fish, *Dat*. You knew we were going to do that. You even reminded me not to get my line caught up in the brush."

"This has more to do with you coming home in the dark at a very late hour, apparently in clothes that were soaking wet."

And there it was. The line they had crossed. Micah knew that he always managed to find it, but this time he'd dragged Susannah with him.

Thomas spent the next twenty minutes leading them through scripture that directed them to be separate, to be set apart, to be holy. By the time he finished, Micah was feeling appropriately chastised. He thought it might end there, but then Thomas stood and delivered his final decree. "Perhaps we should continue this conversation after you've had some time to think on it. I believe a weekly meeting might be appropriate— between the three of us. Do you agree, Susannah?"

"Sure."

"Micah?"

What could he do? Micah agreed. He couldn't leave Susannah to endure the punishment alone, though spending an hour each week being lectured didn't sound like his idea of fun. At least it would be with Thomas and not Atlee. If he'd been told he had to spend an hour with the frowning old guy, he might have been tempted to throw in the towel and walk back to Maine.

Chapter Five

The Goshen Amish community held a barn raising on Friday and Saturday of the following week. Of course, Micah had been to plenty of barn raisings and home raisings, too, for that matter. In Maine, their community was small, which meant that everyone pitched in when there was a need. But the fact that they were small also meant that raisings took a week to complete. Everyone showed up on the first day and then people worked on it as they were able throughout the week until it was completed. Apparently in Goshen they did things differently.

He dropped his grandparents off near the main house, then parked the buggy.

"Where did all these people come from?" he asked Elias Yoder, who was directing buggies.

"There are twenty thousand Amish in Elkhart and Lagrange counties."

"And they're all here today?"

Elias laughed as he chalked a number on Micah's grandfather's buggy—#321. *Wow.* There were 321 families here? He'd actually thought he'd get to spend some time with Susannah today. He'd be lucky if he even saw her.

That thought fell away as he fastened his work belt around his waist and hurried toward the construction area. Though the sun had barely peeked over the horizon, the sound of hammers striking nails rang out and the south wall of the structure was already taking shape. He glanced over to the long string of picnic tables near the house.

The women made quite an image, reminding him of worker bees. They were wearing gray, blue, pink, peach, even green frocks—though everyone's head was covered with the same white *kapp*. There looked to be a hundred or more of them there, many holding babies on their hips and ranging in age from the infants to an old woman he passed, who had to be a hundred if she was a day.

The concerns of the previous week fell away.

He forgot about the meetings he was required to attend with Susannah's father.

He stopped worrying about the many ways that he managed to disappoint his *daddi*.

And maybe for the first time, he let go of his wish to be in Maine.

Micah checked in with the master engineer, who assigned him to the west wall that was just being laid out. The foundation had been poured two weeks earlier. Lumber and hardware had been delivered beforehand as well, and sat waiting to be used in large organized stacks. He passed a group of men sawing floor joists to length. A group of *youngies* would carry the measured and cut boards to men standing on the foundation. Micah suspected that given the amount of workers they had, the frame, including the roof beams, would be in place well before lunch.

Soon he was intent on his section—finishing out the frame and finding a rhythm with the large group of men in his section. Someone started singing, and soon his voice was joined by another and another. Micah became totally focused on the hammer, the nail, the song and the rising sun warming his back. He didn't realize that sweat had drenched his shirt until one of the young boys walked up with a tray of cups and water. He took two, pouring one over his neck and downing the other.

Then the second master engineer was calling out that it was time to begin the actual construction of the wall. The boards were measured and cut. Micah scrambled to the top with a dozen other men as others from the ground lifted the boards into place. The planks were positioned vertically—Micah hammered from the top as a younger guy he didn't know hammered from the bottom.

An hour later, he was once again being offered water. As he gulped it down, he looked around the roof area where he was working. An old man with white hair stood on his left and a young teen on his right. Both reflected the same grin that he felt on his own face.

And then they were working again. Micah straddled a beam so that he could nail from the outside. He looked down and counted four others doing the same. They must look like a ladder of Amish men.

He had no idea how much time had passed when he climbed down and stepped back, trying to take in the whole of what they'd done. "It's like building a house of cards," he murmured.

"Pretty much," the old guy to his right agreed, grinning and straightening his suspenders. "Much sturdier, though."

Soon they were both back on the roof again. The morning passed without Micah even being aware of it. When he heard the lunch bell ring, he scrambled down to the ground, but then he stood there as the tide of workers swept past him. He stared up at the frame of the barn, which was now completely intact.

It really was amazing what could be done when people worked together.

Almost without realizing what he was doing, he slipped his cell phone from his back pocket and took a selfie with the barn rising behind him. Only when he touched the photo button and heard the click did he realize that what he was doing was generally frowned upon. So he stuck his phone back in his pocket and strode off toward lunch.

He'd put it on Snapchat later that evening.

One picture wouldn't hurt anything.

And it wasn't like anyone else in the group had a phone or a Snapchat account. What they didn't know wouldn't hurt them, and it wouldn't land him in trouble, either.

Or, at least, that was his thinking at the moment.

He spied Susannah twice during lunch. Both times he tried to catch her attention, but she didn't see him. Or at least she pretended not to see him.

Was she upset about the meetings they had to attend with her *dat*? He tried to remember if they'd talked about it, but she had been curiously absent when he'd worked in her *dat*'s farrier shop. He'd thought she was simply busy, but maybe she was avoiding him.

He didn't have much time to dwell on it. Before he'd even cleaned his plate, men were returning to work. The afternoon passed as quickly as the morning had. By the time he climbed down from the roof, he was sore in a way that he hadn't been in a very long time. He supposed that farming and shoeing horses didn't use the same muscles as construction. It wasn't that he was getting older. His age had nothing to do with it.

He looked for Susannah as he made his way to fetch the buggy for his grandparents. When he asked Elias, who was once again helping folks with their buggies, he learned that the Beiler family had already left.

Possibly she was avoiding him. So what? Maybe she'd decided that being his sidekick was too risky. The thought depressed him terribly. Hadn't they had fun? Hadn't she enjoyed the evening in the park and the time they'd gone fishing?

He knew she had. She'd laughed and smiled and the serious Susannah had slipped away.

But he didn't doubt that she was making an effort not to spend time with him, which was fine. He'd see her on Sunday. They had the church meeting, and there was no way she could avoid him there.

Fortunately for Susannah, Sunday morning dawned dark and rainy. She could volunteer to stay inside with the babies after service. Then she wouldn't have to deal with Micah.

So she was pretty surprised when she was sitting with Deborah, rocking babies in the Gleichs' front living room, and Micah stepped inside.

"Uh-oh. Looks like someone found you," Deborah said under her breath.

If he felt uncomfortable in a room full of babies, Micah didn't show it. But then was he ever uncomfortable? That was part of his problem—even places where he didn't belong, he still seemed to enjoy. No, that wasn't quite right. Micah Fisher was a man intent on savoring every single moment of a day, and she couldn't really blame him for that. She admired it in one way, but then there was her *dat* to think about...

"Deborah, Susannah. *Gut* to see you both."

"Is there something we can help you with, Micah?" Deborah smiled sweetly and nodded to the fussy baby in her lap. "Or maybe you had an urge to rock a *boppli*."

"I could if you need me to, not that I have any experience. I somehow managed to avoid babysitting my nieces and nephews when they were still infants. Come to think of it, I don't think I've ever—"

Deborah stood and held the crying infant out to him. "Jeremiah is teething and none too happy about it. Maybe he'll respond better to a man. And here's his Binky, which he won't take from me, and also his blanket."

And with an obvious wink at Susannah, Deborah picked up her giant purse and fled the room.

"That was embarrassing," Susannah muttered.

"What was embarrassing, and how do I get this kid to stop crying?"

"First of all, stop holding him at arm's length as if he's a fish you just caught."

"Oh."

"Closer. Snuggle him like you would a newborn."

"I don't know how to snuggle a newborn."

"Okay. First, sit down." She'd been rocking Mary Lynn, a sweet six-week-old whose *mamm* looked as if she was going to fall asleep on her feet. Susannah laid the child in a playpen that had been set up in the corner of the room, covered her with a blanket and then returned to Micah's side.

He was staring at Jeremiah as if he'd never seen a crying baby before. As for Jeremiah, his cries had reached a fever pitch.

"Sit."

"Here?"

"Sit and rock. I'll fetch a bottle."

When she returned to the room, it was quiet. Micah had the baby lying on his belly across his knees and was rubbing his back.

"Huh."

"*Huh*, what? Did you think I didn't know how to quiet a baby?"

"Quite obviously, you didn't. You said as much when you walked in."

"True, but I tried this once with a puppy I found that seemed miserable. I think he'd eaten some hamburger that had gone rancid…"

"Please don't tell me any more."

"The thing had vomited once, and he started howling. Mutt looked so pitiful that I finally went to the front porch and put him across my knees, just like this. And it worked, just like with…" He stared quizzically down at the child.

"Jeremiah."

"*Ya.* Anyway, I've been looking for you."

"Have you, now?" Baby Hannah was happily lying on her back on an old quilt and trying to catch her toes, but Susannah picked her up anyway. She suddenly needed something to do with her hands.

"Come on. Out with it. You're avoiding me."

"Why would you say that?"

"Because it's obvious you are. What gives?"

Susannah sighed. There was simply no avoiding difficult conversations with Micah. He was too direct.

"I've never been called in by my *dat* before."

"I figured as much."

"And I didn't like it one bit. Plus, I'm ashamed that I embarrassed him."

"You didn't embarrass him. I don't think he even really cared. It was that old guy, Atlee, who was stirring up trouble."

"I'm the bishop's *doschder*, Micah."

"And that means you can't have any fun?"

"That means I'm held to a higher standard."

"Sounds like pride to me. Didn't we learn at our meeting on Monday that pride is a sin?"

"Now you're mocking me."

"*Nein*, I'm not."

Baby Jeremiah had fallen asleep, and apparently Micah's knees had, too. He raised the baby to his shoulder, trying to mirror the way that Susannah was holding Hannah. It was such a funny sight, Micah juggling a baby and a blanket and a pacifier, that Susannah had trouble hanging on to her anger.

Anger.

The sermon that morning had been on anger. *The wrath of man does not work the righteousness of God.*

Susannah sighed. It seemed that in matters of Micah, whether she turned left or right, she was facing some sort of dilemma.

"I'm sorry we got in trouble about the picnic and the fishing, but as your *dat* said, it wasn't that we did anything wrong, only that we weren't thinking of how it might be viewed by others."

"So you were listening."

"Of course I was listening. I like your *dat*."

Which made her smile. He said it so simply, as if it were an obvious fact. "I like him, too."

"So would you like to go a movie next week?"

"Uh-uh. No way."

"It's a cartoon. Nothing at all racy about it."

"I'm not going to the movies."

"So you're setting me free to ask someone else? Our deal… It's over?" He smiled slyly at her. "Because I think your friend Deborah might have a thing for me."

"That is ridiculous."

"Is not."

"She left the room as soon as you walked in."

"So she's a little shy."

He was incorrigible. But then again, she had agreed to be his sidekick for as long as he was here. Come to think of it, how much longer was he going to be in Goshen?

"Any news on your moving back to Maine?"

"Now you're trying to get rid of me?"

"I did not say that."

Micah's laugh was sincere and hearty. It came from somewhere deep down in his belly. She'd never met anyone as good-natured as he was. In fact, if she were honest, Micah Fisher was a complete mystery to her.

Tuesday morning Micah still felt like he was in something of a funk. He hadn't been too surprised when Susannah turned him down for going to the movies. It wasn't forbidden, as long as they attended something G-rated or possibly PG, depending on the story. While it was true that most Amish folk didn't waste money on things like movies, it was understood that *youngies* needed to be away from the farm occasionally.

But he'd known before he asked that Susannah wouldn't go. He'd paid attention to her reaction when her *dat* and Atlee had first called them in for The Lecture. That was how he thought about it—with capital letters. It wasn't his first reprimand and probably wouldn't be his last, but it was Susannah's first. There was no doubt about that.

She'd gone instantly rigid.

Sure, she had supported him, but as the meeting had worn on, her shoulders had tensed and she'd clasped her hands so hard that he was afraid she was going to cut off the circulation.

And then in the days immediately following, she'd started avoiding him.

The plan was for them to meet with Thomas every Monday, which they had done twice now. It hadn't been as terrible as Micah had feared. They'd discussed the *Ordnung* in general, events they were looking forward to and how they were feeling about their circumstances. Micah wasn't big on talking about feelings—he had them, same as everyone else. But what was the point in dwelling on them?

Did he feel like he'd been cast out from his home? Yes.

Did he struggle against the restrictions of the *Ordnung*? Yes!

Did he wish to remain Amish? Well, yes, of course he did. He simply didn't understand why it had to be so difficult and confining.

And so, he dithered. That was the only word for it and one his grandmother used—in fact, she'd accused him of that very thing just the day before. *Micah, I love you more than the breath in my lungs, but you can dither more than any man or child I've ever met.* He'd waited until he was in the barn brushing down the buggy horse to look up the meaning on his phone.

Webster's online claimed it meant to be indecisive.

Well, the fact that he was standing in a horse stall using his cell phone pretty much confirmed that he was indecisive—at least about whether to join the church and commit to following the rules of the *Ordnung* for the rest of his life. Moreover, he didn't see why he had to make a decision now. What was the rush? He probably had sixty years stretching in front of him. There was plenty of time to settle down and be a good Amish person.

In the days immediately following The Lecture, he'd told himself none of this mattered.

He often found himself once again calculating the date until his six months was up, but just looking at the days on the calendar filled him with dread. The immense amount of time that was left before he could even think about returning home, the idea of working every morning in the field and every afternoon in the farrier shop, the fact that he and Susannah hadn't done anything fun in nearly ten days…it all depressed him.

On the Tuesday after he'd talked to her in the nursery, he decided he might go crazy if he didn't take a few hours off from the farm. Fortunately, he'd finished up in the farrier shop early. Thomas was having a business meeting with the other members of church leadership—something about the benevolence fund. Micah had the afternoon free, and he'd seen on his phone that the sports store in town was having a clearance sale.

Few things cheered him up like a new hunting rifle or crossbow or fishing gear. His home town of Smyrna was located in the northeastern part of Maine, and was well-known for its fishing opportunities—whitefish, three kinds of trout and two kinds of bass. Just thinking about the fall fishing cheered him up, and he did have a little extra money in his pocket from working for Thomas. Certainly it wouldn't hurt to spend part of it, and he could stop by Jo Jo's Pretzels for a snack afterward.

The thought of a few hours in town had him humming to himself. As he cleaned up and shelved the tools in Thomas's shop, it occurred to him that the only thing that would make his plan better would be if Susannah went along with him. Not that he thought of her in any romantic way—she'd made it quite clear that she wasn't interested in dating—but the girl needed some relaxation time.

Whistling as he walked across the yard, he stuck his head into Susannah's sewing shop, but the place was empty. In fact, it was terribly neat, as if she hadn't been there all day. He started to climb the steps to knock on the front door, but he didn't want to wake the twins if they were napping. They probably weren't, but since it was so quiet, they might be.

Then again, maybe Susannah was around back, working in the garden. He walked down the steps of the porch, around the house, and stopped short when he saw her sitting on the bench next to the garden.

She was sitting in the sun, her head back and her eyes closed. Something caught in Micah's throat. Susannah was a beautiful woman, and she didn't seem to be aware of that fact at all. But it wasn't that awareness that caused him to stand perfectly still staring at her.

She must have washed her hair and was drying it in the sun. Her *kapp* lay on the bench beside her, and as he watched, she reached up a hand to run it through her hair—her beautiful, short brown hair. Then, as if she sensed him there, she turned to look at him. Her eyes widened, and Micah knew that there was no backing out of the situation. So instead he did what he always did: he plunged forward.

It would seem that Susannah had secrets of her own, and he was about to find out exactly what and why she'd been keeping them from him.

He strode over to where she was sitting and straddled the bench. He didn't say anything, deciding to let her lead the conversation, but it was hard to just sit there and wait. He had an overwhelming urge to reach out and run his fingers through her hair. He could see now that it only fell an inch past her ears. The look was so incongruous—an Amish woman with bobbed hair—that he honestly didn't know what to say.

When he'd waited as long as he could, he finally stated the obvious, "Must be hair-washing day."

"*Ya.*"

Maybe it was the way she looked up shyly at him, but Micah could no longer resist. He reached out and ran his hand over the top of her head, trailing the golden brown strands to her neck. Her hair felt like silk in his fingers. He wanted to run his fingers through it, but he knew that would be inappropriate, so instead he crossed his arms and said, "Short hair looks *gut* on you."

"That's it?"

"What?"

"That's all you're going to say?"

Micah shrugged, doing his best to look nonchalant. "I suppose there's a story there, but if you wanted to tell me, you would."

"Astute."

"I am all ears, if you have an urge to share. Finished my work in the shop, cleaned up everything and was just…you know…hanging out."

"You want to go somewhere."

"Maybe."

"And you don't want to go alone."

"I go places alone."

Susannah's grin spread, but then she spied her *kapp* sitting between them and snatched it off the bench.

"Your hair's almost dry."

"Doesn't take very long, not like when I was younger."

And then, he did what he'd told himself he wasn't going to do—he asked.

"Why's your hair short, Susannah? I'm the renegade here, so I know you didn't cut it because of a dare or a wild urge."

"*Nein*. Nothing like that."

"You don't have to explain if you don't want to."

A look of vulnerability crossed her features. Her customary mask—the one that said she knew what the answers were and had no doubt how things would turn out—slipped. Then a bird called out from a neighboring bush, broke the spell and the proper Susannah was back.

"It's not such a mystery, and honestly I didn't know

that you didn't know. Maybe I did realize you didn't know, but then it seemed awkward to bring it up."

"What don't I know?"

She looked left, then right, then out across the garden. When he didn't rescue her from the discomfort of the moment, she met his gaze and said simply, "I had cancer."

It was the very last words he would have expected to come out of her mouth.

"What? When?"

"Diagnosed two years ago, just before my twenty-third birthday. We didn't catch it early enough, so I had chemo before and after the surgery."

"Chemo?"

"*Ya*. It caused my hair to fall out." She ran a hand over the top of her head, as if she needed to assure herself it was no longer bald. "It's growing back quicker than I thought."

Her voice had dropped to a whisper. "Soon no one will be able to tell."

"Who cares about your hair?" The words came out more abruptly than he'd intended. "What I mean is, your hair looks *gut* that way, but more important, how are you? Are you still sick? And why did you never tell me this?"

"Why would I tell you?"

"Because we're friends!" Micah wanted to jump up and pace back and forth, but he forced himself to remain seated. When Susannah still didn't look at him, he put a hand on each of her shoulders and waited until she finally raised her gaze to his. "We're friends. Right?"

"*Ya*. Of course."

"So tell me about this. How do you feel? Will you need more surgery or more chemo? And what is your prognosis?"

"Fine, probably not and *gut*."

Micah let his hands fall to his side. There was something about the way that Susannah was looking at him that made him squirm. As if she were waiting for him to figure it out. But figure what out?

Then it occurred to him. Like a bolt of lightning illuminating a dark night, his mind put the pieces of Susannah's puzzle together.

"This is why you don't date?"

Susannah became suddenly interested in the dirt under her thumbnail. "Maybe. I guess."

"That's ridiculous."

"How would you know?"

"Because it doesn't matter."

"It does matter."

"No, what matters is what type of person you are and whether you have feelings for someone—not that you had cancer and are now in recovery."

Susannah tapped a finger against her lips. Her eyebrows were pulled down into a V, and her eyes seemed to be glistening. Was she going to cry?

"I can't have children, Micah."

"What?"

"Because of the type of cancer I had, I can't have children."

"What does that have to do with anything? Why would that make you decide to stop dating?"

"Because there's no point."

"No point?"

She looked at him directly now, her chin up and her

eyes daring him to argue with her. "We both know what that means to an Amish family, to an Amish man. Sure, I dated before my diagnosis, but now I understand—"

He cut her off, his impatience suddenly overpowering his vow to let her tell the story in her own way.

"You understand what exactly? That no one would want you? Because that's foolish and... Well, it's wrong."

"Is it?"

"Yes!"

"I don't exactly have men lining up at the door."

"Maybe because you keep everyone at arm's length."

"Or maybe because they would want children." Her anger was winning out over her embarrassment.

Micah was almost relieved to see the return of the Susannah he'd come to know—obstinate and strong-willed, sure, but not heartbroken. One more minute of the heartbroken Susannah, and he would have pulled her into his arms and embarrassed them both.

"Not all men want *kinner*."

"All Amish men do. Trust me, I know."

She leaned her neck forward, twisted her hair into some sort of knot and then secured it with bobby pins that were lying on the bench. How did women do that? He couldn't brush his own teeth without looking in a mirror.

She adjusted the *kapp* on her head, then turned and stared at him, as if she was daring him to push further.

Fine.

He'd push.

Because Susannah needed to realize that any man would be lucky to have her as a *fraa*, children or no children.

"Not everyone wants children, Susannah. You can't not date because of that."

"Of course I can, and that's a personal decision, thank you very much."

"So what do you see as your future? Living with your parents the rest of your life? Hiding in your sewing room and making quilts for other families because you don't deserve to have one?"

He knew he'd hit a nerve by the way she catapulted off the bench.

"I'll thank you to keep your nose out of my future."

"Oh, really? Because you're pretty intent on sticking your nose in mine."

"I have been trying to be your friend."

"You've been trying to corral me, to keep me away from anyone in this stupid town, to keep your girlfriends safe from me as if I'm some kind of ogre that might corrupt them."

But Susannah wasn't listening to him anymore. She was storming away as if they were an old married couple having a fight. He didn't know if he should follow her or not, but by the time he made up his mind that he should, she'd gone into the house and slammed the door quite forcefully behind her.

Which pretty much ended any conversation they were having.

Chapter Six

"You haven't talked to him in two days?" Deborah yanked on the yarn she was knitting with. It was a pastel color and self-striping. She was making a baby blanket for her *schweschder*. Someone in Deborah's family was always about to have a baby. It was a good thing that she was a fast knitter.

Susannah had stopped by to drop off some hot pads and aprons she'd made from fabric scraps. Deborah's family had a good-sized produce shed where they sold everything from fresh vegetables to eggs to knitted items. Susannah kept a corner table filled with quilts, pot holders, aprons, even table runners. Though she offered to work one day a week at the shed, Deborah's parents insisted there was no need. They had twelve children, so there was always someone willing and able to work a few hours.

She'd brought along an infant quilt that she was hand sewing the binding to. As she knotted her thread and pulled it through the back of the quilt, she tried to think how best to answer Deborah's question.

"It's a simple yes or no."

"Yes. We haven't spoken since Tuesday."

"Because you're embarrassed?"

"I don't know. Maybe?"

"Why would you be embarrassed, Susannah? It's not like you dyed your hair pink."

"Indeed."

"Anyway, I think I know what's really going on here."

"Oh, you do, do you?"

"It's so obvious." Deborah waved a knitting needle at her and then stuck it back into her next stitch and tugged again on the ball of yarn. "You have a crush on Micah Fisher."

"I do not!"

"I think you do."

"And I think you've been staring at that ball of yarn too long, because you're sounding a little crazy."

"You don't want him dating anyone else."

"Of course I don't. He's trouble wrapped up in suspenders."

"Okay. That sounded plausible when you first told me of your plan to tag along with him. I even admired you for sacrificing your free time to keep him in check."

"I do not keep him in check. Trust me on that."

"Many in our community were perhaps too quick to believe the rumors about Micah, and I'm embarrassed to admit that I might have been one of them. You have to admit that he is…different."

"Oh, I'm aware of that."

"Does he still have the phone?"

"Of course."

"Still wearing *Englisch* clothes?"

"He occasionally swaps out his straw hat for his baseball cap."

"But none of those are actual crimes." Deborah finished the row she was knitting and turned the blanket to purl in the opposite direction. "After he first arrived, when he was sneaking out of his own house, I thought he wouldn't last more than a week."

"The trouble he does manage to get into is so…" Susannah stared down at the needle and thread in her hand, trying to remember what she was doing with it. "Trivial. That's what it is—trivial. Silly stuff."

Deborah stopped knitting and waited for Susannah to look up at her. Lowering her voice, as if she could cushion the blow, she asked, "Did you hear about his picture in the paper?"

"What?"

Deborah reached down into her large purse. She pulled out a paperback book, what looked like a sandwich wrapped in wax paper, a bottle of water and a tube of hand lotion.

"Doesn't that bag hurt your shoulder?"

"Mostly it sits on the ground."

"I still don't understand why you carry so much around."

"If you had eleven siblings, you'd understand."

"I suppose."

"Here it is." Instead of looking pleased with herself, Deborah's expression said that she wanted to apologize. She didn't, though. Without saying another word, she handed a copy of the local newspaper to Susannah.

"Why would I want to read about the city's contract for a new water tower?"

"Not there." Deborah reached over and flipped the

paper so that Susannah could read below the fold. "There."

Susannah actually felt light-headed as she stared down at the photo of Micah standing in front of the barn that was only partially completed. He was wearing his usual cocky smile. In the background it was plain to see several other Amish workers picking up tools or climbing down from the roof. If she guessed, Susannah would say he'd taken it as they were breaking for lunch.

"I can't... I can't believe he'd do this."

"Trivial, as you say, and yet plenty of folks in our community are upset about it."

"Why did you wait so long to show it to me?"

"You've only been here a half hour."

"Still, I would think you'd have pulled it out as soon as I climbed down from my buggy."

"I'm not any happier about this than you are." Deborah resumed knitting. "I don't like being the bearer of bad news."

"I just... I can't believe Micah would do this. He submitted it for photo of the week?" As she continued reading, her mouth dropped open in disbelief. "He won fifty dollars?"

"So it says."

"He doesn't even need the money. I know he's making plenty from my *dat*, and besides, he rarely has time to spend it, since he's working for his *daddi* in the mornings and with the horses in the afternoon."

"It wonders me."

Susannah refolded the paper and held it out to Deborah.

"I'm sorry," Deborah said.

"For what?"

"Ruining your day."

"I'm glad you showed me." Susannah stared down at the paper that they were now both holding, then she jerked it back. "Maybe I should keep it, if that's all right with you."

"Sure. Of course."

Susannah set the offending newsprint down next to her purse. She tried to focus on the quilt in her hands. Sewing always relaxed her. It was immensely satisfying to see random pieces of fabric become something that would warm or comfort another person—often a person she didn't even know. She slipped her needle into the binding of the quilt, pulled it through, then slipped it into the quilt itself. The ladder stitch was one of her favorites, invisibly closing the two seams together. If only life were so easily patched.

Deborah cleared her throat. "So, about your crush…"

"I do not have a crush on Micah."

"Then why did you wait so long to tell him about your cancer? Why did you wait until he stumbled over the fact?"

"I don't know, honestly. I thought about telling him—a few times. But always it seemed like such a downer, or like I would be asking for sympathy."

Instead of answering, Deborah raised an eyebrow and motioned for her to continue.

"And I didn't want his sympathy. You have no idea how tiresome it is to have people pat you on the hand and ask 'how are you getting along, dear?' in that syrupy-sweet voice."

"They mean well, I'm sure."

"Of course they do, but I'm not fragile. I'm not

going to break in two simply because I had cancer. In fact, you know what?" She tugged three more stitches through the binding, tacked down the corner and then stowed her needle by rocking it through both layers of fabric. "I do like being around Micah, or I did, because he didn't know about my cancer. He treated me like he would any other woman."

"Ah."

"Ah? That's your response? Ah?" Susannah realized in that moment that she'd been avoiding examining her feelings toward Micah. Was she afraid that she was falling for him? That was ridiculous. Micah Fisher was not her type, and even if he was, he wasn't staying in Goshen. Still, there was something about him that she'd never encountered before in the few men she'd dated.

"What response did you expect?"

"I don't know. I thought you might understand. You know how it was when I first found out."

"I'm the first person you told."

"And then when Samuel broke up with me."

"He didn't deserve you. By the way, I heard that girl from Shipshe he was dating dumped him."

There was a time when news of Samuel caused her heart to twist, but Susannah realized she wasn't really interested in his dating life. Sometime between their breakup and now, she had moved on.

"I never felt around Samuel like I do around Micah."

"Oh, my. That sounds serious."

"*Nein.* It's not like that. I keep telling you. It's less like when you have a crush on someone and more like I can be myself. Not Cancer Survivor Susannah but... just Susannah."

"I suppose it makes sense."

"What does?"

"This strange attraction you two have, and don't deny that he likes being around you, too. It's plain as day to anyone with eyes and a brain."

Susannah folded her quilt, stuffed it into her sewing bag and sat back in the lawn chair. "Please explain."

"Micah is attracted to you—"

"He is not."

"He touched your hair."

"Whatever. Probably he was in shock. Go on."

"Micah is attracted to you because you're not a risk taker. You're a rule follower. You're the ultimate challenge to a guy like him."

Susannah felt an irrational urge to cover her ears, and yet, didn't she want to hear her friend's opinion? Deborah had always been the one person who would be completely honest with her. Even during her illness, when she was bald and exhausted and looked terrible, Deborah had been refreshingly candid. Instead of claiming she looked fine, Deborah had suggested they add color to her wardrobe. Then she'd proceeded to knit incredibly soft hats and scarfs in blues and greens and lavender, claiming the color gave her a healthier glow.

Susannah didn't know if it had helped her glow. She'd never really thought of herself as a glowing type of person. But the small gifts definitely lifted her spirits, that and the fact that her friend had been honest with her.

"You're an attractive woman, Susannah. And it's not prideful for me to say that about you. It's only prideful for you to think it of yourself." Deborah paused, stared out at the tables laden with goods to sell and then glanced back at Susannah, a smile tugging at the corners of her mouth. "Or maybe pride isn't involved at all. Maybe it's just an observation."

"Danki."

"Where was I?"

"You were explaining why Micah is attracted to me, something that I have to tell you I don't see at all."

"What about the night you were fishing, when you thought he was going to kiss you?"

"I should never have told you that."

Deborah frowned down at her knitting, paused to count her stitches, placed a marker and resumed working on the row. "We've been telling each other about first kisses since we were fourteen."

"You and Josiah behind the schoolhouse."

"Uh-huh." Deborah grinned at the memory. "As I said earlier, I think maybe you and Micah started out as enemies…"

"Scripture reminds us to have an attitude of kindness to all."

"Then whatever you felt for one another moved to friendship when you began to understand each other."

"We're also called to be friends to one another— love your neighbor as yourself."

"And now it's blossoming into something more than mere friendship." Deborah focused on the row she was knitting with a flourish of needles and waited.

Susannah had no idea what to say. Was it possible that Deborah was right?

"Comments? Insights? Objections?"

Susannah felt an unexpected release of the tension she'd been carrying around for some time. Her shoulders relaxed and the headache that had been teasing her all morning dissipated. She had the sense that she was letting go of something that she'd been holding on to for a long while, perhaps since she'd first talked to Micah standing in the road leading to their respective houses.

"It could be you're right. I'm not saying you are, but I will say that I feel…confused. Some days I do find myself thinking that Micah would make a fine husband, and yes, occasionally I drift off into daydreams about that."

Deborah smiled, but she didn't interrupt, and she certainly didn't say the four dreaded words: *I told you so*.

"I realize how silly that is. He's not even staying here in Indiana. If you could hear him go on and on about Maine."

"I have. We all have." Deborah set aside her knitting, walked over in front of Susannah's chair and squatted in front of her. "It's okay to enjoy this time with Micah."

"It is? But—"

Deborah put her hands over Susannah's. "Maybe it will lead to something else and maybe it won't. All we know for certain is that *Gotte* brought you two together during this time in your lives for a reason."

"But I have no idea what that reason is."

"That's okay."

"Then what am I supposed to do?"

"How about you do the simplest of things? Just savor it and stop worrying about where it might or might not lead."

Micah nearly swallowed his gum when Susannah walked into his *daddi*'s barn early that evening.

"I thought you weren't talking to me."

"Why would you think that?"

"Because you walked away."

"Oh, yeah. I did."

"Not that I blame you. I overstepped. I tried to lecture you on your life when my own life is a mess."

Instead of denying that, she simply said, "I might have overreacted."

Which was all the apology he was going to get. But then, maybe she didn't owe him an apology. Maybe he owed her one. Regardless, Susannah seemed to have moved on.

Micah had been oiling and mending one of the harnesses. He set it aside and studied her as she stood there in the doorway to the barn, the last of the day's light splashing over her. She was a sight for sore eyes, that was for certain. He'd tossed and turned until midnight the previous evening, wondering how he was going to survive the remainder of his Indiana exile without Susannah by his side.

"My parents used to have tiffs," he admitted.

"Did they, now?"

"Couple of times a year. Nothing terrible, just a bit of a row and then an awkward silence for the remainder of the day."

Susannah looked intrigued. "My parents never fight, not that I'm aware of."

"Could be because my *mamm* has a temper, or because my *dat* is more stubborn than any mule you will ever encounter." He walked past her, out into the fading sunshine. Watching the sun set in the west, looking out over the fields, he realized that Indiana had a certain unique beauty. Not that it could compare with

Maine, and not that he'd ever want to live here, but he could understand why people did. "It used to upset me when I was a *youngie*."

"What did you do?"

"What most Amish *kinner* do. I ran to my grandparents. This would be my *mamm*'s parents. They moved up to join us in Maine after the first year. You'd think that they would be on her side."

"They weren't?"

Micah shrugged. "Couldn't ever tell, but I do remember what my *daddi* said to me after one particularly loud argument my parents had. I was sitting out near the pond, but not fishing. He came over and told me not to worry. He said if my parents were perfect, they wouldn't have married each other. But since neither one was perfect, I could rest assured that they would forgive each other."

Susannah started laughing, and then Micah started laughing, and then he knew that everything was okay between them. They both sat on the bench under the barn's overhang.

Susannah bumped her shoulder against his. "No perfect people in your family, huh?"

"Not a single one."

"Mine, either."

"Which, I suppose, means we're not perfect."

"Not even close." Susannah pulled a folded sheet of newspaper from her pocket. "And now that we've established that neither of us is perfect, we should probably talk about this."

Micah stared at it, dumbfounded for the space of a few seconds. Then he hopped up, walked across the barn and retrieved his phone from the shelf where he usually stored it. He returned to where Susannah was and attempted to turn it on, but nothing happened.

"Problem?"

"It's dead."

"Ah."

"I don't think I've even used it since the workday at the barn." He waited, expecting her to begin scolding him for using it at all. When she didn't, he sat back down beside her. "There was a time when I checked it every day. Who am I fooling? I checked it every hour. I thought… Well, I guess I thought I was going to miss out on something."

"How so?"

"Well, I have *freinden* on different chat apps."

"Real friends?"

Micah shrugged his shoulder. "They seemed to be at the time, and maybe they were. Or they could have been, if our lives had connected in a more tangible way. I don't know. At the time that I bought this phone, I was feeling like no one understood me. And suddenly there was this virtual community where people did understand. It was nice."

"And now?"

"Now I don't know if any of what goes on through this device is real."

He scrubbed a hand over his face. "If I were to be honest? Now I would rather spend time with you and Deborah and even her *bruder* Elias."

"I didn't know you'd spent any time with Elias."

Micah didn't try to explain that Elias was okay but he enjoyed his time with Susannah more. He didn't know how to say that without making a fool of himself.

As he mulled over that fact, Susannah studied him, and he almost fell over when she started laughing.

"Are you sure you're feeling all right?" he asked. "You're acting a little odd."

"It just occurred to me that your chat apps aren't so very different from the *Englisch* pen pal that I have."

"Now you're just tugging on my suspenders."

"*Nein*. It's true."

"How did Susannah Beiler, bishop's *doschder*, end up with an *Englisch* pen pal?"

"Jayla was in the hospital when I was… We shared a room for a while."

"Did she have cancer, too?"

"*She did.* She's older than me by a few years, African American and already had one *boppli*. We're as different as two people can be."

"Like me and my *freinden* on Snapchat."

"Maybe, which I guess is part of what I like about writing to her. She helps me to see my life from a different perspective."

"And you still exchange letters?"

"We do. We've even met up for coffee a couple of times, when she was back in town for treatment. She lives over by Millersburg, so it doesn't happen as often as I'd like, but I always look forward to seeing her. And her letters—it cheers me up just to see her return address on an envelope." Susannah reached out and poked his phone with a finger. "So, how were you going to learn more about the picture you took from the phone?"

"I was just going to check and see if I could figure out how this happened." He picked up the paper again and stared at it, as if doing so would make the puzzle pieces fall together.

Finally, he handed it back to her. "I don't know how that photo ended up in the paper."

"But you took it?"

"*Ya.* Plainly it's a selfie that I snapped. I even remember taking it. I was thinking I'd like to show it to my family when I get back to Maine."

"Why?" There was no condemnation in her voice, only curiosity. "Surely you have barn raisings in Maine."

Micah was shaking his head before she even finished. "Not like here. That…" He nodded toward the paper she was now holding. "That was a completely different experience for me. In Maine, our communities are much smaller."

"You still help one another."

"Of course, but a barn isn't raised in a day. We might have one big workday at the beginning, but the majority of the work is done as people are able over the period of a week or two." He stood, paced back and forth in front of her for a minute and finally leaned against the barn post, crossing his arms. "I don't know how that picture ended up in the paper, and I know nothing about winning fifty dollars."

"But you think you can figure that out through your phone?"

"Maybe."

Susannah stood and straightened her apron, then stepped closer and smiled up at him. "Perhaps we should go to town tomorrow."

"Town?"

"I heard Dairy Queen has a special on their ice cream."

"Do they, now?"

"Personally, I could go for something cold and chocolate."

"I could probably charge my phone while we're there."

"Exactly."

"What time should I pick you up?"

"We can go whenever you finish your work with my *dat*."

Micah couldn't believe how much his mood had lifted since she'd stepped into the barn. Did Susannah's opinion of him matter so much? And why wasn't she more angry about the picture? She was always lecturing him about staying within the guidelines of the *Ordnung*, but she hadn't said a word about it since arriving. He knew that asking her wouldn't yield answers, and maybe the *why* didn't matter so much after all.

When she'd arrived, the sun was just beginning to set, but while they'd talked, twilight had crept over the fields.

"Let me hop inside and tell my grandparents that I'm going to walk you home."

"I'm pretty sure I can find my way."

"Still…" And rather than explain, he jogged toward the house, returning in a few minutes with a flashlight, a napkin filled with a few of his *mammi*'s brownies and a quart jar full of milk.

"Didn't expect you to bring a picnic."

"Just thought you might like something sweet."

They stopped at the top of the small hill that sat just inside the boundary line on her parents' property.

Susannah was wearing a sweater, and Micah had on a jacket. He slipped it off and put it on the ground for her to sit on.

"Seriously?"

"Wouldn't want you to get your dress…" And then words seemed to fail him as he looked at her in the soft light of the moon. The stars shone as if they'd been flung there particularly for the two of them. He thought of kissing her, then wondered why he'd even have such a thought and then wondered if she'd want him to. Finally, he thrust the brownies at her. "Hope you like walnuts."

"I love walnuts."

They didn't speak again until they'd finished the snack. Passing the quart jar back and forth felt curiously intimate. The brownies were still warm, the milk cold and the sky above them offered a spectacular canopy of the heavens.

He didn't want to push, didn't want to spook her away again, but he wanted to know. For some reason he couldn't put his finger on, he needed to know. And since she didn't seem in a rush to get home, now was as good a time as any. Now might be the best chance he'd get. So he crossed his legs at the ankle, leaned back on his hands and asked what he'd wanted to ask since the day he'd walked up on her drying her short hair in the sun.

"What was it like?"

"Cancer?"

"Being afraid that you might die. How did you get past that every day?"

"I guess during those first few weeks, I was just in shock."

"You didn't realize something was wrong before your diagnosis?"

"Not initially. I became worried when I started losing weight, had trouble eating and then there was the pain." She placed a hand on her stomach.

When she didn't continue, Micah reached for her hand and entwined their fingers together.

"And you had surgery?"

"Ya." Her voice was a whisper, practically a caress.

"That must have been frightening."

"The diagnosis was probably the worst part. After that, it was simply a matter of weighing my options. And my parents were very supportive for whatever I wanted to do."

"Did you have options? Other than the surgery?"

"Not really. But if I'd said I needed time, if I'd wanted to wait, my parents would have understood."

Micah stared down at their hands, which he could just barely make out in the darkness. He rubbed his thumb over hers. "I would never have guessed that you'd been sick."

"Is that so?"

"You're so spunky."

"Spunky?"

"I guess I was a little afraid of you when I first met you."

Susannah began giggling. Snatching her hand from his, she covered her mouth…until she'd worked herself up to a full belly laugh.

"Not that funny."

"It…it sort of is."

Which was followed by more laughter, and Susannah gulping for air, which started Micah to laughing, though he couldn't have said what he was laughing about.

But suddenly it didn't matter why they were laughing, sitting on top of the hill, the stars spread out before them like grains of sand on a beach.

It occurred to Micah then that he should step back. The be-careful voice in his head asked what he thought he was doing.

She's not your type, buddy.

She's out of your league.

She's the bishop's daughter, and don't forget you're heading back to Maine as soon as possible.

As they walked toward her parents' home, he realized that most people he knew would agree with that voice of reason. But when had he ever listened to reason or cared what other people thought?

Never.

And he didn't plan on starting now. He might be in trouble with her *dat* for the picture, but he suspected things would be even worse with his *daddi*. In fact, the picture on the front page of the *Goshen News* might be the final straw. Micah understood he should be worried about that, but at the moment he would rather keep his attention on the beautiful woman walking at his side.

Chapter Seven

When Susannah suggested going to town to charge Micah's phone, she had thought she could sneak away from the farm for a few hours. Normally that wouldn't have been a problem. Unfortunately, the next day her *mamm* was called to a neighbor's to help with a sick *aenti* and her *dat* was attending a monthly meeting of area bishops.

"I'm stuck with these two," she explained to Micah.

"Hey! You're not stuck with us. You love us." Sharon was sticking flower seeds into pots, though in the process, more dirt ended up on her than around the seeds.

Shiloh was sitting on the back porch step, writing her letters on a tablet. "Does this look right, Susannah?"

"Sure it does."

"I think the tail of my g needs to hang down more." She flipped the pencil around and began vigorously erasing.

"Those two are yin and yang." Micah sat in the rocking chair beside Susannah. He kept watching her, like he wanted to say something, but then he would look away. Perhaps he didn't want to talk in front of

Sharon and Shiloh—little pitchers having big ears and all of that.

"Yin and what?"

"They're like flip sides of the same coin."

"Oh, *ya*. They look alike but often act very different."

"Which one is more like you?"

"I don't have freckles like Sharon."

"You called them stardust." Sharon put her dirty hands on her nonexistent hips and cocked her head. "Remember?"

"She has *gut* hearing."

"Yes, they both do."

Shiloh remained focused over her tablet. "I don't have freckles, either, but you said I had the stars in my eyes."

"Yes, you do, Shiloh."

"You told them that?"

Susannah's mind was spinning, trying to keep up with three conversations at once. She finally gave up and focused on Micah. "The point is that we can't go to town for ice cream."

She knew she'd made a mistake the second the words slipped out of her mouth. Her *schweschdern* might be complete opposites on some things, but at other times they merged together into one entity. This was one of those times.

"We want to go for ice cream."

"We did all our chores."

"And you promised we'd do something fun."

"And planting flowers isn't that much fun."

"And I love ice cream."

Micah looked as if he were going to burst out laughing. Fortunately, he held it in or Susannah would have been tempted to dump one of Sharon's pots of dirt over his head. Laughing at the girls convinced them they were entertaining, and from that point there was no turning back.

"We could take them with us," Micah suggested, which pretty much sealed her fate for the day. There was no stopping her twin sisters when they had another adult on their side.

Susannah insisted they walk next door with Micah while he fetched his *daddi*'s horse and buggy. "It'll wear these two out, and as you've noticed they have a lot of energy."

Sharon had repeatedly dodged ahead of them and circled back. As usual, Shiloh stuck close to Susannah's side, though at the moment she was hopping from foot to foot.

Micah's *mammi* actually clapped her hands when they walked up to the front door. "It seems I haven't seen you girls in ages."

"We're going for ice cream."

"Micah's going to take us."

"If he can borrow the buggy."

"Well, of course he can." She reached out and put a hand on both girls, ushering them into the house. "Come in. Come in. Susannah, it's been too long since you stopped by."

Soon they were settled around the kitchen table, and Micah had explained why he wanted to use the buggy. "But only if you don't need it."

Mammi smiled at the girls, then turned her attention to Micah. "I had planned to go and visit Miriam

Hochstettler, who's had a flare-up of her rheumatoid arthritis."

"We can go another day."

"Nonsense. You go on out and tell your *daddi* that you need the buggy. I can visit Miriam tomorrow."

"But—"

"*Nein.* I insist. These two girls look like they've been working hard all day. They've earned a treat."

Susannah couldn't help laughing. "Sharon certainly does look as if she's been working hard. There's more dirt on her apron than in the pots of flowers she was planting."

"Nothing that won't wash out," Abigail assured her.

"And I've been writing my letters," Shiloh chimed in.

"Aren't you a smart girl."

"We have to go to school next year." Sharon's voice dropped an octave and she ducked her head. "Whether we want to or not."

Which earned a laugh all around.

Micah moved to the back door to go and bring the buggy around. As an afterthought, he turned back to Sharon and Shiloh. "Do you girls want to help me?"

He started laughing as they dashed out the back door ahead of him. "I'll take that as a *yes.*"

Susannah and Abigail caught up on what was happening on both farms—which wasn't much.

Glancing at the kitchen clock, Susannah said, "I suppose I should go on out. I don't want to keep Micah waiting."

"Or the girls. They seemed quite excited."

Susannah walked with Abigail out to the front porch, where they sat and waited for Micah to bring the buggy around.

"I've been meaning to speak to you regarding Micah. We appreciate your befriending him."

"Micah's an easy person to like."

"That's what we're a little worried about."

"What I mean is that he's a hard worker and he has a *gut* attitude. Even my *dat* says so."

"I agree with both of those points, but you and I both know that Micah hasn't made up his mind on some very important life choices."

"I'm not sure what you mean."

Abigail set her rocker in motion. "Oh, I pray every day that all of my *family* will stay in the faith, but not all do. That's a truth to be reckoned with."

Susannah started to protest, but Abigail raised a hand to stop anything she might have said. "You're young yet, so it's hard for you to imagine."

"I do have *freinden* who have joined the Mennonite church."

"And it's not my place to say whether that is right or wrong. *Gotte* directs each path. However, if what I know about you and your family is correct—and we've lived next door to each other all of your life—then you have no plans to leave our church or our community."

"*Nein.* Of course not. Well, I've always thought of myself as Plain, and I suppose I will stay in Goshen. Where else would I go?"

"My point is Micah may not stay in our faith."

"He told you that?"

"His actions told me that, and you would arrive at the same conclusion if you'd get the stars out of your eyes."

Susannah sifted through her memories of time spent with Micah, searching for a way to defend herself. She finally settled for "I do not have stars in my eyes."

"Looks that way from here, and normally I would be thrilled at the thought of having you as a part of the family."

Susannah jumped to her feet at the word *family*. Fortunately, Micah pulled the buggy up in front of the porch at that moment.

"I have to go."

"Just remember what I said, Susannah, and guard your heart."

Those words bounced round and round her mind as she climbed into the buggy, made sure the girls were sitting back properly, and listened to Micah discuss a horse he had shoed that morning. Only she wasn't really hearing him.

She was thinking about Abigail Fisher warning her to guard her heart.

The day was warm, and Micah needed to charge his phone, so they ate their treats inside. Susannah and Micah sat on one side of the booth, Sharon and Shiloh sat on the other.

It took a few minutes for his cell phone to come to life. When it did, Micah started punching buttons. Sharon and Shiloh seemed not to notice. They were busy licking at the ice cream cones while at the same time coloring the place mats that the girl working the front counter had given them. Susannah glanced around the restaurant. It was plenty full for three in the afternoon.

One couple sat in a booth across from them. Their young child in a highchair was leaning forward to touch the screen of some small tablet. Across the restaurant another toddler, surely not yet walking, was crying and reaching for his *mamm*'s phone. Even the employee who was supposed to be bussing tables had pulled out his phone and was staring at it, the cluttered table in front of him temporarily forgotten.

She hadn't really paid attention to how much *Englischers* used their electronic devices. What were they looking at? What could be so fascinating? She glanced again at her *schweschdern*. They were adorable, their heads practically touching as they worked on a puzzle on the color sheet. Both were wearing white *kapps* and blue dresses with blue aprons, and for a moment Susannah realized how different they must look to *Englischers*.

She knew it wasn't her place to say who was right or wrong. Her *dat* had often reminded her *not to judge lest ye be judged*. She thought she knew what was right for her, but did that mean that other ways were wrong?

Why did there have to be a right or wrong anyway?

Some people chose to be farmers, some woodworkers. Some people were *Englisch* and others were Amish. What mattered was how they treated one another and how they lived their lives. She glanced at Micah and once again heard Abigail's words. *Guard your heart*. Was she falling in love with Micah Fisher? And even if she was, who was to say that it would end badly?

It probably would end badly.

He was definitely moving back to Maine as soon as possible.

She couldn't imagine living so far from her family, even if he did care about her in that way, which was by no means certain.

Micah turned off his phone and focused on his sundae.

"Well?"

"Well, what?"

"Did you figure it out?"

"Oh, *ya*. I figured it out."

"And?"

He looked at her and smiled as he shoveled in another rather large spoonful of ice cream. "I'm suddenly starved. I could eat two of these."

"You're suddenly avoiding the subject. Out with it."

Micah wiped his mouth with a napkin and cornered himself in the booth so that he could look directly at her. "I took the selfie and posted it to Snapchat the day of the barn raising. As I told you, I haven't even used the phone since."

"So how did it get to the paper?"

"A friend of mine—an *Englischer*—managed to capture the photograph and then he sent it into the paper, pretending to be me."

"Why would he do that?"

"I might have mentioned that I'm running a little low on money."

"My *dat* is paying you."

"*Ya*, and I give all of that money to my *daddi* as I should, since he's feeding me and providing me a place to stay. But that doesn't leave anything for..." He glanced at the girls and cleared his throat, then leaned closer and lowered his voice. "Doesn't leave anything for dating."

Susannah felt her cheeks flame red. She would have stopped it if she could, but she'd always blushed when she was embarrassed. Micah was looking at her as if she was the most important thing in the world, and he definitely noticed her sudden fascination with her ice cream. Instead of saying anything, he squeezed her hand and went back to eating.

He didn't ask her out.

And he certainly didn't clarify what he'd meant.

She had no idea if she was relieved or disappointed.

As they were loading the girls back into his buggy, Micah noticed a car pull up in front of the Dairy Queen and drop off an older woman who toddled toward the door. Micah hustled over to the door, opened it wide for her and spoke to the woman.

When he jogged back to the buggy and climbed in, Susannah said, "What was that about?"

"An idea."

"What kind of idea?"

"The *gut* kind, of course."

"We want to play I Spy," Sharon said, leaning forward over the seat.

"Best sit back," Susannah said.

"Can we play?"

"I spy with my little eye…" Shiloh was practically bouncing on the seat.

The sugary treat must have given both girls an added burst of energy.

Sharon's voice went up an octave. "I wanna go first."

"But I already spied."

"Did not."

"Did, too. I spied that cat over there." She pointed with her finger to a ginger cat sitting on a picnic table.

"Okay, I know what you spied—a cat. Now it's my turn. I spy…"

Micah figured it was best to play along, so they spent the ride home spying another horse and buggy, a red car, two boys riding bikes and even a woman pushing a child on a swing. It wasn't an easy game to play in the buggy, as the thing the person spied was often left behind. When the girls became frustrated, he changed the game to fifty questions, which went much more smoothly.

By the time they reached Susannah's place, he understood how the girls managed to wear her out. He'd barely pulled the buggy to a stop when both Sharon and Shiloh tumbled out. They clamored up the porch steps, rushing to show their *mamm* the paper place mats they had colored.

"Those two are a handful."

"I told you so."

"They're cute, though."

"You don't mind that I had to bring them along?"

"Why would I mind?"

Susannah shrugged, and he wondered if she was thinking what he was thinking. But if he asked, she'd probably just deny it. Susannah was traditional, and she wouldn't admit to wanting to kiss him or even wanting to be alone with him—not that she'd ever lie, but she wouldn't want to be forward.

As if to confirm his thoughts, she blushed prettily and then glanced away. "I should go fetch the clothes off the line."

"I'll help."

Micah set the brake on the buggy and tethered the horse to the hitching post Thomas has fashioned in front of the house. Then he followed Susannah to the backyard, thinking about the girls he had dated before, the girls back home. They had been quite different from Susannah. They'd been flirty and immature. He could see that now. They'd covered their insecurities up with bold words and *Englisch* clothes, but they hadn't shared their dreams or fears or hopes for the future.

They'd tried to prove to him they were different, that they were *the one*. The pressure to choose and settle down with one girl had begun when he'd turned twenty-one. His parents didn't understand what he was waiting for. Honestly, he didn't know, either. He'd always felt different from everyone else.

Now he wasn't so sure about that.

Underneath, wasn't everyone the same? Everyone wanted to be liked, to be respected and to have their opinions count.

But it was more than that.

Everyone wanted to connect in some authentic way. Maybe that was what he'd been looking for on social media. He wasn't certain. He only knew that he wasn't finding satisfaction there, but when he was with Susannah, that itch felt as if it was being satisfied. Just watching her fold clothes brought a goofy smile to his face, and he was powerless to stop it. He was confused about his feelings when he was around her, but he was also content for the first time in his life.

How could he feel both things at the same time?

Susannah laughed when she saw the way he was folding the towels.

"Do not tell me I'm doing this wrong."

"Okay."

He looked at the neat stack she'd placed in her basket, then at the towel he'd folded into a football shape. "I'm doing this wrong. Show me."

Instead of pointing out he most certainly did not know the proper way to fold clothes, she walked over to where he was standing.

"Hold the towel up like this."

He picked up a towel and mirrored what she was doing.

"Now fold it like this."

He thought he did what she did, but looking down, he must have twisted it somehow.

Susannah started laughing—a sound he dearly loved to hear. "This is impossible," he growled.

"Of course it's not. All you need is practice."

"Uh-huh."

She quickly folded the last of the towels, and they carried the two baskets of fresh laundry to the back porch.

"Are you going to tell me what your *gut* idea was? The one you had when you held the door open for the *Englisch* woman?"

"Hmm... I'd rather wait and see if it pans out."

"So, you're not going to tell me."

"I will say this..." He stepped closer, glanced at the windows to be sure no one was watching and then dipped his head and kissed her softly on the lips. Why did she taste like strawberries? He didn't ask about that. Instead he said, "If it works out, I'll have the money to take you to dinner."

"Will you, now?"

He wanted to kiss her again, but Sharon and Shiloh sprinted out the back door, squealing and running to the swings that had been set up under the branches of a large maple tree.

Susannah stepped toward the porch. "I should probably help with dinner."

"And I need to go and talk to my grandparents about that newspaper thing."

"I suppose it would be best if they hear about it from you before a neighbor takes them a copy."

"And I'll talk to your *dat* tomorrow when I come over."

Which he realized was a change in how he did things. Usually he avoided such conversations. But what was the point in that? Best to stay ahead of trouble if that was even possible, though in this case it might already be too late for that.

Micah knew the minute he stepped into the house that he was indeed too late in beating the bad news home. A copy of the *Goshen News* sat on the kitchen table, where supper should have been. His *daddi* and *mammi* were sitting at the table, obviously waiting for him.

"I was coming home to talk to you about that." He slid into a seat at the table.

When his *daddi* finally looked up, Micah's heart sank. He saw an entire world of emotions in the set of his mouth, the weariness of his eyes and the frown lines that seemed permanently etched on his forehead.

Mammi sat with her hands cradling a cup of coffee. Supper was on the stove, but apparently no one was expecting to eat anytime soon.

His *daddi* sighed heavily, as if he were carrying the weight of the world and needed to set it down. "We're disappointed, Micah."

"But I can explain."

"How can you explain that?" His voice remained a low growl.

Micah could have handled a raised voice. Hadn't he just told Susannah about how his parents would holler at each other? But always, always they would make up before darkness fell on the day. No, what his *daddi*'s voice told him was that he'd already made up his mind, already decided on his judgment and there would be no arguing.

Still, he had to try.

"I did take the picture."

"With the *Englisch* phone."

"I had never been to a barn raising with so many people, and I wanted to show my *schweschdern*."

"We make quite an effort to keep the *Englisch* photographers at bay, only to have you splash our doings on the front page of the local paper." *Daddi* grabbed the paper from the table and shook it at Micah. "I don't know what you were thinking, but I do know that I warned you."

"But I didn't—"

"We are to remain separate, Micah. Do you not understand what that means?"

"I did *not* send that picture in to the paper."

"Now you're denying taking it?"

"*Nein*. I took it, but someone else sent it in."

"That makes no sense."

"It was a friend of mine."

"An *Englisch* friend, no doubt."

"He thought he was helping me. He thought I could use the money, but he didn't ask me first. I had no idea he would do such a thing."

"You should have considered that possibility before you took the photograph." *Daddi* dropped the paper and slapped the flat of his palm against the table. "If you hadn't taken it to begin with, we wouldn't be having this discussion."

"What is so wrong with people seeing that we help one another?" Micah knew his temper was winning out over his common sense, but he couldn't help it. He couldn't sit there and not defend himself.

"Go and get the phone."

"What?"

"You heard me. Go and get the phone."

Micah didn't have to go and get the phone, since it was still in his pocket from having gone to town. He handed it to his *daddi*, thinking that perhaps he was going to keep it awhile or hand it over to the bishop or mail it back home to his parents. He never once thought that the man would drop it on the floor, stand and crush it beneath his foot.

"Are you crazy? Do you know how much that cost?"

"Perhaps you should learn to use your money more wisely, then." He didn't bother to pick up the pieces. Instead he snatched his hat off the hook on the wall. "I'm warning you again, Micah. You step outside the lines one more time—"

"And are those lines that you've drawn? Or the bishop? Because last time I spoke with Thomas, he was quite happy with my work."

"Your work—yes. But your actions outside work? You should stop and consider the repercussions of those, Micah. As far as I'm concerned, you're on your last chance." *Daddi* didn't even turn to look at him. Something about the stoop of the man's shoulders pulled guilt strings in Micah's heart, and if he'd even turned and given him a hint of compassion he might have let his sympathy for his grandfather win over his anger.

But he didn't turn.

He didn't look at him.

And Micah quickly brushed away any such thoughts of sympathy. His *daddi* was obstinate and unfair. He did not deserve anyone's sympathy.

"Go against our *Ordnung* one more time, and you'll have to find another place to live."

"You're kicking me out?"

Now *Daddi* did turn. The stump of his right arm rested in the pocket that *Mammi* had sewn from the sleeve. His left hand was tanned and strong. At the moment he was using it to rub a circle on his chest.

"Maybe you should calm down, John." It was the first words his *mammi* had spoken.

"I'm fine." He never took his eyes off Micah. "The crops are in. I won't need your help around here except for feeding the horses and cleaning out the stalls."

"Meaning what?"

"Meaning I want you to find another job." And with that final jab, he turned and left the house.

Micah sat staring at the door his *daddi* had walked through.

Why did life have to be like this?

Why did his grandfather make a problem where there was none?

Mammi stood, fetched the broom and dustpan and swept up the pieces of phone. She held the dustpan out to him. "Want what's left of it?"

He waved her away.

"Your *daddi*…"

"I know. He wants what's best for me."

"It's true, Micah. Whether you can see it or not, it's true."

"Is it also true that he doesn't need me around here

to help him? Or does he just not *want* me around to help him? Because it's pretty plain to me that he can't stand the sight of me."

"You're being unfair."

"*He*'s being unfair."

His *mammi* had never been particularly demonstrative with her emotions, but now she sat down beside him and pulled his hands into her lap. "He's a *gut* man, your *daddi*, and I won't have you disrespecting him."

Her words were softened by her touch as she reached out and untwisted one of his suspenders. "John's not a proud man, but he sees things as black-and-white. He wants you to put away your childhood things…"

"By stomping on them?"

"Become a man and put away childish things."

"And get another job."

"Only for the mornings. You'll continue to help Thomas in the afternoons." She patted him on the shoulder, stood and walked to the stove. "Dinner will be ready in thirty minutes."

Micah wanted to say he wasn't hungry, but in truth his stomach was gurgling. Refusing to eat would be childish, plus he would go to bed hungry. There was no use trying to avoid his *daddi*, and he wasn't ready to move out. The thought hadn't really ever occurred to him.

He'd thought of moving home, but not of moving out.

Where would he go?

And how would he afford it?

Nein. He needed to find a way to make this work until he could return to Maine, which meant he needed a job. He remembered the older *Englisch* woman, the car that had dropped her off, the sign in the window of the car.

The idea he'd had would put extra money in his pocket and satisfy his *daddi*'s demands. As to whether they would approve of what he hoped to do, time would tell.

Chapter Eight

Susannah did not plan on telling her *mamm* about the kiss.

But as they were sitting at the kitchen table later that evening—her *mamm* knitting and Susannah stitching together the top of a nine-patch quilt—the details of the day came tumbling out of her mouth.

If her *mamm* was surprised, she hid it well.

"You've been kissed before."

"*Ya*, but it's been a while."

"Since before your cancer."

"Just about two years ago, which doesn't say much for my dating life."

"You know, Susannah, you're not damaged goods."

"Why would you say that?" Susannah pricked her finger with the needle, jerked her hand away and inspected it to make sure she wouldn't bleed on the fabric.

"I sometimes think that you have the opinion that no one would want you, that you're not whole."

"I'm not whole. The doctors removed part of me, leaving me not whole."

"Not true." Her *mamm* shook her head so vigorously

that her *kapp* strings bounced. It reminded Susannah so much of Sharon that she couldn't help smiling. "You are fearfully and wonderfully made."

"Is now really the time to quote Scripture?"

"If it fits, then yes, it is."

Susannah ducked her head to better see the seam she was attempting to stitch. In truth, her mother's words brought tears to her eyes. Some days she hated that she cried so easily, that she was so emotional. Other days it seemed as if she was viewing life from a distance and couldn't feel a thing. She wasn't sure which was worse.

"After my diagnosis, Samuel treated me differently, almost as if I was contagious."

"It's obvious now to both of us that you and Samuel were not meant to be anything more than *freinden*."

"I wish it had been obvious then. At the time, the way he treated me and then our breakup... It just—well it hurt."

"And if I could have spared you that hurt I would have."

"It doesn't bother me much anymore, not really. I've moved on." As she uttered those words, words she'd probably said before, Susannah was surprised to find that they were true in a new way. Thinking of Samuel didn't bring the old ache that it had at one time.

"My point is that your cancer wasn't something that *Gotte* didn't see coming. It wasn't a mistake on His part."

"How could it have been intentional?"

"I don't know. Most of the whys in life I don't understand."

"What you're saying doesn't make any sense."

"Do you think that Caroline Byers's *bruder* is a mistake?"

"Because he has Down syndrome? Of course not."

"He's not damaged goods?"

"You know that no one thinks that." She glanced up to see her *mamm* studying her very closely. "A person who is born different isn't damaged in the way that a buggy might be after a wreck."

"I'm glad you feel that way."

"We all do. We all love Stephen. Have you seen how he is with their sheep? He's named every one, and they come to him when he calls them. Stephen isn't damaged. He's special."

"So *Gotte* didn't make a mistake with him?"

"I don't know why he's different, but the fact that he is doesn't cause anyone to love him any less. So no, I don't think *Gotte* made a mistake."

"You'd never throw him away."

Now her *mamm* was teasing her. Sure enough, when Susannah glanced up, she noticed a smile tugging at her *mamm*'s lips.

"I would not, and no one who knows him would."

"Then how are you any different?"

"I don't follow."

"Only because you're being stubborn."

Instead of asking her *mamm* to explain, Susannah allowed a silence to permeate the room. She became aware of the sound of her mother's knitting needles, the crickets outside, the creak of her father's rocking chair from where he sat on the porch.

Finally, Susannah gave up on the seam that was growing increasingly crooked. She stood, heated water on the stove and brought two cups of tea and a plate of oatmeal bars to the table.

"Danki."

"Gem gschehne."

And those words, that tradition of gratefulness and kindness, seemed to loosen the cat's grip on Susannah's tongue.

"I don't think I'm damaged, but I do think I'm different."

"Every one of *Gotte*'s creatures is unique."

"And maybe it wasn't a mistake that I had cancer. Maybe *Gotte* has some grand plan, some greater good that will come from it."

"He used Balaam's donkey. I'm sure He can use your cancer."

"But I am different, *Mamm*. There's no more use in denying that than there would be in denying that Stephen is different."

Her *mamm* nodded and reached for an oatmeal bar.

"So what are you really worried about?"

Susannah sipped her tea, then sighed and closed her eyes for a moment. When she opened them, her *mamm* was studying her.

"That the kiss meant nothing to Micah and everything to me. That the kiss meant everything to both of us. That he doesn't understand the baggage that I carry around with me—that there is a chance the cancer will return."

"And there's an even better chance that it won't."

"Regardless, I will not be able to have children."

Her *mamm* didn't answer right away. In fact, Susannah thought she wouldn't. They finished their snack, her *mamm* stood, rinsed their cups, covered the oatmeal bars with a dish towel and finally sat down across from her again.

"If Micah loves you—and I'm not suggesting that's

true or that enduring love always follows one kiss—but if he does, then it won't matter to him whether or not you can have children."

"How can it *not* matter to him?" As hard as she tried to blink away the tears, they insisted on coursing down her cheeks. Her *mamm* reached forward and thumbed them away, then kissed her on the forehead.

"Because love doesn't work that way."

Micah spoke with Thomas early the next morning. As he laid out the details of his plan, he noticed Thomas's hesitancy and expression of skepticism.

"I'd like your approval to just try this—give it a few weeks, a month at the most. If it doesn't work, then I'll try to find employment at one of the businesses in town."

"And you've spoken to your *daddi* about this?"

"*Nein.* I wanted your approval first, and I also still need to speak with Widow Miller and finalize the details. Once everything is in place, I'll go to *Daddi* and explain the entire thing. You have my word on that."

Thomas clasped him on the back. "And you've prayed about this?"

"I have, and I feel that *Gotte* put this idea in my mind. I certainly would have never thought of it on my own."

"All from seeing a driver drop a woman off at the Dairy Queen." They were sitting in the farrier shop. Thomas had been working on his accounting books. He picked up a pen, clicked it twice and sat it back down. "Coincidence or possibly *Gotte*'s guiding hand."

"I honestly think it's something I'd be *gut* at. I have

a lot of energy, it drives me crazy to sit still and I have an outgoing personality."

"That you do." Thomas glanced around his farrier shop. "I can take care of today's work. See if you can get the details of your plan worked out."

"Danki."

Micah was almost to the door when Thomas called him back. "Perhaps it would help if we switched your hours with me to the morning. That way you could work on your new business into the early evening when necessary."

"You'd be willing to do that?"

"Sure. Seems to me you'd have a more flexible schedule then, to accommodate your customers."

"What about our meetings, you know, where I'm learning to be properly Amish?"

"I suppose we can talk while we're working, like we are now."

Micah wanted to jump and shout at the same time. Instead, he smiled his thanks and headed down the lane. Widow Miller lived two miles away. He'd be walking that distance twice a day, but Micah didn't mind. He could cover a mile in twenty minutes, and the exercise would do him good.

He'd met the older woman when he and Thomas had gone to her house to shoe her buggy horse. The gelding was not getting enough exercise and generally wasn't being looked after as well as he should have been. Nothing neglectful, really, but the horse could use a good brushing and the buggy definitely needed to be cleaned.

It took him ten minutes to explain his plan and another twenty to work out the details. Thirty minutes later, he was ready to go to the Goshen Library to make some flyers and copy them, but first he needed his *daddi*'s approval.

"Just once, why can't you do something normal?"

Micah had dared to hope that his *daddi* would be as open-minded as Thomas. Apparently that was hoping for too much. He tried to tap down his anger—count to five, take deep breaths, be patient. It wasn't working. He could feel his pulse accelerating and sweat running down his back.

How he would love to storm out of the barn, but that was what a child would do. He was a man now, and he was ready to act like one. He was ready to stand and fight for what he wanted to do.

"You want me to go and work at the RV factory? Or maybe you see me riding over to Amish Acres every day, showing *Englischers* what it's like to live simply."

"There's nothing wrong with either one of those jobs."

Micah took a deep breath. "I didn't say there was, but I think my idea is something I could be successful at."

"And Thomas approved of it?"

"He did. He even offered to shift my hours to mornings."

His *daddi* turned back to the plow blade that he was sharpening. He'd positioned the blade in a bench vise to hold it steady. It was amazing what the man had learned to do with one arm.

"And you'll be splitting what you earn with Widow Miller?"

"Fifty-fifty. Seems only fair since I'll be using her buggy and horse. Plus, it'll be better for the horse."

"So you explained."

Micah waited, and it seemed that his *daddi* had forgotten he was there. Finally, he raised his good arm and made a motion as if he was shooing away a fly. "I expect you to make good on what you told Thomas. If you're not seeing enough business in two weeks…"

"We agreed to a month."

"And if the widow is unhappy with the deal for any reason, then you abandon this plan and get a real job."

"Done."

If he'd been expecting his *daddi*'s blessing, he might have stood there a long time. Instead, he took his grandfather's grunt as permission, hitched their mare to the buggy and headed to town to make it to the library before it closed.

Susannah and her *mamm* had planned to go to a sew-in the following Monday. She hadn't seen Micah on Sunday, but then perhaps his grandparents had lunch with someone else. It was their off Sunday. She was a little surprised that he hadn't stopped by, but then it wasn't like he'd promised he would.

The sew-in would be a nice distraction. Sharon and Shiloh were excited to see their friends, but if Susannah was honest with herself, she was rather dreading the entire thing. There was no doubt that she'd be grilled about Micah's comings and goings. He seemed to be the talk of the town these days, which just proved that very little was happening in May in Goshen, Indiana.

But her mother was looking forward to her day off the farm, and Susannah knew that begging off would make things harder since she wouldn't be there to help keep an eye on the twins. It would actually be selfish for her to do so when there was no good reason not to go, and besides she'd just have to face everyone at the next Sunday meeting. Might as well get it over with on a beautiful summer day.

The sew-in had been scheduled so they could complete half a dozen quilts that they planned to donate to the school auction held every summer. That event attracted *Englischers* with money to spend on authentic Amish items. The funds raised helped to pay for school supplies as well as any needed repairs to the building.

She found herself growing more excited as her *mamm* drove the buggy toward Widow Miller's, where the sew-in was to take place.

After they'd parked the buggy, Susannah asked Sharon and Shiloh to help her. "Can each of you carry in one of our lunch dishes?"

"I can carry the big one." Shiloh stood up straight and tall as if to prove her strength.

"Better give me the little one," Sharon said. "I drop sometimes."

"Both of you hold the dish with both hands and walk—don't run."

Taking their task very seriously, they walked toward Widow Miller's front porch and up the steps.

"They're *gut* girls." Her *mamm* hooked her arm through Susannah's. "You've been rather quiet today."

"Have I?"

"Anything you want to talk about?"

"I'm dreading everyone asking me questions about Micah."

"And why would you dread that?"

"First of all, because I'm not his keeper."

"But you are his friend, and it's normal for people to be curious."

"I suppose. And second, folks seem to assume the worst where Micah is concerned. I guess his first impression wasn't a particularly *gut* one."

"You can set the record straight."

And then they were in the widow's house, and the large group of women assembled there naturally separated into smaller groups by generational lines. Susannah supposed that was because friendships had formed many years ago, and there weren't that many chances to all get together and catch up. Sometimes it seemed to Susannah that she knew more about her cousins in Ohio than she did about someone living down the street.

She went out the back door. Two quilts had been set up on standing looms. Around one was most of the sixteen-to-eighteen-year-old group. She remembered how she'd looked forward to these days when she was first out of school. She hadn't missed sitting in a school desk for the majority of the day, but she'd certainly missed seeing her friends. Watching that younger group brought a sharp pain of nostalgia that she hadn't expected.

Did she miss being so young?

It wasn't as if she was an old maid now.

But then she turned toward her group, which was gathered around a double-wedding-ring quilt that had also been placed on a quilt stand. They were situated more toward the side yard, with a view of both the back and the front of the house. It seemed to her that over half the group was pregnant. Many of the others had babies in carriers on the ground beside them. Only Susannah, Deborah and three other girls remained unmarried.

Perhaps she didn't really fit in with either group, which was a rather depressing thought. Regardless, there was quilting to be done.

She clenched her teeth and prayed for patience.

Strangely, no one asked her a thing about Micah.

There was plenty of "How are you today, Susannah?" and "What a pretty apron. Is that new?" and "I saw your *schweschdern* flitting around here. They certainly are growing."

She felt herself relax, so much so that when she saw looks passing between others—knowing looks—she convinced herself that it had nothing to do with her or Micah.

They'd sewn for most of the morning when she heard the clatter of buggy wheels.

Again the knowing looks, and then as one, they stopped sewing and turned their attention toward the front of the house.

And that was when she saw him. Micah was driving Widow Miller's buggy. When he pulled to a stop, he jumped out, walked around the buggy and helped out Old Sally. It was when he closed the buggy door after her that Susannah saw the sign.

It read Amish Taxi, followed by a phone number.

Micah had helped Old Sally up the porch steps. As he returned to his buggy, he stopped and waved— whether at Susannah or the group in general, she wasn't sure.

He looked inordinately pleased with himself.

And Susannah suddenly wished she could melt into the ground because conversations had erupted to her right and her left, and they were all about Micah and his new business.

* * *

She didn't have a moment alone with Deborah until they were eating lunch.

As usual, Sharon and Shiloh had finished in record time, so Susannah took her plate of food out to the picnic table that was situated next to the swings and seesaw, long ago remnants of a time when Naomi Miller had *kinner* and *grandkinner* around. Now all of her family lived in Shipshewana—close enough to visit, but not as often as she'd like. Susannah wondered why she hadn't moved with her family. Before she could think that through, they were surrounded by loud, energetic children. The afternoon was filled with a dozen girls and boys running and shouting and using up their abundance of energy.

Deborah nudged her with her shoulder. "You really didn't know?"

"I really didn't."

"It was the only topic of conversation before you got here, and then I tried to get your attention."

"You did?"

"*Ya.* I was…" Deborah pantomimed raising her hand above her head and bringing it back down over her *kapp.*

"Thought you were swatting at a bee."

"Word is he started this morning, but he put out flyers all over the community on Saturday."

"Good grief, word travels fast."

"You know the Amish grapevine."

Susannah momentarily covered her face with her hands.

"It's not so bad."

"Not so bad? Amish Taxi? It sounds like a bad joke."

"But it is honest labor, and to hear the girls talk, he had your father's approval."

"What?" Susannah's voice rose so high that both Sharon and Shiloh turned to look at her. She waved at them to go back to playing. "My *dat* knew and didn't tell me?"

"You've told me before that he's very private about things that he discusses with others."

"That's true."

"Seems to me it's honest work, and what else is he to do? The crops are in and…"

"And there are at least a dozen people hiring in Goshen to help with summer tourists."

"I suspect he'll have a line of folks waiting to ride in an Amish Taxi. He'll be helping with tourists plenty." Deborah started laughing and then, against her better instincts, Susannah joined her. It was rather funny if you thought about it.

It wasn't until they were all back home and had finished eating dinner that she had a chance to talk to her *dat* about it. Sharon and Shiloh were upstairs preparing for bed. Playing with the other children all day had certainly worn them out. They'd practically fallen asleep with their *kapp* strings in their soup.

"Seemed like a rather *gut* idea to me," Thomas said. "He's splitting what he earns with the widow, since he's using her buggy and horse."

"He is?"

"The horse needs more exercise, and Widow Miller can certainly use the money."

"She needs money?"

"It's not easy for the older ones." Her *mamm* filled their mugs with decaffeinated coffee.

"What do you mean?" Susannah asked.

"About what?"

"About it not being easy on the older folks. I thought we… Well, I thought that we provided for those in our community who had less."

"We do, as is right and proper." Her *dat* pointed an unlit pipe at her. He'd had it for as long as she could remember. She'd asked her *mamm* about it once. The pipe had been his father's. He only actually smoked it once a day, only after the evening meal, and only out on the porch. "The Scripture tells us as much—to care for the orphans and the widows."

"Many of our elders have family close by, but for those who don't, finances can be tight. They'll never want for house repairs or groceries, but even Widow Miller likes to have a little extra change in her pocketbook."

"She has family in Shipshe."

"That she does, but there's some difficulty there. She doesn't ask them for extra because she doesn't think they have it."

Susannah shook her head. "We're getting off topic here. How is Micah's business even supposed to work?"

"Maybe you should ask him yourself." Her *dat* pointed the pipe toward the window, where she could just make out Micah crossing the field that separated her parents' home from his grandparents.

Susannah ignored the smile that passed between her parents, excused herself and met Micah before he'd made it to the porch.

"Amish Taxi? Really?"

"I'm sorry I didn't get a chance to tell you myself."

"You certainly don't owe me an explanation." The

words came out snippier than she intended, so she looked up, down and around, and then asked, "Wanna look at Shiloh's kittens?"

Instead of answering, he entwined his fingers with hers, and that seemed so right, felt so natural, that she couldn't possibly hold on to her frustration. Fifteen minutes later they'd examined each kitten. There were five in all—four striped and one white.

"We never had any cats growing up." Micah ran his finger from the top of the white kitten's head, along its spine, to the tail. He was rewarded with a purr that resembled a small power motor. He glanced up at her and smiled. "This one likes me."

"You never had barn cats?"

"*Nein*. My *mamm* was allergic. If we had church in a member's barn and they had cats, she'd start sneezing and her eyes would water, and she'd have to excuse herself and go outside."

"You don't seem allergic."

"Guess not." He placed the kitten down next to the mama cat. They walked outside and stood looking at the near-dark sky.

Susannah could make out the first star, but there was still enough light for her to turn and study Micah. "Tell me how this new business of yours is supposed to work."

"Pretty simple, really. Widow Miller lets me know ahead of time if she will need the horse and buggy. Mostly she only drives to church or the grocery store or sometimes a doctor's appointment. It was one of the things that made me think of it. Her horse—Sunny Boy—needs more exercise. He almost seemed depressed when your *dat* and I went over to shoe him last time."

"Okay. So you walk to her house, harness Sunny Boy to the buggy and then…"

"I bought another phone, but not like the last one. This one doesn't even have the internet. It's only for making and receiving calls." He had to explain to her about his *daddi* crushing his cell phone and insisting he get a job.

"I'm sorry, Micah. I had no idea he was so strict."

Micah shrugged. "I don't think it's about me as much as it is about him coming to terms with the changes around him."

"That's awfully mature of you to say."

"I've never been accused of being mature before." He stepped out from under the overhang of the barn. "Want to walk a little? For some reason, I'm feeling restless."

So they walked, and they talked some more as the moon rose and darkness fell properly over the fields.

He'd had a dozen rides his first day of business.

He'd made two hundred dollars.

Half of that he gave to the widow when he returned the horse and buggy.

Susannah thought of what her *dat* had said about helping the elderly. Micah was certainly doing that.

"This morning I worked a couple of hours for your *dat*, and when things slowed down, he told me to go on to town and get started on my new venture."

"I can see why my *dat* gave you his approval, but I'm a little surprised your *daddi* went along with it."

"Guess he felt like he didn't have a choice, since the bishop had approved."

"But he wasn't happy."

"Nein."

"Maybe he will be, when he sees how you're helping folks."

"Half of my customers were *Englisch*, just wanting to ride in an authentic buggy."

"That's pretty common around here."

"Not so much in Maine." Micah's voice turned somber. "*Daddi* thinks we should be separate. I'm sure that's the part of my plan that he doesn't approve of… as if being around *Englischers* will rub off on me. Next thing you know, I'll be wearing blue jeans and carrying a cell phone."

"You were wearing blue jeans the first day I saw you."

"True."

"And you had a phone in your back pocket."

"See? I'm already corrupted, so what harm can come?"

What harm indeed. Susannah had heard every possible scenario as she'd sat in the sewing circle. Everything from he shouldn't be alone with *Englisch* girls to he might put Timothy Zook out of business. Timothy ran a buggy ride for *Englischers* during the summer, and Susannah knew for a fact that he had more business than he cared to have. He had refused to extend his hours and had even cut his days back to three a week. Micah would actually be filling a gap that needed to be filled, and he'd be helping Amish folks at the same time.

She understood in that moment that Micah was a good person. It was only that he considered things from a different perspective than most. Who else would have thought of being an Amish taxi driver?

She walked over to an old tree that held a tire swing.

"Get in," he said.

"What is it with you and swings?"

"Just get in already. I'll push."

"I'm not even sure it will hold me."

Micah tugged on the rope, looked up at the limb and declared it sound.

He turned the tire upside down and ran his hand inside to make sure there was no water or critters, then he held it high as she wiggled her shoulders through. And the next thing Susannah knew, the tire swing was going up, then down and twirling and then back up again, and all of the responsibilities that she carried on her shoulders—or thought she did—fell away. Suddenly she was simply a young woman in a swing being pushed by a handsome young man. And above her the stars seemed to wink their approval.

Chapter Nine

What Micah didn't share with Susannah was that he was giving his grandparents half of his portion of the day's earnings. Out of two hundred dollars, the widow received one hundred, his grandparents fifty, and he kept fifty. It seemed like a fair enough arrangement to him. His grandparents were providing him a place to stay and feeding him. He also received a small amount each week for working with Thomas Beiler in the farrier shop. Between the two jobs, he felt like he was pulling his weight.

He would be lying to himself if he didn't admit that he thought his grandfather would thank him, or at least acknowledge in some way that he'd done well.

Instead, the next morning his grandfather had ignored the money sitting on the middle of the table. When his *mammi* brought it up, he'd simply grunted and told her to put it in the mason jar she kept in the pantry. "Something's bound to break soon, and we'll need it."

The meal passed in silence, the way most of their

meals did, and then without another word, his *daddi* stood, pushed in his chair and walked out toward the barn.

"Has he always been like this?" Micah asked.

"Like what?" His *mammi* stood and began clearing away the breakfast dishes.

"Solemn, taciturn, grumpy."

Mammi had her back to him as she filled the kitchen sink with warm water and then a splash of dish-washing detergent, but he could still make out the heavy sigh.

He carried the rest of the dishes to her and picked up a dish towel. "I'll dry if you wash."

Which seemed to ease her burden a bit.

Was it that easy?

Did helping with dishes make that big a difference?

Or was it more that his grandmother wanted to be seen, that she wanted to be thanked for her labors the same way that Micah wanted to be thanked for the fifty dollars sitting on the table? When was the last time someone had thanked her for making a meal or putting clean sheets on the bed or sweeping the floors?

"Breakfast was *gut*."

"*Ya?*"

"*Mamm* never did learn how to make biscuits from scratch."

Mammi started laughing. "I tried teaching her, and I know her mother tried, as well. She always seemed to forget at least one ingredient, and there aren't that many ingredients in biscuits."

"I might have starved if Becky hadn't taken over the cooking."

"Your *schweschdern* are all *gut* girls. It's funny

when you think about it. I suppose we all have things that we're good at and other things that we never can quite get the hang of."

They continued washing and drying, and Micah was surprised to find that the silence between them felt comfortable. He realized he'd miss this when he went home—this time with grandparents that he barely knew.

"I wish I could figure out how to talk to him. Everything I say seems to irritate him one way or another."

"Your *daddi* never was much of a conversationalist."

"So it's not just me?"

"*Nein*, though..." She shook her head, as if she wished she hadn't started the sentence that she couldn't bring herself to finish.

"Might as well say it."

"It's only that he worries about you. Your *dat* was our only son, and now you're his only son."

"I'm supposed to carry on the family name."

"I don't know about that. If the Lord wills it..."

"But..."

"But you do have a responsibility to your family, even to your *schweschdern*."

Micah was shaking his head before she'd even finished. "They're all older than me. Trust me—they're not depending on me for anything."

"That's not true." *Mammi* pulled the plug on the sink water and watched it swirl down the drain. "It might seem that way now, because of your age. And you'll always hold a special place in their hearts because you're the baby *bruder* they hoped and prayed for. But when you're older—when you're forty or fifty or sixty—it won't matter that you're the youngest. They'll look to you for advice. It's just the way Amish families are."

"Hard to imagine."

"I know it is."

The sun was peeking over the horizon, and he had chores to do before heading over to work at the bishop's. Hopefully, his afternoon would once again be full of taxi customers. He was looking forward to the day, and he felt some better about his grandfather. He might never understand him, but at least he could sympathize a little with what the old guy was going through.

He'd given his grandmother a quick hug, fetched his hat and was headed out the back door when his *mammi* called him back. "Keep an eye on him for me."

"Daddi?"

"Ya, just…let me know if you notice he's not feeling well."

"Is he not feeling well?"

"Nothing that he would admit to." She walked over to him, straightened his hat and stood on tiptoes to kiss his cheek. "But as you so clearly pointed out, he's grumpier than ever. It could be that he's feeling worse than he's letting on."

As he walked to the barn, Micah realized that it wasn't *Daddi's* amputated arm that *Mammi* was talking about. *Daddi* had been dealing with that longer than Micah had been alive. No, if he wasn't feeling well, it was something else, and it was something that he wasn't even talking to *Mammi* about. The question was whether it was anything serious, and if it was, how they'd convince him to see a doctor about it.

The next day, Susannah stood and stared at the calendar on the wall. She'd had the day circled since her last visit, six months before.

"Are you sure you don't want me to go with you?" Her *mamm* was sewing new dresses for Shiloh and Sharon on the old treadle machine they kept in Susannah's shop. Susannah had offered to do it, but in truth, she was better with quilts than she was with garments.

"*Nein.* I can go by myself."

"We'll go with you, Susannah." Sharon was sitting on the floor playing with a ball and jacks.

"We can hold your hand," Shiloh said from her chair beside the sewing machine, where she was watching her mother sew each stitch.

"By the time you get home, these two girls will have nice new frocks."

"Because we're growing," Shiloh said.

"Like weeds. That's what *Dat* said. 'You girls are growing like weeds.'" Sharon's imitation of their *dat* caused everyone to laugh and eased the worry that Susannah was feeling.

As she directed their buggy horse, Percy, toward town, she realized she wasn't terribly worried about what the doctor would say. There was always a chance that her cancer would return, but wouldn't she know it? Wouldn't she feel different?

The fear of what might happen was something she'd learned to live with—at least some days. Other days were a bit harder. All she knew for certain was that she felt better, healthier than she had in a very long time. Her cancer no longer was something that she thought about constantly. It no longer defined her, or at least she didn't think it did. She was enjoying being a normal young woman, and she wasn't ready for that to change. Not yet. Maybe not ever.

She'd stopped by for blood work the week before.

Today she would have an examination and then meet with the doctor to discuss her test results.

Dr. Kelly's office always made Susannah smile—it was decorated with pictures from her patients, some who were obviously quite young. The drawings sported stick figures holding a stethoscope, large hearts decorating each person and flowers taller than the people.

As the doctor walked in and picked up a folder, Susannah was overwhelmed by a fluttery feeling in her stomach—it wasn't fear exactly, but some emotion just as powerful.

"Your test results look good."

"They do?" The butterflies in her stomach scattered, replaced by sudden and total euphoria.

"Were you expecting something else?" Dr. Kelly had black skin, shoulder-length hair and kind eyes. She seemed ageless, but the picture of two teenage boys on her desk—boys Susannah could tell by one glance were her sons—indicated she had to be close to forty. "Talk to me, Susannah. Having you been feeling poorly?"

"*Nein*. I feel fine, and I wasn't expecting anything else. I always hope and pray the tests will come back fine, but I also try to prepare myself. You know…"

"Go on."

"Well, I try to weigh myself a couple of times a week to make sure I'm not losing weight, because last time…"

"I remember how thin you'd become when you first came to me."

"And I keep the journal you had me start…saying how I feel each day."

"That's good, Susannah. It's good that you're being

vigilant about your health and keeping your appointments. Everything here looks fine. In fact, you seem healthier—and happier—than I've seen you in a long time."

Dr. Kelly waited. She didn't check her watch or tap her fingers against the desktop. If anything, she relaxed into her chair, indicating Susannah could take her time sorting through her emotions.

"Can I ask you a question?"

"Of course."

"How many of your patients, patients my age, go on to live happy lives—happily married lives?"

"That's an interesting question. I'd say roughly about the same percentage as those without cancer."

"Oh."

"I just read a study that Americans are waiting longer to marry, and more people than ever before are choosing not to marry at all. But that's probably not true among the Amish."

"It's not true among the Amish I know. Most Amish pair up by the time they're twenty, and they stay married for life."

Dr. Kelly sat there, her fingertips steepled together, for another moment. Then she crossed her arms on the desk and leaned forward. "I can tell you my opinion, but it's based on purely anecdotal evidence."

Susannah nodded, though she wasn't completely sure what anecdotal evidence was.

"It seems that my patients put their lives on hold when they first receive their cancer diagnoses. If they're young and just beginning to consider marrying, they put that out of their mind for a while. If they're older and were thinking of retiring and traveling the

US, they put that on hold. They press the pause button on their lives and deal with their cancer."

"And then?"

"And then the vast majority of them move on. They press the go button. They take up where they left off. Not all of them, of course. For some people, a cancer diagnosis becomes a new identity and changes the way they view every facet of their lives. They don't know how to move past it." She stood, smiled and walked around the desk, before sitting in a chair across from Susannah.

"I have a feeling that what you're experiencing, the thing that's worrying you, is that you are ready to press that go button. And if you're looking for my permission or approval to do so, then you have it. You've always had it. Now all you need is to find the courage to do so."

Susannah didn't remember driving home.

Once there, Shiloh and Shannon pounced on her, insisting she sit in the living room until they ran upstairs and tried on their new dresses. Her *mamm* knew she had good news before she said a word, and when her *dat* came in for dinner, he immediately enfolded her in a hug.

"*Gotte* is *gut*," he murmured, and Susannah nodded her head in agreement.

The rest of the evening passed in a blur. It was when she was kneeling by her bed to say her prayers, which sometimes felt childish but mostly felt necessary, that she realized she was ready to push that go button Dr. Kelly had talked about. She understood in that moment that she was tired of worrying about what might or might not happen.

Would her feelings for Micah grow even stronger? Did he feel the same?

What would they do when he moved back to Maine? What if her cancer returned?

And beyond all those questions, there were several that had been in her mind since she'd first learned she had cancer. Would someone really want to marry her knowing that she couldn't have children? Would it be selfish of her to do such a thing? How would she know if any marriage proposal was motivated by true love or something done out of pity?

As she knelt there on the hardwood floor, she didn't receive any answers straight from heaven, but she did resolve to stop worrying and trust that God had a plan.

Micah's afternoons driving Amish and *Englischers* grew even busier than that first day. The following week, Old Eli actually flagged him down from the side of the road. "Heard you're giving rides, and my wife says I can't drive anymore on account of my cataracts."

"I'm headed back to town now. Want a lift?"

"That's why I'm standing out here flagging you down."

Micah generally didn't quote a price for his rides. People paid what they could—most offered something between five and ten dollars. It added up quickly. When he didn't have any Amish folks who needed a lift, he drove to downtown Goshen, parked near the Old Bag Factory and put his cardboard sign out.

Amish Taxi.

$10/person for twenty minutes.

Inevitably, there was a queue of people by the time he returned with the first passenger.

The day flew by. He lost track of how much he'd made, but he thought he'd exceeded the previous day's total. It seemed word was spreading quickly, and he already had rides lined up for each day the next week. After he'd dropped off the last *Englischer* for the day—a lady who simply wanted to drive through the countryside and look at the farms—he stopped by the general store.

"Can I help you?" One of the Amish girls from their church district was working the register. She looked to be about sixteen years old and had freckles across her cheeks and nose. Micah might have been introduced to her at church, but he couldn't remember her name.

"I guess I need a calendar."

"Like a wall calendar?"

"*Nein.* Something I can put in my pocket."

"I know just what you're talking about."

Unfortunately, they all looked pretty girlie to him— the outsides decorated with flowers and hearts and motivational slogans. He settled for the one with kittens, since it reminded him of the white cat he'd held at Susannah's. He bought a pen as well, and at the last minute he spied a display of rose-scented goat lotion. "This stuff work?"

"I guess. My *mammi* uses it."

So he added a tube to his purchases. When was the last time someone had bought his *mammi* a gift? Probably not in the last ten years, since it seemed his *daddi* had been in a bad mood at least that long. He carried his purchases to the register.

"The calendar must be for your Amish taxi business."

"It is."

"I think what you're doing is so smart. Some people say it's a travesty—that's the word Ruth Lapp used when she was in here earlier—but I'm not sure what that means."

"It's bad."

"I gathered as much. Still and all, if you're going to be Amish in this day and age, you have to learn to adapt."

"Not something we're well-known for."

"I'm aware."

"I'm Micah, by the way."

"I'm Lydia." She smiled at him, her cheeks a rosy red.

Did she think he was flirting with her? The old Micah would have been. Maybe out of habit he'd done or said something that she'd taken the wrong way.

"Can you ring me up one more of those tubes of lotion?"

"Sure."

"It's for my girlfriend, Susannah Beiler. Maybe you know her?"

"*Ya*, I know Susannah. I didn't know you two were stepping out." She fetched another tube of the lotion, and then placed all of his items in a bag and counted out his change. "If it doesn't work out with Susannah, you know where to find me."

It was a rather bold statement coming from an Amish girl, but somehow the way she said it, the words seemed more friendly than flirty.

Instead of responding, he waved goodbye and moseyed out to the buggy. The week had turned into a fine one even if it had suffered a rocky start. Maybe by the time he got home, his *daddi* would have found something to smile about, or maybe he needed to stop worrying about whether that would happen. He hadn't caused the old guy's unhappiness; at least he hadn't caused all of it, so there was little chance he could help him get over it.

He returned the buggy and horse to Widow Miller, counted out her portion of the money and turned down oatmeal cookies and milk.

"*Mammi* serves dinner pretty early. Wouldn't want to ruin my appetite."

But as he drew close to his grandfather's place, he saw a van parked in the lane, and he knew that he wouldn't be eating anytime soon.

He rushed up the front porch steps, where his *mammi* stood on one side of the screen door and a reporter for the *Goshen News* stood on the other.

"Micah, I've told this woman that we're not interested in being interviewed. Now, please see her off our property."

"Micah, I'm so glad to meet you. I'm Phoebe Jackson with the *Goshen News*."

The *Englisch* woman turned her attention toward him, and he tried not to squirm under her gaze. Her eyes were heavily made-up, and she had several earrings running up one ear. Her hair was cut in a short spiky style. Her lipstick reminded him of the pink taffy candy he'd loved as a child. She didn't look that much older than him.

"My editor sent me out here to ask a few questions about your Amish taxi business. Can you tell us how you got started?" She pushed the microphone in his direction and then glanced at a skinny guy, who looked to be about twenty and had terrible acne. "Charlie, you're rolling, right?"

"Uh-huh."

"So, Micah…"

Micah put out a hand and gently pushed her microphone down. Then he turned to the cameraman. "Charlie, stop rolling."

"But…"

"Stop, please."

Charlie looked at Phoebe, who nodded once—curtly.

"*Danki*. Now, if you'd be so kind as to leave my grandparents' property." He stepped off the porch toward their van, and Phoebe followed as if they were tied together by some invisible string.

"But this is a big story, a human interest story. People want to know how you got started."

"They can take a ride in my buggy and ask me then."

"You're from Maine, right?"

"How did you know—"

"Do they have Amish taxi drivers there?" Phoebe had once again pushed the microphone in his direction. "I couldn't find anything on the internet."

Micah stared pointedly at the microphone until she took the hint and dropped it. "In general it's difficult to find Amish businesses online since we don't own computers."

"But…"

"Look, Phoebe, I appreciate that you need stories to fill your paper."

"It's called the news for a reason." She trudged back toward her van as she stuffed her microphone, notepad and pen into a large shoulder bag—eyebrows drawn together, pink lips in a pouty frown.

Micah sighed and followed her. "I know that you're only doing your job, but my grandparents are very private and very old-fashioned."

"And what about you?"

"What about me?"

"Are you private and old-fashioned, too?"

Micah shrugged. "A little of both, I suppose."

Charlie had loaded his camera in the van. Phoebe opened the door, tossed her shoulder bag inside and then turned to give Micah a once-over. "Not too private to submit a selfie to our paper and win fifty dollars."

Micah shook his head. "I can explain that."

"What's to explain?" She hopped in the van and slammed the door shut, then rolled down the window. "Seems to me that if you're being paid for it, then you have no trouble being in the paper."

"I didn't submit that photo, and I'm sorry if I've offended you in some way."

"Oh, I'm not offended." She checked her lipstick in the mirror, dabbed at the corner of her mouth and looked again at Micah as she slipped dark sunglasses on. "I'm a reporter, Micah. I will get my story. In this instance, I'll just have to interview your customers since you're not willing to go on the record."

"On the record? What do you think this is…a television show?"

"So you know about those, too." She tapped a finger adorned with bright pink polish against her lips. "Are you sure that you're really Amish?"

Micah felt his temper spike, but for perhaps the first time in his life, he brought it under control.

Phoebe reached into her bag, pulled out a business

card and held it out the window until he took it from her hand.

"If you change your mind, give me a call."

And then they were gone.

Micah stood there, watching the red taillights disappear down the lane and trying to figure out how he was going to explain this to his *daddi*.

Chapter Ten

As May gave way to June, Susannah and Micah settled into a pattern of sorts. He would come in the morning to help her *dat* with the horses. Before he left, he'd stop by her quilting room, and they would make plans for the evening or the weekend or whenever they could find time to be together. It was becoming increasingly more difficult because his taxi business was doing so well, or at least that was the only reason she could think of that would cause him to be out every evening. He was no doubt running *Englischers* around until sundown.

He didn't share the particulars of his business with her, but she could well imagine that by the time he returned the buggy, walked home and ate the cold dinner waiting on the stove, it was too late for them to see each other.

Susannah assured him that she understood, though he was looking increasingly exhausted. Dark circles had formed under his eyes, and it looked to her like he'd lost weight. When she asked him about it, he only said, "I have a plan, Susannah."

"Care to share it with me?"

"I do." He glanced at the watch he'd begun wearing. "But not yet. Not now, when I'm rushed. We need to talk soon, but when we're not in a hurry or distracted."

He was certainly both of those things. She shrugged as if *soon* was fine with her. "But how do your grandparents feel about your long hours?"

"I don't know. *Daddi* barely speaks to me. He probably hasn't said a dozen words since he smashed my phone with his work boot."

"And your *mammi*?"

"She seems preoccupied. He doesn't seem well, and I think she's worried about him. For reasons I can't fathom, he refuses to talk about it."

"Should he go to a doctor?"

"Maybe. She's suggested it, but he won't even consider seeing a doctor. The last time she suggested it, he glowered at her and said, 'Does it look like I'm bleeding, Abigail?'"

"I could ask my *dat* to go over and—"

"I don't think that's a *gut* idea. At least not yet. But *danki*." He pulled her to her feet and into his arms, lowered his head to hers and inhaled deeply. "I sure am glad you offered to be my buddy when I came to town."

"Is that what I am to you?" Her voice was teasing, but Susannah knew that he heard the seriousness behind her question. They had kissed on several occasions since her visit with Dr. Kelly, and she was trying to let things unfold naturally and at their own pace. Some days that was easier than others.

"Yes…" His lips found hers, and for a moment, she forgot what she'd asked.

Then she pulled away. "I'm not sure it's appropriate for buddies to be kissing."

"Is that so?"

"Maybe."

"I guess we need to change your title, then."

"And what would we change it to?"

Micah rubbed at his chin as if he couldn't think of the word. Then he snapped his fingers. "I've got it. Girlfriend. You'll be the girlfriend, and I'll be the boyfriend."

Susannah rolled her eyes and turned back to her cutting table.

"My boyfriend should get going then, or you're going to be late for your first taxi client."

He walked up behind her, slipped his hands around her waist and lowered his voice. "I have a plan."

"You do?"

"Yup. And if it works, and I think it will, then I will have plenty of financial resources. I won't be at the mercy of my parents or my grandparents. And then you and I will sit down and decide what happens next."

She pivoted in his arms, looked in his eyes and marveled that she'd managed to fall in love with someone she was hoping wouldn't stay in Goshen more than a few weeks.

For the next three hours she focused on the quilt on her design table. She was working on a patchwork-star quilt the librarian had hired her to make for her soon-to-arrive grandbaby. Unfortunately she was having trouble focusing. Her thoughts insisted on wandering back over Micah's words.

What plan? What did he mean when he said *if it*

works? And what was he thinking when he said they'd have to decide what happens next?

Was he hinting about marriage?

Was she foolish to jump to that conclusion?

And why hadn't she just asked him?

The questions tumbled through her head, but she soon pushed them away and immersed herself in the process of choosing fabrics, cutting squares and meticulously sewing them together. As for Micah, whatever his plan was, time would tell. He'd share the details with her when he was ready to. Until then she'd pray for patience, and that whatever he was cooking up was firmly in line with their *Ordnung*. The last thing they needed was another run-in with his grandfather.

Susannah woke to pounding on the front door and then the murmur of voices downstairs. She grabbed her robe and hurried to the living room, arriving in time to see Micah's grandmother leaving. "What is it? What's wrong?"

Her father had already returned to his bedroom, presumably to dress, since all of the lanterns seemed to be on.

"*Mamm*, what's wrong?"

"It's Micah." Her mother pulled her over to the couch. "He's been arrested."

"Arrested?"

"He's at the Goshen Police Department now. Abigail came and asked your *dat* to go down to the police station and see if he could work out the misunderstanding."

"What misunderstanding? Why did they arrest him?"

"It seems there's been a robbery."

"What?"

"And Micah was in the vicinity. The police pulled him in for questioning and decided to book him."

"Can they do that?"

"Apparently."

Her *dat* walked into the room, kissed her *mamm* on the head, then did the same to Susannah. "Try to sleep, and if you can't sleep, then pray."

And then he was gone, leaving Susannah wondering what had happened and what, if anything, she could do about it.

Micah looked up when he heard Thomas's voice. He couldn't hear what was being said. When no one appeared in the hall that led to the cells, he finally moved back over to his cot and sat down.

He stared down at his ink-stained fingertips. The photographing and fingerprinting seemed to have happened days ago. He became convinced this nightmare of an evening would never end. Once his initial fear had subsided, a sort of numbness had settled over him. It was almost as if he was standing a few feet apart from himself—watching the arrest, booking and jailing happen to someone else.

He'd never been in an *Englisch* jail. It was both better and worse than he'd imagined.

Better because he wasn't forced to share it with any petty criminals—the Goshen municipal jail allowed each person their own four-by-six concrete space. The stories of motorcycle gangs and hardened criminals roughing up the innocent Amish boy melted away into the night. No doubt, these stories were told to *youngies* to keep them on the straight and narrow.

And that was the worst of it. He'd finally committed his life to the straight and narrow, and look where it had landed him.

He heard footsteps and glanced up to see Susannah's *dat*.

"How are you, son?"

"I've been better. Did you come to get me out?"

"I came to try, but the officers are claiming they have video evidence."

"That I robbed the general store? That's not possible, because I didn't do it."

"Gut. Gut." Thomas reached into his pocket, pulled out an old pipe and stared at it a moment. Stuffing it back into his pocket, he glanced up at Micah and smiled. "My *dat* used to say the truth will out."

"The truth will out?"

"Ya."

"What does that even mean?"

"That given enough time, the truth will work its way out. If you didn't do this thing—"

"I didn't."

"Then you have nothing to worry about."

Micah looked around his cell—the small bed, the toilet and sink. It was all so humiliating. He turned his attention back to Thomas.

"Ya, I know. Just think, though. You're in good Biblical company."

"I am?"

"Paul and Silas spent time in jail."

"Oh, I suppose I remember that now that you mention it."

"Joseph, Samson, Jeremiah, Daniel, John the Baptist…"

"I didn't remember those, though I doubt they were in jail because someone thought they'd knocked over a general store."

"I would like to pray with you. Would that be all right?"

"Ya." Micah sighed and walked toward the bars separating them. "I could use some prayers right now."

He never expected to fall asleep, but he woke to someone in an adjacent cell complaining about instant eggs, and the guard telling him that this wasn't the Ritz. Whatever that was. He washed up at the sink, pulled the single cover up on his thin mattress and sat on the bed. Within a few minutes, a tray of runny eggs, cold toast and what had to be imitation bacon was delivered to his cell.

"Probably not what you're used to at home," the officer said. He almost sounded like he cared. The tag on his uniform said Officer Wright. The expression on his face said that he'd seen it all, and he probably had.

"Nein. It's not."

"Hopefully you won't be here long enough to get used to the food."

Micah cleaned his plate because he was starving. His restlessness grew as he realized that he was missing his taxi appointments. No doubt everyone had heard by now, though. He'd be lucky if anyone trusted him enough to ride in his buggy.

His heart felt as if it dropped somewhere close to the floor when he realized Susannah would have heard, as well. He wished he could get a message to her. She wouldn't believe him capable of doing such a thing. Susannah was a fair person. She wouldn't turn her back on him. Thinking of her made him feel better, and knowing he would see her again helped him to resist falling into a state of despair.

An hour later he was sitting in an interview room, Thomas next to him on one side of the table and two officers sitting across from them. One was in uniform and the other was in regular *Englisch* clothes.

"For the record, this interview is being recorded." The man in *Englisch* clothes straightened the sheets of paper in his folder. "Please state your name."

"Micah Fisher."

The man nodded toward Thomas, who tapped a finger against the table, smiled and said, "Thomas Beiler."

"And are you related to Mr. Fisher?"

"*Nein*, I'm his bishop."

"I'm Detective Cummings and this is Officer Decker. This interview is occurring at 9:35 on the morning of June 10." Cummings was tall and thin with red hair that had been recently buzzed. Decker was a woman in her forties and had yet to smile. "Mr. Fisher, please confirm that you've been read your rights."

"As officers were slapping the handcuffs on my wrists."

"A simple yes or no will do."

"Yes, I have."

"You are being held on suspicion of breaking and entering of the general store."

"Which I didn't do."

"We'd like to go over your statement, and then we'll talk about what happens next."

"What happens next is you let me go. I did not rob the general store."

Thomas's hand on his shoulder caused Micah to shut

his mouth, which he supposed was the good bishop's purpose for being there. He took a deep breath and scrubbed his hand over his face. If ever there was a time he needed patience, it was now. And he needed it fast!

"Understandably Micah is upset." Thomas's voice was quiet and his tone neutral. It worked to calm Micah down. "I'm happy to vouch for him. He's a *gut* worker, and he has never been in trouble before."

"We'll get to that. Again, just to confirm, Mr. Fisher, you waive your right to an attorney?"

"Yes."

Thomas nodded in agreement. "As I'm sure you know, we prefer not to become entangled in legal matters. Our goal is to remain separate and yet be *gut* members of the community."

"Yet you are entangled." Decker sat back, crossed her arms and waited until she was sure she had everyone's attention. "I've been on this police force for twenty-two years, and I appreciate and respect your culture. But you know as well as I do, Bishop, that we've had our share of Amish teenagers step over the line."

"And we've always cooperated and done everything in our power to compensate anyone for damages and see that the youth received counseling as needed."

"We're not talking about underage kids drinking beer behind the Dairy Queen. We have video evidence of this young man robbing the general store last night."

"That's not possible, because I wasn't at the general store."

"All right." Cummings tapped a pen against his pad of paper. "Give us your alibi, then. We'll verify it and we can have you out of here in time for lunch."

"My alibi?"

"Tell us where you were and who you were with."

Micah opened his mouth and then shut it. "I can't do that."

"Why?"

"Because I can't."

Susannah's father tilted his head toward Micah and lowered his voice, though, of course, the detective and office could still hear what he said. "It would be in your best interest if you would—"

"I can't, Thomas. I just…can't."

"All right. We seem to be at an impasse here. Micah, for whatever reason, can't tell us where he was, but if I understand *Englisch* law correctly, he doesn't have to prove his innocence. You have to prove his guilt."

Detective Cummings nodded at Decker, who pointed to a television on the wall and then hit some buttons on her cell phone. At first, the video was dark, showing little except for the front of the general store.

"This was taken from the store across the street twelve minutes before the alarm went off in the general store."

As they watched, a horse pulling an Amish buggy stopped in front of the general store. A young man stepped out, though the camera was too far away and the scene was too dark to tell who it was. The man was approximately Micah's height and build.

Decker paused the video. "Now, is there something you want to tell us?"

"*Nein*, because that's not me."

As they watched, the young man pulled out a crowbar, busted the lock on the front door and hurried inside. They couldn't see in the store or what was happening, but suddenly the wail of a siren could be heard on the video.

"That was activated by the alarm attached to the cash register," Cummings explained. "The owner disabled the security alarm to the front door because it kept going off at random moments, but he left the one on the cash register drawer."

The time meter at the bottom of the video continued to roll forward. Not long after the alarm went off, the Amish person ran out of the store, jumped into the buggy and drove off. Decker stopped the video and looked at Cummings, who focused on Micah.

"Son, it goes better for everyone if you just confess to what you did. Plead guilty, and I will personally speak with the judge and request the minimum sentence."

"I am not your son, and I wasn't the person in the video."

Cummings sat back with a sigh, as if it pained him greatly to hear Micah's words. Not even looking at Decker, he motioned for her to keep going. She pushed more buttons on her phone and another video came up, this time showing the opposite side of the buggy. The buggy had paused at a road crossing, directly underneath a streetlamp.

"A business on the next block has CCTV."

"What is that?"

"Closed-circuit television—it's a security measure so they can record any activity in or around the store when it's closed. We were able to pull this video and establish that it occurred in the same time frame as the first video, but it gives us a different point of view."

"So?"

Officer Decker looked at him for just a moment, as if he might be the dumbest person she'd ever encountered. Thomas had gone completely still, his eyes focused on the video. With a sinking feeling in his stomach, Micah turned his attention to it. He watched as the buggy came into view and then proceeded past the camera's field. Decker pushed more buttons on the phone; the horse and buggy moved backward. She then paused the video and zoomed in.

The first thing Micah saw was the scraped paint on the front fender. He'd asked Widow Miller about fixing it when he'd first started using her buggy. Her answer had been "Why? It travels the same whether the paint is perfect or scraped."

The second thing he saw was the passenger-side window, and taped to it was the sign that he had placed there, which read Amish Taxi.

He didn't know what Thomas said to the detective or what the detective said to him after that. His mind was spinning, and it was as if he couldn't process anything else.

It wasn't until he was back in his cell, until he heard the bars clank shut and the lock turn, that he managed to bring his attention back to the present.

Officer Wright had apparently escorted him back. Now Wright was studying him with a resigned look. "Guess you'll have time to get used to the food after all."

"What do you mean?"

"Do you have the money to post bail?"

"Nein."

"Neither does your bishop, apparently."

"So?"

"So that means you're staying until the judge is

in court again, which will be two more days. Might as well make yourself comfortable." Officer Wright stepped closer to the bars, and something about his demeanor or the look in his eyes reminded Micah of the old men in Maine who sat around and told stories of the early days there. Something in his eyes spoke of experience and wisdom. Whatever it was, it caused Micah to listen—to really listen.

"I don't know what you did or why you did it. The why doesn't matter so much at this point, and I can guarantee you that Judge Johnson isn't interested in whether you were mistreated as a child or are suffering depression. Johnson's an old-fashioned kind of judge. You do the deed, you pay for it."

"And what if I didn't do it?"

"Then you need an alibi, because from what I heard, they've got you on this one from three different directions."

Micah didn't answer. He was thinking about the buggy and the Amish man and the sign on the window.

"All I'm saying is that this place is not so bad. Food's terrible and you don't have TV or a library, but it's not that bad. But where you're going? It's not where a young man like you should spend a year or two. Do yourself a favor and wise up before the judge gets here."

And with those words of comfort, Micah found himself once again alone.

Susannah couldn't believe it. She tried to process what her *dat* told her. She could tell he wasn't holding anything back, but she couldn't believe what he was saying. There was no way that Micah was guilty of breaking into the general store.

She tried to speak to his grandparents. John Fisher took one look at her and headed to the barn. Abigail stepped out on the porch, but the conversation went nowhere.

"I know you love your grandson."

"Of course I do, but Micah has never seen the world as the rest of us see it."

"You're saying you believe he did this?"

"I'm saying he might have convinced himself it was okay. I don't know. Sometimes what a person is capable of will surprise you."

"Have you been to see him?"

His *mammi* shook her head once, and that was the end of the conversation. She turned and walked back into the house, leaving Susannah standing there and wondering what to do next.

Visiting Deborah didn't go much better.

"He didn't do this, Deborah. I know he didn't."

Deborah held up her hands in surrender. "I don't want to believe it, either."

"He didn't do it."

"You said he's been out late a lot."

"So what?"

"So four other stores have been robbed in the last two weeks."

"What? And you think he did that? You think Micah was traveling up and down Goshen knocking over stores? Why would he even do such a thing?"

"You're the one who said that he has a plan. Didn't he say if it worked, he would have financial resources?"

"Which could mean a lot of other things besides robbery."

Deborah stopped separating dollar bills in the cash

drawer of her family's vegetable stand. She walked around the table and put her arms around Susannah, who had determined she would not cry. She was not going to cry about Micah, because he did not do this.

"Have you tried to see him?"

"I have." She brushed her sleeves across her eyes.

"And?"

"He saw me the first time—that was yesterday. Told me that he didn't do this, and that he would be out by the weekend, so I should have the fishing poles ready."

"Maybe he will. Maybe he is innocent. I'm just so sorry you're going through this."

"Then he asked me not to come back."

Deborah stepped back, hands still on Susannah's shoulders, as if she needed to get a better look at her best friend's face. "Why would he say that?"

"Because he said that without an alibi…" The tears resumed streaming down her face. "Without an alibi, they just might pin this on him, and there wasn't anything he could, or would, do about it."

"All right. So we know where to start."

"What do you mean?"

"I mean, you're going to see him again this afternoon. Didn't you say the judge is in court tomorrow?"

"Yes."

"So go to him today. Go now. It's important that you see him before he appears before the judge."

"What am I supposed to do? What am I supposed to say?"

"You're going to convince him to explain where he was and who he was with."

Chapter Eleven

Micah didn't look up when he heard the guard open the outer door. Whoever was in the cell at the end of the hall had a large family. They'd all come to see him. He couldn't hear much of what they said, but what he did hear was like a knife in his gut.

"We know you didn't do this."

"We're going to get you out."

"Dad's working on the bail money."

"Mom knows a guy who knows a guy who's a lawyer."

Whoever that person was had a very engaged family—a family who believed in his innocence. Micah didn't know if the person was guilty or innocent, but he did know that he was a lucky man to have so many people on his side.

Only two people had come to visit Micah.

His bishop.

And his girlfriend.

He hadn't seen or heard from his grandparents.

He'd used his one phone call for the bishop, so he hadn't spoken to his parents, and he wasn't sure he wanted to. What could he tell them? How could he explain this situation that threatened to change the course of the rest of his life?

And then the scent of rose lotion pulled him away from his dark thoughts.

If anything, Susannah looked prettier than the day he'd seen her standing by the mailbox with Sharon and Shiloh. She wore a light blue frock and a white apron and, of course, the ever-present white *kapp*.

"Why are you smiling?"

"Just remembering the first time I saw you without that *kapp* on."

"Five minutes," Officer Wright said. He offered to bring Susannah a chair, but she shook her head no and thanked him.

"Why did you come back?"

"Because I needed to see you." She pulled in her bottom lip, and he knew that she was fighting back tears, which caused his defenses to crumble.

He stared at the ceiling, and when he looked at her again, he'd regained control of his emotions. It wasn't that he was afraid of crying in front of her. He wasn't one of those guys who believed that men shouldn't ever show their emotions. It was more that he felt if he let go of the reins that were holding them in, he might never regain control again.

"Things were going too well," he whispered.

"What things?"

He only shook his head.

"Come over here."

Micah could hear the trembling in her voice, and it nearly undid him. He closed his eyes for a moment, but when he opened them she was still there.

"If you are going to do this to yourself, to us, then you owe me this much. Come over here and look me in the eye."

"I can't tell you where I was. I—"

"You can't tell the judge. I know. You said that before. But if you can't tell me the when or where, then you can at least tell me the why."

So he stood and walked to where she was waiting. They weren't supposed to touch. The poster on the wall proclaimed that rule loud and clear. But then Micah had never been good at following the rules. Susannah's hands were wrapped around the cell's bars. He ever so gently wrapped his hands around hers, figuring they had one minute, maybe two, before one of the officers came busting through reminding them to stand three feet apart.

"Tell me why." Her voice was soft, and when he looked in her eyes he saw a whole world of hurt.

But he also saw something else... He knew that she trusted him or at least she wanted to.

"I can't tell you where I was..."

The rattle of keys at the end of the hall told him the officer was coming through.

"I can't tell because I promised I wouldn't. I gave my word, Susannah. And what kind of man would I be if I couldn't keep my word? You deserve better than that."

She swiped at her eyes. "Okay."

"Okay?"

"*Ya.* Okay."

The officer separated them before either could say anything more, but what Micah saw before she walked away almost sent him to his knees because it wasn't judgment or disappointment or anger—it was love.

* * *

Micah stood in a type of waiting room next to his court-appointed lawyer. The man was definitely under thirty years old, and he looked as if he'd slept as little as Micah had. When Micah had refused to give an alibi, he'd only asked, "You're sure?" When Micah confirmed that he was very sure, the man—Rafael Rodriguez—had grinned and said, "Chances are you're going away to prison, but we're going to make them earn it."

He opened the door, and they walked into the main courtroom.

The judge had apparently been working for several hours already. He glanced at the clock, as if he was wondering whether he could take a lunch break. The man was in charge, wasn't he? Couldn't he just order the court adjourned? Or perhaps Micah was remembering the single court scene he'd watched on television wrong.

Judge Johnson was older, white haired, and Micah could tell in a second that he did not suffer fools.

The bailiff called Micah's case, and he and Rafael walked forward to stand before the judge.

It was a moment that Micah understood he wouldn't forget if he lived to be a hundred. It was surreal, standing there before a man who had the power to free or imprison him. There was a spiritual lesson here that wasn't lost on him—the power of forgiveness and the sacrifice of Christ standing before the one and true God. He'd heard it preached often, but at that moment, he felt it clean through to his soul.

"Mr. Rodriguez, does your client still refuse to provide an alibi?"

"He does."

"Mr. Fisher, you are charged with aggravated burglary." Rafael had explained that *aggravated* meant he had a weapon—in this case, a crowbar that could be seen in the video and was used to break the lock on the front door. "How do you plead?"

"I plead not guilty, Your Honor."

Rafael had told him what to say word for word. They'd even practiced.

"I assume you still have no means to post bail."

"That's correct, Your Honor."

"Then I have no choice but to remand you to the Elkhart County Jail until…" He must have consulted a calendar, because he picked up some half-glasses, perched them on his nose and stared down at something. "Looks like it'll be July 18 before you can have a jury of your peers."

He took the glasses off and looked at Micah—really looked at him—for the first time.

"Mr. Fisher, you're certain that you want to remain behind bars until that time?"

"I don't see as I have a choice, Your Honor."

"You most certainly do. If you can prove that you weren't the person in the video…"

"Objection, Your Honor. The accused is not required to prove his innocence, but rather—"

"I know the law, Mr. Rodriguez." Johnson shook his head as if he needed to rid himself of a pesky fly. "I've seen the video, and I have to say that the evidence here is strong. Strong enough to hold Mr. Fisher over for a trial."

"You can't know that's him."

"That will have to be proved at the trial. Until

then..." He raised his gavel to strike it against the desk when someone spoke up from the back of the room.

"I can provide Micah with an alibi."

Relief washed over Micah in that moment because he knew that voice. His legs felt suddenly wobbly and his hands shook so that he had to clasp them together.

Rodriguez stepped closer and said, "Steady there. Don't faint on me, Fisher."

But Micah understood what Rafael Rodriguez and Judge Johnson couldn't—what they would very soon know. Micah understood that this nightmare was over, and that he'd be able to go home.

Thomas walked on one side of him, Susannah on the other, as Micah left the Goshen Municipal Jail.

"How about we have some lunch before we go home?" Thomas nodded at a coffee shop across the street.

Susannah squeezed his hand. "We heard the food wasn't so good in there."

"You heard right. I'm starved."

They ordered hamburgers, fries and shakes before they got down to business.

"Levi Hochstettler?" Susannah was sitting across from him. No doubt she wanted to be able to look into his eyes while he explained the last few weeks. "You were with Levi? I wasn't aware you even knew him."

After thanking the waitress for the shakes she left on their table, Thomas asked, "And why was that so hard to admit?"

"The first time I picked up Levi for a ride, he had me drop him at this old barn over on the east side of town. It was an *Englischer*'s place, from the look of it."

"What was he doing there?"

"Rebuilding the engine on a 1956 Mercedes."

"Levi always was *gut* with small engines," Thomas said.

Susannah leaned forward. "And you helped him?"

"Not at first, but after the third ride, he figured he could trust me." Micah had already consumed half of his shake. He didn't realize how bad jail food was until he was a free man and eating good food again. "I did some engine repair up in Maine, so I offered to lend a hand. This was last week, the same week that my business first got off the ground."

"This is why you've been so tired."

"I knew I was stretching it—burning the candle at both ends as the old folks say—but it seemed like too good an opportunity to pass up."

Thomas grunted, but he didn't interrupt.

"So I was helping Thomas in the morning, running my buggy service in the afternoon and helping Levi at night. We were about halfway through with the rebuild…"

"And then?" Susannah was twirling her *kapp* string, completely engrossed in his story.

"Then Levi found a buyer. An *Englisch* guy who was willing to pay top dollar."

"Which was, no doubt, a lot of money."

"It was, and the *Englischer* put down a deposit, so we knew he was good for it. But the problem was that he needed it for some race this weekend."

"A race?"

"Some race with old cars. They give you a map at the last minute. I didn't really understand that part."

"The Great American Race." Thomas smiled when

they both turned to stare at him. "I'm a bishop, but I'm still a man. This race has been around since the eighties."

The waitress brought their food, and for the next few minutes, no one spoke as Micah made up for lost calories. When he finally pushed back his plate, Susannah and her father shared a smile.

"Don't say it, *Dat*."

"Growing boy needs his food."

They all laughed, and it felt good. Micah wanted to pull Susannah into his arms. He wanted to thank her for standing by him, but he understood that doing so in the middle of a burger joint in front of her father probably wasn't a great idea.

"So the *Englischer* needed the car fast. He was willing to pay good money and Levi was willing to share what he made." Susannah shook her head. "What are you not saying?"

"Levi's parents." The bishop ran his fingers through his beard.

"Exactly." Micah took up the story. "Levi's parents are quite strict. They were already unhappy that he was working on car engines."

"I've talked to them about that," Thomas said. "Levi is good with his hands, good at fixing things. If he'd been born *Englisch*, there's no doubt he would have been an engineer of some sort. It seemed to me that allowing him to use those talents in a way that was acceptable would solve the problem."

"But it didn't?" Susannah had pushed her plate away and was again leaning forward, no doubt ready to pull the rest of the story out of him.

"I'm only sharing this because Levi told me as we

left the courtroom that I should tell you everything." He glanced at Susannah but directed the next part to the bishop. "He's thinking of leaving the faith. Well, not leaving exactly. He has an *onkel* who is Mennonite and has a shop in Ohio. Says he can give Levi all the work he needs. But he insisted that if Levi really wanted to do it, then he would have to save the money for the bus fare as well as a deposit on a place to live. They have eight young ones, so there's no room at their house."

"But if he could sell the Mercedes…"

"Then he'd have enough money to go." Micah finally pushed away his plate. "He's going to come and talk to you tomorrow."

Thomas nodded as if that settled things.

"Okay." Susannah held up her left hand and began counting off points. "You were helping Levi. He was sharing the profits with you. You were definitely not in Widow Miller's buggy, and you did not rob the store…"

"I never doubted that," Thomas said.

"Why couldn't you just explain that to the judge?"

"Because I promised Levi I wouldn't tell. I gave him my word that I would not be the one to tell his parents. He wanted to do it, in his own way, in his own time."

"You didn't want him to get in trouble? You were willing to go to jail for that?"

Micah didn't answer right away. When he looked at Susannah and Thomas, at these two people who had come to mean so much to him, he knew that he could be completely honest.

"I've been on the outside most of my life. I'm not really sure why. Rebellious nature that needs taming, or maybe…maybe I hadn't met the right person who could settle me down." He paused and looked directly at Susannah—smiled and resumed his story. "I know what it's like to walk a tightrope at home, and how important it is to have one person who you can trust with your real self, with who you really are. You two have been that for me, and I have been that for Levi. It was important for me to honor that commitment."

"When Levi stood up for you in court, when he provided your alibi, he also put himself on the line with his parents."

"Exactly."

"You know, Micah. The one thing that you can give and still keep is your word. It seems to me that you showed maturity and wisdom today."

Which seemed to settle the matter as far as Susannah and Thomas were concerned. Micah didn't know what would happen when he went home to his grandparents.

And he certainly didn't know who had stolen Widow Miller's buggy and broken into the general store, but he did know that it wasn't him, and that it was time to do what Levi was doing. It was time to stand up and be true to who he was. He would probably never be a traditional Amish person, but he loved his faith and he had the support of the bishop for his Amish buggy service. If that wasn't good enough for his grandparents, then perhaps it was time he accepted he was bound to disappoint some of the people who meant the most to him.

Their disappointment might hurt, but it wouldn't change who he was.

Micah stared at his *daddi* in disbelief. "You can't make me do that."

"You're right. I can't. However, I can issue an ultimatum."

"An ultimatum?"

"*Ya*, for sure and certain."

"That's not… It's not how we do things."

"How would *you* know?" His *daddi*'s voice rose like a wave crashing over them. "How would *you* know how we do things? You've spent the last three days in an *Englisch* jail."

"For something that I didn't do."

"You have only one foot in our world. The other is firmly planted in the *Englisch*."

"That's your opinion."

"*Nein*, son. It's a fact, and I will not stand for it any longer."

Micah glanced at his *mammi*. Was that sympathy he saw in her eyes? Perhaps, and yet she didn't jump to his defense.

"You will inform Thomas of your decision to join the church on Sunday morning."

"I haven't made that decision yet."

"You will inform him on Sunday or before Sunday, or you will find another place to live—perhaps one of your *Englisch* friends will take you in."

His *daddi* pushed himself up from the table with his one good arm, and that was when Micah noticed that his hand was shaking. He shifted his left shoulder, as if it pained him. Micah had the sudden realization that his *daddi* was not a young man, that he was aging. He felt a stirring of sympathy for him, which was immediately wiped away by the man's next words.

"I've given you time, Micah. We all have."

"And I have done what you asked."

"You think this life is a game of some sort—a long procession of parties and reckless decisions and stepping back and forth across the line that our community has plainly drawn to keep us separate." He reached for his hat and crammed it on his head. "That is your choice, but I won't abide it a moment longer. We've all coddled you much too long. It's time for you to make a decision. Choose the life you wish to live."

And with that final declaration he stormed out the back door.

Neither Micah nor his *mammi* moved. Finally, she sighed and stood, beginning to clear away the dishes.

"Tell me you don't agree with him."

"Doesn't matter if I do or not."

"It matters to me."

Mammi placed the dishes into the sink and stood there for a moment, staring out the window. When she turned back toward Micah, he saw such conflicting emotions in her eyes that it tore at his heart.

Was this really all his fault?

Was he tearing his family apart? The memory of his last week at home in Maine threatened to rise, but he quickly pushed it down. They'd understood him little more than his grandparents.

Instead of lecturing, *Mammi* walked over to where he sat, pulled a chair up close and sat so that their knees were touching. She reached for his hand and stared down at it a moment. When she finally raised her eyes to his, Micah's heart sank.

She was on his *daddi*'s side.

He knew what was coming.

"Your *daddi* isn't wrong, not in his intent. Perhaps his presentation could use a little work." She attempted to smile, but it slid away. "He loves you, Micah. We all do. However, you are twenty-five years old. You're a man, not a *youngie*."

"I know that." His throat was suddenly tight. He had to push the words out. "I know I'm not a child."

"And yet you so often act like one."

Coming from his *daddi*, the words would have stung. But the words were whispered by his *mammi*, and the look she gave him? It held only compassion.

"He's feeling older these days. The mornings are hard because he wakes so stiff, and then some mornings, like today, the indigestion bothers him."

"I'm sorry he isn't feeling well, but it gives him no right…"

"It gives him every right. He doesn't complain, and I'm not telling you this so you'll feel sorry for him. Though, of course, you should have sympathy for others, especially your family. I'm telling you this so you'll understand."

She ran a wrinkled finger under his suspender, straightening it, and patted his shoulder lightly. "What your *daddi* understands, which you don't, is that this life is but a fleeting matter, like a passing mist. You think that you have all the time in the world to decide the course of your life, but none of us has an unlimited amount of time to make our choices. Today is the day for you to make your decision."

She patted his shoulder again, then pushed herself into a standing position. That was when Micah knew that all was lost. She would not intervene on his behalf.

He felt numb all over.

Why did it seem that everyone was against him?

First that foolishness about the break-ins, as if he would do such a thing. And now this.

His *daddi* was actually going to force him to join the church. He'd actually been considering doing so, but now... To have it dictated to him put a sour taste in his mouth. He couldn't make a decision like that because someone said he must. It would be a lie.

The one thing you can give and still keep is your word.

Thomas's words came back to him like an arrow to the heart. When he made a decision to join the church, he was giving his word, so he needed to be certain. Didn't he?

And what was the alternative?

Or did he even have one?

Chapter Twelve

He spent that afternoon and the next morning in a bit of a fog. He saw Susannah when he stopped by her *dat*'s farrier shop, but he didn't speak to her of what was happening with his grandparents. He wasn't ready. What if she agreed with them?

There was little work for him in the shop, so he took off early and headed to town to hopefully pick up some Saturday passengers in his buggy service. He lasted less than an hour. After he took one Amish girl to the wrong store, and an *Englisch* woman asked why they were traveling in a circle around the same block, he knew his mind wasn't on his work. Apologizing, he dropped her off where they'd started—free of charge.

He simply couldn't focus.

The anger and sense of unfairness grew until he thought that he might explode. He picked up his Amish-taxi sign and made his way back across town, returning the horse and buggy to Widow Miller's and making his way to his grandparents' house. There he paced back and forth in the barn for the better part of a half hour.

Only ten thirty in the morning, and yet it felt like

the day had lasted forever. He walked inside, looked around and headed back out. He was barely aware that he'd grabbed his hat from the mudroom, and he didn't realize he was walking toward Susannah's until he caught sight of her playing outside with her little *schweschdern*. Sharon and Shiloh spied him at the same moment and dashed toward him.

"We found a grass snake in the garden." Sharon grabbed one of his hands. "We placed rocks around him so that we can watch what he does."

"He can't get away," Shiloh added, standing close and worrying one hand inside the other. "I was scared at first, but Susannah says it won't hurt us."

He followed them to the edge of the garden. The grass snake was only a few inches long and bright green. He'd probably been sunning himself when the girls had noticed him and quickly built a perimeter— one that the snake would have no trouble sliding over or through, but Micah didn't bother telling them that.

"I'm going to get him some grass." Sharon bounded off toward the edge of the garden.

"Susannah said he eats frogs. I'm going to see if I can find one." Shiloh dashed toward the water trough they used to irrigate the garden.

"Watch out for snakes," Susannah called from her place at the north end of the garden.

"Too late for that advice." Micah plopped down on the ground beside her.

She rolled her eyes. When he didn't say anything else and only sat there brooding—that was the only word for it—she bumped her shoulder against his.

"What's wrong? Did your favorite baseball team lose last night?"

"Nein."

"I thought you'd be in a fine mood today, since you're no longer considered the bandit of Goshen."

"And yet I'm still the black sheep." The unfairness of it seemed to press down on him. Why couldn't people simply accept him like he was? Why couldn't he be Amish without following every one of their silly rules? Why were rules even necessary?

"Something has happened." Instead of pushing him, Susannah waited, which was something she was very good at.

It was one of the things he appreciated about her. While his mind dashed back and forth, her steady presence helped to calm him down. He stared at the garden for several minutes—a part of his mind hearing the girls giggling over the snake, a part of his mind still back in his grandparents' kitchen.

Finally, he blew out a noisy breath and told her everything.

Susannah wasn't exactly shocked at what Micah told her. She'd suspected such a thing might happen sooner rather than later, but she was disappointed that it had happened the morning after he'd been proved innocent of the break-ins.

"I'm a little surprised you're taking it so hard."

Micah jumped to his feet and began to pace back and forth. "Taking it hard? I'm about to be thrown out on my own."

"Just last week you were talking about having a plan and not being dependent on your grandparents anymore."

"But I need more time. I'm not… I'm not ready yet."

When she smiled at him, he collapsed on the ground beside her. "Maybe I should have seen this coming. I'm not sure, to tell you the truth."

"It seems to me that your grandparents are simply forcing the issue—an issue that you were already thinking about."

"They're saying I have to decide between being Amish or *Englisch*. That I have to decide now."

"They're saying if you're going to stay in their home, you have to decide now. No one can force you to make the decision to join the church, Micah. You can take as long as you need, but the process of deciding… Well, it must be hard on them."

He flopped onto his back and shielded his eyes against the sun. "I know you're not on their side. You've stood by me through all the ups and downs since I've been here. You even visited me at the jail."

"Twice."

He stole a peek at her and made a valiant effort to keep the perturbed expression on his face. "Twice," he conceded.

"You've had a difficult week. I definitely think you deserve a break."

He pulled up a handful of grass and tossed it at her, and Susannah couldn't help smiling. He had changed so much from the young man she'd seen step out of an *Englischer*'s truck in downtown Goshen. He had stepped into adulthood when he'd begun his own business, when he'd begun planning for the future, and certainly when he'd put his integrity over his freedom.

But the playful Micah lurked underneath, and maybe that was okay, too. Many adults were too serious. She loved that he was able to lighten her mood with a touch or a smile or a silly suggestion. Amish Taxi? She couldn't believe he'd come up with that. She was beginning to think of him as her Amish rebel. And rebels weren't such bad things—they kept everyone on their toes, weighing their decisions rather than following blindly along.

Still, she understood that it was hard to leave the carefree years of *rumspringa* behind, to embrace being an adult and accept responsibility for all of one's actions. Her cancer had forced that role upon her earlier than most, and something in Micah's upbringing had allowed him to put off any such change again and again. Perhaps it was because he was the only son in a family full of daughters. Perhaps it was simply his personality.

Regardless, she rather agreed with his grandparents that it was time for him to decide. They could have suggested such a thing a bit more tactfully, but John Fisher had never been known for his tact.

"You refuse to cut me any slack," Micah muttered.

"Is that what you want?"

"*Nein.* I like that you're honest with me."

She shrugged and the look he shot her caused the heat to rise in her cheeks. Just like that, the subject of remaining Amish was behind them, and the playful Micah was back.

"You worry me when you get that look in your eyes."

Sharon picked that moment to dump two handfuls of grass onto Micah's stomach. He launched himself off the ground, chasing her around the garden until she fell into Susannah's lap squealing and laughing. Shiloh had plopped down cross-legged beside them and rested her head in the palm of her hand.

"I think we should take our snake to the pond."

"Do you, now?" Susannah reached out to tug on her *kapp* strings.

"Actually, that's not a bad idea." Micah sat up straighter. "But I've heard that what snakes really like is rivers—especially grass snakes, because…you know, there's lots of grass growing on the banks of the river."

Susannah tried to catch his eye, but he was avoiding looking directly at her. "I don't like where you're going with this."

"It's Saturday. What else do you have to do?"

"I'm supposed to be minding Sharon and Shiloh while our parents are visiting church members."

"And you will mind them at the river."

Which, of course, started a chorus of "Please" and "Can we?" and "We promise to be good."

"No fair," she laughed. "It's three against one."

"I'll even help you pack a lunch." Micah pulled her to her feet, stepped close enough to scoot her *kapp* strings back over her shoulder. "Maybe we can wear these two out, and they'll take a nap."

"I hate naps," Shiloh murmured.

"We're too old for naps!" Sharon jumped from one foot to another. "Oh, I know. I'm going to get a box to put Simon the Slippery Snake in."

She dashed off toward the house in search of a box. Shiloh stood clasping her hands and watching Susannah. "Are we going? I think Simon would like the river better than our garden. If you think it's okay."

It was probably the look on Shiloh's face that made up Susannah's mind. She was such a sweet, serious girl—maybe too serious. A few hours at the river would do them all good.

"All right, but we need to be back well before dinner. I promised *Mamm* I would have food on the table by five. Besides, it's supposed to rain."

Micah waved away any concern. "A summer shower can't stop us from having fun."

Twenty minutes later, Susannah had changed the girls into older dresses, Micah had helped to pack the makings for a picnic lunch and they were traipsing across the field to the back of her parents' property. She'd left a note telling her *mamm* where they were going.

The clouds had begun building toward the west.

"Weather's changing." Susannah pointed the fishing rods she was carrying toward the darkening sky. Shiloh and Sharon were walking in front of them—Sharon carrying the box with the snake, Shiloh carrying an old quilt they would use to spread across the ground.

"Still a long ways off. We'll be fine, Susannah." Micah shifted the picnic basket to his right hand and slipped his left arm around her shoulder. His fingers trailing her neck caused goose bumps to cascade down her arm. She deftly stepped to the left, out of his embrace.

Micah laughed. His melancholy mood over the argument with his *daddi* seemed to have passed. She'd learned that was both a strength and a weakness of Micah's. He had the ability to move past things in a way that she envied. She tended to dwell on things too long.

But he also moved on without ever attempting to resolve the problem. She knew from experience that such a course was akin to kicking the can down the road. It only postponed what needed to be done, and many times that indecision had a ripple effect, causing even worse problems and more difficult decisions.

But now wasn't the time to tell Micah that, if it was even her place to do so.

He was laughing, assuring her that a little rain wouldn't hurt them and predicting they would catch enough fish to feed her entire family.

They crossed one field, then another. The path to the river that they used skirted around and then behind an abandoned barn. She hadn't been in that thing in years. Her *dat* kept saying he was going to tear it down, but looking at it now, she felt a rush of affection for the thing. It seemed to be leaning gently—its boards weathered to a soft gray, and she realized she enjoyed seeing it there. The old barn was a symbol of permanency, a fond memory from her childhood. She'd played in it many a summer as a young girl.

She led her way around it, then down the path that led to a lower pasture and the river. Perhaps Micah was right. Maybe it was the perfect day for a picnic.

Micah felt in his element walking toward the river at the back of the Beiler property. Perhaps the argument with his *daddi* wasn't as bad as he'd feared. Oh, he understood his *daddi* was serious, but as Susannah had pointed out…he'd been thinking of moving into town anyway. That had been part of his big plan—independence and hopefully a chance to live his own life.

It wasn't that he didn't want to be Amish.

But why was everyone pushing him to choose such a narrow path so soon? The day before, he'd been in the Goshen jail. Didn't he deserve a day or two of rest? Why couldn't they just enjoy a Saturday fishing on the river?

Well, the answer was: they could.

They spent the next hour setting up their picnic area, releasing Simon the Slippery Snake and helping the girls put the fishing lines in the water. The sun was now obscured by the clouds, and a westerly wind had picked up.

"Perfect day for a picnic," he murmured, lying back on the blanket with his hat over his eyes.

"Not exactly."

"You're sweet, Susannah, but I don't think you'll melt in the rain."

"Perhaps we should start toward the house."

He tipped his hat back enough to peer at her. "Seriously? We just got here."

"The storm seems to be coming in sooner than they predicted. I wouldn't want to get caught."

"Can you stop worrying for a few minutes?"

The words came out sharper than he'd intended, and he could tell that he'd hurt her feelings by the way she pulled in a breath and sat up suddenly—her posture ramrod straight.

"Don't do that."

"Do what?"

"Get your feelings hurt because I have a big mouth."

"Oh, do you, now?"

"We both know I do." He found her hand and entwined his fingers with hers. He glanced at the girls, still standing with their backs to them, staring at their fishing line. Could he sneak in a kiss before they turned around? Because Susannah suddenly looked quite kissable.

Susannah's voice dropped. "I do realize that I tend to be a bit too serious. You're not the first one to suggest such a thing."

"I didn't mean anything by it. Only that I wish you could relax."

"You mean you want me to be more like you?"

"Yes! Exactly. Then there would be two of us renegades in the Goshen Amish world."

When she laughed, Micah knew he was forgiven.

"Perhaps we should eat before this storm soaks everything."

Micah's stomach gurgled, and he realized he'd not eaten breakfast. He'd been too busy worrying over his *daddi*'s ultimatum. He helped her to make peanut butter and jelly sandwiches, then convinced the girls to leave their poles resting on the bank.

"What if we catch a big one?" Sharon was jerking her pole up and down in the water. "I want to be here to pull him out."

"I promise to run and catch him if some whale starts to pull your pole into the water."

Which caused Sharon to laugh. They joined Shiloh and Susannah on the blanket and the next hour was spent enjoying the food while playing a game of I Spy. It was only when he noticed Susannah attempting to hold down the corners of the blanket that he noticed the wind had picked up quite a bit.

"I truly think we should go back." Susannah began loading the leftover food back into the basket, the wind tugging at her *kapp* and her skirt and the edges of the blanket.

It was in that moment that the weather abruptly changed.

"It stopped, Susannah." Sharon clapped her hands. "The wind stopped. So we can stay. Right? Please…"

But suddenly Micah wasn't thinking about fishing

or picnics or even finding a private moment to kiss Susannah. He jumped to his feet and strode away from the picnic, away from the trees, where he could have a better view of the sky.

The edges of the storm had turned an ominous olive green. He checked the tops of the trees again, as if to confirm what the back of his brain was telling him. Maine only averaged two tornadoes a year, but he vividly remembered 2017, which had been one of their worst years in terms of weather. An unusually high number of tornadoes—seven in all—had touched down that year, one within sight of his parents' farm.

He knew the signs.

A green sky.

Sudden drop of wind.

Unnatural stillness.

And then he saw it, dipping down from the western sky.

"We need to go." He ran back toward the picnic, grabbed Shiloh in one arm and Sharon in the other. "Leave that, Susannah. We need to go now."

And then they were running across the field and toward the abandoned barn.

Chapter Thirteen

Susannah saw Micah running toward them, hollering at her, though she couldn't make out his words. He'd picked up the girls and was urging her to do something. She put her fingers to her ears, attempting to yawn and pop them, and that was when she heard the freight train bearing down on them.

Then he'd run back and was shouting in her ear, "We need to go."

She dropped the basket and ran with him. How was he able to carry both girls? She'd tried to pick Shiloh up just that morning, to set her on a chair and tie her shoes. They'd laughed that she'd staggered under her *schweschder*'s weight.

They were halfway across the lower field, Micah leading the way, still holding both of her *schweschdern*. Susannah stumbled, dropped to the ground, and that was when she looked back. The funnel cloud seemed to be nearly on top of them. She sat there on the ground, gawking at it, frozen.

The noise was tremendous.

The sight was terrifying.

She barely realized that Micah had once again turned back and was squatting beside her and yelling something. It was the sight of Shiloh and Sharon that brought her back to her senses. Both girls were wide-eyed, their arms wrapped around each other, tears streaming down their faces.

Susannah jumped to her feet.

"The barn," she screamed.

And then they were running, Micah again carrying Sharon and Shiloh. He didn't put them down until they'd reached the barn door. He struggled against the wind to pull it open, and Susannah thought, *This is it. We're going to die here because the door is stuck.*

Her heart cried out to God then. It wasn't so much a prayer, not words that she would later remember. It was the cry of her heart—for Shiloh and Sharon and Micah and, yes, for herself, as well. Because she realized in that moment that she wanted to live. Her fear of cancer and the uncertainties of life were whisked away and she felt an actual pain in her heart.

She wasn't ready yet.

She didn't want this to be it.

She wanted to live and embrace life and see her *schweschdern* grow into fine young women with families of their own.

The door didn't open so much as it flew out of Micah's hands, and then they were tumbling inside.

Susannah didn't know if it had been a good or bad idea to shelter in the decrepit barn, but there wasn't time to second-guess herself, and there wasn't anywhere else to go. Her eyes met Micah's for a brief second, and she saw there the same fear and yearning and love that she was feeling.

But before she could process anything, before she could attempt to speak or reassure Shiloh and Sharon, Micah knocked them all to the ground. He threw himself on top of the three of them, and then the noise seemed to become an entity unto itself—roaring and crashing and colliding. And the structure—the barn that she had such fond memories of—simply broke apart.

She must have passed out.

She gradually became aware of Micah shaking her. She opened her eyes to find his tearstained face close to hers.

"You're alive."

"*Ya*, I think so."

She attempted to sit up. The world seemed to tilt, and she dropped her head into her hands. "I think I'm going to…"

And then she vomited up everything she'd eaten sitting on the old patchwork quilt as the girls fished in the river.

The girls…

She jerked upright, and a tremendous weight shifted from her head to her heart.

Sharon sat beside Shiloh, crying and holding her *schweschder*'s hand. Shiloh's arm was twisted at an awkward angle, but it was the blood running down her face that caused Susannah to gasp.

She didn't run so much as crawl over to Shiloh's side.

"She's still breathing." Micah squatted beside her. "I tried… I tried to stop the bleeding." It was then she noticed he'd taken off his shirt, compressed it into a bandage and placed it against Shiloh's head. "Her arm, it's broken, but it's the cut on her head that I'm worried about."

Susannah glanced up at the roof, but it was gone. Instead of the storm they'd fled, she saw clouds broken here and there by blue sky.

"How long…"

"Fifteen minutes. I've been trying to wake you. I didn't want to leave them."

"Go. Go now."

"Are you…"

"I'm fine, Micah. Go and get help for Shiloh."

Susannah didn't watch him leave. Her attention was completely focused on Shiloh and Sharon. Shiloh had yet to move or open her eyes. Sharon was crying so hard that she'd begun to hiccup. Susannah pulled the young girl into a hug.

"She's going to be okay, Sharon. Micah has gone for help."

"I was so…so… I was so scared."

"We all were."

"Uh-uh." She wiped the back of her hand across her eyes. "You weren't scared. You stood up and ran, just like Micah. But I was so scared that Micah had to… He had to carry me. And now Shiloh is… Shiloh is dead."

She broke down into sobs. Susannah put a hand on top of her head. She'd somehow lost her *kapp*, and her hair was a tangled mess, but none of that mattered. "Micah didn't carry you because you were too scared to run."

"He didn't?"

"*Nein*. He carried you because his legs are longer, so he can move faster."

"He saved us."

"*Ya.* He did." Susannah took Sharon's hand, opened her small palm and placed it gently on Shiloh's chest. "Can you feel her breathing?"

"Uh-huh."

"She's going to be okay."

"But she's bleeding."

"Something must have hit her on the head. She's going to need stitches, and she'll probably have a big headache."

"She will?"

"*Ya.*"

"Her arm looks funny. What's wrong with her arm, Susannah?"

"It's broken."

"Broken?"

"The doctors can fix that, Sharon."

"Micah went to get help?"

"He did."

"What can we do?"

"We can pray. Do you want to do that with me?"

Sharon had been crouching on her knees. Now she plopped onto her bottom, placed her palms together and squeezed her eyes shut. Together, they began to pray.

A part of Micah's mind noted the destruction that he ran through. A line of fencing, gone. The chicken coop to the side of the garden was now sitting in the middle of the lane. He skidded to a stop at the garden, where they had all been sitting just hours ago. It looked as if the ground had been freshly tilled. Every plant, every seedling, every tomato post had simply vanished.

Which was when he glanced up at the house and saw that the side of it facing the garden had no wall at all.

He could peer inside, like an *Englisch* dollhouse he'd once seen in a store. He craned his neck back, stared up at the second floor and into Susannah's room.

What if she'd been there?

What if they'd all been there?

The question paralyzed him for a few seconds, until sirens began to echo through the air.

How many had been hurt?

Were his grandparents all right?

And how was he going to get help to Shiloh?

He sprinted to the east pasture. Percy, the buggy horse, was gone—of course he was. Susannah's parents had taken him to visit church members. He put his hands on his knees, attempting to draw in deep breaths, and when he glanced up he saw it—Susannah's bicycle leaning against the side of the barn.

Micah jumped on it and sped off down the lane.

Later he wouldn't remember bicycling the two miles or dashing into the phone booth. He didn't recall picking up the phone, dialing 911 or dropping the receiver.

The ride back to the old barn was a blur.

All he knew for certain was that he had to get back to Susannah. He had to be there with her and he needed to help with the girls.

He pumped the pedals of the bicycle, sailing back down the road, turning into the lane, jumping off when he reached the yard and sprinting back across the field, back to the old barn.

He skidded to a stop in the doorway of the barn, though there was no longer a door. There weren't even walls so much as there were piles of debris. The roof was gone completely, the windows blown out, glass glittering on the ground.

What if the glass had blown in?

What if the entire thing had collapsed on them?

He understood in that moment that he would never forget what he saw when he stepped into the main room of the barn. Susannah was holding Shiloh in her lap. The head wound had bled through the shirt he'd pressed against her head. Shiloh raised eyes that were dazed, that seemed not to see him, but then she smiled, and the fear that had seized his heart melted away.

"Micah, I hurt my head."

"And her arm. Her arm is all wrong." Sharon darted toward him, snagged his hand and pulled him across the room—toward Shiloh and Susannah.

He knelt beside them, and that was when Susannah raised her eyes to his. When she reached out and touched his face, the tears that he'd been holding back, that had been strangling his voice and blurring his vision, began to flow freely.

Micah didn't know how long they sat there, huddled together. He was suddenly aware of the sound of a vehicle approaching and the blip of a siren. He kissed Susannah on top of the head, squeezed Shiloh's hand and said to Sharon, "Let's go tell them where we are."

By the time they stepped out of the barn, two paramedics were jogging across the field, carrying a child's gurney and a medical box. They'd left their vehicle on the side of the road. Micah could just make out the strobe of its red lights.

It wasn't until they'd placed a splint on Shiloh's arm, put a clean compress on her head and were loading her into the back of the ambulance that Micah thought to ask, "Are there more injured?"

"We've had a lot of calls, but so far no fatalities."

Micah put a hand on the back door of the ambulance to keep the paramedic from shutting it. Sticking his head inside, he assured Susannah, "I'll stay with Sharon. We'll find your parents and tell them. We'll all be right behind you."

Susannah seemed about to say something, but instead she nodded her head and turned her attention back to Shiloh.

And then the door was slammed shut, the ambulance was pulling away and Micah was left standing on the side of the road, Sharon's hand clutching his.

Susannah knew her way around a hospital. She'd spent enough time in one when she'd gone through her cancer diagnosis and treatment. She understood the reason for the X-rays that the doctor insisted on taking. She wasn't bothered by the IV they started in Shiloh's arm or the fact that they had to shave a swath of hair to clean the wound and stitch it up.

"Now our hair will match," she assured her *schweschder*, which earned her a smile.

She was able to explain the machines that beeped, noting Shiloh's heart rate, blood pressure, oxygen saturation, respiration and temperature.

"What does it all mean, Susannah?"

"It means you're going to be okay. Are you feeling better?"

"I didn't like that needle."

"*Ya*, needles are no fun."

"And now I'm so—" she paused for a huge yawn "—sleepy."

"Close your eyes and rest."

"But…"

"I'm not going anywhere."

"You'll wake me when *Mamm* and *Dat* get here?"

"If you want me to."

"I want you to."

Shiloh's right arm was still in a splint. She turned onto her left side, placed her hand under her cheek and closed her eyes. She was asleep before the clock on the wall had ticked off another minute.

A thousand questions crashed through Susannah's mind.

Was their house okay?

Had anyone else been hurt?

What about Percy and the chickens and the barn cats?

What about her neighbors?

For the first time in her life, she wished that she had an *Englisch* phone so that she could know what was happening. But then she realized she didn't need to know. *Gotte* knew. *Gotte* was in charge, just as He had been when He'd watched over them. She didn't need to know every detail this minute. She only needed to trust Him.

So she did what she'd done in the barn with Sharon. She prayed—for her parents, her neighbors, for Micah and Percy and her *freinden*. She prayed for the doctors and nurses. She prayed that the break in Shiloh's arm wouldn't be too painful.

By the time the doctor came in—a young woman sporting a name tag that read Dr. Emir—Susannah felt calmer and ready for whatever news the doctor brought. She was petite with long black hair pulled back in a simple ponytail holder and large owlish glasses.

After introducing herself and confirming that Susannah was Shiloh's relative, Dr. Emir said, "Your sister was very lucky. The head wound wasn't too terribly deep, and the arm was a fairly clean break."

"So both will heal quickly?"

"It's amazing just how fast young ones heal. If it was you or me, it would take a while, but Shiloh shouldn't have any trouble at all. We'll need to cast her arm, of course."

"Her favorite color is purple."

Dr. Emir smiled. "I'll see what I can do."

Then the doctor cocked her head and asked, "Are you sure you're okay? I can have someone look at…" She raised a hand to her own face, and that was when Susannah remembered that she'd been cut from some of the debris.

"Oh, I think it's fine."

"Best to clean it up anyway. You wouldn't want infection to set in. You're going to have your hands full taking care of your *schweschder*." And that—the doctor's use of their word—eased Susannah's heart more than she could explain. They were Amish and *Englisch*; of course they were. But they were also one community that pulled together in times of trouble.

As the doctor turned to go, Susannah asked, "Have you heard anything else? About injuries, or…" She couldn't bring herself to say the word *deaths*.

"The emergency room has been pretty busy. They're saying it was an F2 and that it left a pretty wide swath of destruction. Fortunately most of it was farmland."

Susannah nodded. She wondered how long it would be until her parents arrived and whether Micah was still with Sharon. And then her mind slipped to the realization she'd had as they ran toward the barn—that she loved Micah, that he was the person she wanted to spend the rest of her life with.

Today wasn't the time to tell him that, to explain to him how she felt, but wasn't that what she'd learned in that moment of terror when the tornado dropped out of the sky?

Life was precious, and it was best to take nothing for granted.

As a nurse stepped into the room and cleaned her wounds, Susannah promised herself that she would hold that lesson close to her heart and in the front of her mind.

She'd spent too long caught in the past. Starting this moment, she would plant her feet firmly in the present.

Chapter Fourteen

Micah wasn't sure if he should stay and wait for Susannah's parents or go check on his grandparents. Based on what he could see, the tornado had veered off in the opposite direction. He was sitting on the front porch steps with Sharon when Susannah's parents pulled up in front of the house.

Sharon flew into her mother's arms.

Micah tried to explain what had happened. He'd reached the part where the ambulance had arrived and picked up Susannah and Shiloh, when Thomas interrupted him. "Get in. You can tell us the rest on the way to the hospital."

"I should check on my grandparents."

"Of course. We'll drop you off."

"*Nein*. Go. Go to the girls, and tell them both I'll be there as soon as I can."

He realized as they pulled away that neither of Susannah's parents had commented on the destruction of their home.

Homes could be rebuilt.

Their one concern had been for their daughters.

He was thinking of that as he crossed back toward his grandparents' farm. It was the people in your life that mattered, not the things. It didn't at all matter what he wore, or whether he owned a phone, or if he drove a buggy or a car. What mattered was how you treated the people you cared about, and he realized with sudden clarity that he had not treated his grandparents well.

In fact, he'd taken them for granted—eating their food, staying in their home, allowing his *mammi* to wash his clothes and his *daddi* to provide his transportation. It was true that he'd given them money, but had he given them his respect and his gratitude? In truth, he'd thought they owed it to him, but no one really owed anyone else anything. It was their love for him that had provided for his needs.

And what had he done in return?

He'd mocked their way of life.

Shown a complete lack of respect for their years of hard work.

Argued at every possible turn.

He'd been a child, as surely as Sharon and Shiloh were children. When he'd realized that it was up to him to get Sharon and Shiloh and Susannah to safety, he'd left that side of himself behind in the path of the tornado. The storm had done more than threaten their very lives, it had pushed Micah into the world of being an adult—of being responsible for someone else and embracing that responsibility.

There would be no turning back.

He let out a breath he didn't realize he'd been holding when he saw his grandparents' house. It was completely intact, without so much as a tree limb littering the yard.

He took the front porch steps two at a time.

His grandparents were in the living room—*Mammi* sitting next to *Daddi* on the couch, holding a glass of water and pressing it to his lips. As for his grandfather, his face was an ashen gray and his breathing seemed labored.

"What happened?"

"We heard the…the tornado. John figured you went over to Susannah's. He was going to check on you when he collapsed on the front lawn. I managed to get him inside."

"*Daddi?* Can you hear me?"

His grandfather opened his eyes, though he seemed to have trouble focusing. His breathing was ragged, and though it wasn't hot at all in the house, sweat ran in rivulets down the side of his face.

"I shouldn't…shouldn't have said…"

"Not now, *Daddi*." Micah clasped his hand. "It's forgiven and forgotten. Now, we need to get some help."

He sprinted out of the room, to the barn where he kept the replacement phone he'd purchased. He only hoped it was charged. Had he even used it since he'd arrived home from jail? He pulled it from the shelf where they kept miscellaneous tools, powered it on and ran out into the yard.

Two bars and 8 percent power.

It should be enough. It would have to be.

For the second time that day, he tapped in the number 911.

The person who answered took down the information, told him what to do and insisted on staying on the line until the paramedics arrived.

He found the bottle of aspirin in his *mammi*'s medicine cabinet. After Micah had given one to his *daddi*, the emergency dispatcher walked Micah through checking his pulse, which was weak but steady.

"It's important that you keep your grandfather calm. We have an ambulance on the way to you right now."

Five minutes passed, then ten, and then finally he heard the scream of the siren coming down their lane. He wasn't too surprised when the two paramedics who hopped out of the vehicle were the same ones he'd seen earlier.

"Busy day for you," the woman said, patting him on the shoulder before rushing past him and into the house.

They stabilized his grandfather and loaded him into the ambulance.

His *mammi* looked a bit dazed. "You can go with them, *Mammi*."

"I can?"

"I'll bring the buggy."

"*Danki*, Micah." She pulled him into a hug, clung to him fiercely for the space of three heartbeats and then she, too, was gone.

Micah wanted nothing more than to hitch up the buggy and tear out after them.

But what would his *daddi* want him to do?

After all, he would only be waiting and pacing at the hospital. They wouldn't even let him in the room for the first hour or so. Instead of rushing off, he walked through the living room and into the kitchen. He found a pot of red beans cooking on the stove, so he turned the gas burner off. He covered the pot with the lid and pushed it to the back of the stove. The clock above the sink said that it was nearly five in the afternoon, when his *daddi* always looked after the animals.

So Micah did those chores, too.

Finally, he walked into his grandparents' room to see if there was anything there that they might need. His grandmother's purse and sweater were hanging on a hook near the door. He grabbed both and had turned to go when he spied her worn Bible on a nightstand. Picking it up, he ran a hand over the cover. The corners were worn and the letters on the front were barely discernible.

Sinking down onto their bed, he opened the book and stared at the inscription.

To Abigail, the love of my life.
John
October 15, 1978

His *daddi* had been a young man then, younger than Micah was now if he'd done the math correctly. And yet he'd known that Abigail was the woman he wanted to spend his life with. He hadn't questioned his love for her or her love for him. And look at them now. They'd survived the terrible accident that had taken his arm, raised a houseful of children and now they were helping to raise Micah.

He realized in that moment how much he respected his *daddi*. Micah might not always agree with his opinion on things, but he admired how he'd spent his entire life caring for and providing for his family. He recalled the look on both of their faces as *Mammi* had sat beside him holding the cup of water. There was simply no doubt how much they loved each other.

Micah wanted that.

He wanted that kind of consistency in his life.

He wanted someone who looked at him like his *mammi* looked at his *daddi*.

And he was absolutely certain he knew who that someone was.

Susannah had moved to the waiting room and was sitting with Deborah by the time Micah found her. He explained about his grandfather—the doctors had assured him that his condition was stable, but that he didn't need more visitors at the moment. "How's Shiloh?"

"*Mamm*'s in with her now, and *Dat*'s taken Sharon to get something to eat and then outside to check on the horse."

"What about you?"

"What about me?"

"Have you eaten anything?"

"*Nein.*"

Micah reached for her hand, pulled her to her feet and then told Deborah where they were going. The room was virtually filled with *Englisch* and Amish. The latest reports were thirty-four people injured, but no fatalities. Three homes had been damaged—two Amish and one *Englisch*, though it sounded like Susannah's had taken the most direct hit.

"I'm sure I have something to eat in this bag." Deborah hoisted her large purse off the floor and onto her lap. "*Ya.* I have gum and peanut butter crackers and…"

Micah leaned down and said, "*Danki*, but I'm going to take Susannah to the cafeteria to get her some hot food."

Deborah raised her eyes to his, glanced at Susannah and then smiled. "*Gut* idea. You should do that. I'll just stay here, and if anyone is looking for you two, I'll tell them where you are."

"Danki," Susannah said, enfolding her friend in her arms. She then left with Micah, tucking her hand in the crook of his elbow.

The cafeteria was staying open later than usual, owing to the aftermath of the tornado. They both grabbed sandwiches and coffee, and Micah carried their tray to a table in the corner of the room.

Susannah took a couple of bites and then sat back, studying him instead of eating.

"You should finish that. You're going to need your energy. Your *schweschdern*, they can be a handful."

She could tell he meant it in a teasing way, that he was trying to lift her mood, but she wasn't ready for that yet.

"Micah, I need to thank you."

"Nein. You don't." He closed his eyes and rubbed his forehead with his fingertips. Finally, he pushed his tray away, crossed his arms on the table and focused on her. "I shouldn't have talked you into going to the river. I'm always doing that. Trying to find a way to goof off and dragging someone along with me, and today the result was that Shiloh was hurt. That's on me. That's my fault."

She could tell he was surprised when she reached across the table and covered his hands with hers. "I didn't see our house, but they told me. Half of it's gone. Is that right?"

"Ya."

"So if we'd been home, if we hadn't gone to the river, there's at least a fifty-fifty chance we'd have died in that house today."

"Please don't say that." His voice was husky with emotion, and when he raised his eyes to hers, she saw tears sparkling there.

"You saved us, Micah, and I am grateful that you did. You saved your *daddi*, too. *Gotte* has used you today, and… I'm just glad that He brought you here."

Micah swiped at his eyes, then sat up straighter and squared his shoulders. "Are you saying that you'll go fishing with me again?"

"I could be talked into it."

She'd tried to match his light tone, but it was a facade that was simply too hard to keep up. He reached for her hands, pulled them to his lips and kissed them.

"I love you, Susannah Beiler."

"You do?"

"Tell me you haven't known that for some time."

"I hoped, but *nein*, I wasn't sure."

"I let you teach me how to sew."

"You're not very good at it."

"Susannah, I'd be interested in alpacas if it meant I could spend more time with you."

"I don't have any alpacas."

"Not my point."

They sat there another ten minutes, until they became aware that others needed their table. Susannah wanted to tell him how she felt, but how was she supposed to do that in the middle of the crowded cafeteria? Then they were walking down the hall, and Micah stopped abruptly. He glanced left, then right and then pulled her into an alcove, wrapped his arms around her and held her close.

"I was so frightened," he admitted.

"Me, too."

"And when I realized..." He framed her face with his hands and kissed her softly on the lips. "When I realized that I might lose you, I understood how important you are to me. I knew when I saw that tornado dipping out of the sky that I would do anything for you, for your family, for us."

He kissed her again, then thumbed away the tears slipping down her face.

"I love you, too," she whispered.

"You do?"

"Don't act surprised."

"I thought you were dating me to keep your friends safe."

"That was the original plan."

He kissed once more, and she felt safe again. No longer worried about what might fall out of the sky. He kissed her, and she knew that somehow everything was going to be all right. Then he pulled her back out into the hall. Together they walked toward the waiting room, knowing that whatever news they faced, they would weather it together.

Shiloh was released from the hospital the next morning.

Micah's grandfather stayed an additional three nights, and then was only allowed to go home when he promised to rest and stay off his feet. They'd put in a stent to clear up a blockage in his main artery, and the doctor had started him on a statin medication.

Micah was in the room when the cardiologist had said, "You've had a heart attack, Mr. Fisher. As we discussed, that means your heart is damaged. You're going to need to give yourself a few weeks to build your strength back up, and I expect you to be in my office in seven days for a follow-up."

Once they were home, his *daddi* insisted on sitting on the front porch while Micah unharnessed and cared for the horse. When Micah had checked everything and closed up the barn, he climbed the steps to find his *daddi* still there. The sun was dipping toward the horizon, and through the window Micah could see his *mammi* heating one of the casseroles a neighbor had left.

"I'd like to talk to you, Micah."

Instead of arguing, as he might have the week before, Micah sat in the adjacent rocker and waited.

"I meant what I said when you found me the day of the tornado. I shouldn't have spoken to you as I did that morning. I shouldn't have tried to force your path."

"You care about me."

"I do, but I see now that your path is different from mine. Doesn't mean it's wrong."

Micah fought to hide his surprise. When his *daddi* caught his eye and smiled, Micah admitted, "You're not the only one who needs to apologize. I see now that I've been bullheaded out of habit and immature because I could be."

A red bird landed in front of them in the yard, hopping back and forth as it pecked at the dirt.

"I'm going to ask Susannah to marry me."

"She'll make a fine *fraa*."

"Not yet, though. I won't ask yet. I want to give her time to recover."

His *daddi* sighed, then pushed himself up and out of the rocker. "If there's one thing I've learned, it's never assume you have more time."

Micah understood what his *daddi* was saying, but

he also appreciated what Susannah had been through. He didn't want to take anything for granted, least of all her. He also wanted to be sensitive to her feelings.

Three days later, Detective Cummings stopped by to say they'd found the person who had burglarized the general store as well as quite a few others. "Not an Amish kid. He thought that by acting like one, by looking like one, he could get away with it."

"And he almost did."

"His mistake was stealing Widow Miller's buggy twice. She saw him driving out of her place, and she walked to the phone shack."

"Good thing it's across the road."

"She called the police, and we caught him as he drove into town."

Which seemed to end the matter as far as Micah was concerned.

Two weeks later, a workday was held at the Beiler place. They began before the sun came up, and by the time it was setting, a new home had been framed. They'd been staying in a *dawdi haus* over on the Hochstettler place, and Micah knew they'd be glad to move back home.

Each day of the next week, Micah went over in the afternoons to help finish the house. Each time he arrived, a different group of men were nailing up Sheetrock or painting rooms or finishing the porch. By the end of June the house was completed. They'd opted for a one-story design, since Susannah's parents didn't see themselves having any more children.

Micah tried to stay away, but he found he couldn't.

He was drawn to the Beiler place. It felt like home to him. He needed to be there.

He arrived after dinner, their first dinner in their

new home. Shiloh and Sharon insisted on showing him their new room. "We have window seats," they squealed, then insisted he sit there while they brought him a pillow, blanket, three books and two dolls.

Susannah stood in the doorway laughing.

It wasn't until the girls were in bed and Susannah's parents had moved to the front porch to enjoy the cool evening, that he asked her to go for a walk. And it was there at the pasture fence, under a covering of stars, that Micah asked Susannah to marry him.

"You're sure?" She reached up and touched his face. Micah wanted to memorize the way that her fingers felt against his skin. More than that, he wanted her this close to him every day for the rest of his life.

"I've never been so sure of anything."

"Even though…"

"You can't have children? *Ya.* I'm aware."

"That's a big thing, Micah."

"It's not as big as my love for you. Now, if you said you didn't love me, that would be a big thing."

"Of course I love you."

"Then you'll marry me?" He felt as if he'd laid his heart before her. He felt as if, with Susannah by his side, he could do anything.

"*Ya*, I'll marry you."

"*Gut.*" He kissed her once, then again, and then pulled her into his arms. "We can build here or on my *daddi*'s place."

"You've thought that far ahead?"

"I need to provide for my family."

"What about Maine?"

"It'll still be there, but I can't leave now. Not with *Daddi* needing help. I don't want to leave."